I0657346

Future Fugitives

Endless Tempest, Volume 0

Mark Landon Jarvis

Published by Mark Jarvis, 2024.

FUTURE FUGITIVES

First edition. August 9, 2024.

Copyright © 2024 Mark Landon Jarvis.

ISBN: 979-8986701295

Written by Mark Landon Jarvis.

Toward the Turncoats, who don't yet even exist.

Chapter 1: Sneet

February 2030

Lark looked through his reflection to the traffic outside the restaurant. The gray wet day was framed in a sunburst of his wild red hair. All day he had been questioning himself why people would not stay home. Sleet made a mess of things, and it made all these goobs stupid. Some of them saw sleet as cold rain, so they braved the elements. Others saw it as light snow—no reason to change plans on a Wednesday afternoon. No one cared it had been *reeting* and *slaining*. They did not even notice until they'd left their cars parked for a while.

They would return to their cars, lugging shopping bags, and simply gaze all around, astonished as if they only now noticed everything around them was layered in dripping ice. His customers sometimes started cars and came back in for another coffee while the defroster worked its wonders. Lark wished for heavy snow, a good blanket of the white stuff on top of that layer of ice, but he knew even that would not get him a snow day as a server at Mack's. He'd shuffled and tromped ten blocks to take the apron from the overnight hag—ten blocks one way in the snow—but it was too slick to bike and he refused a ride from his mom.

At least Mack's lunch crowd had been sparse. At least Lark knew ninety percent of the drink orders would be coffee. Most of the people he was waiting on were regulars, and he knew their orders before they did. Mack's did not get big crowds, not even the after-church mob. That herd went across the street to the Perkins, where golden lights and overstuffed booths wooed people in from the weather.

A tall guy outside caught Lark's attention, standing at the window. He smiled right at Lark, and with the superimposed red hair, he looked like a lunatic relative. Lark busied himself with a

1

table, trying to ignore the goob who was now waving both arms like a bird.

Sometimes Henny or some other punk from school would do this, usually only because they knew how he felt about it. They'd stand at the window and watch him work, like bussing tables and listening to the old farts place orders was some kind of performance art. When he'd first lost his hand, it felt like crowds gathered to see if he could still wait tables, like they were just waiting for him to fumble a tray of plates or slosh coffee all over the place.

Lark was grateful that the Fergusons were at the register. He beat the other server, Stacy, to the front. They were his customers, after all. Stacy stuck out her pierced tongue and moved on. Some cheery chatter, the old routine of punching in the digits—just what Lark needed to forget about that freak at the window. He even saw them to the door, sharing a good guffaw. "*Sneet!*" Old man Ferguson was saying, "Lark, you'd be a good weatherman some day!"

The smile froze on Lark's face as he turned to see Stacy had seated the tall crazy at one of his tables. As they passed, she gave him a wicked smile. "Don't blame me," she said. "He asked for that table."

"I did at that," the man said. He was shrugging off his coat. He kept his gloves and his knit cap on. He could have been a cancer patient. He didn't have any facial hair, not even eyebrows.

"Hello, Larkin Wayne Fortune! Some call me Gary Sackerson, but you can call me Sack." Then he stuck out his hand, as if to shake. His *left* hand.

Lark took a step back from the table, bumping into a passing customer. "Who are you? How do you know—"

"Pleased to meet you, Lark." Gary Sackerson gave a little head toss toward his extended hand.

Lark reached out as if he were about to touch a ghost. The handshake was sure and firm, if not a little creepy through the glove. "How'd you know?" They both glanced at Lark's right wrist.

"Have a seat," Sackerson said. "We have a lot to talk about."

Chapter 2: Why, Why, Why

"**I** mean, really! Whatever happened to being a doctor or a veterinarian?" her father had asked her on one of his weekends. "What kind of kid says they want to be a federal agent?"

The kind that spent the summer dodging a pack of agents, she'd thought, but kept to herself. Sometimes it just went easier if the 'rents didn't know everything. It was even easier with her family since they never seemed to keep it straight which weekend she was to be where, or what story she was sticking to.

Now Krystal was sitting in her mom's Volvo, using her mom's opera glasses to spy on a man she was just sure was yet another agent. Why were they coming around again? "Why, why, why?" she asked aloud.

"That's what I want to know," Henny said, peeking up from the back seat. He smelled like McDonald's, and he looked worse. Normally, she wouldn't be caught dead with Kenny Hinman. At least she'd convinced him to hide in the back. "We won't be so obvious," she had persuaded him. "They'll be suspicious if they see us both." Surveillance made strange partnerships.

"Why's he after us?" Henny continued. "Why'd he start with me?"

"We still don't know that he *did* start with you," Krys reminded him again. "We haven't caught up with Stu."

Stu wasn't answering his phone or responding to texts. Then again, why would he answer hers? It had been a nasty breakup. And anyone might ghost Henny, just because.

She peered again through the gaudy little binoculars. The stranger was chumming it up with Lark, just like he had with her last night. The guy was a Spook; she was sure of it. He knew too much to be—what had he told her? *"A man on a mission,"* he'd said. He knew all their names. He knew all about the space junk caper. He had to be some kind of agent, though he'd never said as much. He just had to be a government man, even if he didn't dress like one. Krys studied him more, but her attention kept turning back to Lark. He was clearly uneasy.

"How's Lefty taking it?" Henny asked for yet another report.

Krys turned half around to stare him down. "Do you call him that to his face?"

"Wha—you mean—Lefty?" Henny rolled a shoulder and sat up a bit. "Yeah. Sure."

"I've never heard you call him that. You never called him that last summer."

"Everybody calls him Lefty." Henny fished some paper-wrapped horror from his McDonald's bag. "Hell, Coach didn't even know his real name. Called him Lefty all fall semester."

I'd never call him that, Krys thought. She returned to the opera glasses, to watching Lark squirm. She couldn't remember seeing him like this in Mack's ever before. He usually seemed so in control there, like it was his own restaurant. Now Lark kept brushing back his red mop, kept glancing all around the restaurant like he was looking for a lifeline.

Krys weighed and measured. It was just across the street. Nobody she knew went to Mack's. She could go in alone. If she were lucky, she wouldn't even get much slush on her new shoes.

Still, something about the agent seemed especially... menacing. He'd put her in a cold sweat when he'd mentioned her birth mother. *Nobody, but nobody,* knew about her.

She sighed as she watched Henny in the rear-view mirror, chewing something. She tried not to think of the societal consequences of what she forced herself to say next.: "Maybe we should go in there," the words caught in her throat like a sharp corn chip, "together."

Henny shuddered, as if he was repulsed by the idea of being seen with her, too. "I don't wanna get near that guy again. This is close enough."

Chapter 3: Afternoon drive

Instead of Wednesday night church, Stu always took a Wednesday night spin. He was, in a word, *religious* about it. While some of his family would watch football or play Gin Rummy, Stu would be out on the back roads, sizing things up. He'd been faithful to this tour of county roads for over two years, since his daddy first let him take his truck off their land. Now he had his driver's license, and the only thing slowing him down was the mucky roads.

Most Wednesday drives were just for the sheer joy of driving. His dog, Spud, would hang his head out the passenger window, and Stu would hang his arm on his windowsill, and they'd enjoy the fresh air. Even on cold winter days, the whir of the heater and the roar of his truck helped him think straight. He did his best thinking outside like this.

Sometimes, however, like this Wednesday, his thinking got the best of him. His head was as clouded as the windows, and his thoughts tossed back and forth like the wipers. Even Spud was no help at all, just curled up in a ball like he would rather be home.

Stu wiped the frost off his side window, surprised to see he was already driving by Hinman's place. He hadn't set out for it—or had he? "Don't stir the pot," his mom always said, but here he was, right back where it all started.

Stu downshifted and eased out the clutch after rounding a turn. He could still make out the gray government-issue t-posts, even in the sleet. Since he was here anyway, he might as well circle the whole thing. About every quarter of a mile—except where they'd been stolen or the barbed wire fence was down—a sign would remind trespassers that this stretch of Oklahoma red dirt was under the Bureau of Land Management. Everybody just called it "The Strip" now. Some seven miles long and a mile wide, the former housing development and golf course was now fenced weeds. It blocked off a couple of Stu's favorite roads. The whole Strip was off limits.

When he saw the dome, he slowed to a stop. Off in the distance, smack in the middle of the field, was a huge, white geodesic dome. Nearby a massive concrete rectangular building dwarfed the dome. They didn't even bother painting it. On a day like this, it blended in, but there would never be a time it belonged out here. It was fenced off tighter than a bug, even had a six foot high chain-link fence up closer to "the Installation," as the government guys called it. There was one good gravel road that led from the blacktop over by Hinman's grandpa's place, right onto the property, but it still had locked gates and solar cameras.

From where he sat, Stu could just make out his tracks from last summer, when he'd tore off through a gap in the barbed wire, zipped all over the Strip, and spun circles around the Installation. It had been a stupid thing to do, but he liked showing off the 4-wheel drive for Krystal, and it was one of those *"in your face, taxman!"* pranks he so loved. It was just the immature kind of thing she pulled up time after time when they were breaking up, too.

He picked up the mobile phone on the seat between him and Spud and thumbed through her texts again. Nothing since that last "I'm sorry" in October until last night.

Then there'd been a flurry of messages. "Need to talk," they started. "Something weird's going on," she'd written. "Feds are back and looking for you," she'd sent him, during church. He kept returning to the last one, however painful it was to read: "Meet me at Perkins."

At one time, Krystal had said Perkins was *their place.* Stu hated Perkins. For that matter, he hated Guthrie. Every park they'd sat around at, every restaurant they'd been to. He was glad he went to the consolidated rural school district, far from all the drama—and from her. Now she just had to see him? She expected him to ditch his drive and just come to her like a cow coming in at night?

"It just ain't right," he said aloud to Spud. The dog raised his eyebrows, sighed, and resettled. Spud was used to it. He'd always been Stu's sounding board. "Who's she to tell me what to do, huh? What do I need with more trouble?"

He threw it into gear and slid around on the road. He raced the engine and spun a few circles, throwing mud and slush far up in the air behind the oversized tires. The truck sloughed off into the ditch, then up over the road and into the other ditch, and Stu whooped and laughed the whole time. Spud, bracing himself with one paw on the dash, another on the window, probably did not think it was quite so funny.

When the mud settled and the truck straightened back out on the road, Stu found he was heading toward town. "Trouble it is, then," he said. A quick glance in his rear-view mirror confirmed the rifle was still in his gun rack.

Chapter 4: The Milk Man

Lark came back to the table with a milk, as requested "a big one, in a glass glass, no plastic." He set it down, then he sat across from Sackerson.

"Would you look at that!" Sackerson said. "Grade A, 100% whole white milk."

Lark raised his eyebrows but said nothing.

Sackerson couldn't take his eyes off the glass. "You should have some. You like milk."

"You don't know what I like."

Sackerson raised his head, eyeing Lark. Then he took off his gloves, almost laid them on the table, then tucked them into his coat. He clasped both hands around the glass and grinned. "You like milk, but only if it's cold, like this one. Not chocolate milk or raw milk or goat's milk or soy milk. You like milk so much you have "Got Milk" posters up in your room...but just the girls."

He waggled his eyebrows, or what would have been his eyebrows. This close up, Lark realized Sackerson didn't even have *eyelashes*. He had a big, almost playful, face. Even though he was odd and obviously some kind of government man, he didn't come off as too scary.

"So, you're some kind of super sleuth. Congratulations, Sherlock. I'll admit it, I like the white stuff."

Sackerson looked a bit offended for a second, then he smiled down at the glass. "You know, where I'm from smoking's illegal in public areas. Milk," he hefted the glass, "you just can't get it like this anymore."

Lark looked around for someone—anyone—who needed a coffee warmed up or a plate bussed. Old man Lawton smiled but

10

hovered his hand over his coffee cup. Only a handful of others were left in the restaurant. No one was paying them any attention.

When Sackerson took his first sip, he closed his eyes and savored it. "Oh," he sighed "That's the stuff. Ours is so processed. Well, technically, it's not even from the same animal as you're assoc—"

"It's from a cow, right?"

"Well, yes, but a highly modified, genetically engineered cow. One that's fed a diet, custom tailored to its lactation cycles and yield. Then the processing just takes all the joy out of it. You've had skim milk?"

Lark leaned forward. "Why are you bugging me? What do you want?"

"Gawd it's good." He took another drink. "You can almost chew it." Sackerson belted back half the glass and then set it down firmly. "Okay," he said. "Down to business."

"It's about last summer, isn't it?" Lark sat back, tucked his hair behind his ears, left, then right. He was supposed to wear a hairnet, but he didn't.

"Yes, and a whole, *whole* lot more." Sackerson seemed all serious now, but he had a milk mustache.

"Listen, we didn't mess with anything. We didn't see anything. We didn't steal—"

"Lark, you're already on record with all that." Sackerson glanced out the window. When he looked back at Lark, his eyes were flint. "I want to know about your dad."

"My dad? Works all the time. Why are you asking me about him, when he's already sold out to you guys?"

"When's the last time you saw him?" Sackerson wiped his lip, folded the napkin, and put it in his pocket.

"What's it to you?"

"Everything."

"Where's your badge? Aren't you supposed to flash some credentials?"

"I'm... unaffiliated."

Lark didn't like the sound of that. He slid over to get out of the booth. "Dude, I think we're done here. Milk's on me."

"I'm going to catch up with your dad, and you're going to help me. This is do or die, shock and awe stuff here, Lark."

Lark stood, glanced over Sackerson's shoulder at the off-duty cop swilling down coffee.

"Sergeant Burns?" Sackerson snickered under his breath, "are you kidding me? The guy can't even jog a block. Poor excuse for law enforcement."

Lark blinked forcibly. *How did this guy do it?*

"Let's order something, really talk it out. What do you say?" Sackerson stood, towering when he stood so close.

"I got work to do."

The cowbell over the front door clanked loudly. Sackerson smiled beyond Lark at someone just coming in. "We're going to need a bigger booth," he said. "The gang's all here."

Lark turned and moaned out loud at the sight of them. The three stooges.

Chapter 5: Questions

October 2027

"Fortune," he announced, holding his photo ID before him, "Dr. Christopher Fortune. Colonel, USAF, retired." Sometimes the "doctor" opened doors, especially at a medical facility. Usually the "colonel" commanded attention, particularly in military environs. Though this was a military medical operation, Chris Fortune's impressive credentials had little effect. The clerk, a sleepy-eyed private in scrubs, did not stand at attention or wave him through.

"You on the list?" she asked.

"You have my son. Larkin Fortune. Something happened to his hand?"

"Why didn't you say so?" The clerk called up his records on the laptop before her, then picked up her mobile phone and snapped his picture.

"What's with the picture?" he asked as she directed him down the hall.

"New protocol... as of tonight."

Rushing down the corridor, Chris said to himself, "Everything's new as of tonight!"

"We was out hunting. Jackrabbits. Coyotes." Henny was wearing a hospital gown. It was not a pretty sight, a beefy defensive tackle in a floral hospital gown. "Stu was watching the comets and not the road, then we was in the ditch. Rolled at least once."

"Confirmed," one man across the table said to the other, scrolling through a screen on his computer. "Twice, end for end."

"And then?" The main interviewer was all Matrix about everything. He was even wearing sunglasses in the interrogation room.

"Then BOOM." Henny slapped the steel table between them. "I mean, damn! I've been at tractor pulls and drag races, been outside when lightning hit pretty close, but I never heard nothing like that!"

"Bright light, knocked you out, got it... but then what?" The computer jockey was in a hurry.

"Then I started looking for Stu. I couldn't even hear my own voice when I yelled for him. It was like I was in the bottom of a pool. You ever holler—"

"What about the car?"

"I didn't even see it at first."

"Did you notice anything at the time?"

"You're talking about the hole in the side, but no. I was half blind, and it was really dark. Dirt was so thick you could taste it," he slapped at his arms as if expecting dust to rise off them. "I didn't see that hole until your fellas showed it to me." Henny glanced at one man, then the other. "Your guy said it just missed me?"

"Correct."

"Made a hole as big as a half dollar?"

"About 5 centimeters, yes."

"Where's the rock? That would be something to show everybody—here's the meteor that just about killed me."

"There were no measurable pieces of debris."

"See, that's what I can't figure. I mean, the sky was lit up like a concert with all this space junk, and now there's nothing out there to pick up?"

"That's right. If it truly was a meteor fall, most likely it all burned up as it entered the atmosphere, and if not then, upon impact. Meteors disintegrate into shards and chunks that are moving so very fast—"

"None of us need a science lesson, Maxton," the computer guy said. "Now, Kenneth, we need to know everything you saw, everything you might think you saw."

"I've been through all this with the first guy, that Mr. Starky guy," Henny groaned. "I'm hungry."

Krystal Price looked at her nails again. They were in terrible shape. Two were so roughed up she couldn't see her reflection. Her thumbnail was broken. She'd done the whole inventory—before they'd made her change into this hideous gown—lost a shoe and her purse. Scraped her elbow somehow. She felt covered in dust even after the shower. Her hair was ruined. They didn't even offer her any conditioner.

She shut one eye, then switched and shut the other, trying to focus, though she knew what was wrong with her vision. She wasn't telling them anything, not even that she'd lost one contact. She had refused to talk to them. "Not without my lawyer," she had said, as if she had personal counsel on retainer.

Krystal heard some scuffling outside the room they'd left her in. It was a small room with cinderblock walls. One table, her chair, two others. One door, no windows. She wanted a window. It had to be mid-morning by now.

The door popped open and yet another crew cut suit walked in. "Someone to keep you company." He growled, then stepped aside.

Stu Wiebe winked at her. He had a black eye. He was wearing a jumpsuit and was shackled. They led him to the table, and he dropped into a seat. "Rough night," he smirked.

"Dad?" Lark sat up in bed.

"Lark, what happened?" Chris rushed around, bedside and put a hand on his son's shoulder. He couldn't help glancing down toward Lark's hand.

Lark teared up, twisted his mouth around. His chin wrinkled, as it had done since he was a baby. "I was just out there for the meteor show, like you said."

"No one predicted it was—the trajectory was—" but he didn't have the right words. "I'm just glad you're okay."

"I'm not okay." He held up his bandaged arm. "My hand's gone. Just gone!" Tears poured down his face as he looked at Chris for answers. "How could my hand just be...gone?"

"They said nothing hit you, but that it's burned off? What can you tell me, son? What happened?"

"Where's mom?"

"She's coming. I sent someone for her."

"Where are we, on base?"

"Yes. They'll let her in, though."

"I'll wait." Lark sat back, pressed the back of his head into the pillow, and seemed to have nothing else to say.

Nurses came and went. He was there for Lark whenever the boy was ready. They were giving him twelve hours before they started their interviews. In that time, Chris was charged with mining his son for information. All he wanted to do was hold him. He wanted to say something that might matter to him. All he could think of were questions. He just sat there like an idiot—an idiot astrophysicist.

Chapter 6: No... Stranger

February 2030

Stu didn't like anything about the situation. He thought Mack's was an ashtray of a restaurant. He didn't care what Krystal wanted. He didn't give a rip that Lark Fortune was in trouble.

He didn't like the look of the stranger at the table. Who shaves their eyebrows? Some lunatic, maybe.

"I know you all have questions," the guy started, "and so do I. Let's do this: give and take. I'll start. I'm Gary Sackerson. I'm here to follow up on the Guthrie Fall of October 2027."

"So why bug us?" Stu asked.

The guy looked right at Stu and beamed. It made him uneasy.

"Hey, Stu," he said, softly.

Stu had never seen the guy before, and here he was, being all warm and fuzzy. "Do I know you?"

"Not so well as I know you."

"Let's start right there," Lark jumped in. "How do you know us all?" He was standing at the table, acting like a waiter. "You've been spouting off stuff that's not in any file anyone could keep on a guy. How do you know all that?"

"Like, how'd you know where to find me?" Henny asked.

Krystal chimed in: "And my phone number? How did you—"

"Listen," Sackerson put up his hands to calm them all. "I admit I'm very well informed. I have to be."

They were in a round corner booth, Sackerson in the middle, Krys and Henny on either side of him. Stu was crowded to the edge of the seat by Henny, who was keeping his distance from the stranger.

"So, *how* do you know so much?" Stu pressed. "And what's so interesting about us?"

"Yeah, we're just a bunch of kids," Henny added.

The stranger smiled, looking from face to face. "A bunch of kids," he repeated. "You're so much more."

"You're creepy," Krys said, then like Henny, she slid farther toward the edge of the booth.

"If you were legit, you'd have dragged us back to the base," Lark said.

"Or out to the Installation," Henny said, and that brought them all to silence.

Mack's was a narrow, smoky, low-ceiling place, like a trailer house turned into a restaurant. They'd come in the regular front door, but Stu watched customers exit to the street at the far end, streetside. He figured there was a third door off the kitchen to the alley out back.

Lark seemed to look the same way, Stu thought. He caught a subtle nod he and a pudgy little guy shared. It took him a second before Stu recognized Burns, out of uniform.

When Stu turned his attention back to their table, he was shocked to find Sackerson staring at him, then Lark, then back at him like he was warning them.

"Go clock out," Krystal said to Lark without looking at him. She was doing her best to glare at Sackerson. "We're leaving." She pointed a finger at the guy's long nose. "Don't mess with us."

"I'm the least of your problems." He flashed her a stiff smile. "Besides, where can you go that I cannot find you?"

"We know places—"

"—to hide?" Sackerson closed his eyes, as if reading from a file in his head. "Krystal—stepdad's cabin. Stu—under the pulpit at church. Henny, well, you're not one to hide." He looked up at Lark, "And you... used to run home to mommy about now."

"I got tables to wait on," Lark growled, turning away.

Sackerson slid out fast, sending Krystal staggering to her feet. He grabbed Lark's elbow.

Everybody in the restaurant stopped, coffee cups hoisted midway, mouths gaping open. Stu reached for the buck knife, holstered in his belt. Henny clutched a fork in each hand. Burns was getting up as sly as he could.

"You *used to* run away, Lark. I can give you a very compelling reason not to."

"I doubt that," Lark said, moving on.

"Your father—*our* father—is about to die because of the space junk caper."

Chapter 7: Don't Ask

October 2027

Stu flexed his hands, wincing at the pain from the scuffs and scabs earned in his dustup with the law. He knew his daddy was there, somewhere on the grounds, but he didn't know if he wanted to hear from him or not. Would he be the Deacon and chew his butt, or would he be the Rancher and back him up? Hadn't he always told Stu to never give up his guns? Didn't Rancher Wiebe hate the government with a passion?

He tried to push all that to the back of his mind now, however, for he was sitting across from Krys, that hottie who'd been out star gazing with the hippie kid. She was alive and well, even if her car was junked.

"They got you, too, huh," Stu said.

"What happened to Lark?"

"I dunno. I don't even know what happened to Henny. I was just running for help when—"

Krys scowled, pointing to the ceiling.

He followed her finger to a black panel among the fluorescent lights in the ceiling tiles. Krys cupped her ears and pointed again at the black panel.

Stu continued, "...when I saw Elvis and eight tiny reindeer."

The two of them had a chuckle.

· · · ·

HENNY YAWNED. "WELL... I, uh... I told you already I didn't see anything. Told you every little thing I did see. So when can I go home?"

"That's part of the bargain we made, if you'll recall," the computer guy said, scrolling through his notes, then reading them back. "Unconditional release, no record of incarceration, and various incentives forthcoming."

"We're cutting you a deal, Kenneth, not for what you saw, but what you might see later on. Got it?" Matrix guy smiled a little bit.

"And for that, I get a 'get out of jail free' card?"

"Yes. That's today. And any time you can further our investigation, we can sweeten the pot."

Henny squinted his eyes and asked, "How sweet?"

The agents looked at each other. Computer guy gave Matrix guy a single nod. "We're authorized to give you anything," Matrix said.

"So, let me get this straight. You want me to spy on Stu and them, and if I tell you stuff—rat them out—you'd give me anything I want?"

The agent took off his shades and said again, "Yes, Kenneth. Anything."

"Anything, huh? Like a steak dinner kinda anything, or a new car kinda anything?"

"Yes, and more."

Henny leaned forward, put his elbows on the table that separated them. Both agents were right there with him, like they were ready to close the deal. "And if you give me all that, what if I, maybe, forget or change my mind? What then?"

Computer guy sighed and turned back to his laptop. Clearly a skeptic.

"You cannot renege. We cannot allow it."

"Whaddya going to do about it—kill me?"

The room was still. Computer guy quit typing, yet his fingers were hanging over the keys, like he was wanting to get the next thing out of his partner's mouth just right. Matrix guy put back on his sunglasses, and said only this, "What do you think?"

• • • •

LARK KEPT HIS EYES closed. His wrist hurt like hell, but he'd fake a coma to get out of more prodding. It was easier this way. No dealing with his dad or the nurses or the uniforms outside his room. It gave him time to think.

In the history of teenagers, had there ever been a date that was such an epic failure? He didn't know any 'moves.' He didn't even own a car. But somehow, he'd ended up sharing a tight-fitting sunroof with none other than Krystal freaking Price. Looking back, Lark couldn't even remember asking her out. However, he would never forget that moment when they ran out of small talk and patience for meteor showers—for that led right into fireworks!

First was a blast of dirt clods, pounding the two of them flat on the roof of the car. Blinded by a bright flash, Lark wriggled back down inside, ramming the shifter with his tailbone in the process. He was pulling Krystal down when the concussion rocked her little sports car like a toy boat, and glass exploded everywhere. She flopped against the driver's side door—limp, her eyes shut, her mouth open.

Another explosion, this one farther away, kicked a cloud of dust over the field.

Then it was quiet.

Overhead, through the brown haze, hundreds of streams of light were scorching closer and closer to earth. "Meteor fall," Lark screeched, and he pushed into the driver's seat with Krystal. The keys were in the ignition, but nothing happened when he turned them. No lights on the dash. He realized the radio, just seconds ago offering the soundtrack for their real-life movie, was mute. "EMP," Lark said aloud.

A lightning-bright blast was followed by a deafening boom not 100 yards away. Dirt rained down on the car. They had to get out of there. Lark fished behind her and found the door handle, but when he pried it, she tumbled out on the ground. He squirmed around the wheel and crawled over her body. She was dead weight, impossibly heavy for such a petite girl, but he pulled her on out.

He sat with his back against the car, looking at her. Even sprawled in the dirt, hair frayed out everywhere, she was the most beautiful girl he'd spoken to. Though it scared him more than the meteors, he felt her neck. It was bizarre to touch her but exhilarating to find a pulse.

Another crash landing rocked the car, kicked dirt in his face, choked him with dust. Lark got to his knees and felt around for Krystal's wrists, and began dragging her across the field. They'd never get far this way, but if he could just get her to shelter, he could then go for help.

Several meteors hammered the field all at once. Though blinded again, he could feel them impacting the ground through the soles of his feet, and the concussion pounded his chest. It seemed forever far to the edge of the field. He had to stop pulling her once to wipe his eyes and catch his breath. Through the haze, he saw what was left of Krystal's car—pieces.

Finally, he stumbled into the ditch and found the culvert pipe. He didn't like shoving her in there, but at least she might be safe. He didn't want to leave her or the safety of the ditch, but he had to. He had to save the day, had to be the hero. He didn't feel very heroic, however, when he noted that he'd peed his pants.

That never happened in the movies.

Chapter 8: Awkward

February 2030

Krystal suppressed a giggle, even so much as a smirk, as the off-duty officer hitched up his off-duty utility belt and sauntered up. "Problem here?"

"No," both Lark and Sackerson said at the same time.

Our Father, he had said. She had heard right, hadn't she?

Lark was fidgeting like a kid on meth, and he was staring at Sackerson. Probably everyone was staring at Sackerson, but Krystal was trying to get a read on Lark.

"Well," the cop searched their faces, "good." He patted the phone holster on his hip. "If you need me, Fortune, call."

By now Stu and Henny were standing, too. Krystal could feel the testosterone hanging as thick as the smoke in the air. *A couple of jocks, a cop, and a federal Spook walk into a bar...*

"We're good, Officer Burns," Sackerson said. "We were just funning around."

Funning around? Who talked like that? What did it even mean? Anyone with half their wits could have glanced at a snapshot of them just then and known there was nothing fun here.

Krystal had to fight back a double take, however, when the cop broke into a smile and backed off. "Okey dokey," he said, returning to his table.

"I told you," Sackerson said to Lark in a raspy whisper, "this is serious stuff. Now come on, let's sit down."

It was clumsy, but they managed to get situated. Krystal did not like being at the back of the booth, but that's where she ended up. Lark did not like being next to her on one side, but neither did Stu on the other. She was sandwiched between two guys she once thought she liked, two guys who would rather eat glass than talk to her. Henny rounded out the booth, as always, at Stu's side, like a faithful puppy.

Sackerson had pulled up a chair on the aisle side of the booth, effectively blocking all of them in. She realized despite his age and size, until this moment he'd seemed quirky, sure, but not so much in charge. He hadn't seemed like much of a threat. "Okay. That could have gone better."

"What do you mean, 'our father' is in trouble?" Lark began. "You my long-lost brother or what?"

"Sounds like a cult," Stu said, nodding.

"It's complicated. More important is that his situation is life threatening."

"What does that even mean?" Krystal asked, then regretted it, for everyone at the table looked at her like she was interrupting. Maybe she was, but it was driving her crazy.

Sackerson pulled off his snowcap and sighed. Bizarre tattoos covered his bald head. It looked like a maze or complicated circuitry webbed all over his scalp.

"You really are in a cult, aren't you?" Stu asked, puzzling over the numbers and barcodes.

"Lark, he's going to be killed. He may be... gone... already." Sackerson put his head in his hands, dropped elbows to the table, and rubbed his bald head, then his face. To Krystal, he seemed pretty shook up.

"That's ridiculous!" Lark smirked. "He's a telescope jockey. A nerd. Who'd want to kill my father?"

Our father rang in her ears. Krystal wanted to hear them both say it, one, then the other. She thought they pronounced it the same, a little too much like the Lord's prayer.

When Sackerson looked up at them again, he did not seem like an agent of any kind. He looked beat. "This was a dumb idea," he said, "selfish of me."

"Selfish?"

"Yeah, selfish. I thought this would be kind of a reunion, you know? Relive a moment. Solve everything over dinner."

"Every time he opens his mouth, it gets weirder."

"Shut it, Henny," Lark said. He leaned in and said, "So, getting us together, this is selfish on your part?"

"A reunion?" Stu scowled.

"I know." Sackerson sat up straighter, looked them over. He glanced at a clock on the wall nearby. "Listen," he said, "I may not live to see tomorrow, so let's just get it all out on the table. You still got it for her. He's still got it for her. She's not sure what she wants—never is. So, you hate him, Krys, and he thinks you're misguided." Sackerson turned his attention to Henny. "And you... I have a hard time even sharing a table with you."

"What'd I do?"

"What's even more insane is that even I got it for her," Sackerson said, shaking his head. "Even now."

Krystal felt her face burning. She wanted to melt under the table.

A rap at the window and a splash of movement got her attention. Everyone's attention. A big black bird was flapping its wings, cawing and tapping on the window glass at the Mack's logo.

"Aha!" Sackerson saw it, too, and waved it away. The bird perched on a parking meter, snapping its head to glare at them with one eye, then the other. It cawed again.

Sackerson continued, "I thought we could all pull together, you know?," he said, talking faster. "I didn't want to do all this alone either. I don't think I *can* do this alone. Problem is—" he paused as the cowbell rang over the front door. He nodded as if he expected it, then glimpsed over his shoulder at the door. "The problem is, I was shortsighted and put you guys in harm's way."

Two men in long black coats were at the register waiting to be seated. Krystal knew they were not from around Guthrie. They were better dressed than feds. They carried themselves the same way, if not even more suspiciously. One with dark glasses panned the room. She looked away when the other man tried to make eye contact.

"Yes." Sackerson nodded to her. "That's right, Krys. That's 'harm' you're looking at."

"This is such bull—"

"Henny, it's only because I have questions for you that you're even around."

Henny waved his arms and made a face. "What?" he bellowed.

"They coming our way now?" Sackerson asked Krystal. She peeked over his shoulder and nodded.

"Guys, this is going to get *really* crazy," he whispered, frantic. "Go through the kitchen and don't look back. Go fast, and when you hit the alley—crazy time! You'll be okay, though. I'll find you."

He pulled on his hat, threw back his chair, and whipped around to face the two.

"It's the bear!" one of them said, dropping to a knee and pulling a gun. The other man ducked behind a booth.

About everyone in the restaurant was scrambling for safety. An old Einstein-looking guy seemed amused by it all, just sitting there, but Officer Burns dragged him under cover.

Time stopped. A baby cried but was quickly muffled. Someone coughed.

Dead still inside Mack's, so Krystal fixated on the crow outside—the one Sackerson called "Aha." It was agitated, slamming the window like a cardinal once did at her bedroom window. It was hitting so hard it was losing feathers. She wished she were out there, so that she could calm it or shoo it away.

Then, with an exaggerated shrug of its wings, the bird perched again on a parking meter. It nodded once.

Sackerson seemed to take it as a cue. He threw open his coat and pulled out long silver pistols. "Hello, boys!" Sackerson greeted them. "Kiss, kiss," he yelled, firing twice into the air. "Bang, bang!" He popped off two more shots.

The sound was deafening. People were screaming all around. Bits of ceiling tile were sprinkling down. Everything was a mess. Stu was pulling Krystal out his side of the booth, and Lark was urging her to follow him. Henny might as well have been on the gridiron. He was bulldozing people out of their way as they scrambled toward the kitchen.

Behind them, Krystal heard more yelling, and just as they crashed through the double doors into the greasy kitchen, more gunfire. All three boys were cursing as they pushed her past the fry cook. They ran into Stacy, who couldn't keep the coffee cups balanced on the tray she held overhead. Cups were bursting on the floor at their feet, splashing them with hot coffee as they passed.

"This way!" Stu called, kicking open the back door.

The gray afternoon was suddenly a radiant crisp blue, and Krystal was shocked by a bright blue flash as she crossed the threshold to winter. She thought she stepped in a puddle of slush, and then—POP!

• • • •

THE FOUR OF THEM WERE wrestling in a jumble, kicking and pushing apart from each other, cussing and disoriented. They were in a pile of hay in some old building, not the alley. One second they were at Mack's, another and they were not.

"I've been here," Krystal gasped.

"Yeah, it's my daddy's barn!" Stu surveyed the place. "We're in the hayloft. Again."

Lark sat up, brushing straw from his crazy mane. "Awkward."

Chapter 9: The Other Guy

"**N**o, you can't go back for your coat, Lloyd," an officer blocking the door argued. "That's a crime scene. You're a witness. We got processing to do."

Detective Shae Ward shouldered through a knot of police and Lloyds and Floyds and Hanks and Bubbas. She flashed her badge, more as a show for the patrons than for identification, since the Doorstop was also her office mate, second cousin, and third baseman on her co-ed softball team. "Bart," she said, "how bad?"

"Already cold," he grumbled. "And Burns is the best you got in there—if that tells you anything."

She pressed on inside, hoping Mack's had been clamped down before it was too sullied. She knew better. Even when she heard it on the scanner, *"shots fired, 2nd and Central, inside Mack's,"* Ward knew people would have traipsed all over her crime scene. Sure enough. As she had pulled up, the ambulances were leaving, their lights churning, their sirens muted. Gurney tracks in the snow. It was the way things worked here. No reason to gawk over the bodies. That was disrespectful of the dead. Policy and procedure, evidence and common sense—all out the window here. *More respect for the dead than the law.*

"Burns!" she called in the empty restaurant. The place always smelled like her husband's parent's house: stale cigarettes and fried food. Now it layered with the smell of cordite and the copper, too. As she made her way down the aisle, she noted overturned chairs, cold food still on plates, and then, one to her left, the other to her right, large dark puddles of blood on the worn carpet. Brass shell casings were localized there, too. A plate-glass window, street-side, was shattered, letting in sleet and road noise.

Sergeant Mike Burns came out of an alcove midway down the interior paneled wall. She was aware that it was the bathroom, and based on the sound of the flushing stool, she was certain that room was not going to be pristine.

"Tell me what happened here. I heard you were first on the scene."

"Shae, I *was* the scene. I was sitting right over here, and they was shooting on either side of me."

"You were here? When it all went down?"

"Right smack there. Saw the whole thing, then secured the scene."

"Good work," it pained her to say.

"Called it in. Kept everybody contained, too." Burns said, "That was the hardest part."

It had been a shootout like the town had not seen in her lifetime. Three men firing openly in a public restaurant on main street. All of them strangers. One of them was at large and associated with some local kids. Good kids.

"Two of them, over here?" Ward asked. "Behind this booth here, the other one behind that chair?"

"That's right. The other guy—"

"Two against one? They fired, what... two clips each?"

"I... I figure so. The other guy didn't even take cover. Just hollered and fired like mad."

She made her way back by the booth, past yet another overturned chair. She faced the front doors. She noted the distance to the bloodstains, not even thirty feet away. "He was standing right here?"

"That's right," Burns nodded.

Ward counted what appeared to be six bullet holes in the ceiling. There was no brass at her feet. "How many shots did he get off?"

"I couldn't count. It was a madhouse in here, Shae. We was all—"

"How many 'you think he fired?"

Burns shrugged. "Ten? A dozen? Maybe?"

"And he got away?"

"Yes. Took off after Lefty and the rest of them. Right through the kitchen," Burns gesticulated, "sorta."

"Sort of?"

"I don't know what to tell you. You can ask 'Berto and Stacy. They were back there." Burns bowed and shook his head. "Guy went through the door, then he was gone."

"Yeah, yeah." Ward had heard such justifications a hundred times. It was too dark. They had the high ground. "He was just too—"

"No, I mean... *gone*! Disappeared. You can go ask Barry and Chet. They're still out there looking for trace."

"Burnsy," Ward smiled, "you better sit down. I think all this is getting to you."

"No, I will *not* sit down. Shae, I'm telling you the truth. I wasn't ten foot behind the guy. I was coming in the kitchen when he was going out that door, and then he was gone."

"Disappeared?" she repeated, looking back toward the kitchen now. "You can't stick to that, you know. Not if you ever hope to get on full 8's. If you put that in a report, Mike, you're through."

* * * *

SHE MADE SURE IT DID not get put into print, but Sargeant Burns' claim was not dispelled by any evidence. There were no footprints, no fingerprints, nothing but a size 12 boot print on the inside of the kitchen door. Both of the other witnesses corroborated his story. No one from the street had seen *anyone* exit to the alley.

No one could find the kids, either. The gunman had been sitting with them when the whole thing erupted. Some witnesses reported a little trouble between them, especially between the gunman and the waiter.

It made Ward sick to her stomach. She stepped outside twice to call home. The first time, she made her husband lock up. The second time, close to bedtime, she talked to each of her girls.

They let the last of them go from Mack's by 10 p.m. Attention was turning to the kids. They found the Price girl's car and the Wiebe boy's pickup right across the street. Neither car was locked. Both were clear. Wiebe had an unregistered handgun under the seat and a rifle in the rack, but who didn't around here?

Family were being held and questioned at the station, all the parents, stepparents, even some grandparents. Dale Wiebe was being difficult. The Hinmans had been drinking. The Fortune boy's father could not be found. None of them had ever heard of a tall, bald man with tattoos all over his scalp. Not one of them could think of any reason their child would have associated with such a stranger.

The dead men weren't talking either. Neither one had any identification. Serial numbers on their weapons had been filed off. It would be 48 hours to get their prints back from OKC.

The other guy was going to keep Detective Ward up all night. What kind of man could appear in her town, gun down two men, then kidnap four kids—all in broad daylight—and disappear?

Shae knew who might have the answers: a tabloid junkie, a conspiracy nut, a man who would still be up at all hours. Buzz Lawton, her dad, would have loved this one... but when she dialed him up, he didn't answer. She called her mom, woke her, only to learn her dad had gone out for afternoon coffee and not yet returned. He did that now and then, had done so all Shae's life. AWOL for days.

The timing seemed especially suspicious.

Chapter 10: Cold Delirium

L ark closed his eyes again tightly. If only he could close his ears. They'd been going on, back and forth, for what seemed like an eternity. "So, you're saying he took the ladder down?" Henny continued. "Tried to trap us up here?"

"Are you going to make that jump?" Krystal asked.

They had all thought about it, surveyed the situation like Henny continued to do. It just took Henny a little longer to process things. It was at least thirty feet to the cement floor of the barn. The ladder was propped far across the tack room below. Whether it was Sackerson or not, whoever moved it must have known it would be aggravating to see it there, out of reach.

"And somehow he doped us?" Henny asked, back on the question they all had.

"How else can you explain it?" Krys said.

"Maybe something to do with this," Stu said. Lark opened one eye for a peek, only to see Stu reaching up to touch something.

"NO!" Lark dived into Stu, and they fell back in the hay. Before Stu could even react, Lark was on his feet, examining the curl of blackened wire dangling from the rafters. "Never touch one of these!" He warned them. "Ever."

"Pretty good moves, Lefty," Henny said.

Krystal stood slack jawed.

Stu was getting to his feet, glaring back at Lark as if he was about to throw him over the edge. "What is *with* you? What do you think you're doing?"

Lark was asking himself the same things, but more, he was asking himself questions about that wire. He had only seen one once before like this, *still hot*. He sniffed for bleach, but it was masked by the odor of the barn.

"And what, exactly, is that?" Stu continued. "When did you put it here?"

"Wasn't me," Lark said, studying a charred bump on the wire. He wanted to pinch it in his fingers to see if it would crumble, but he dared not touch it.

"What is it?" Krystal came closer now.

"If it wasn't you, what's the big deal? Huh?" Stu poked Lark in the chest.

"I wish I knew," Lark said. "Just don't touch it."

"Why not?"

Lark raised his right wrist, started to explain, then changed his mind. He turned from them and waded away through the hay. "I just wouldn't," he said.

"You're such a freak," Henny smirked.

It was true. He'd always been a freak, always the new kid, from one base to the next, from one lab to the next. Nobody got him. Nobody tried. He was that weird red headed kid. He sat in the hay now, looking at the three of them. Once they'd actually had something in common, even inside jokes. Now they looked at him like he was something new at the zoo again, just like everybody else did.

"You know something, Lefty, and you're going to tell." Stu grabbed the wire and jerked it free from the rafters. He held it out in Lark's face. "Why's it warm?"

"I dunno."

"But you *do* know," Stu crouched close. "I'm starting to think you're in on something with that nutjob."

"Was that thing hooked up to something that fried our heads?" Henny asked, "You know, made us lose our memories on how we got up here?"

What he knew to be true about the wire was even more ridiculous. Lark inhaled, readying himself for a long explanation that might work... then he stopped himself. He looked back and forth at Henny and Stu. *Dumb and dumber.*

Krystal came up, shouldered Stu out of the way, and sat down, close enough Lark could smell her perfume. "C'mon, tell us." She switched on her anime eyes. "We're all kind of lost here."

It was the first time he'd been this close to her since the night of the Fall. He wanted to tell her everything, but his mouth failed him. He felt like a Muppet with a big terry cloth tongue.

She put her hand on his arm. "Please."

• • • •

OCTOBER 2027

Lark tripped again, but this time he found his leg tangled in wire as fine as hair. This field must have been an old landfill, he'd thought, for he seemed to have tripped over all kinds of things in his mad dash across it.

He took this minute to catch his breath, pulling the wire from his legs, then from the sandy soil. Rising to his feet, he stuffed a length of wire into his pocket, and forged ahead.

This was otherworld stuff, like walking through a live action video game, or being in a war movie. Explosions would knock the wind out of him, then he'd be pummeled with debris. He'd get back up, reeling from it all, and just trudge on. Relentless. The big hero on forced march.

A strange, high-pitched whistling passed overhead, so unlike the roaring and crashing. The object making this sound was a flaming ball, like the others, but when it crashed, it shattered into thousands of little rocks. The impact was far enough away that Lark wasn't instantly shredded by them, but had he been closer... it would have been like a shotgun blast. As it was, it felt like a barrage of tiny hail.

Lark picked up a few of the little white rocks. They were not pebbles but perfectly sculpted little oblong shapes. Had he not known better, he would have mistaken them for Tic-Tacs. As he had with the wire, he shoved a handful of the little rocks into his pocket.

A meteor hit him.

His thigh and hand were instantly scorching hot! He rolled onto his back. He jerked his hand from his pocket. No meteor. A glowing red wire was wrapped around his wrist. He screamed out in pain when the wire flared white hot, his hand blast bright blue—then it all was gone. Except the pain. Lark flopped to the ground, writhing and howling, holding his wrist where his hand had been.

• • • •

HE COULDN'T TALK ABOUT it with the medical staff, with the agents, or the air force, or even his mother.

His therapist, Bertha Lorde (he saw the subtext of her name, even if she did not see the humor in it), asked him to put it in writing. Lark tried writing it out. She always urged him to switch it to first person, to own what had happened, but he couldn't quite get it right.

It never made sense. Nothing he wrote made sense. He could never capture it all, so he ultimately gave up even trying to write it out linear. She said to give it a go with a poem, so he did, again in third person, but he penned:

Cold Delirium
Would be a good brand of beer
But he was here
Blended into the soil.
He was planted.
Transplanted.
Hymns offered him
No more pain.

There was no getting up.
A boy on his back
Oppressed by more than
The gravity of it all.
Had he wished himself dead?
A tang in his nostrils
A bright light with no heat
Burning his eyes.
Pressure released with a
jolt—Decouplers—frangible bolts!
Himself jettisoned.
But it was all backwards:
Himself ascending
Himself a shrug and wave away.
Then he was again alone
With the pain pushing back.
Hard ground.
Cold night.
A good place to
Black back out.

Chapter 11: Bupkis

Officer Davis Cole was cold to the bone. He'd been stationed at Mack's back door since 16:00, leaning against a utility pole. Now that it was dark, he amused himself by watching the ember of his cigarette glow brighter as he inhaled.

It was that boring on watch.

Forensics had left hours ago. They'd fired up the shop lights about an hour before they left, and Cole was standing near one, hoping to draw some heat, but that didn't work.

He couldn't park his car in the alley, they said. It might mess up the evidence. Funny thing, there was no evidence. No matter how many times the guys had tried to pull a footprint from the snow or anything from the door, they got bupkis.

Cars weren't even circling the block anymore. Rubbernecks had all turned in for the night. It was just Cole and the pole he leaned against. And it was cold.

He fumbled for his mobile phone. Sure, he was breaking protocol, technically even breaking the law, but it was something to do. Posting updates. Cigarette clamped in his mouth, he fought his gloves off and posted to his socials.

Something cracked him in the side of the head, and he went down hard. When he could focus, he was hurting. Bad. He was lying in the alley, soaking in the slush. His vision was bloodied, and he did not raise his head, for he saw a shadow move. The floods were out, but he saw someone at the back door.

"Anything?" a voice behind and above Cole asked. Cole clamped his eyes shut and did not move. It had to be his attacker.

"Mmmmmm..." the other one said.

Cole chanced a peek. Through blood and snow, he saw the perp at the door was running his hands over the doorsill.

"Try the bricks, Maxton," the one by the pole said.

"Got it!" he was prying something from the grout between the bricks above the doorway. "Old school Hot Wires."

"Hot Wires—two of them? I didn't know you could—" the attacker suddenly leaned over Cole, shaking his head. He was a clean-cut man with cropped dark hair and dark eyes. "Davis Cole!" he read his nametag. "Don't be a hero." Then he reared back and kicked Cole in the head. Hard.

Chapter 12: Answers

Krystal was a little more than kind of lost. Being stuck in the loft with the three boys did nothing to help. Stu had been swaggering around for an hour about his daddy's barn being one of the best in the county, if not the country. Wood milled right here. "Grandpa still tells about the barn raising. Man, that had to be something..."

Henny proposed Acme-patented escape after escape, each more ludicrous than the last. He wanted down from there, urgently.

Lark was also too tightly wound, but when he tackled Stu, Krystal thought he'd lost it completely.

She just wanted some answers! They were finally going to get somewhere. Lark was surrounded, the answer man. He was taking in a big breath, like he would do in their speech class last semester. It was true confession time.

"What the—?" he blurted, and they turned to see the last of a blue flash. Shuffling sounds below brought all four of them to the edge of the loft. It was getting dark, and though she thought she saw someone leaning against the barn doors, she couldn't be sure.

The barn was striped by shafts of moonlight coming in through the barn's planking. Krystal so wanted to flip on a light switch or pry open the barn doors below.

"Someone's down there," Henny whispered.

"Thanks, Captain Obvious," Stu said aloud. It was probably no secret they were in the loft anyway. Every time they moved, a little bit of hay would drift to the floor. "Who's down there?" Stu shouted.

The person stirred, then fell. A stripe of moonbeam over his shoulder confirmed what Krystal was guessing. "It's Sackerson. That's his coat."

The heavy wool coat was not moving.

"Oh no. Not on our place." Stu tromped to the back of the loft, rummaged around, tossed hay bales aside. He returned with a coil of rope.

"Are you kidding me?" Henny asked. "You had this the whole time?"

"Stu, we've been here for-freaking-ever!" Krystal said. She had needed to go to the bathroom since they were back at Mack's.

"I wanted some answers," he said, unapologetically. He tied off one end of the rope to the very same rafter the wire had been on. "Didn't get any yet." He squinted his eyes at Lark, adding, "I'm hoping for more from the other freak."

With that, he gave them his patented prom king smile and shimmied down the rope. It was that kind of bravery and charm, a combination of stupid and cute, that had first drawn her to Stu.

"Wait for me!" Henny said, grabbing the rope and following Stu.

Krystal watched the rope jerk and twist as the two boys descended. Lark was not so quick to go down, and neither was she. They didn't know what to expect... but they knew Sackerson had a gun. She looked at Lark for an idea of what they should do next. He shrugged, "Test dummies."

It seemed too long before she heard anything below. "He's out," Henny's voice seemed so far away. "I think he's hurt."

"Let's see," Stu said, and a solid clack was followed by several large lights snapping on, glowing orange as they warmed up.

Sackerson was lying on his side. At his waist, his coat had a growing dark stain that had to be blood. His head was cockeyed and his hat askew. Krystal wondered if he might have a broken neck.

The two boys were standing over him. Stu nudged him with his foot. Nothing.

She felt her pulse pound at the thought that Sackerson might be dead. She had never been in the same room as a dead person. She didn't even go to funerals. Krystal stepped back from the edge of the loft and sat on a bale. The big barn lights buzzed loudly.

She appreciated Stu's plan, now that it was too late, now that everything was back in motion again. While they were stuck up there, they were on an island in limbo, just the four of them working it out. Even though they hadn't worked out anything, in retrospect, that had been a comfortable, if not tense, time. Now they had a dead man in the barn and a lot of explaining to do.

Explaining. Again.

Lark was watching them below, but talking to her, or maybe to himself. "I dunno what to do. What if he's faking? What if he whips out a pistol again? Up here, we're trapped. Down there..." He looked back at Krystal then, as if remembering she were there. He took a couple of steps closer and said, "I'm so sorry I got you into all this."

"Hey Lefty! You comin' down or what?"

He ignored Henny, crouched on one knee in the hay. His eyes were brimming with tears. He said, "Sackerson's right about all of us, you know."

"What do you mean?"

"We're all hooked—"

The ladder thumped against the loft, then it shook as someone climbed it. Lark stood up, between her and the ladder, clenching his fist.

Henny popped his head up. He lumbered onto the loft and sat on a bale. "Stu's gone for help." He mopped his brow. "Wouldn't want to be him, telling his daddy there's a stiff in the barn, calling the cops."

"Did you see what's wrong with Sackerson?" Lark asked. "You sure he's really... dead?"

"Well," he huffed. "He didn't move, and Stu clocked him pretty good in the head."

"He *what*?" Krystal asked.

"Kicked him in the head."

"Oh. My. God."

Chapter 13: Bones

"Criminy!" Stu said. It was cold and wet, and his coat was... where? Back at Mack's, maybe? Back in his truck? "Spud!"

His dog would know what to do, but he was stranded back in town, probably bored out of his gourd. As Stu trudged across the farmyard, he couldn't help but wonder what Spud was up to. He scoffed at the thought of Spud using the two-way, slobbering all over the knobs. Howling and panting over the radio out of boredom.

No boredom here, just a frickin' dead body in the barn. Stu had made it across the farmyard to the shop, keeping an eye on the lights in the windows of their house, not far away. No one had noticed him yet. That was good. Dad's truck was gone... and that was probably bad. Where would he be on a Wednesday night? *Out looking for him,* Stu feared.

He made his way through the shop, around the grain truck and the lawn tractors, between his grandpa's old milking equipment and his dad's welder. Even in the dark, Stu knew everything in there, laced through it like a defensive line, for everything was in its place, right where he had left it. That was the way it always was at their farm: tidy. His job was keeping it that way. In a few years, his dad said, he would grow into the rest of it.

Stu didn't even want to think about what his dad and grandpa would have to say about the current mess out in the barn. He plucked the wheelbarrow from its mount on the wall and rolled it back the way he'd been. "Guy just broke in, right when I was showing my friends around," he rehearsed, but it didn't hold water. Even his dad knew the Fortune kid was trouble, a military brat from a broken home. Try as he might to hide it, probably even the cattle knew things had not gone well with Krystal lately.

"This friend of Henny's..." he started, but no one would believe that, either. Stu was his only friend in the world. He hesitated at the

45

shop door, looking long at the house again. It looked so warm in those glowing windows. He thought about slipping in to snag a work coat but dropped the idea when he saw his mom's silhouette just off the kitchen.

He could lie to anyone in the world but her. If she caught him, with just a raised eyebrow she would get a full confession: "Strangest thing, ma. This freaky bald guy was bugging us at Mack's, then started shooting up the place, and next thing we knew, we just... woke up in the loft."

He shook his head. Sometimes the truth was the hardest thing to believe. He couldn't believe it himself.

A cat was rubbing against him, one of the ones nobody'd bothered to name. Stu picked it up and rubbed its ears. The cat squirmed away, tried to jump from his arms, but he grabbed its back feet, holding it like a dead rabbit. The cat was whipping around, jack knifed up to grasp Stu's arm. It stuck its claws through his sleeve a little deeper than it needed to.

Stu winced at the pain, grabbed the cat by the scruff of the neck with his other hand, and held it up to his face. "Now what, eh?" he said, eye to eye with the cat. It had released him and was just passively looking back at him. Stu looked toward the house again, then the barn, then back to the cat. "I mean, c'mon. Where can I put a dead guy that you won't find him?"

The very idea. He'd seen something like it in a horror movie, where cats and dogs had gone feral and ate the faces off people in their sleep or something.

He let out a sigh that clouded the cat in steam.

"Guess I *could* ditch him in the burn pile," he said aloud to the cat. "Between you guys and the coyotes, he'd be gone in a couple of days." It wasn't a perfect plan. Hell, it wasn't even a good plan, but it was more than he'd had when he told Henny he was going for help. It was better than just rolling a corpse around the yard in the wheelbarrow with no idea what to do next.

He put the cat down and scanned around in his memory of the shop. Feeling around under a bench, he found what he was looking for: a five-gallon can of gas. Stu loaded it in the wheelbarrow and set off for the barn.

He would tidy up this whole situation.

· · · ·

OCTOBER 2027

Henny didn't answer him, no matter how many times Stu yelled his name. He wasn't anywhere to be found around the wrecked pickup. The radio was still blaring, a tire still spinning—but Stu had set off for help. He kept falling down as he ran across the field. The way his side ached now, he had to have run a half mile or more, full tilt. Every few seconds, the sky would white out, then he'd have the pins kicked out from under him as the ground quaked. He could not outrun the meteors, he knew, but he was running for help, cross-country. In the distance, he could make out the bright lights of a feedyard. Someone there could help, he hoped. Maybe they could call for an ambulance.

Stu had first approached the fiery ruins of that car in the field, but when he recognized it, realized he knew whose it was, he just could not poke around. If Krystal Price was in there when it happened, there'd be little of her left now. It made him sick to think about.

So, he did what he could do: run. He was running the ball downfield, a quarterback sneak—but the defensive linemen were giant flaming cannonballs. One had been so close he was sure he was singed down one side.

Then it was quiet. Either that, or his ears were blown. He stopped, panting. He could hear his own pounding heart, his gasps for air. He could hear cattle, far ahead, though he realized now that even the feedyard had gone black.

After he got himself together, he resumed running north, toward the feedyard and eventually town. It had been so loud and so bright. Now, except for the crackling car far behind him, it was quiet. Fires were dying out all up and down the stretch between the mile road and the feedyard. He guessed himself to be half-way down the length of the corridor where most of the meteors had hit.

Something flashed bright, like an M80, about 100 yards ahead. The flash was followed by a terrible scream. Stu stopped... listening. The scream faded away. It was guttural like a coyote howling from taking a hit, but then—it sounded like a voice.

That's when the voice turned into unmistakable crying... and that's when Stu ran the other way.

• • • •

FEBRUARY 2030

Back in the barn, Stu realized just how cold it was outside. A guy could get frostbite. A guy could lose fingers and toes in this weather. Maybe a whole limb. Stu tried not to focus too much on Lefty's stump, but he wondered randomly if it hurt when the weather changed. He wondered what it felt like, day-to-day. He rubbed his hands together to warm up, realizing that was something Lark Fortune would never do again.

Lefty sneered at him, as if he was reading Stu's mind.

"And just what do you plan to do with that?" Lefty asked, eyeing the gas can.

"What do you think? Burn down the barn, with ol' Sackerson in it," Henny said, approvingly.

"Hell no!" Stu corrected. He would rather a SWAT team storm the property and haul him off for murder. He would rather tell his mom the whole thing. Anything was better than burning down the barn.

"So... burn the body?" Henny ventured.

"Eww," Krystal said.

Stu set the gas can aside and gestured to Sackerson. "Guys, help me load this carcass."

The three stood there, cow eyed.

"I'm going to put it out back, outside the tree row."

"You mean, *him*," Krys corrected, "not it."

"Whatever," Stu said, crouching down. He rolled the man onto his back and folded his arms so he looked like some guy in a casket.

Lefty shrugged and waggled his head. "And then?"

"Coyotes will do the rest," Stu said, matter-of-factly.

"You think of everything, don't you?" Lefty said, a little too snarky for his own good.

"Got a better idea?"

"What about the bones?" Lefty asked, but he crouched down with Henny, and the three of them hefted the body into the wheelbarrow.

Bones. Stu thought about that as they all stood around the corpse. Sackerson looked like he was asleep in a lawn chair. Sleeping it off. Dirt nap. Other than the blood that soaked his torso and coat, the guy was no worse for the wear.

"I'll go dump him," Henny offered, and he hefted the handles of the wheelbarrow. "Burn pile, right?"

"Yeah, but go around the long way, Henny. I don't want—"

"Wait a minute," Krystal interrupted. "You're going to burn the body?"

"What?" Stu hadn't thought of that. It wouldn't work, anyway. Bodies burnt right up in the movies, but when they'd tossed dead livestock on the fire before, it usually left most of the corpse behind anyway. "No, no."

They were looking from him to the gas can.

"No, that's to clean up. The blood, you know, there—" he pointed to the puddle, now turning darker, "and to clean the wheelbarrow."

"And your hands? And clothes?" Krys asked. "What about the blood all over them?"

Henny shrugged and rolled out of the barn.

Stu hadn't thought of everything, but he couldn't tell her that. Bones. Blood. It was a grizzly mess that was hard to hide, but it had to be done. Things had to be tidy. "Find some rags," he said. "We gotta clean this floor."

Chapter 14: Minimizing Risk

Lark was startled when Henny burst back into the barn. Henny was blanched and trembling. He did a double take when his eyes darted to Lark. He shrank back toward the barn door, just about to scream...and then he threw up, projectile vomited, in their general direction. He twisted quickly and lunged again for the barn door just as it was kicked open. Henny fell back, slipped on his own pool of puke, and toppled into Stu and Lark. The three of them fell to the floor.

Sackerson was back.

"What the hell, man?" Stu said, scrambling out from under Henny. Then he, too, saw Sackerson, and sat back on the floor, paying no mind to the spilled gas can, the blood, the vomit...

"Back from the dead!" Sackerson said, beaming. "Whew, that cold air was bracing, wasn't it, Henny?"

"Yeah, I don't... you just... I uh—"

"Shhhhh," Sackerson admonished him, a finger to his lips, shushing. He patted his bloody coat. Lark noted the bulge, remembered the pistols. "Don't say anything you'll regret."

"I don't understand," Krystal squeaked, clutching her head.

Lark stood up, a gas rag still in his hand. "So... you're... okay?"

"Never felt better—well, not lately, anyway," he smiled like a Cheshire cat. "And how about you, Lark? A little confused, maybe, but no worse for the wear?"

Stu stood and eyed Sackerson's head.

"Yeah, you gave me quite a love tap there, Stewey, but I... heal fast."

"You were sh-sh-shot," Stu stammered. "A lot."

"One thing you're all going to find out, guys, is that things are seldom what they seem."

Henny remained a heap on the floor, fighting back tears. Lark had never seen him look so helpless. Afraid.

"Listen, I don't know who you are, or how you're doing all this—" Krystal was interrupted by the single finger Sackerson held up.

"Hold that thought," he said, and turned to shut and lock the barn door. "Now," he continued, "where's my hat?"

Stu held it up, and with a shrug of apology, extended it to Sackerson.

"Ugh. No thanks, man," Sackerson sneered. "You ruined it."

He truly had ruined it, Lark noted, having used it to scrub the barn floor.

"Well." Sackerson looked all around. "I'm going to need a hat."

"Who cares?" Krystal said. "Tell us what's going on, right now!"

"I don't know quite what we see in you, sometimes," Sackerson leered at her, then turned his attention to Henny. "Hinman, ol' boy. I'll be taking that fine hat of yours."

Henny curled up in a fetal position, moaning.

Sackerson swooped down and snatched the hat from Henny's head. He pulled on the red plaid trapper hat and nodded approvingly to himself. Then he turned his attention fully to Krystal.

"Okay, m'lady. But I gotta make this fast. Lark and I need to skedaddle."

"What?" Lark said. He felt as if he would never catch up to the conversation again.

"You're next, Lark. But we'll have the luxury of time, as they say."

"Then spill," Krystal demanded. "Or I'll scream."

Sackerson smiled broadly but splayed his hands in surrender. "Okay, okay," he said. "It's like this. I'm a freelancer, just trying to set things right. Our protagonist, Dr. Christopher Fortune, Colonel,

US Air Force, retired, is being pursued for his knowledge of the most important scientific breakthrough, well, maybe... maybe ever! Thing is, he doesn't even know what he knows. He has no idea how it's going to—how disruptive—" Sackerson just shook his head. *Was he at a loss for words?*

"That's just so much bullshit," Lark interjected.

"That's what everyone's going to say, probably already has been saying. The fact that he hasn't brought it home or that it hasn't made it to the papers yet... well, it gives me hope."

"Hope?" Krystal tipped her head.

Sackerson belted out part of an old hymn, "My hope is built on nothing less than daddy's love and righteousness."

Lark saw something out of the corner of his eye, and he hoped it wasn't what he feared it was... but it was.

Stu had somehow found one of the big chrome pistols, and now he was holding it with both hands, pointing it at Sackerson.

"So that's where that went!" Sackerson said. "Where was it? Over in the hay? Did you pick it off me when you were going to toss me out?" He gestured for Stu to hand it to him. "Fork it over."

"You freaky bastard. I don't know where you came from, but you don't belong here. Get off my farm."

"Daddy Dale's not here to back you up, you know. I already scouted around out there after Henny and I talked outside."

"I don't need him," Stu said, but the pistol was quivering in his hands.

"Shooting him didn't seem to work," Lark said.

"Henny! Tie him up."

Henny just sat there, wagging his head. "No way."

"If you're here for Lark's dad," Krystal returned to the subject, as if all the testosterone in the room was irrelevant to her, "then why bother with us? And... and how did you get us all here... to the barn loft?"

Lark kept an eye on Stu, who refused to put the gun down. Lark's father had always instilled in him a respect for guns. He was not the kind of kid to have one hidden in his book bag or strapped to his moped. Stu, on the other hand, had been escorted from school, from a ball game, even from prom, for packing weapons.

"Drugs," Stu said.

"Nope," Sackerson replied. "Technology."

"My eye!" Stu snorted. "What do you mean, technology? You like... like, brought us out here on a flying saucer or something?"

"Or zapped us here..." Krystal mused. "Like a transporter?"

Sackerson stood a little taller, appraising her. "Well, I'll be—yes, Krys, that's exactly it! Yes!"

"Sci-fi baloney," Stu said.

"Now, it's a little hit and miss. I mean, I set up a dozen or so before I even came calling on—"

Henny moaned.

Sackerson squinted his eyes at him, and Henny was quiet immediately. "So, like I was saying, you take one of these—" he pulled a tiny white object from his pocket. "—and some high tensile wire, titanium is best, like this—" and he extracted a coil of wire from his other pocket. "And when you hook it all up like this, you got a little teleportation window!"

"Let's prove it," Lark said. He was moving before he even realized what he intended. He snatched the pistol from Stu and dropped it through the wire loop Sackerson was holding.

And just like that, the pistol vanished in a flash of blinding blue.

Everyone was quiet. Even Henny.

Lark looked at his stump, then back at the wire that was now black and smoldering on the barn floor. It smelled of bleach.

"That was a very expensive demonstration," Sackerson said. "But yeah. My pistol probably went to the same place as your hand."

They exchanged a long look.

• • • •

LARK TURNED TO THE others and said, "I'm going with him. You guys just keep your mouths shut."

Sackerson glared at Henny, "Especially you, got it?"

Henny swallowed hard. "Got it," he said, getting to his feet. "Lark, be careful."

Krystal grabbed his arm. "Really, Lark? You sure?"

He didn't know if he was sure. All he did know was that he wanted to get this guy away from her to keep her safe, but he couldn't put it into words.

"He's looking out for you, guys," Sackerson said it more directly—then even more directly. "Minimizing risk."

"Let's go then," Lark said, and made for the door. Sackerson was right behind him.

"You know, Creeper, you could 'minimize risk' yourself if you took us with you," Stu said. "Keep a lid on things."

Lark turned back, astonished. What was Stu thinking?!

"Yeah," Krystal seconded.

"No," Lark countered.

"Besides, I know where the truck keys are, unless you're gonna whip out a flying car," Stu added. "And if Henny's with me, he's good. Keeps him contained. Right?"

"Kenny?" Krystal took his hand.

"I... I don't wanna go," he eyed Sackerson suspiciously. "But I guess if you guys wanna—"

Sackerson shrugged. "Okay then. Let's Scooby-do this!"

"We'd be better off alone," Lark insisted. "This is ridiculous."

"Or genius," Sackerson held the door open for them all. "There's a fine line between the two."

Chapter 15: Deadly Force

"That's right, Detective. There's no other explanation," repeated the local ballistics expert, Ed Bonfy, who was *in no way officially associated with law enforcement.* Shae had told him that the moment he showed up and offered his services. He was a "gun nut," plain and simple, but he was here—and now—and Shae needed both if she was to quell the locals... and if she were ever to sleep well again.

"Because of the trajectories," she summed up, somewhat distracted by her current project, the unwrapping of straws. "And the bullets match."

"Well, yes, and no. Fatal shots were from very close range and directly from the perpendicular—"

"Meaning not from across the room."

"That's a yes. But no, we won't really know about the bullets matching anything until there's full ballistics, of course, but I can tell you from looking at your dead back there," he thumbed vaguely toward the funeral home, "and the holes in the walls here—" Bonfy walked over to the wall and gestured toward holes marked with yellow tags "—they're probably the same caliber."

"And you're saying from across the *aisle*, not across the room?" Shae produced four straws she had shoved together end-to-end and joined him by the bullet hole. She stuck one end of her long straw in the hole, a fairly snug fit, and together they followed the trajectory across the aisle to a bloody place behind the register.

"Right. From right over there... and probably just a .22 by the look of them."

"I can't tell you much, but I can confirm that," Shae shared. "Garden variety .22 automatics, filed."

Bonfy grimaced something of a smile, then continued, "But look at *them* holes, all over the ceiling, and up around the room back here, by this wall, and the one that popped the storefront glass—big bore." He looked at her, then away, mumbling, "Uncommon."

Shae was absently scanning the holes that peppered the restaurant's entry and walls. Head height or higher. More like cover fire than someone aiming to kill.

"How uncommon?"

Bonfy shuffled some broken glass underfoot. He looked uneasy.

"Ed? How uncommon?"

"What's the timeline on reporting a stolen firearm?" he asked sheepishly. Though it was just the two of them in Mack's, he was practically whispering now. "And... well... how *private* can that reporting be?"

"Are you saying—" she stopped when she found herself whispering, and more than a little frantic. Detective Shae Ward cleared her throat and asked in a normal, composed tone, "You had a gun stolen?" She gestured around the room. "This gun?"

"Guns." He couldn't look her in the eye for a minute. "Matching pair. S&W 500's."

Big revolvers. That's what witnesses had said. It matched. It might be the break she was after. "Ed, is that why you showed up tonight? You knew it was your guns?"

He looked so pained. "I always try'n help the law."

"Yes, I know."

"An' I can't have the fellas get wind of this, that my guns was the ones some loony toon did all this with."

"I know, Ed," Shae said, reaching to pat his arm but thought better of it. "This is an active case and a hot crime scene. You're a civilian who told me something in confidence here. Nothing gets out until this is solved, you know, and even then, well... some details might be left out."

Ed visibly relaxed. "Can we?" he gestured to a couple of chairs at a nearby table. "There's more."

Shae wanted to pull out her notepad but resisted. He was going to tell her things that he clearly did not want on the record.

They sat opposite each other at a table that had been undisturbed. Sometime earlier, patrons had sat here eating. One had an open-faced roast beef sandwich, the other a club. Their half-eaten food was now sprinkled with flecks of ceiling tile. One glass, she guessed of water, had toppled. She sized it up and waited him out.

"People talk. You know that, Detective. They say the damnedest things."

"That they do," Shae could write a book on the topic.

"They been talking about the guns the tall guy had already. I know they have. People have been asking me."

"Well, you are something of an authority—"

"Those two were special. Nickel plated, 8-inch barrel. Could blow through an engine block. Drop a bear. And... and they're unregistered." Ed stopped the conversation with that last word and swallowed hard. *First admitting his weapons had been stolen and now confessing they were not entirely legal.*

"Well..." she did not have a professional answer at-the-ready. She could not talk in any official capacity about the fact that about half the guns in evidence were not registered, nor about how she and Rob had two unregistered handguns at home. "I guess that's good, right? No direct link to you, even if this would leave the room?"

He seemed a little surprised by that but continued, "Now, I don't know how many people would have known I had those two. You're right. Lots of folks know I have lots of guns... that I got a conceal carry on me always... but also... knowing that... they tend to leave me alone, if you catch my drift."

She knew Ed Bonfy was a widower, a veteran, a former part-time Sheriff's deputy. She knew he didn't need one of those little signs in the yard or stuck on a window that advertised some home security system. It was common knowledge. He could recite the Castle doctrine of deadly force.

"The thing is, Ms. Ward, the man who took those guns knew just what he was after. He knew right where they were." He looked around the empty restaurant, leaning in to add, "Those are hobby pistols. You'd know that, right? Fifty-caliber handguns? Can drop an ox! More for bragging rights, I'm ashamed to say, than anything. *Most powerful handgun made today.*" He scoffed, as if chiding himself. "There's no good reason a man would steal those over others in my cabinet unless he was some cocky kid or a gun collector."

Shae noted he had said "the man" who took the guns.

She also noted he was becoming more agitated.

She risked it and went out on a limb. "You saw him, then?"

Bonfy took a deep breath and sighed. "Yes, yes, I did. It was the same man as here today, from all I heard. Tall. Thin. Bald." He swallowed again. "And I froze when I caught him leaving. Didn't do a damn thing when he was backing out the door."

"That was very wise, Mr. Bonfy. He was an armed perpetrat—"

"I think *that's* why I didn't move. Just like you, just now—he called me 'Mr. Bonfy,' like he knew me. Said it like he'd always known me."

She knew her best detective work had always been on instinct and emotion, to hell with what they said in the academy. This was one of those times she felt they were on the edge of a break, maybe. She forced solid eye contact with him. "What do you mean by that? What exactly did he say that made you feel that way?"

"Mr. Bonfy. I'll be taking these guns."

"That was it?"

Bonfy sighed, then continued, "I taught middle school science for thirty years."

He was going to leave it at that? She nudged, "Yes, I know."

"Those kids. When they'd say my name... well, I know it sounds silly, but the man in the foyer said it just like that."

"So, you're saying... he was once a student of yours?" It was 1:00 a.m., and she had hours of paperwork to do. "Is that why you didn't... intervene?"

"I'm sure of that, maybe more. Maybe like some kid I'd had out to the place to paint or mow or had in Sunday School or something. But it's like he knew me, like he was glad to see me, almost. Like he knew—in spite of all the shine about me always packing heat—he knew I wouldn't hurt him."

"And you're pretty sure you're not reading anything into this?" She had to ask, for if Ed Bonfy was right, the limitless pool of tall bald men was now narrowed down to Guthrie's local men, middle school graduates from the last thirty years.

"Either that," Bonfy said, "or he just didn't care. Like some psychopath." Ed smiled and sat back in his chair. Confession concluded.

Shae couldn't help but raise an eyebrow. The stranger in town was getting stranger by the minute.

Chapter 16: Improvisation

"**A**nd that undoubtedly makes you Daphne—"
The chiming of a cell phone interrupted Sackerson's lecture on Scooby-Doo. It was Stu's, Krystal knew the ring tone, and before he could even get it flipped open, Sackerson swatted it to the floor. "No calls. Okay? No trouble."

Stu had let off the gas and was eyeing his phone on the floor. "If I don't get that, we'll be in trouble like you never knew."

"Pretty sure it's an after-curfew check-in," Krystal offered. "I texted my mom hours ago."

"You did what?" Sackerson said. "I want your phone too. I want everyone's phone. Now!" Sackerson picked up the phone and flipped it open. Krystal could see "DAD" on the display, even from the back seat. He hesitated, then handed Stu the phone. "Tell him you're fine and you're going to be unavailable, got it?"

Stu flipped the phone, popped it to his ear. "Yeah?"

He had pulled over. All of them were straining to listen in.

"I told you, Dad. Spending the night at Hinman's."

They heard some un-Christian yelling from the other end of the phone.

Stu looked at Sackerson, held his phone at arm's length, and shrugged as his dad continued his tiny cellular tirade.

All the boys, Sackerson, too, looked a little panicked.

Krystal put her hand over the phone and whispered, "Tell him we're getting back together. We're with my mom."

Stu looked at her wide-eyed, then at the rest of them for input. "Dad. Dad. I'm sorry. I—"

Another blast of righteous condemnation from the phone, but when it slowed, Stu jumped in again: "Listen. I was... I am just a little embarrassed, is all. Remember Krystal Price?"

Stu was pressing the phone to his ear. She could not make out the response on the phone. Stu was biting his lip. Listening.

"Yeah, that's her." He let out a sigh. "Yeah, well... tonight the time just got away from us, Dad. We've been talking about getting back together—"

More listening. It looked from Stu's expression like it wasn't going well. Stu, Lark, and Henny all looked like frightened little boys. Sackerson caught her attention and waggled his eyebrows.

Krystal let out a big sigh, and she grabbed the phone from Stu. In a stern and righteous voice, she said: "Hello? Hello!"

The boys were audibly astonished. She shushed them with a glare. It was her best mom glare, and it was just what she needed to get into character. "*Mister* Wiebe! Dale, isn't it?" She cleared her throat and continued, louder, over the frantic shouting coming from the phone. "Mr. Wiebe, I have never in my life been spoken to in such a way, and I won't have it now. Do. You. Understand?"

Stu was mortified. Sackerson was loving it.

Krystal thumbed it to speakerphone just as it fell quiet on the other end of the line. "Ma'am?" a gravelly voice finally said.

"Yes. Am I to understand you have questions about our children being together so late?"

"Mrs. Price?"

Krystal held the phone out between them all so they could hear. Everyone's face was awash in the light of the little phone.

"Yes," she said with confidence. "About tonight. I can assure you—"

"Oh, no ma'am. I... I had no idea they was—"

"Of course, you didn't," Krystal sneered her words. "How could you?"

Sackerson was playing charades. He put his hands together, as if in prayer, tipped his head on them. He then gestured an arch, then pointed at his wrist. Krystal was trying to keep up with him and listen to Stu's dad too.

"...highly irregular's all. You see that, don't you? Upstanding young man, my pride and joy—"

"And my Krissy would never be out so late, trust me. They were sitting in Stewart's pickup truck in the driveway at ten, and I flagged them in from the cold."

Sackerson was now mouthing the words he wanted her to say. It was outlandish, outright crazy, but so was this call, this night. Everything.

"Well, thank you for that. Kids don't have sense to come in from the rain."

"Yes, yes. Well. I made them some cocoa, and we visited a while. Eventually, they asked my advice on their relationship." Krystal covered the phone as Stu's father said something. "Watch this," she whispered, now fully in her element. "And eventually," she interrupted him, "eventually, we fell into prayer."

She covered the mouthpiece again, and everyone fought off laughter, except Stu, who rolled his eyes in distaste. He eyed the phone in distrust.

"That's a kindness," Dale Wiebe stated. "And I thank you."

"So easy to lose time, you see, sir?"

"Oh... oh yeah. Yes." He paused for a long while. "So... may I speak to my son again? I believe I owe him an apology."

"Of course, Mr. Wiebe, of course. But one more thing? Would it be alright if he just spends the rest of the night here on the couch?"

"Pardon me?" The ire was bubbling in his voice but not boiling. "Tomorrow's—"

"Oh, rest assured, we'll have him at your farmstead by time for chores in the morning."

Stu's dad sounded flummoxed. He growled some kind of agreement, yet another apology, and Krystal switched the phone off speaker and handed it summarily back to Stu. Her palms were sweating.

"Yes. Right, Dad." Stu was cupping the phone close again. "First thing."

Then Stu looked even more shocked, if that could be, and he stammered, "Love you too, Dad." He caught her eye in the rearview, then snapped shut the phone.

"And that, boys, is how we do it," Krystal proclaimed.

"Women!" Henny said. The men all shook their heads.

Sackerson grabbed Stu's phone and asked for the rest. Lark could not have afforded one, she knew, and Henny said his was broken. She checked hers one more time for any reply from her mom—there was nothing all evening—and for a moment, Krystal wished her mom was half the mom she had just pretended to be on the phone.

She tossed the phone into the front seat and wedged back in between Kenny Hinman and the door. She stared out the window as the truck resumed speed.

• • • •

"SIMPLE RULE IS: EAT *as-is*." Sackerson was carrying on about nutrition, of all things, when she paid attention again. "If you gotta process it, even so much as cook it, then you're ruining it."

"Raw foods," Krystal offered.

He turned back to her and smiled. "Yes!" He thought a little. "Guess it's coming in from the coasts about now, eh?"

"I read about it in Vogue," she said. Krystal shook her head absently. Her mother had always said staying on trend was important. Now, here she was discussing healthy eating with three boys and a potential kidnapper as they raced for the Kansas border. *Unbelievable.*

"Well... trust me. Especially you athletic types," he gestured at Stu and Kenny. "You want to be preserved, then stay away from preservatives. Eat clean. Live long," he chuckled, adding, "and prosper!"

"I'm more of a pizza and pop kind of guy," Lark said, with little interest.

Henny pointed at Lark. "And beer. And cheese. I love—"

"This is really fascinating and all," Stu said, "but I still want to know where we're going."

"I told you. We're going to save Lark's dad."

"And where, and how, do you propose to do that?" Lark asked.

"Keep heading north, about an hour yet... get over the Kansas border. Tomorrow then, or the next day, we'll zip back down here, find your dad, save the day."

"Kansas border? *'Zip back'*... how?" Henny perked up. "Like the way we showed up in the loft?"

"Yeah," Stu said. "Like how exactly did *technology* land us in the barn?"

"And how did you make that gun disappear?" Krystal added.

"And where is it now?" Lark said.

"Okay, okay," Sackerson blocked with both hands, palms out. "I got it... and I owe you." He twisted in his seat so he could better see them all, his back pressed against the front passenger door. He looked each of them over individually. His gaze returned to, and rested on, Kenny.

"Guys," Henny moaned. "I gotta bail."

"What?" Stu swerved a little.

"What do you mean, bail?" Krystal asked, turning to look him in the face. He looked pale and unhappy.

"I mean, I can't go with you," he said, but Krystal thought he was leaving something out. Something big. When no one spoke, he added, "I think I'm gonna be sick again."

"Great!" Lark growled. "Just what we need—"

"What am I supposed to do, just let you out on the side of the road? That's crazy," Stu said. "I can get you to Perry, anyway. To the Pump n' Go."

"Leave me at the rest stop, just ahead."

"The rest stop?" Stu asked. "I think it's closed."

"It's urgent," Henny moaned. "I gotta bail. I'll hitch home. Done it before."

Krystal smelled his sweat and the old vomit caked on him. It was overpowering, and now he was huffing and squirming.

"Might be both ends, Stu," Henny said. "Rest stop. Now."

Krystal nodded in the mirror.

Sackerson was nodding too.

"Don't be so glum, hun," Sackerson said. "He'll be fine."

· · · ·

THEY HAD MADE IT INTO Perry, despite all the drama, leaving Kenny Hinman at the all-night cafe. He had to be scared, and lonely, and Krystal worried that leaving him there was just throwing him to whomever was chasing them. "It's just wrong. We could have waited him out."

"You heard him. It's what he wanted," Sackerson said firmly.

Krystal had heard him call Kenny *some other name* when the two of them were standing out in the sleet, strangely chummy. Even stranger, Sackerson held Kenny at arm's length, then pulled him in for a big hug just before they left. Lots of patting him on the back. She was still so shocked, now nothing was coming clearly to her. What had he said, *So long, Judas?*

It was oddly quiet for a few miles. Everyone was left to their thoughts. Krystal felt all she had in her head were more questions.

"Okay, what I'm about to share is some strange stuff," Sackerson began. "I had to spend my first week here just getting my bearings."

"Whatever," Lark said. "We aren't new to strange. We get dragged in by the Feds every time there's a—"

"Terrorist threat," Sackerson finished his sentence. "Yes, I know."

"But just *how* do you know?" Krystal asked. "And if you know, maybe you can tell us why they always bug us about everything."

"Okay, okay. I told you there's something big cooking in the lab, right? That Dr. Fortune is about to break something like the world has never known."

"From the space junk?" Lark asked. "He's been obsessed with it."

"Yes, exactly that... and sort of not at all... but that's getting into the weeds a bit. Point is, he's going to hook up a Hot Wire, like back at the barn, only he's doing it in a lab environment, for the government."

Krystal heard his bitterness. "So, you think—what—that the government's going to do something?"

"Something like that. It's messy. No actual records to work with, just blanks to fill and people to visit."

"What's that supposed to mean?" Stu asked, looking from the road to Sackerson.

"It means I don't know what happens. I just know what happens *later*."

"Like what?" Krystal pressed.

"Like Dr. Fortune disappears, for starters," Sackerson said. "And all his research disappears with him... but some of the more intuitive types, artists in their own right, I suppose you could say, well, they improvise based on what they saw and did there at the ol' lab."

"And you're from that camp, I'm guessing," Lark said. "The artists."

Sackerson nodded thoughtfully. "Sort of. I'm sort of taking improvisation to a new level."

"Again," Stu growled, "what's that *mean*?"

"Honestly," Sackerson chuckled, "I just like the sound of that one."

"Okay, so you think Dad's going missing, maybe going dark, and you know that because of some leak in security at the lab. I still don't see how *we* are going to do anything about it."

"If all that's even true," Krystal said. "Didn't you say, 'Things are seldom what they seem?'"

"Yes, yes, I did. Krys, you are one sharp cookie."

"Well?" Lark asked after a long pause.

"Well, it *seems like* some crazy guy kidnapped you, shot up some guys in the restaurant, and is now going into hiding in Kansas. It seems like I'm crazy because I'm talking about teleportation and the boogie man getting Doc Fortune. That about sum it up?"

"There's your freaky looks too," Stu said. "Your head's got crazy written all over it."

"And the whole thing about knowing us like some kind of spy or something," Krystal said. "That's the creepiest part of it all."

"What if none of it was true?"

"Aww, c'mon. Do I have to say it again?" Stu said, "What's—"

"What's it mean? It means this: I am not some crazy kidnapping creep. We are not going to Kansas. Feel free to turn around, Stu. Let's go to the cabin you lease out during deer season... or better yet, let's go to the last place they'd ever look. Warm. Plenty of food. Police protection too. Let's hole up in the basement of Mack's. What do you say, Lark?"

He seemed too stunned to argue.

"Good," Stu said, wrenching the truck around. "I hate Kansas."

"Can we get Kenny?" Krystal asked.

Sackerson sobered. "Afraid not. He's not quite what he seems either."

"Aww, c'mon," Stu said.

"Trust me. I am one of the good guys. The fact is, I might be *the only* good guy. Well... not counting you three. I know what's going down, lots more than I can let on. I just don't know *what* I can tell you. Nobody's really sure about all this, but I'm *living* it, and I can tell you—straight up—everything you've been told about the Butterfly Effect and disrupting the 'space-time continuum' is just so much science fiction."

"You're talking now about... time travel," Lark said.

"I am."

"So... you're saying you're from the future?"

"Yes, and that makes me...makes all of us...future fugitives. It also accounts for why I know so much about you. Research. Lots of research. Lots of planning."

"So, it *seems* like you know things in advance, but really... really they happened one way, and you're just working it out that way, or changing it up. Is that what you're saying?" Krystal asked, her head about to explode.

"Yes. It's also why I feel like I know you guys so well. It's why I volunteered for this gig." Sackerson was giddy. "You guys are my heroes, and I'm here at the start of it all. Like an origin story in a comic book."

"So, this teleportation thing, it's also a time travel thing?" Lark asked.

Sackerson laughed aloud.

"What?" Lark groused. "How should I know how all this works?"

"That's just ironic. Comedy is irony, you know... and you're the punchline more than you'll ever know."

"You didn't answer his question," Krystal interjected. "Is it the same?"

"That's the improvisation. I kind of just tried something out here... and it worked!" He laughed again. "I'm right *where* I wanted to be, *when* I wanted to be, and the odds were a million to one—maybe more!"

"What's he talking about?" Stu flashed a glance at Krystal and Lark in the rearview mirror.

"I have no idea!" Lark said.

Chapter 17: Leads to Follow

"**A**re you in trouble, son, or are you safe somewhere?"

"Yes. Right, Dad," Stu's voice stated over the speaker phone and then confirmed, "First thing."

The first thing... the kid was saying... *trouble.* The kidnapper must have been right there during the whole call.

It was obvious that Dale didn't know what to say. He was hunched over the speakerphone, lost. His eyes pleaded with Shae, who sat opposite him. She nodded sympathetically.

"Love you, son," he said, still in shock.

She wanted to chastise him for not having called the boy before. She wondered just what stubbornness was at the root of such behavior, but his expression brought her up short. Clearly, he truly did love his son very much.

She had missed visiting with the other parents, but she wasn't too unhappy about it. The only one she felt she'd missed out on was Dr. Chris Fortune, but some Air Force suits whisked him away just as she had pulled into the station. He came and went in the time she had been away.

• • • •

HAD SHE NOT FOLLOWED up with Mike Burns, she would have had that time with Fortune, but then Burnsey's lead had been interesting. He had called her down to the Magic Dragon, of all places, Guthrie's hole in the wall bar. She showed up about 1:30, and to her surprise, there were more than a dozen cars still on the street. Officially, bars closed at midnight here, she knew, but that just meant they officially quit serving alcohol.

Nothing was official tonight. Through the haze of smoke (in a community that had voted to outlaw smoking in public places), she found him easily enough. He was at the bar with a lanky man everyone just called Skip. It looked as if Burns had just bought Skip another unofficial round.

"I'm off duty," he explained, as she approached.

"Me too," she sighed. "Can a girl get a White Claw around here?"

"A what?" the bartender sneered.

"How about a wine cooler?"

"How 'bout a lite beer, miss?" He popped the top and handed it to her before she could protest.

She took a long drink from the chilled bottle and closed her eyes.

"Long day, huh?" Burns asked.

"I'm soooo beat, Mike," she sighed, but she did not relax. The Dragon was full of drunk men, and more than a few were eyeing her not-so-slyly. She could feel the weight of her sidearm, tapped her boot to the brass rail to confirm the backup was handy.

"My adrenaline's been going like crazy ever since—well, you know," Burns raised an eyebrow and surveyed the occupants of the bar.

"So, I guess we're here for ol' Skip, am I right?" Shae saluted him with her beer. He smiled. It was a tired smile of a compliant old man one step from sleeping on the streets. She knew all about him, but for the moment, she tried to give him the benefit of the doubt.

"Ol' Skip's got word for you," Skip said of himself. "About the shoo—oo-ter." The sing song extra syllable made Shae doubt herself and Burns.

"Did you know Skip here used to have a jewelry store, Shae?" Burns asked. "Well, he did. Down by the old Sears store."

"That must have been... a while ago?"

Skip was doing the math, but Burns continued, "Long enough lots of people forgot about it." He recoiled at what he had just said. "No offense, Skip."

"None taken." Skip tipped his head and repeated, "None taken, Mike."

They talked for too long about jewelry and diamonds and just how much inventory he'd carried back in the day. Shae continued with her beer, relaxing into it. The fellas at the Dragon weren't so bad. Once they realized she was just here to unwind and have a drink, they went back to their own drinks and stories. Darts and pool.

"So, here's where it gets interesting," Burns leaned in a little.

"Real interesting," Skip said, his head nodding a little.

"Shae, you know who didn't forget about ol' Skip's jewelry store? The one guy who's brought it up in probably ten years?"

She just looked at him, waiting. Burns was all about theatrics, and at this hour, it was about all that was keeping her awake. "No. Who?" she finally asked.

Burns pulled back, out of the way, and let Skip have at it.

"Tall kid. About my height," Skip said. "Few days ago. He saw me on Main Street, just came up to me and started talking like he knew me. Friendly enough."

"Tell her what he wanted," Burns prompted.

"Said he knew I did engraving. He wondered if I could engrave something for him." Skip continued, "Well, I still have lots of my older stuff, you know. And I still live above the store. And... well... I could use a few bucks, I tell myself, so I take the bait."

"Tell her what you engraved, Skip." Burns was squirming now.

"Kiss Kiss," he said, "and Bang Bang."

"On a couple guns, Shae!"

"That's right. Big pistols. Heavy. Had me engrave the barrels, one with Kiss Kiss, the other with Bang Bang."

Shae was on full alert now. "Did you confirm an ID, Mike? Is it the same guy?"

"Oh, it's him, Shae," Burns said. "From what Skip's told me about him, I'm sure of it."

"I just remembered something else," Skip volunteered. "He just gave me a hundred dollar bill, outright. Didn't want the change. Don't that beat all?"

"Do you still have the hunnert?" Burns asked.

"Drank it," Skip smirked.

· · · ·

AND SO, AS SHE STOOD by Dale Wiebe now, a man full of equal parts remorse and wrath, Detective Shae Ward offered little consolation, "Mr. Wiebe, you did the right thing. We know more than we did, and your son knows you care. There's nothing more important than that right now."

Wiebe offered her a wan smile. "Right."

"And things are coming together. Fast." In fact, Shae felt she was living in a movie. She had never been on a case where things were coming together so quickly. She'd never catch up writing it all out.

The shooter showed up a few days ago. He paid a visit to Ed Bonfy, who swears the man was familiar. Shooter takes the stolen guns to an ex-jeweler who he somehow knew too, and he has some stupidity etched on the pistols and pays cash. She was kicking herself; she could not get her hands on that hundred dollar bill, or the pistols, or anything with his prints.

Now she knew the kids were still in trouble. At least one of them, Dale's boy, now knew that his father knew they were in trouble. It might give the boy something to hold on to.

She also had heard from Bart that Mrs. Wiebe had called in that her husband's *other* pickup was stolen. That's what had led Dale to make the call. Meanwhile, they put out feelers (Wiebe wouldn't allow anything official) for the truck, his 1971 Dodge crew cab.

She hoped they'd have it, and the kids, and the crazy gunman, all by breakfast.

Despite how well it was going, she wasn't going to hold her breath.

Chapter 18: Off the Team

December 2028

"What is it with you, Fortune?" one officer asked. "There's lots more interesting finds at the Installation than those... those pellets."

"Worthless. Inert. Common." Another summed up from across the table. He was flipping through a printout. "Why bother?"

Christopher Fortune had no answers. That was what bothered him. From the first night, everything else seemed to have some explanation, no matter how outlandish. But the little white pills defied explanation; even the most speculative theories failed to explain them.

"Velcro," he said, and nothing more.

At this stage, he knew his funding was to be withdrawn. It had been over a year, and he had failed to get on board with the team that was trying to recreate the debris of what they thought was a propulsion system. He refused to attend meetings over the scraps of what some thought to be the heat shields of what had to have covered what could only be a vessel.

"Velcro?" a third man in the room said, sardonically. He was 'down from DC,' as they had introduced themselves. Suits.

Chris stood from the table to pace. He assumed his lecture tone from his days at the Academy in Colorado Springs, "1941. George de Mestral, an electrical engineer, was on a hunting trip with his dog when he noticed how burdock seeds stuck to his Irish Pointer's fur. He simulated the miniscule hooks on the seeds, and now we have Velcro."

"Uh-huh," said Ben Canole, the head of the division and, for that matter, the Installation overall.

"Charles Goodyear, ever hear of him? In 1839 he goofed, spilling gum rubber and sulfur onto a hotplate. When it hardened, he had created the rubber that served on tires for over 100 years." Dr. Christopher Fortune was in his element now. "Don't you see, gentlemen? I could go on and on. The Slinky. The microwave oven. Penicillin. All were happy accidents. Most are derived from things otherwise overlooked."

"You're saying then, ignore the obvious and poke around in the weeds for... what exactly?" Dr. Graber was as close to an accomplice as Chris had found here, and even he was skeptical.

"Yes, I am saying ignore the obvious. We know something extraterrestrial crashed here, something that was crafted of unknown materials and assembled in unexplainable ways."

Everyone around the table was nodding.

"We know, given time, we'll figure out how it all fit together, right?"

"Presumably—"

"Except for these," he shook a vial of the little white 'rocks.' "We have absolutely no idea what these are."

"Hell, Fortune, they could be the equivalent of bug guts on a bumper, just debris that stuck to the ship," Canole chuckled.

"Our best guess is insulation," Graber offered. "There's a lot of it, and it might have—"

"Except it hasn't any impressive thermal properties."

"And they don't weigh enough, even all together, to have been ballast."

"Insulation. Ballast." Chris scoffed. "Guys, what if these were the cargo?"

Everyone at the table sat back in their chairs. A couple of them were shaking their heads sadly, as if sorrowful Chris had lost his mind. Graber would not make eye contact. Canole actually seemed amused, but he was trying not to show it.

One of the suits, not a uniform, not a lab coat, spoke up. "We invited you in on this because you—"

"Because I was already here... I know the truth."

"Because you had skin in the game," Canole interrupted. "Your son has suffered a terrible loss from the whole incident."

"However," the man directly across the table, who had said nothing, now laid it out, "you are not performing, Dr. Fortune. You have not generated anything we can use."

He was the heavy from Washington, Chris knew, and he didn't know the team or the struggles or the mystery of it all. He just served as an intermediary on a mid-level project of interest. He was the one who delivered verdicts from on high, and from his perpetual frown, Chris figured this guy, Smathers or something, was only in the business of delivering bad news.

"Not only that, but your tinkering has been expensive!" Smathers said. "First you brought on the college kids for the dig."

"Well, that paid off, didn't it? We harvested most of the objects in question from as much as a foot underground."

"One hundred thousand dollars?"

Canole spoke up, "We had to route it to DC and back, and when it came back, it was tagged as a research grant and honorarium."

"And there were a dozen grad students, for an entire semester at that," Chris added. "Two hours from Norman, so there was transportation, food, sometimes lodging..."

"And for what? More and more of something that's come to nothing."

"But we don't know that yet, do we?" Chris argued. "If we'd left them in the ground, who could guess the result? At least from the dig, I think we retrieved 90% of it."

"Moving on," Smathers said, aggravated. "Non-destructive testing. Running them through all manner of radiation..."

"And how many spectrometers?" one of the suits asked. "Broken?"

"Inaccurate at best." Chris defended, "These things just don't cook out like we—"

"Experiments off the edges of the periodic table," someone read. Chris wilted. He had written that in a prosaic flight of fancy, early on, when he was so optimistic.

"And this... Sending some to CERN with you as an escort. What exactly was that, Dr. Fortune?"

Chris shrugged. "A hunch?"

"Maybe an all-expenses paid trip to Switzerland?"

"I don't need this," he gestured at the table, "all this snark!" Chris said, making for the door. "I was doing you a favor, Ben."

"Don't forget your NDA," Smathers said, in a 'don't let the door hit you in the ass' tone.

He darted back to the table, scrawled his signature on the paper Smathers held out to him, and gave his colleagues a last look. "You're going to ignore them? Over 100 pounds of mystery pebbles? Probably just relegate them to some storage drum somewhere?"

"Probably dump them in a landfill," one suit said.

"Not all of them," Chris said to himself on his way out the door.

Chapter 19: Carnival Ride

February 2030

Lark stepped aside as Stu barged into their little circle. They were huddled shoulder-to-shoulder, trying to stay warm. "Not five minutes!" Stu said. "Where'd he go that quick?"

"Are you sure he doesn't have a phone on him?" Sackerson asked. "He should have a phone on him!"

"He would have coughed it up when you asked for them," Lark said.

It was cold, dark, and wet with sleet. The cinder block structure of the shabby diner was a poor wind break. Stu had been through the whole place, even the kitchen and bathrooms, he said, and had just reported back that Henny was gone. Just like that. Krystal refused to even step inside, based on the smell alone.

Sackerson seemed impatient. He kept going out to the intersection and looking down both highways. He would return, warm up in the foyer, then go back out, clearly expecting something.

Lark watched him as he ventured across the highway to a darkened gas station. The lot was huge, once maybe serving as overflow if there had been a time the diner had thrived. Tonight, it was crowded with semis parked close together. He had seen this at rest stops and just off interstate exit ramps. Truckers going as far as their legal time behind the wheel, then sacking out, roadside. Sackerson seemed to be milling around between them all, still looking for something.

The rest of them huddled on the leeward side of the building, in the middle of the night, wondering about Henny's whereabouts.

Lark doubted foul play, but Stu said he was seriously concerned. Krystal was just sure he had been abducted and said as much.

"Now THAT would be true irony," Lark said, "to be abducted from your kidnapper."

"Not funny," Krystal said.

Lark thought it was, actually, pretty close to amusing.

• • • •

SACKERSON CAME FROM the restaurant with hot drinks. He knew Stu liked his coffee black, that Krystal preferred hot cocoa. That was surprising enough, but he had made up the tea just like Lark liked it, lukewarm, twist of lemon. How could he know that?

"If he *did* have a phone on him," Sackerson said, "I think I could rig something to track him down."

"Or just call him," Stu countered. "He never shuts off his ringer."

"So, he *does* have a phone on him!" Sackerson said.

"Call him. You have our phones."

"That's not going to work," Lark said, flatly. If they hadn't found him yet, what good would it do to call? Regardless, Sackerson fished both of their phones out, recognized which was Stu's, and handed it to him.

"What about me?" Krystal asked, holding out her hand.

"Nope. Sorry. Besides, I already had to pull the battery. Too easy to trace. You can never really shut the location beacon down on those phones."

She stomped away in a huff.

"Try calling first, and if that doesn't work, I'll jack with it."

Stu flipped it open and punched a number on speed dial. They listened to it ring over and over on speaker phone setting. Nothing. He dialed it again and waited and watched.

"If you're so worried about us being tracked, then do you think this is a good idea?" Lark asked.

"You got a better idea, Lefty?" Stu said, looking up from the phone.

"It's probably not my best idea," Sackerson shrugged, "but it should prove a thing or two."

"Like what?" Stu asked.

"Like that Henny ratted us out and got a ride home," Lark sneered.

"You're full of it, Fortune. He wouldn't do that."

"Wouldn't he?" Sackerson asked.

"You're both full of shit," Stu argued. "He was right with us, all along."

"I can't say I've been with him much since then," Lark said. He knew the same was true of Krystal.

"He went through the same interrogation we did," Krystal added. "And he's no good at hiding things."

"You mean, like the phone he lied about?"

"Listen. He was with us when we got shot at," Stu continued his defense. "Nobody shoots at their own."

"And he was really freaked when you hopped out of the wheelbarrow," Lark conceded. "I'll give him that."

"I might have given him a little more than that to be scared of—"

"Guys!" Krystal was pointing. "What's that?"

Though he could barely make it out, Lark heard a faint ringtone, some Sports Center theme, and saw the curbside slush was strobing. All four of them approached it.

Stu picked it up and wiped it on his jeans. "Henny's," he said.

Sackerson looked over Stu's shoulder. "Take it," he said.

Stu looked at the phone long and hard.

"Stu!" Krystal prodded.

He flipped it open and accepted the call.

• • • •

LARK HAD A THING ABOUT stereotypes. He speculated that those who fit most readily into them were possibly the least stereotypical on the inside. He knew, for instance, that people thought of him as some kind of wild child, and he played into it with his crazy hair and fashion sense. If anyone really knew him, however, which they did not attempt, they would have found him to be much more conservative than he seemed.

He confirmed his theory repeatedly. Nerds were often quite adventurous, given the opportunity, often closet pharmacologists and pervs. Every Priss he got to know was self-conscious, sure, but some were honestly introspective and ran much deeper than they let on. Valley girls, his dad had once categorized a few of Lark's classmates, were commonly intelligent and shy, despite their veneer.

Krystal had certainly proven his theory out, even in the brief time they shared on the night of the Fall. Especially tonight, she was revealing herself to be much more mindful of their situation, much more caring, too, than daddy's little rich girl. She was, as some old song went, "only human after all."

Lark thought Stu was trying too hard to be the rough and tumble hayseed kid. The extra effort betrayed him.

But Henny simply lived his stereotype. He was the quintessential sidekick, an extra, an NPC. Sure, he was part of the football team, but never the star. He was the big kid with nothing inside but stuffing. Lark had tried to make conversation once or twice, when Henny came in Mack's with family. He'd offered to help him with homework. He'd asked him about college. But Hinman wasn't having it. He was a big lug, an enigma. Placid, cool if everyone else was, but egging on a fight if that was the thing to do. Henny was a lackey.

Except tonight.

It would have freaked anyone to have a dead man climb out of a wheelbarrow, Lark knew, so he could understand Henny's fear. Then there was something between him and Sackerson, like maybe they'd had words at the burn pile before Henny came running back into the barn. *Had they?* It just didn't all add up. Henny had agreed to ride along. He lied about his phone. He was faking being sick—Lark was sure of that. And now he was gone.

Kenny Hinman had broken character.

• • • •

"ARE YOU SURE ABOUT Kansas?" the voice asked through the phone, cold as the wind itself.

"Uhhhh," Stu looked from face to face.

Lark rolled his eyes.

Sackerson shrugged.

Krystal was gesticulating like they were playing charades.

"I can't hear you good," Stu said. He was holding it out in speakerphone mode, and he acted like it was a grenade.

"KANSAS!" the phone barked. "ARE THEY IN KANSAS?"

Everyone was shocked... except... Lark noted, Sackerson.

Stu was without words. He held the phone out to the rest of them, pleading with his eyes.

Krystal huddled closer and whispered something in his ear.

Stu looked at her, puzzled. She whispered again, looking deeply into his eyes.

Lark almost took the phone, then thought better of it.

"*Are* they in Kansas?" Stu repeated back to the phone, questioning, as if this could not be what the caller had said.

Krystal nodded and smiled with encouragement.

"Last word was they're headed that way. Have they reached the state line?"

No one seemed to know how to answer that. They all snugged up from the wind in a communal shrug.

Sackerson was nodding, raising his bare eyebrows at Stu.

"Uh... yes...."

"And can you confirm the make and model of the vehicle again?" There was some audible clacking on the line. "We aren't finding it."

Lark gazed out at the truck. *Find it? How were they even looking for it?* Before Lark could stop him, Stu spouted off "1970 GMC Scottsdale crew cab."

"Plates?"

Krystal practically jumped in his arms to stop him from saying more. She cupped her hand to his ear and said something. Stu held the phone up a little closer, taking her direction, and said, "What's in it for me?"

Sackerson gave them the thumbs up.

"You name it, Kenneth," the voice said, smoothly. "Do you remember the plates?"

Stu covered the phone and asked, "Should I—"

"Sure. I don't care. Tell him where it's parked if you want to," Sackerson said. "We're moving on to a new plan." He walked off toward the parking lot, adding over his shoulder, "And when you're done, ditch the phone."

Stu held the phone limply at his side, watching Sackerson stroll away.

"Don't tell them anything," Lark said with no regard for the open line. "Make 'em work for it."

Krystal nodded.

Stu looked suddenly determined. He snapped shut the phone and pounded it on the diner wall in a blast of obscenities mixed with unpleasant outcomes he intended for Henny.

Krystal patted his shoulder, saying, "I'm sure he had his—"

Stu whirled on her. Lark thought he saw tears in Stu's eyes, but his expression was otherwise so fierce that he stepped back and looked for Sackerson.

Krystal asked, "So guys... what do we do now?"

Lark was asking himself the same thing. Going over the border until this cooled off was not even an option now, thanks to Henny. Did they take Stu's family's truck home? The one everyone was now looking for? With or without Sackerson?

"Find Henny and beat his—"

A loud blast from a semi-truck air horn sounded from the parking lot. From the passenger door, Sackerson was waving them over. "Got us a ride!"

"You gotta be kidding me," Krystal said.

"No way," Stu growled. "I'm not riding in that thing."

Even in the darkness, Lark could make out the garish paint job and the crazy lettering that emblazoned the entire rig. It was a circus truck, repurposed for who knew what.

"I guess you could stay here or ride off in the truck you just told Henny's friends about," Lark said. "I'm joining the carnival."

As they approached the truck, it was obvious now that the parking lot was bristling with idling trucks that truly *were* part of a carnival. The trailer rigs sported various thrill rides and entertainment. Strapped to Sackerson's choice semi were boxes and booths and bangles, in an altogether random hodgepodge.

"Sometimes, Lark, it's best to hide in plain sight, and you can't miss this thing!" he said, hopping to the ground to greet them. "What luck, eh?"

"I thought you..." Lark began. "I thought you were into research and planning and plotting all this from... from the future?"

"That was before ol' Judas sold us out. Now we're off-script. Actually, it will throw them off."

"Throw who off?" Stu asked.

"Exactly," Sackerson said and gestured them toward the semi cab. "We could wait and find out... or we could ask my new friend here to get us on down the road. Put some space between us and them."

"Wait a minute," Krystal asked, stepping up to Sackerson. She had to crane her neck back to look him in the eye. "You set us up, didn't you? You used Henny, too, didn't you?"

Lark noted her fists were balled up. Maybe she had forgotten he had one pistol yet. Maybe she failed to realize he might well be their best hope, even "off-script" now.

"It's important that we keep them guessing, but it's also vital that we know who it is we are keeping guessing... so yeah, I guess I did sorta set this up."

"You set up Henny?" Stu asked. "You know where he is now?"

"If I were to guess, I'd bet on the Kansas border, looking for us," Sackerson looked North. He switched on his biggest grin and swung open the door of the truck. "But for now, kids, we have Oleander Dollarhide to thank for a ride. Right, Mister Dollarhide?"

Lark thought the driver looked spent, foreign-looking with a long white braid trailing down his back. "Room for everyone in the berth," he squeaked at them, in a surprising falsetto. "She's a full-on sleeper cab."

"See for yourself," Sackerson said. "C'mon in. This baby has all the comforts of home."

Lark started up the ladder, but Krystal pulled him back.

"Conference," she ordered and pulled both him and Stu some distance away. They hunkered down behind a neighboring truck, sheltering from the cold. Diesel fumes were stronger there, but the idle of the trucks might help drown them out.

"Henny's gone," Stu started. "Guys are shot up at Mack's. It's 2:30 in the morning, and everybody's out looking for us."

"To say nothing of Sackerson. No offense," Krystal said to Lark, "but if you're related, I gotta tell you, the guy's a psycho."

"Time travel!" scoffed Stu.

"Hey, he's right about the other thing, the teleportation," Lark offered. "Saw it for yourself."

"What I saw was you and him doing a magic trick with a gun."

"Really?" Krystal interrupted. "What about us just... just showing up in your barn, Stu? How else do you explain it?"

"Guys," Lark said firmly. "I don't think we have time for all this. Somebody's coming for us, and I don't think they're people we want to find us. If Sackerson can get us out of here, then... maybe later, like morning, we can get away from him if we need."

"Dad's got people looking for us," Stu muttered.

"What?" Krystal and Lark asked at the same time.

"Other than the cops." He squinted his eyes. "I told him we were in trouble, and I know he's got the Boys out looking."

"The boys...?" Krystal trailed off.

"Who, exactly?" Lark asked.

"My people. Neighbors. They'll be out all over the place, and they'll find us. They'll know dad's truck. They'll talk to everyone from here to hell and back."

"That's all good and well, but right now we have to make a choice," Krystal said, shaking them both at the shoulder. "Stay here, or go with him?"

Before Lark could even reason through an answer, she continued, "I vote for going. I am going. Whoever was on that phone... well, I don't know..."

Stu growled. "I vote we stay. They're heading to Kansas. We can just tool around the back roads until morning, then work things out. Better without the freak show, if you ask me."

Lark looked at them, back and forth. Finally, he said, "I have too many questions... and he thinks Dad's in trouble..." Resolve was brewing in him. "So, I'm going to go with Sackerson. You two do what you want."

He took Krystal's hand and asked, "You in?"

There was a slight crinkle in the corner of her eyes, almost a smile, when she looked down at their hands. "Yeah," she said. "I am."

"Fine," Stu grumbled and pushed past them, rounding the corner and climbing into the truck ahead of them.

"All aboard!" Sackerson-the-conductor said.

Lark followed Krystal up into the cabin. In the strangest of ways, he felt a little more optimistic than the situation should merit... and he was okay with that.

Chapter 20: Derailed

Stu had to admit that Sackerson was persuasive. Somehow, he had first convinced Oleander they needed a ride, then together they used the broadband radio to motivate the whole caravan to get rolling a good four hours early.

He had never considered the mechanics of a carnival, not given any mind at all to the fleet of vehicles it took to move those elaborate rides from town to town. There were nine vehicles in the ramshackle fleet, five semis, a repurposed (and repainted) moving van, two passenger vans, and a Suburban, and from what Stu could tell, all of them were late model vehicles. It reminded him of the custom cutters that rolled across the plains every summer.

Krys and Lefty were sharing a laugh with Sackerson, but he was having nothing to do with it. He sat up front, riding shotgun with old man Dollarhide. He pretended, even to himself, that he might like it up there, watching the three vehicles in front and, in his side rearview mirror, the rest snaking along behind them.

He preoccupied himself by wondering about the life of a carney rat. They usually only worked from April to October, then they'd drift back to their main settlements and ride out winter. Olly Dollarhide had explained to Stu that they were wise to winter in Texas, not Florida, like so many "in the entertainment industry." Florida was a resort state, an escape, and in anyone else's perspective, a great place to hang out and ride out the off season. "The Family Circus," as Dollarhide referred to their troupe, took the off-season to rebuild, invent, and—very important apparently to Olly—paint. "We repaint the whole damn caravan every year. I'm the pin striper." Texas was hot and dry, just ideal for their winter goals. "Cain't do that in Florida cuz it rains about every day."

Stu had heard stories about the carneys, and he wanted to confirm them one by one. Were they even American citizens? Was it true they were wife swappers and inbred? What was the trick of throwing rings over bottle necks?

He was about to ask if it was true, that they lived to be over 100, when he noticed a strange behavior in the trucks at the end of the line. They were playing leapfrog, passing one another and exchanging positions like NASCAR racers.

Olly caught his attention with an abrupt downshift and hooted, "Nobody's passing us. Not on my watch!"

Stu looked over his shoulder at the others to see if they noticed. Krys was buckling Lefty's seatbelt, then fidgeting with her own. Sackerson was smiling back at Stu. He asked, "Learning anything about the biz?"

"Yeah," he muttered, turning back to the front. "Plenty."

Everyone was pressed back into their seats when Olly floored it, and their truck surged ahead of the one in front of it. They were gaining on the next one. They were going to at least be the front truck, if not in the lead, even ahead of the Suburban.

They were neck and neck with a semi that looked to be painted orange and pink. The driver was a slumped and wrinkled old woman. She flipped Stu the bird and pressed ahead.

"Old Olga's a mess, ain't she?" Olly cackled.

"Your wife?" Stu asked, but thought she was so old she might even be his mother.

"Oh no, no, no," he answered. "That's my cousin. Odd one, she is. Never cut her hair since her husband died."

Olly floored it again, shifted again. He couldn't catch her. Black soot was bellowing out of the stacks on her truck as she drew more and more from it.

"Guess it's been a long while," Olly continued. "Her hair drags behind her like a long white wedding dress when she takes it out of that kerchief."

"Tell him about the sideshow," Sackerson leaned up to suggest.

"Oh, yeah!" Olly chuckled. "Crazy times. See, gas was so high that year, we couldn't even afford to run the rides. But what's a carnival without rides, right? We were out in the middle of nowhere, honestly somewhere around these parts, I think, when we was flat broke. Somebody had the bright idea, just to even make gas money, why not set up a side show... so we did. All of us had to cook up our own gimmick, see? It was a crazy time."

"You mean... like a freak show?" Stu asked.

The vehicles behind them continued to lace between one another, often blaring their horns at each other. Once in a while, a car coming from the other way would tame them down. Mostly, however, it was pandemonium.

"Nah, we're not into S&M or all that 'nail through your head' stuff." Olly frowned, "And we didn't want a circus, a real circus, with a bunch a stinkin' animals." He smiled then at Stu, obviously the precursor to a punchline, "We're animals enough."

Lefty was looking car sick. Krys was looking bored. Sackerson was leaning in on them upfront again. "I'm sure you were the barker, right? What was Olga, the bearded lady?"

Olly chuckled, turning to them with his reply, "She was the Fat Lady, back then." He tugged at the air horn controls and blasted long and hard. "Outta our way, Knuckles!" Olly shouted to the Suburban. "Now, Knuckles, he loved the side show summer. Some of the rest of us could have just sat that one out, but he was the Boxer from Biloxi. Went the whole season un—"

Olly screamed. A blast of bright light, some kind of explosion ahead on the highway! He pumped the brakes and clutch and tugged at an emergency brake, practically all at the same time. They were tossed all over the cabin, then the sideways skidding finally stopped, and the truck dropped back on all 18 tires.

"Oh my god, oh my god!" he was yelling, and he burst out the door. Sackerson blasted past Stu and followed Oleander.

"What just happened?" Krystal cried out.

"Wreck!" Lefty pointed out the windshield.

Stu had already unbuckled and was popping open his door. "You guys should just stay here," he said. "It looks bad."

When his boots hit the highway, Stu knew it wasn't over. A loud thundering rhythm shook him and made the pavement tremble. A terrible screeching sound ahead and to the left was followed by crashing and more earthquake-level rumbles.

He ran toward the lights and screaming ahead. As he ran past the Suburban, then the U-Haul, it all came into full view.

Train cars were still streaming across the highway, but then it sounded like they were plowing into one another off in the dark down the tracks. The front semi, Olga's semi, had been demolished.

Stu could not contain his adrenaline. He was running from vehicle to vehicle, person to person, offering his help. Some looked at him like he was a lunatic. Others just bowed their heads and wept.

When he came up on Sackerson, he could only say, "What happened?"

"Train. It didn't stop. Crossing never activated." Sackerson was scanning the total scene, alert. "No accident. This was *sabotage*."

The rest of the train cars tore through and crashed into oblivion. Then, the clanging railroad crossing relented, the lights quit flashing, and the road was open again. Moments later, it was quiet, save for the wailing of the carnival family.

Together, Sackerson and Stu crossed the tracks, trailing behind Olly. The cargo trailer had taken the brunt of the hit—as if the truck was almost across the tracks before impact—but that had only catapulted it off into the ditch at full tilt. It looked as if it had rolled from what was left of it. Tires were still spinning. It reeked of diesel.

"Empty," Olly called out after climbing up to look inside the cab.

"Nobody around," said another carney. He shouted, "Where's Olga? Where's Kiko?"

The cars from across the tracks moved ahead and parked. Their headlights bathed the scene in a flat whitewash.

"Get the others," Sackerson commanded. "Get in the 'burban."

"But—" Stu stopped, and turned back, though he kept watching over his shoulder.

Sackerson was consoling Olly. Then he was waving away the onlookers. Even from a distance, even though he barely knew him, Stu could sense that Sackerson was wary. He noticed that the big, nickel-plated gun was out, but not directed at the people pouring from their cars, at least not yet.

"What's going on?" Lefty asked. They had caught up, and now Stu was coaching them toward the Suburban.

"I think we're leaving," he said. "I think—Sackerson thinks—maybe this was no accident."

Krys and Lefty were taking in the wreckage.

Stu tugged them along. "We're to get in here."

The Suburban was half in the ditch. Doors were left open, and the headlights pointed at the sky. The engine was still running. When he looked inside, Stu recoiled. The cab was full of vibrant clothes and blankets, like a costume shop. It was littered with food and trash. It smelled of weed and sweat and alcohol. Above it all, he smelled something plastic burning.

Krys fished a half-smoked cigarette off the floor and tossed it out. She shrugged and clamored inside. Lark joined her on the back bench seat. They immediately bundled up with whatever they could find. Stu had ended up in the driver's seat.

"Now what?" Lefty asked.

"Now we wait for Sackerson, I guess."

He surprised himself then that he did not just drop it into gear and leave it all behind. He felt sickened by the wreck, and even though he'd never so much as spoken to her, he was worried for old Olga.

People from the caravan were swarming the scene, sometimes passing the Suburban and looking in on them, puzzled. They were too alarmed to do anything but run toward Olga's truck. They huddled and milled about, talking to one another in clouds of steam made white by headlights.

"There he is," Krys said, pointing.

The wait had not been long. Sackerson emerged from the crowd, standing a foot taller than the others, walking against the tide, walking stiffly and directly to them.

A crow was perched on his shoulder. It looked like the crow he remembered seeing outside Mack's. Stu shook his head in wonder. *Where did it even come from?*

Stu opened his door and started to go around to the passenger side. He stopped when Sackerson pointed him back inside. "You drive," he commanded.

As soon as the doors were shut, Sackerson began, "They'll stop at NOTHING. Absolutely NOTHING. That was a freight train, and the engineers said their system went black, but they were in northwest Nebraska. Nebraska! Then just-like-that, they were rolling through here. They had no idea this was a crossing, no instrumentation. One of their guys is just a bloody mess..." Sackerson frowned hard and looked away. "At least Olga's alright. Just came strolling up out of the snow, carrying Kiko over her shoulder like that girl was..."

"You said it *wasn't an accident*?" Krystal asked.

"The timing," Sackerson said. His crow nodded emphatically. "The simple truth of it all. They knew we were in this caravan. I think they even thought we were in Olga's rig."

"That means...," Stu said with an awareness that drained his blood from his face, "That means that this could have been us?"

"No doubt about it," Sackerson said. "Now get us the hell out of here."

"But... but it's not even our car," Lefty protested.

"I already told Knuckles where to find it, but I asked him to give us until first light," Sackerson said, then added, "Assuming we make it that long."

Stu dropped it into drive and floored it. He corrected the Suburban up out of the ditch. They were spinning and sliding on the wet highway, and then they shot off like a rocket sled toward Guthrie. "We'll make it," he said, but he lacked conviction. "We will make it," he said again, more firmly, for their sakes.

Chapter 21: Bigger Emergencies

Krystal couldn't stop the tears, and the boys looked as if they were also on the brink. Teleported, being hunted, and now, some lunatic was hurling trains at them?

"We could have died," she wept openly. She knew she was an ugly crier, and she was aware of the snot and sound and mess of it all.

"But we didn't," Stu said from the driver's seat. "And we won't." He was proud of his 'elusive maneuvers' as he called them, the backroads he bragged he knew so well. No one could find them now, he had claimed.

"Why, why, why!" She continued, "What'd we ever do?"

Sackerson reached back and put a hand on her shoulder. He had incredibly long arms. "We met. We conspired. We ran. We gave them the slip."

"All because of you!" she cried out and wrenched his hand away.

"In all fairness—"

"There's no *fairness*, Lark. Nothing's fair about this."

"Think about it, though. Where would we be without him?"

"Dead at Mack's, I figure," Stu offered. He turned from the windshield to Krys, then nodded at Sackerson. "Guess we owe you."

"Don't thank me too—"

"Don't thank him at all!" Krystal shouted, then curled up in a quilt. "It's all your fault."

She put her hands over her ears and did her best to ignore the calming tones the three were offering. She was trying to think. Everything was unraveling so fast.

Krystal growled and pulled away when one of them outside the quilt tried to pat her back. He kept it up, pestering. Poking and prodding. She whipped back the quilt, and the crow burbled in her face. It was strangely soothing.

None of it seemed possible. That she was even in the same space as Stu and Lark was unlikely. And that Henny, tubby, lovable Kenny Hinman had sold them out? It was such a stretch. She longed for her brother, the sounding board. If only she could bounce all this off him, Kev would have known what to say.

Instead, she tried to sniff back her crying and calm her breathing. She ventured to put a hand on the crow's back, as she'd seen Sackerson do. The bird was a bundle of nervous tension, his eyes alert. He seemed more anxious than she was. She patted him absently.

She listened to the others in the Suburban. They were visiting in muffled tones now about mundane things like how far they could get on a quarter tank of fuel and whether it was safe to eat the open bag of chips they were crunching on.

"Where's your Boys now?" she heard Lark, beside her, asking. "Be nice if they could swing by." The answer was not clearly audible, but Krystal could hear the defeat in Stu's voice. Something about changing vehicles twice now, and something else about it being too late.

Their conversation came and went, but after a while, her interest was again piqued. Sackerson was answering someone's question, "That's what he said. Just blacked out the whole thing. Garmin. Cell signal. Even radio. Said he couldn't even talk to the front."

Krystal listened, but only caught a fragment of what Stu was saying up front with Sackerson. They seemed to not be worried much about including her or Lark.

"Sabotage then?" Stu said. Then, "...they could do that—train crossing...?"

She pulled the quilt down from her head and said, "Obviously, they're from the same place he's from."

Everyone looked at her. Sackerson gave her a tight-lipped smile, like he was proud of her again, but a little less lit up. "Yes, and no."

"Same *time* as he's from," Lark corrected.

Sackerson nodded.

Stu just shook his head. "I'm still not buying that, Sack. Time travel!"

"But you can't deny the teleportation," Sackerson said. "Moved the needle that far, right?"

Stu was shaking his head slowly.

Krystal had been mulling over a lot of things, and when she did so, some of it often escaped her. "About that," she said, with a start. "Why can't we just teleport away from all this? Why just to the hayloft?"

"I've been thinking about that too," Lark said. "Take us to Stu's cabin or somewhere."

"Take us to *yesterday*," Stu chided, "so we won't be in this mess this time." His tone was just oozing with doubt.

"Whatever," she tamped him down. Then she blurted, "Sackerson, you did say you set up a dozen of those, right? Let's use one to get out of trouble."

"We can work our way out of this," he said. "We have to save the ports for the big emergencies."

"Emergencies?" She could hardly stay in her seat. "What's bigger than this? We're on the run from—well—from everyone, it seems. You say they've tried to kill us with A TRAIN."

"And Henny handed us right over to them," Stu grumbled.

"Guys," Lark was saying, looking out his window into the night. "Guys!" He was tapping at the glass. "What's that?"

Everyone looked out the east windows, following Lark's gaze. Far off toward the horizon, but getting closer quickly, was a bright blue light in the sky.

"It's been tracking, changing up, following every turn we take," Lark said with wonderment.

"That," Sackerson said, "is one of those bigger emergencies."

• • • •

SHAE FINALLY PUT HER head on a pillow at 3:45 a.m. On nights like this, *especially* nights like this, she whispered in her husband Rob's ear to decompress:

"Seems like we have two factions, if you will, these guys in the black coats—I know, right, get a less obvious wardrobe, change it up a bit—and this tall bald guy with the guns."

At least 6'4", rail thin, packing two Smith & Wesson .50 caliber nickel-plated 'hobby' pistols, she recalled, but continued to Rob:

"He's got the kids, and he's got as far as that rest stop up north. That we know from tracking their phones.

"Then all hell broke loose with that train wreck and Dollarhide's Amusement—all after you and the girls hit the sack, but it's gotta be all over the news now—and some people claim they saw the bald guy and the kids there. Except we've got Kenny Hinman cold at the Kansas border on their cams at the toll booth... and we haven't really *found* anyone all night. If they're over the border, we're out cold. Hell, even over the county line and I'm toast..."

She flopped flat on her back, continuing, "Even out in the county I'm stepping on toes, but you know what? Maybe this is worth a few territorial types getting butt hurt.

"So instead of chasing our tails, I gotta regroup around what we know, like you always say. That is that this guy has been around town a while and that he seems to know everybody... and somehow these kids—the same ones from the Strip last year—are all mixed up in this.

"Then there's the unknowns, like the black coats... probably with the government and maybe—but those two at Mack's just don't add up." She yawned and stretched luxuriously, then pulled the covers back over him and tucked him in. She pulled them over herself, too, but just stared at the ceiling for a while.

"The bald guy's obviously a loose cannon... packing cannons! I can tell by his guns. I mean, 'Kiss, Kiss, Bang, Bang,' What's that all about? Witnesses say he shouted that out when he opened fire... But honestly, I don't really know if he's a killer or even a kidnapper. We don't even know if he's an accomplice or what. But everything Bonfy's said, and everything we heard at the morgue, suggests he did not kill the shooters at Mack's, that, get this... *they killed each other*.

"I just have a feeling, Rob," Shae said, curling up now, "I'm in way over my head."

• • • •

DECEMBER 2028

Christopher Fortune followed the last of his boxes as Julian, from maintenance, wheeled them to his Forester. Another load with a few dozen cardboard boxes, full of completely unremarkable books and materials, reams of paper, files, and three-ring binders. His stuff could have belonged to virtually any office worker in the building.

Yet those documents could frighten any man, woman, or child on the planet. With his scopes and prognostics, he could forecast cataclysmic events better than any actuary. Yet now denied his research post and stripped of his role here, Dr. Fortune might just as well have been anyone. Julian probably thought he was an Accountant.

As the woman from maintenance was navigating the dolly outside, it tipped radically, and one wheel dropped off the curb. Both of them righted the load, but one box escaped them and tumbled to the street. It spilled tiny packing peanuts, but Fortune insisted nothing was broken. He took personal care to sweep up after himself, as best he could with his bare hands, while Julian neatly stacked the rest.

He shut the hatch on the car, shook hands robustly with Julian, and left the facility. Only when the lab was in his rear-view mirror did Christopher Fortune truly breathe freely again. He was sweating; even his upper lip was beaded with sweat. He was no secret agent. He was a nobody now.

But his car was full of teeny tiny bits of stolen alien technology.

Chapter 22: Car Wash

"No, Stu, it's not the Interstate," Lark insisted. "It's moving."

"We did just pass County 66," Sackerson said.

"And a couple miles over, on 35, that's where there's a big exchange. Lots of streetlights."

"You're both right," Sackerson said. "It is a bright intersection about two miles that way, but that light is most definitely chasing us."

"What is it?" Krystal asked.

Lark had several theories, and he wasn't throwing out flying saucers... at least, not tonight. Whatever it was, the light zig-zagged, lower to the ground than anything but a crop duster would dare.

"Helicopter," Sackerson guessed. "Probably from Perry. Think the hospital has one there?"

"I know they do," Stu said. "They had to LifeWatch my uncle from Perry to Tulsa. Boating accident."

"Why would a hospital helicopter be following us?" Krystal asked. By the time Lark turned from the window to her, she had a revelation. "You don't think—"

"Commandeered," Sackerson said. "By the same scum that tried to swat us with a freight train."

"Yeah," Stu said. "Maybe. But maybe it's just going on an emergency run to town. To Guthrie. We are getting pretty close."

Lark moved as much as his seatbelt would allow, craning his neck to see what Sackerson was doing in the front seat. He was working on something, but whatever it was, he was handling it gingerly.

"So, Stu," Sackerson said, not looking up from his work. "Just south of the high school. You know that intersection with the pet store and the U-Haul?"

"I go to Consolidated... to Coyle," Stu replied.

"I know the place," Krystal spoke up. "Why?"

"There's a car wash there. You gotta hook around on Hill, then come back at it from the south."

"Car wash?" Stu looked over at him quizzically.

"It's on us!" Lark shouted, as the bright light tore overhead. The sound was, indeed, that of a chopper, and it sounded like it was going full throttle. The craft was operating flood lights, so they could see below and ahead. As soon as it passed, the helicopter twisted back toward the highway.

"Just a couple more blocks," Sackerson said. "Just after the high school, I'm going to bail."

"You're what!?" Lark and Krystal said together.

"Don't even stop," Sackerson said. "Don't stop at the high school intersection. Don't stop at Hill. Just twist back up the access road—fast—and roll right in the car wash."

"Are we going to try hiding in a car wash?" Krystal asked.

"One better," Sackerson said, gathering up his materials. He rolled down his window and took a series of measured deep breaths of the frigid air. "We're gonna..." but the helicopter roared again overhead, and Lark missed out on his comment.

Sackerson looked after it in the sky, turned back to wink at Lark, then threw open his door and jumped out.

"Jesus!" Stu said but whipped the wheel left and right to slam the door. He jammed the brakes and spun the wheel.

The crow cawed as if concerned for Sackerson. In the panic of its flapping wings, a few feathers drifted in the cab. Lark was thrown against Krystal. She yelped and righted herself and Lark.

"What's he doing now?" Lark asked, looking ahead wide-eyed.

As Sackerson had described, they were passing a U-Haul and the pet store, both lit only by their storefront signage. A single stall brick car wash squatted north of the pet store, and Stu cranked the wheel toward it.

Lark spied Sackerson inside the car wash bay. It looked as if he were doing jumping jacks.

Again, the helicopter roared overhead, but this time, it had crisscrossed from the southeast, and it came to a sudden stop, hovering over the highway right behind them.

Lark patted Stu on the shoulder and said, "Go for it, man."

It seemed like that was all Stu was waiting to hear. He stomped the gas pedal and covered the last two parking lots in a riotous, bouncing, curb-popping dash.

"Hang on!" Lark shouted to Krystal, expecting a gut-wrenching sudden stop inside the car wash.

Instead, it sounded like the helicopter had hit the car wash. They were all blinded by scorching white light, bright as lightning itself. The suburban lurched and veered, twisting as if Stu had completely abandoned the wheel. Lark could hear crashing sounds as they came to a sudden stop. Steam rose from the crushed Suburban hood. It smelled strongly of bleach and anti-freeze.

Lark did a double take. In the flickering light of an alley streetlight, one that he knew well, he surveyed their surroundings. They had crashed through a swing set and pinned a barbeque grill against the back deck—of his dad's house.

"This can't be!" he said.

"Where are we?" Krystal wondered.

"We're in Norman," Lark said. "We're in my dad's backyard."

"Norman! That's an hour away!" Stu shouted.

"We just teleported like 60 miles," Lark said. "Just like that."

"Where's your dad, Lefty? He's not gonna like—"

"His dad?" Krystal asked. "Guys. Where's Sackerson?"

C ontext File
     Bloodsport has had the fancy and imagination of man for millennia. Since recorded history, man has pitted animal against animal in a fight to the death. Cockfighting, for example, has been enjoyed as a sport in ancient Asia, and introduced in Greece around 500 BC. Bloodsport among men has been a thrill since long before the well-known Gladiators of Rome stepped into the arena.

In the first century AD, women were commonly found in the ring, though most often pitted against dwarves and animals. Animal slaughter was, by modern standards, horrific and extreme, with over 11,000 animals being brutally butchered in a 100-day ceremony that celebrated the opening of Rome's great Coliseum.

The legendary Gladiators did not always fight to the death, for they were celebrities in their own right, and they were heinously expensive to house and train. Though some became lauded as heroes simply for their rate of survival, any Gladiator who lived into his late twenties was rare.

Fighting to the death fell out of fashion, and by the time the West was won, even dueling was illegal in the United States. Animal fighting, particularly cockfighting, however, is still legal in many countries. In the United States, cockfighting, a billion dollar-a-year industry, remains legal in Louisiana, New Mexico and Oklahoma.

One especially gruesome chapter of European animal fighting is often overlooked. On the south bank of the Thames at Bankside, which later became London's theater district, arenas were erected exclusively for bear-baiting. These pits were lined with eager audiences placing bets on just which animal would survive: the bear staked out in the center of the arena, or a pack of wild dogs which attempted to tear the bear apart. This practice, which by modern standards seems uncouth, attracted the same crowds as those who attended Shakespeare's theatrical productions.

The rich and famous gravitated to the bear-baiting bloodsport, and they often owned the most fierce and long-lived bears. Like their predecessors, the Roman Gladiators, some of these bears became the stuff of legend. Several were touted as nigh indestructible. They were given names that were emblazoned on posters and pamphlets.

One such bear was known to be the most bloodthirsty and indefatigable of all. Adopted by Queen Elizabeth I, this infamous bear, the great and mighty "Sackerson," was cited by name in William Shakespeare's play *The Merry Wives of Windsor*.

Chapter 24: Gone Cold

Stu figured they had spent half an hour at the house already, fumbling around the yard, looking everywhere for Sackerson. Under the truck. Under the deck. In the trees. There was nothing, not a sign of him.

Stu imagined Sackerson poised heroically on the Suburban roof, backlit by the moon. The crow was on his shoulder. He was bare chested, grinning madly. He still had Henny's Elmer Fudd hat on, and he was brandishing his big guns in the air.

He glanced up there, just to be sure. Nothing. "No Sack, nowhere."

"I even miss his stupid bird," Lark commented in exasperation. It had flown off as soon as they opened the Suburban's doors.

"Know what else is missing?" Krys asked. She was staying warm in a cocoon of brightly colored quilts.

Stu and Lefty looked at each other, then back at her. He shrugged.

"Neighbors," she said. "In my neighborhood, security would have been on this before the truck stopped."

Lefty waved that down. "Nope," he said, and scanned the yard and beyond. "Whole thing's a sham. Empty houses. Like Doom Town, out in Nevada."

They followed him through the yard to a storage shed, which the Suburban had scarcely grazed.

"Most of these houses are empty." Lefty continued, "And those who do stay here are like my dad. Scientists and researchers who do nothing else. Go in early, stay late..."

"But still—" Krys looked at him funny. "We crashed a 6,000-pound truck in the yard!"

Lefty shrugged. "Anybody around here slept right through it. Sleeping pills. Alcohol... or they have their nose down in the books so far, they're just out of it."

"You're kidding!" her quilts were unraveling from her astonishment. "You're saying nobody cares?"

"That's about it. No neighbors. No friends. Nobody over for the night. No family cookouts on the deck... like that grill you were worried about?" He looked at Stu.

It looked to have been a nice one, a high-end pellet feeder.

"It's all for looks. Props." He studied a padlock on the shed and shook his head. "This is real enough, though."

"What exactly are we doing?" Stu asked, as Lefty tossed more and more junk from the back of the Suburban out into the snow. A sleeping bag. A duffle. A little accordion.

He did not answer but kept at it. Colorful piles were building behind the Suburban. When he emerged with a tire tool, Stu thought he looked a little crazy.

His crazy paid off, however, when together they pried the hasp and lock from the shed. Lefty insisted they should hide the fluorescent pink and lime green Suburban. So, they rummaged around in the dark shed. It seemed like home to Stu, everything so well arranged and shelved. If you knew what you were looking for, you could find it in the dark.

Lefty couldn't find anything, though. He admitted he'd never even been in the shed before. Krys finally found some white canvas drop cloths, neatly folded. They draped them over the truck and shoved debris underneath. From a distance, it might just look like a lot of snow, an avalanche maybe, had plowed through the back fence, the garden, the swing set...

Stu was so cold he vowed to never be without a coat again. He even considered putting on a red and yellow striped carney coat he was kicking under the drop cloth.

It bothered him a little that Lark was more worried about hiding than he was about his own dad. Had they crashed at the farm, Stu would have done that first thing.

Except he hadn't, had he?

Stu was more than happy to go inside, finally. They had to crunch through the broken glass of the patio door, but once inside, it was a little warmer.

Stu flipped a couple of light switches. "Power's out," he announced.

"What happened here?" Krys asked, panning the room. Kitchen drawers had been pulled out and dumped on the floor. Cabinets had been emptied. Their doors were left open. It looked like some had been thrown open violently, for they hung by a single hinge. Everything that looked like it might have belonged on the countertop was on the floor. As Stu stepped over a mess from the fridge, he thought that every last thing must be on the floor.

"The truck didn't do all this," Lefty said absently, setting a kitchen chair upright. "I think he's been robbed."

"I don't think so," Stu said. He picked up some tongs, and with them a wallet, which he held before them. "It's still got cash and cards."

"Your dad's?" Krys asked Lefty.

"Yeah," he said, snatching the wallet away.

"He must've put up a real fight!" Stu said.

Lefty gave him a cold, empty glare. "That's not his style."

"So... someone just trashed the place?" Krys asked, "A warning maybe?"

"Maybe," Stu said, still reviewing the damage. The kitchen table was overturned. Beyond that, comfy furniture was ripped open, the stuffing strewn all over the family room. "Maybe they were looking for something."

A syrupy mess puddled on the floor. Stu dabbed it with the toe of his boot. It looked like chocolate sauce.

"Blood," Krys said, crouching over the puddle.

Stu took a knee, peered at it closely. Dark maroon.

Lark rushed over. "Whose blood?"

"Who knows," Stu said, looking up at him, "but it looks like it's been here a while."

"Or," Krys said, then exhaled, open-mouthed, and gestured at the steam, "it's just gone cold."

Chapter 25: It Takes Two

Chris Fortune had made a breakthrough.

It wasn't what one would expect. It was absolutely accidental. Somehow, one of those little Tic Tacs had dropped from the lab counter into a trash basket, a wire mesh basket, with holes so small that the Tic Tac fell in just a way that it was wedged in the mesh.

Dr. Fortune witnessed it in a split second: the entire basket flared blue-white and the contents of the trash can simply disappeared. Then the trash basket wires went from red to black, and the little basket crumpled on the floor. He distinctly smelled bleach, not melted wire or anything hot.

"I'll be damned," he said, "Eureka!"

Finally, the little nothing tablets had done something.

He spent weeks on the remains of that original mesh basket. What surprised him most was, despite how many tests he ran, there was absolutely no trace of the trash that had been in that basket. There were no remains of the crumpled pages he had tossed. Not a drop of coffee from the cup that had been there. Not a staple nor paperclip nor gum wrapper. There was not so much as a fiber of the tissue paper. Everything that had been within that basket had quite simply vanished.

An experiment, to be truly valid, had to be replicable. Chris tried and tried to make it happen again. He wedged the pellets, one by one, between wire elements of every type and in every configuration, in carefully controlled laboratory situations.

Connect the tip of the pellet to the wires.

Connect the wires to a series or mesh of other wires.

Simulate. Isolate. Repeat. Vary conditions.

He thought for a few days that perhaps he had been trying too hard to isolate the reaction with lab conditions, special wire, and so on, so then he revisited the *same table* and spent days brushing Tic Tacs into wire baskets of the same manufacturer. He filled waste baskets with contents as nearly identical to what he could recall as in the original. He tried and tried to get a Tic Tac brushed from the table to actually land just like the flaming one had done, wedged between the mesh. He found, through trial and error, that this only would occur once in about one thousand swipes. When one would land just right, he would set that basket gently aside, then swipe at another.

At the end of the week, he had twelve baskets as nearly identical to his original as he could imagine. Yet none of them reacted at all.

Still nothing. Inert. Nondescript baskets of trash.

He returned to the Tic Tac swiping, racking his brain as to what condition was not identical to that fateful night the basket had burned. He tried brushing the Tic Tacs at the same velocity. Left-handed. Right-handed. Backhanded. Different hand soaps. Different laundry detergents. Different times of the day or night.

In every instance and interval, Dr. Christopher Fortune took meticulous notes in a cryptic cipher he and his twin had invented when they were only seven years old. He kept it on his person at all times, an old leather-bound notepad.

• • • •

AT THE INSTALLATION, Dr. Christopher Fortune specifically asked to head the research team on what everyone had come to call "Tic Tacs." He would conduct materials tests on them, running every conceivable test on them. He was incredibly tedious about his work, absolutely dependable in his research, and thorough.

All of this would simply buy him more time for the real work he was doing in his basement.

His work at the Installation informed his private practice. By day, he was a quiet man in a lab coat, operating methodically according to scientific method and theorem. At night, he remained this same man, but his experiments went beyond logic and reason... and he wore a Hawaiian shirt.

Over the ensuing months, he lost a lot of weight. His power had been cut for non-payment twice. He had been put on notice at the lab. His ex-wife was the only one who looked in on him, bringing him groceries once in a while. Though he could not confide in her, she once summed up what she knew to be his underlying motive: this was somehow about Lark and how he had lost his hand. He denied this, of course, but after twenty years of marriage, he knew she knew his true character.

Three months had passed. Then five. All of his house plants had died, he noticed one day on his way out the door. Being unusually alert that day, he also took down notices stuck on his front door from utilities and two citations for his lawn being out of control. He eyed the well-cut lawn, then read a third notice: the city had cut his lawn and charged him $200.

He was getting in his car when he noticed the lawn had also been sprinkled with tiny white grains of fertilizer. For some inexplicable reason, this instantly consumed him. He tossed his lunchbox and notebooks in the passenger seat and then crouched down to study the fertilizer.

On his hands and knees, then laying down on the sidewalk on his belly, he examined the fertilizer long and hard. The little grains of fertilizer were mostly on the ground. A few had been lodged in the grass and suspended there. He could not readily find a pattern in their distribution.

Then it hit him.

He bolted up from the ground, bumping his head on the bottom of the car door. He did not bother with the car door, nor the door to his house. He did not bother resealing a secret panel door to the basement. He stumbled down the stairs and set to work with explosive vigor.

Two of the little grains of fertilizer had been touching.

The experiment required two Tic Tacs, one to fall into the wire mesh, the other had to have been brushed in at the same time, yet it had fallen on down in the wastebasket. It took two of these little pellets to make a circuit!

To his dismay, he learned again that it was not that easy. He hypothesized that not only was the activation of the circuit to require a pair of Tic Tacs, but it also had to be the right combination of these two.

Dr. Fortune spent the next few weeks dropping the Tic Tacs, one-by-one, into each of the twelve baskets.

Chapter 26: Wired

Detective Shae Ward sat opposite Officer Davis Cole in an empty interrogation room. Between them was an assortment of evidence, all of it neatly bagged and labeled. One cellophane envelope was fiber (but oddly, no hair) from the gunman's booth. It had been run against clothing examples and descriptions from the parents of the four teens and isolated to now definitively belong to the gunman at Mack's. It had proven to be nothing more than a standard Army surplus wool coat.

More substantial, and yet not surprising, another dead end: a black watch cap in a zip-lock bag. Even sealed in the bag, it emitted the strong smell of gasoline. It had been retrieved by Mr. Wiebe from his barn, and so it was now out of context, tampered with, and the gasoline voided any hope of DNA testing. His very hat, and yet it was getting them nowhere.

Other baggies held blackened coils of wire. No matter how much she had heard about them, they still made her curiosity spike.

"Why are you here again, Cole?" Shae asked the officer across the table from her. "Why aren't you on leave?"

"Leave?" he groaned. He glanced at the two-way mirror, skeptical. "You mean 'cuz of the posts?"

"Yes, exactly," she said. "Generally, it's frowned upon to livestream from a crime scene."

He chuckled at her accidental rhyme. It made her furious. Useless evidence and a sloppy cop. A cocky, sloppy cop at that. "Wasn't a livestream, just some updates."

"You might as well get a megaphone and tell the—"

"Chief says if I cooperate with you and the feds, I got nothing to worry about."

"Is that right?" Shae said.

"He says if I tell you about the alley, I can take a few days PTO before I go back in the car."

She already knew about the alley. Perhaps worse even than the smattering of evidence between them was the impossible alley. Four kids and a strange man bolt out the door, so say the cook and server and a few diners. Five people go through a door, and yet, absolutely nothing after that proves they set foot outside.

"I know all about the alley," Shae said. "You gotta do better."

"Sure." He sat up and leaned forward. Slow and casual, like a big sloth, Cole slid one of the evidence bags apart from the rest. "One of these was in the alley."

She shook her head. She had read every report. There was no report of a burnt-up wire in the alley. "You aren't improving your situation here, Davis."

"I saw it with my own eyes. I swear."

"You saw a wire, but we don't have this wire?"

"Saw 'em take it. Two square cut military guys. I'd bet on it."

Shae had heard about this claim, though it was just a rumor if it wasn't in writing. She had her own dozen such tidbits that were not going to make it into the record. Cole's rumor, however, had concrete truths to it, like suspicious footprints at the scene in the frozen slush, corroborating his timeline and the contusion Cole liked to show everyone.

"So, two guys pried a wire just like this out of the brick wall around the back door, and then?"

"Took it an' left, I guess." He pulled back his hair to show her the bruise. "I was out of commission. Don't know what they did next."

She eyed the two packets with crusty black wires rolled up in them. One had been retrieved from Wiebe's barn, by the doors. The other was found in the loft. A third was said to be in evidence the Feds were keeping tight. Since it had to do with a stolen vehicle, they could cloister it away indefinitely, citing all kinds of transportation citations.

Cole leaned in, catching her eye. "Guy called 'em 'Hot Wires,' whatever that's worth."

Shae kept turning one packet over and over. The contents just looked like burned up guitar strings. Rob played the guitar, and he was always restringing his. Coils of wire not much different from these charred ones were common at her house.

Something about these, however, was anything but common.

Chapter 27: Spinning Wheels

Lark didn't have any idea what they were really after. It seemed futile to search a house that had been so thoroughly ransacked. Surely the Spooks had found whatever they were after. Certainly, they had taken his dad with them. Lark felt awkward, for he did not know which he was most curious about: his dad's whereabouts or whatever it was the Spooks had hunted for.

Then they found the secret door.

Krystal was the one who ultimately tripped some hidden switch. A wall panel snicker-snacked and opened a little. She was making some comment about Harry Potter, just goofing around, when she made the discovery.

The three of them opened the doorway more and looked cautiously into the darkness.

"Basement?" Stu asked.

"We already did the basement, from the stairs off the pantry," Lark said.

Krystal felt around the inside of the door frame and flipped a light switch. Nothing. A staircase descended into the dark. "*Second* basement," she said, stepping out onto the landing.

The stairs were steep and wooden. They seemed homemade, just a notch better than a tree house ladder. It was crisp and quiet down in the basement.

"Who has a second basement?" Stu asked from behind them.

Krystal found a pull cord for a basement light, and on instinct, pulled it. To everyone's surprise, the light came on, revealling a space that had not been discovered by the looters. This second basement was small, just a dozen feet wide. The walls were covered in shelves, and the shelves were covered with various scientific instrumentation, books, reams of paper, and cases of ramen noodles, canned goods, and beer.

"Independent power supply?" Krystal marveled. She ran her hand down a counter that had several blinking instruments.

"Your dad's a prepper?" Stu asked. "Cool."

"No, he's not a prepper," Lark corrected him. "He's a workaholic."

Lark was determined to not leave that second basement without some answers. The mess—and particularly the blood—upstairs was numbing. The impossibility of the teleported Suburban out in the yard was... unnerving. Fear of being chased by men like those who shot at them at Mack's, even fear of Sackerson himself, left Lark terrified.

Here, however, he could put all that aside. Here, he had a singular purpose: to figure out what his dad had been up to. As they looked around, Lark was surprised it had come to all this. Sure, after he got out of the hospital, his father had already been reassigned to the Installation. That had led to security clearances and protocol that made him feel less and less welcome at his dad's. Even when he had called ahead and his mom had made plans, most of the time, his dad had forgotten, had not left work, had made last-minute changes.

Now, Lark thought he knew why. Something in this space was really, really important to his father. It was so special that he had secretly made this whole room; in fact, Lark had had no idea it even existed until now. His father had devoted everything to something here, and Lark wanted to understand both what it was, and why it was so very important.

"Looks like Greek or something," Stu said, flipping through an open notebook. "Check it out."

All three of them examined the strange characters on the pages. "I've seen lots of other languages," Krystal said. "I mean, I had a poster of the Rosetta Stone above my bed as a kid—"

"What?" Lark said, "Who has a poster of the Rosetta Stone, period?"

"What's the Rosetta Stone, anyway?" Stu asked.

"The point is," she said, with some exasperation, "I've seen a lot written out, and this is just... strange."

"Yeah," Lark mused, "strange, but it does kind of look... organized. It's not just gibberish, right?"

"Pppfft!" Krystal said, "I dunno."

"It's not like she's some kind of codebreaker!"

Krystal gave Stu a glare. "I bet I could, though. I could break this. If I had the time, I bet I could totally figure this out."

"Why would your dad write like this?" Stu looked at Lark suspiciously. "Is he... are you... foreigners?"

"Aliens!" Lark said and waved his hand in Stu's face.

"That's not even funny," Krystal said. "Considering everything else we've been through tonight, you being an alien isn't even a joke."

"At least there's pictures," Stu said, turning the page. "What do you make of this?"

He was pointing at a drawing, but even when Lark turned the notebook around, he could not quite tell what it was a drawing of, exactly. "Tornado?"

"Some kinda drain or something?" Stu asked.

"Look at this part, though." Krystal ran her fingernail through the loops, then followed a thin line right off the page. "It's like this was sucked through a funnel or something."

"Like a spinning wheel, maybe," Stu added. "Wool here... yarn here."

"Hey, that's pretty good," Krystal said. "So, he's drawing out some kind of process, maybe?"

"That could be anything," Lark said. "Like some doodle while he was waiting on test results."

"Looks like more than a doodle," she said, then turning the pages, she added, "For one thing, this line, this yarn, goes on for pages. Man, I wish I could read what he was writing about here."

The characters on these pages were more erratic, as if scrawled quickly and with a dull pencil. In places, it was clear the lead had broken. It went on like that for page after page: frantic words cut through with the yarn line.

"Seems like he was pretty worked up about something," Stu said.

Lark turned the page, and then it was nothing but full pages of neatly written 1s and 0s for the rest of the notebook. Several other notebooks were entirely filled with these same numbers.

Each of them flipped through the number notebooks. For several minutes, the only sound was the turning of pages.

"I can't see any kind of pattern," Lark said, after a few minutes.

"Think it's Binary?" Stu asked.

They looked at him quizzically.

"What, can't I say smart things? My sister's in Computer Science, you know."

Lark didn't know. He didn't even know Stu had a sister.

"I think he's maybe right," Krystal said, "but I don't know the first thing about Binary."

"Dad would," Lark said.

All three of them nodded, as if this was an obvious fact to acknowledge.

"Maybe Sackerson was talking about this stuff when he said they'd be after your dad," Stu said. "Maybe they'd make a trade?"

"Who says they got him?" Lark asked.

"Maybe he got them," Krystal stated.

"I'm just saying," Stu continued, "someone wanted something upstairs. They wanted it really bad. I say it was this." He held up the notebook he was rifling through. "I say what we have here gives us the advantage."

"Or," Lark said, "it puts us in even more trouble."

"How's that?" Stu asked.

"Because once they find this room, they'll figure we did too, and they'll still be coming for us, thinking we know more than what they do. They'll think we're holding out."

"Maybe we should," Krystal said. "Maybe we should just take as much as we can carry and run."

"Why?" Lark asked. It seemed like a terrible idea, like rubbing bacon grease all over and running through a pack of hungry dogs. "So they'll chase us?"

"Might give us some space," Stu said. "We could probably make deals with these. You know, 'step back and wait,' and we'll give you a page at a time."

"Or they could kill all three of us and have it all," Lark said.

Chapter 28: House call

Something about boys. They would be going all out, like the argument between Stu and Lark. Then they'd just fall asleep, like they were now. Both of them were sacked out in Dr. Fortune's trashed family room. One was draped over a love seat, the other crashed in the recliner. Krystal just watched them saw logs. They might as well sleep, she thought, for this was nothing but a waiting game.

Less than an hour ago, by her estimation, they'd been yelling and cussing at each other. Lark was insistent they stay here and wait for Sackerson. Stu wanted to go—anywhere—and call home. They bickered about everything, including how flakey Sackerson was and how unlikely it might be that he would show up at the house.

Krystal's concerns that someone else might find them were just a sidebar in their argument, just dismissed out of turn. Lark insisted they couldn't just abandon his dad, that they had to keep hope in Sackerson, for he seemed to know at least something that would have happened to his dad, even if it was in the future.

Replaying that in her head still didn't make any sense: *would have happened—in the future.*

Most of the yelling, thank goodness, had taken place in the little basement lab. Stu finally just stomped up the stairs like he was leaving, but they found him in the kitchen rummaging through a cabinet. He had a bag of chips and a pop with him, and he flopped down in the recliner. "What?" he barked at them. "I need to think."

Krystal followed Lark down a dark hallway to a bedroom. He ducked in, then back out into the hall before she could follow. He opened the door to the bathroom, growled, then darted across the hall to another room.

"What are you looking for?" she asked.

"I don't know, Krystal. I don't even know the house. *My own dad's house*, and I don't even know my way around," he grumbled. He was shuffling around in what must have been Dr. Fortune's study. A desk was overturned. A light crunched underfoot. Papers were everywhere. "What am I looking for?" he muttered under his breath, "Clues... maybe?"

She watched him digging and soon found herself joining in. It surprised her to find a bowling ball bag empty, but the ball was nearby. In different circumstances, she might have asked Lark about it. He was, however, obviously not in the mood. She found model ships that, sadly, had been smashed by the looters. One ship in a bottle was preserved, though she did not know how. Almost everything in sight had been rumpled, tossed, crushed. It had been a malicious search, she thought.

Most surprisingly, she found an unopened, undamaged Christmas gift with a tag addressed to Larkin. She hefted it for weight. She shook it to listen for what might be inside. It did not attract Lark's attention, and she knew better than to hand it to him, so she just placed it out of the way for the moment.

Krystal noted a tangle of cords near the desk. She recognized one as a computer cord. "Do you think they took his computer?"

"You think?" he said. She did not like his tone.

"What is with you, Lark?"

He just looked at her for a second, then resumed his rummaging around. He took a little extra time crouched over a pile that must have once been on the desk.

Lark got up, a telephone receiver in hand. It was an older model cordless home phone. Lark thumbed the button, then tossed the phone away. "Dead. Like all the lights, all the power, except down there."

He moved past her out into the hall, then into yet another bedroom. Lark gathered up a comforter and pillow and pressed by her in the doorway. "Might as well get comfortable," he said to her gruffly.

"What did I do?" she said, reaching out to him.

"Nothing. That's just it. You just can't pick a side, can you?"

"Pick a side..." Then he was gone, back to the living room.

The house was creepy. He had left her in the dark hall. She imagined some poltergeist had trashed it. She picked up her step on her return to the guys.

Stu had curled up in the chair, turning his back to them. Lark was trying to get comfortable on the short loveseat. Krystal picked a cushion off the floor, brushed it off and replaced it on a chair. Then she sat opposite them. She still had the quilt from the Suburban, and she curled up in it.

"Now what?" she asked.

"Now we wait," Lark said.

"No plan—*that's* a stupid plan," Stu grumbled to the wall, but said no more.

• • • •

THEY WOKE TO A POUNDING sound. It was daylight now, and the room looked even worse than in the dark. The pounding again at the front door. Stu and Krystal looked at Lark. He shrugged his shoulders but got up.

He shuffled groggily toward the door. Stu was right behind him, holding a fireplace poker. Krystal stood and hid behind a partial wall, where she could get a view of the front door.

The pounding again.

Lark and Stu whisper-bickered, then at Stu's behest, Lark called out, "Yeah, be right there." The boys were in an animated yet silent argument. Stu shook his head and showed Lark the fireplace poker.

Lark turned to the door, took a deep breath, and pulled himself up tall. Stu assumed a position behind the door, on the hinge side, the poker over his head. Stu nodded. Lark opened the door.

"Good morning," a man in coveralls said. "I'm here on a house call... a service call."

"Oh," Lark said. "Good morning."

"Your neighbors, the entire neighborhood, it seems, suffered a little blackout early this morning."

"Yeah... yes. Yes, we did, too." Lark nodded his head. "Power's still out."

Krystal could see an orange utility truck in the street beyond. An orange safety cone was set out in front and another in back. Yellow lights were flashing on top, as were the hazard lights. She could not get a good look at the man from the power company.

"Yes... well... I need to check your meter, maybe look over your transformer. Your place is on the main, you know, so that transformer splits off to the whole block."

"Sure. Sure," Lark said. "Go ahead."

"Here. It's a slip we leave on these checks. Give it to your dad."

"Right," Lark said, making to close the door.

"Oh, and sir—" the utility man interjected.

"Yes?"

"You have a Jim Dandy day," he said and turned back down the porch as Lark closed the door.

"Geeeeezzzzzzzzz," Stu said. "That freaked me."

Lark gestured for him to be quiet.

Krystal stepped toward them, noting the fright on Lark's face.

"What is it?" Stu asked.

"Give it to your dad," Lark said, softly.

"Did you see his shoes too?" Krystal added.

"What about them?" Stu whispered.

"They're all wrong."

"Aw, great," a voice behind them said. "Sharp eye, kid." Krystal whirled to see another utility worker had stepped into the kitchen. She was astonished that he had crept in, unheard, through all the broken glass and rubbish on the floor.

She was more shocked, however, at the gun he leveled at them. "Maxton!" He shouted out the patio door, "Jigs up!"

"You kidding?" Krystal heard the other man call back, rounding the house. "What was it this time? My accent?"

"Shoes. We got the wrong shoes."

"Aw, cripes," the one called Maxton said, stepping inside. He, too, had drawn a menacing black pistol. "The shoes, again?"

"It's attention to detail," his partner said. "We just gotta be more on point."

"And would you look at this mess?" Maxton said.

"Amateurs."

"We... *we* didn't do this," Lark said.

"Really?" the man from the back door asked, kicking aside a toaster. "Then who did?"

"Ironical isn't it, Turner?"

"What's Ironical?"

"When affairs or events seem all deliberate and contrary to what you expect. It's often laughable."

"I mean, what do *you* think is so ironical, Max?"

"That we're here to find such and such, but we're critiquing them that did it, beat us to the punch."

"Aw, never mind," Maxton said. "Kids... over here." He waved them back into the living room. "Have a seat."

"And ditch the stick, cowboy."

Stu set down the poker and followed Lark and Krystal. They all jumbled together on the loveseat. She was again wedged in the middle.

"Good looking kids, huh, Turner?"

"Yeah, they are."

"Which one of you's the Fortune kid?"

Krystal cleared her throat.

"We know it's not you, toots," Maxton said.

"It's you, right?" the other man pointed his pistol at Lark. "I knew it from the stump."

"That's coarse," Maxton said. "Don't call it a stump."

"Well, what should I—"

"Hey!" Krystal said. "What's going on here?"

Both men turned their attention to her.

"What's going...? What's going on here?" Maxton asked. He chuckled, "Well, babe, we have us a—"

"And what's with you, being all misogynistic?" Turner interrupted.

"Mysogi—what?"

"You. Calling her 'toots,' and 'babe,' and—"

"Whaddya want me to call her? Mizz?" Maxton frowned. "And what's with you? Making fun of the kid's hand? Calling it a stump?"

"Just shut it."

"You just shut it."

"Why don't you just let me do the talking?" Turner said, more loudly.

"You do the talking? Who died and made you—"

"You can't get anything right. That's why I'm doing the talking. You can't even get the shoes right!"

"Oh yeah? Who's the one who flipped the wrong house? *Got the address wrong*," Maxton mocked.

"Like I told ya, all these houses—"

"It's attention to detail, Turner, like you just said," Maxton sneered. "Wasted a lot of time. We wouldn't be in this fix with these three, if it wasn't for—"

"Fix? Because of me, now we got leverage, stupid!"

Krystal couldn't understand why the two men were so volatile. They kept at each other, their tempers rising, until they broke out in a brawl.

"All. Your. Fault!" Maxton was swinging his pistol at Turner.

"Somebody beat us to it!"

Turner clocked Maxton with a lamp. They were growling and cursing and pounding each other.

Krystal wanted to look away, but she couldn't. The outrage that flared between them was so sudden, so unbelievable!

"Let's go!" Lark whispered, tugging at her quilt.

"Truck!" Stu said, and on their way out the door, he grabbed the fireplace poker for good measure.

They skipped stairs on the porch and ran flat out for the utility truck, but when they reached it, the three pulled up short.

Sackerson was in the driver's seat now, smiling and waving them in. He had on that stupid hat of Henny's, and he had a cigar clenched in his teeth.

Stu hesitated, his hand on the passenger door handle. "Guys?" he asked.

Then there were shots fired inside the house, and the decision was made. They bolted into the truck cab.

"Drive!" Krystal shouted.

"As you wish," Sackerson said with a cackle.

Chapter 29: Spun Honey

May 2029
        Chris Fortune was humming an old tune he had learned at some Bible camp as a child. It was unlike him to hum, even less like him to hum a hymn, and it took him a good while to even remember the words. "It was the Touch of the Master's Hands," he sang aloud, once it came back to him.

In the song, an old violin at an auction was not getting highly bid upon, at least not until an old man stepped forward and played a beautiful song on it. Then everyone wanted it.

Chris was that old man.

The Tic-Tacs were the old violin.

He was the master who had found value in those little bits of debris the Installation disregarded. After a year of public and private research, he had finally found their true nature.

The reason virtually every test was inconsequential was that the little white capsules were new, different, and Fortune was sure now, extra-terrestrial.

Though they gave off virtually no detectable electromagnetic force, there was a very, very limited instance in which he discovered them to have the slightest magnetic property: they each had a single partner pellet.

That first zap in the wastebasket was an absolutely random fluke, that a matched pair of pellets had combined through an arc of the basket's wire mesh.

One night, he did the math. He had, over time, taken home six boxes of the pellets, and each box was two feet, square. That gave him about 48 cubic feet of pellets. He converted that to about 38 bushels, for he readily found a bushel of wheat (each kernel being about the same size as a Tic Tac) contained a million grains. He had close to 38 million Tic Tacs, or possibly 19 million pairs.

Initially, they were just stacked in boxes in his basement, but when he learned they were potent, whether it was electric or whatever it was, he decided it was time to hide them.

But where to hide 40 bushels of pellets?

The house he had bought after the divorce was a quick-fab developer's home, like all the rest in Shallowbrook. While most every other home around him had only a partial basement, Chris had bought one that had never moved on the market, one that had been a show home when the development changed hands, the only one with a full basement. Norman was close to Murray, known as one of the most tornado riddled communities in America. Every house in the region had at least a partial basement.

Chris Fortune set about making his basement identical to all the rest. It took him weeks, and he had to watch a lot of YouTube and practice his carpentry skills. Eventually, he had crafted a secret, second basement with a separate, hidden entrance.

Even if someone were to find this space, no one would find the Tic Tacs. He had taken a cue from Graber, back at the lab. The walls were 2x4 stud walls, like all the rest in the neighborhood, except his were insulated with the pellets.

• • • •

HE HAD BUILT DOWNSPOUTS into the stud walls, and these were hidden with the mop boards of the room. Whenever he wanted to extract some pellets, he would pull away a mop board, open the downspout, and they would flow freely. The basement had a suspended ceiling, and it was easy enough to lift a tile and pour pellets back into the stud wall. The entire operation, all this storage, was undetectable.

Tonight, like every night, he would pour a quantity of pellets, then sit at his workbench and sift through them, seeking even the slightest signs of polarity. He watched to see if one would spin end-to-end to tap into its partner. He looked closely for them to be in any way attracted to each other. If he would have had a lab anymore, he could have sped up the process with any number of mechanisms. This manual, observant sifting, however, gave him ample opportunity to think. To imagine.

He often returned to the question of why two partner pellets did not just arc if they ever found each other. It baffled him, but the best he could guess was that they required a secondary conductor, like the wastebasket wire. He had already studied that wire exhaustively, finding it to be nothing special, just a low-grade steel mesh.

He wondered, more than anything, where the contents of that first basket had gone. To even dream that material just disappeared violated the laws of middle school physics—matter was neither created nor destroyed. He knew this to be true, but he had no explanation for the litter. He asked himself if Lark's hand had somehow gotten mixed up with a pair of pellets, for it, too, was gone without a trace. When he allowed himself to entertain the idea that the bright blast that somehow destroyed matter had only taken a limb, Chris was both relieved and terrified.

What would happen if partnered pellets could be harnessed? Weaponized to destroy everything between them? It made him shudder.

It also made him all-the-more cautious and secretive about his work. If it fell into the wrong hands, he could not fathom what might come of it.

• • • •

IN WEEKS OF SEARCHING for partnered pellets, combing through them, sliding them around, matching them end-to-end like beads, he had found only a pair. After another month, another two pairs. In close to a year, allowing for his pace to quicken from impatience, simple machines, and being let go from the lab, he had now amassed a full 100 pairs. He stored these in lengths of aquarium hose, and he laid those inside a nondescript cigar box he kept on the lab table.

On nights he was discouraged, he would open the box and look at them with wonder. He would write about them, capturing all his wildest speculation about them, in notebook upon notebook, all in his childhood cipher. Occasionally, he would pull a notebook from the shelf and re-read its contents, annotating and illustrating things he had learned or imagined.

One afternoon, sitting in his easy chair, he was watching reruns of "How It's Made" on the television. He was drinking a beer, one of many that day. He was only half attending to the show, but he was sure to look away when it transitioned to commercial, for he would see his frumpy, fattened reflection in the TV screen. Too much down time, sedentary desk work, and too many beers—it was taking its toll on him.

He looked back when the show resumed, only to see a segment on the manufacture of fiber optic cable. His mind was free associating, from molten glass to spun honey to spinning cotton candy to a spinning wheel. He caught up to his thoughts and again to the program, just as it was espousing the merits of fiber optics: "smaller, lighter...carry more information...fewer repeaters...and unlike copper cables, they're immune to electromagnetic interference. They're also hard to tap without being detected...all based on a very simple principle: Light traveling through glass."

Dr. Christopher Fortune had done it again. He tipped his beer to the television, then got up and made his way down to his lab and began sketching and coding his latest breakthrough.

Chapter 30: Valentine's Day

February 2030

"How's your Eskimojo?"

"I'm sorry, what?"

Rob slid a placard in front of her. "See?"

They were at Eskimo Joe's in Stillwater, at 'their table,' as Rob had called it, though Shae remembered it differently. This was the place he had proposed, on the day he had proposed, just ten years before.

The table tent between them was raising trivia questions about the place. She turned it around to find an ad for an "Eskimojohito" on the reverse.

"Happy Valentine's Day, babe," he said with his warm and funny smile. What would she tell a sketch artist, that he smiled like some kind of big, happy Shar Pei? That his face looked, remarkably, like Eskimo Joe himself, with the eyes squinted to slits when Rob would turn his smile full-on? She sighed as she admired him. He was so happy. He was her happy place.

"Happy Valentine's," she returned, though even saying it made her feel guilty. She had accepted the card he and the girls had made... and the flowers... and she was surprised her folks were babysitting. She loved the new dress, and she was even okay with dressing up and going out, even on a lunch date, but Shae had conditions she was yet to reveal. It was totally out of their way, but maybe she could sell him on a side trip to Perry as part of their time together.

"Remember the Avocado burgers?" Rob asked, taking her hands in his. "Remember how that server kept saying ah-VA-ca-do?" She did not, but she smiled and nodded. "Well, anyway, I ordered them. Not even on the menu anymore, but I special ordered them!"

She did love a good avocado burger. As he knew, it was her favorite, as it had been even back then. The server had brought her another Pineapple Express. "I shouldn't," she said, but Rob insisted.

"Relax, Shae. I'll drive. You need to just fall into it, sweetheart." Once he had serenaded her with a song that had that as a chorus, something about "fall into me," and it had been his catch phrase ever since. Whenever she let herself, she had to admit it felt pretty good.

"To you, Big Squeeze," she toasted him.

"And to you." He lifted his glass of water, and they clinked them together. "And to your case."

A little frown tweaked her nose. "Case?"

"I don't *always* sleep through your debriefs," he said, looking around the room as casually as he could, then added, "and I can tell this one's really got you."

"So..." She was more surprised by this than the elaborate Valentine's Day arrangements. "So, what do you know about my case?"

She thought it cute the way he cast his eyes about, furtively, as he spoke. "You think the guy from Mack's is okay? You're wanting to do more to prove it, but it's moved out of town, so you're just working a cold case."

"I wouldn't call it that, but yeah. I'm frozen out at the city limits. Jurisdiction."

"Yeah," Rob grimace-smiled then, something he usually only used when he had to tell the girls bad news. "Yeah, I suppose that's frustrating."

"What is it?" Shae asked. She knew there was more than empathy there.

"Thanks for agreeing to all this... I mean, I know I'm cheesy sometimes and all. And I know you can't just let work go." She waited him out. "So," he said at last, "I got you something *different* this year."

Rob pulled a red envelope from his jacket pocket and placed it on the table. The server popped up with their meal, so Rob pulled the envelope back to his side. He and the server exchanged the usual pleasantries about the food, the need for anything else, while Shae puzzled over the gift. He had already given her a card. What was in this envelope? It was obviously something lumpy.

He made her wait through the entire dinner, even through after-dinner drinks. Her head was spinning when she licked the last of the third Pineapple Express from her lips. She couldn't help herself, finally saying, "Gimme, gimme, gimme!"

He tossed her the envelope, and she ripped it open. A key on an old school motel fob fell out onto the table. He was beaming.

"Why, Robert Ward! Just what are you proposing this time? An afternoon tryst in a motel?" she giggled.

He reached over and turned the fob around in her hand. She read, "Cherokee Strip Hotel and Casino?"

He tapped it, and she read more, "Perry, Oklahoma?"

"Yep," he said, and nothing more.

"Rob," she shook the tropical blur from her head. "What's this—"

"Dollarhide Amusements," he said, with a faraway look in his eyes. "I hear they're staying there for a day or two while all that settles down about the accident up there."

"Rob!" she smiled a smile to rival his. "How did you...?"

"I'm in a network of Stay at Home Dads, you know, and we talk. I just mentioned to the guys that I was shocked to hear about that train wreck, and the fellas came through."

"You're kidding," she laughed. "Really?"

"Our room's on their floor. I'm sure you can get plenty of time to talk with them... off the record and all."

Shae wiped a tear from her eye and laughed again, marveling, "Stay at Home Dads!"

• • • •

FINDING THE CARNIVAL group was easy. Shae had had
enough to drink that asking them down to the casino bar, *Strip and
Chips*, for another round was not hard either. Everything was coming
easily, it seemed, until she asked one too many questions about the
tall bald man.

The old man shook his head, and the table got quiet. Shae didn't
feel shut out, though. It seemed more like they were mourning him.

"You're not really askin' about the train, then," the one with the
broken nose stated. "You're asking about Sack."

She raised her eyebrow, feeling this might be big, but she asked
nothing.

"Salt of the earth, that one," an old lady chimed in. She was the
chain smoker, sitting directly under the 'No Smoking' sign. "Helped
me find my Kiko."

"And Kiko is...?" Shae asked, pencil poised.

"I'm Kiko," said a girl in her twenties, slightly built, who sat by
the prizefighter. "And Sackerson was everywhere, like some kind of
paramedic or something."

"Sackerson?" Shae asked for clarification.

"Yeah," old Mr. Dollarhide said, "Never caught his first name,
but he rode with me and the kids."

"Kids?" Rob asked, unable to help himself. He put down his
coffee cup.

"Yeah, three of 'em," Mr. Oleander Dollarhide said. He was the
patriarch of the group, that was clear. Sitting at the head of the long
table, when he wasn't answering questions, he was allowing others to,
sometimes with eye contact, sometimes the subtle nod of his head.
"Good kids. Probably from around here," he continued. "Pretty sure
one was from around here. Had his damn boots on my dash like he
owned the place."

"Remember any names?" Shae asked the old man.

"Nah!" Dollarhide shook his head. "Two boys and a girl."

"And the crow. Don't forget the crow," someone offered from down the table.

Shae looked around the table. "Anyone remember anything else about them? The kids?"

Most of them were looking at their drinks, lighting cigarettes, waiting for Dollarhide's leadership.

"One kid might've been Sack's," Kiko said at last. "Looked a little like him."

Others nodded. Knuckles offered, "The Cripple."

"Cripple? What do you mean?" She knew what he meant, but she wanted confirmation.

"I went to shake his hand, and... well, he only had the one," Dollarhide said in his reedy voice. "But you wouldn't know it otherwise. He weren't no cripple, if you ask me."

She filled them in a little, on the kids' names and how there was a lot of law enforcement out looking for them. When she told them Sackerson was a kidnapping suspect, the whole table revolted.

"I'd give him my firstborn!" someone at the far end of the table said.

"I'm your firstborn!" Kiko retorted. Several of them chuckled. "And I'd go with him, sure."

"Gave the guy the 'Burban, and I know he'll bring it back when he can."

Shae sat upright in her chair. No reports had mentioned anything after the accident. It was as if the four of them had been spirited away by the drifting snow. She tried to compose herself, but her pencil was shaking.

"Burban?" Rob asked, his baritone rising. "Like a Suburban?"

"Yeah," it was the one they called Knuckles again. "He offered me a wad a' cash, but I just told him to hold on to it. Acted like he needed to move on in a hurry. Told him to leave it here when he was done with it."

"We hole up here sometimes, between things," someone offered. "Cheap food and rooms."

"And gamblin'," someone else added.

Many at the table affirmed this, "Gamblin'!" like a table of pirates.

Shae waited to ask more about the vehicle, but Rob spoke up first: "So... he's coming back here with the Suburban? When?"

"We've been here two days, 'way it is," the oldest woman said. "Lots of reports, between the highway patrol and the railway."

"We kinda need to move on," Dollarhide said, "but I figure he'll catch up to us."

Shae and Rob looked at each other.

"Catch up? Back here... or on the road somewhere?"

"Man of his word, I figure," one of them said. "He'll come around."

"What's this Suburban look like?" Rob asked, and laughter erupted around the table. "What?" he asked.

"Can't miss it," Knuckles said. "Looks like the rest of the fleet."

"Yeah, I guess that stands to reason," Rob smiled sheepishly.

"So," Shae played a hunch, "the Hypo's don't know anything, do they?"

"Not a damn thing," one of them said proudly. He got a look from Dollarhide.

Another one, closer to Shae, missed the stink eye and continued, "They only asked about the train wreck—"

"So that's all we told," Kiko said. She riveted Shae with a glare, nodding her head, "And that's all we told you, right?"

· · · ·

SHE FINISHED HER SHOWER, glad to have scrubbed all the smoke out of her hair, and called to Rob for a towel.

He was there, holding out a towel, but distracted by his cell phone.

She dried, but then let the towel drop to the floor, immodestly.

He had not even noticed.

"What is it?" she asked, looking at his screen.

"Strangest thing," he mused. "I'm pretty good at this, you know, but all I can find on 'Sackerson' is a bunch of stories about a bear."

"Rrrrrowr!" she said and dragged him to bed. "We can worry about that in the morning."

It had been her best Valentine's Day in recent memory.

She hoped to remember it in the morning.

Chapter 31: Historical

S tu was struggling to find something to hold on to. The four of them were packed tight in the utility truck's bench seat, and the pickup was lurching and swerving constantly. Stu kept getting cracked in the knee by the gearshift. "You ever drive a stick before?" he asked Sackerson.

"Probably," he said. "Besides, I'm a quick learner. I blame the snow packed streets."

"Right," Stu said, clutching at the dash.

"Where've you been, anyway?" Lark asked from the far door.

"Me?" Sackerson chuckled. "Right back there."

He thumbed over his shoulder at the truck's bed. Stu craned his neck to look. It was a high sided utility bed, toolboxes and ladders and spools of wire pretty well filled it up.

"For how long?" Krys asked, turning back to the front.

"Probably what... three... four hours?" He shrugged and smiled around his cigar. "How long's it take to get here from Guthrie?"

"An hour... maybe," Stu said, confused.

"You were back there all that time?" Krys asked.

"And then some. Had to hide before they took off. Had to hide once we got here. I'm not saying I didn't get a little stiff, all folded up back there, but I'm good in tight spots."

"What about the cold?" Lark asked. "Weren't you freezing?"

"Are you telling me you rode here with them?" Stu thought there would be no end to it. One unbelievable story after the next. "Why didn't you just pop down here like we did?"

Sackerson's head bobbled, and he grunted. "Well..." he navigated a particularly unsettling turn, in which they drifted half a block. "The truth is, guys, I never really know where you're going to end up when we use those Hot Wires."

"What?!" Krys said.

"Again, what happened to researching all this," Stu scoffed, "like from your time travel machine?"

"Improvisation," Lefty said at the same time as Sackerson.

"Exactly that," Sackerson said, winking at him. "Sure, I set up a dozen of them, but it's kinda random as to which one you come out of when you go in. You could've gone here first, after Mack's, before the barn. You might've 'ported from the car wash to... any of the rest of the presets."

"So, even if you would've used another one, you might not have gotten here, at least not efficiently," Krys said, nodding like it was making any sense at all.

"If it's all so random, how'd you know we'd end up here from the car wash, eh?" Stu was no dummy.

Sack slapped him on the knee. "You got it, Stu! There's no way in all creation I'd have ended up where you guys did, at least not for sure."

"And yet here you are," Lefty said.

"Along with those guys with the guns," Krys said. Stu could hear the accusation without looking at her frown. He could feel it burning right by him.

Sackerson pulled over, actually slid over, and bounced off the curb. "I gotta admit, Krystal, I don't like it either. Never knowing much, trying to second guess and outsmart everything. This time I just fell in to follow them."

"Follow them..." Lefty was putting something together. "So, they *do* know where we're going when we use those things?"

"They sure seem to know more than I do," Sackerson said. "At least, they seem to crop up with unusual accuracy."

"You said you worked from historical records, right?" Krys asked. "Like what, exactly?"

"Everything I could get my hands on," he said. "Phone records. Police records. Every kind of artifact."

"Did you have Dr. Fortune's journals?"

"No..." Sackerson said. "Why do you ask?"

"Why didn't you?" Lefty jumped in. "If everything's about Dad and some discovery, wouldn't you have his stuff in the future?"

"It'd be priceless!" Sackerson said. "But it all burned in the lab."

"Burned?" Lefty asked.

"What lab?" Krys asked.

"Maybe a better question is, when did that happen?" Sackerson said.

"Guys," Stu was tired of the ping-pong questions. "Let's just go back and show him what we found."

"What you found?" Sackerson asked, dumbfounded.

"Probably a thousand pages of stuff, if you ask me," Stu said.

The cigar fell from his mouth.

• • • •

SACKERSON'S DRIVING was even more erratic. He used the truck like a bulldozer, plowing over yards and fences as he turned it wide like a tank. They filled him in on the secret door and the second basement, none of which was in any records he had seen. As they pulled up to the house again, Krys was just saying, "Those two just started fighting!"

"Both of 'em. Ballistic!" Stu said.

"Yeah," Sackerson said, opening his door, "I have that effect on people."

The front door was still wide open, and Stu could smell cordite from the porch. "I heard them shooting when we were running out," he said.

"They're terrible shots," Lefty said, peering inside. He wretched then and turned aside. "Or worse."

Stu stepped inside right behind Sackerson. Both the utility guys were shot dead on the floor of the family room. The tan carpet was soaking up blood around them.

Krys did not even look. She stayed at the door with Lefty.

"Look at it like this, guys," Sackerson said, picking up their pistols and wiping them off. He tucked them into his coat. "Better them than you, right?"

"Right," Stu said, but the others were just moping around the entry.

"Who did this?" Krys asked. "And where are they now?"

"Don't freak," Sackerson said. "I'm pretty sure they shot each other."

"I still don't think we should stay here," Krys said. "It's the middle of the day. Somebody around here had to call the police."

"Wait, wait, wait," Stu said, holding up his hands. "If you know so much about... about the past... how come you don't know all this happened? Happens. Whatever."

"Like I told you, Stu," Sackerson said, "we're off script. This never happened before. Not like this. This is not historical."

"No one found the basement lab," Lefty said, coming cautiously inside.

"We better get what we can and go!" Krys said. "I think I hear sirens."

All of them stood stark still for a second, listening. Stu couldn't hear anything, but Lefty said he did, and he took off down the secret stairs, Sackerson right behind him. Stu looked back at Krys. "You coming?"

"I'm going to stay up here," she said. "I need some air."

"Suit yourself," he said. He grabbed a roll of trash bags from the floor and took the stairs down as fast as he could.

Lefty and Sack had armloads of the notebooks. They gladly dumped them in his trash bags and scooped up more.

"What about the equipment?" Stu said. "We may not have time to get it."

"With any luck," Sack said, "we can buckle up that door again and no one will be the wiser. Like last time." He swept everything he could off of the bench and into Stu's last bag.

• • • •

THEY HAD PULLED AWAY from the curb before the first police car was in sight. Stu was a little worried that they'd left the cones behind. He was worried they'd be able to catch up to them once they put two and two together.

"Wish I could tell you," Sackerson said, struggling with the wheel. "None of this is historical."

"You want me to drive?" Stu offered.

"I got this," he countered. "Trust me."

"Thanks again," Krys said. "That's twice you've gotten us out of trouble."

"Three if you count the helicopter," Lefty added. "And you were right, by the way. They *are* after us."

"Those guys called us 'leverage,'" Krys said.

"To get to your dad," Stu said to Lefty. "Like hold us hostage or something."

"Or something," Sackerson said.

"How is it they're like, everywhere?" Krys asked. "They just swarm around. Guthrie. Perry. Even here."

"And they can read a Hot Wire's residue, somehow," Sackerson said. "I didn't know that until I was tagging along."

"So, if we use one, and they find it, then they'll find us?"

"That's the only way I can figure they knew to come here," Sackerson said. "Unless they were just hedging their bets, digging around the house."

"I think there were two crews," Stu offered. "The early guys that tossed the place, then these utility guys."

"And maybe someone was hurt in the first group," Krys said. "Remember the blood in the kitchen?"

"I just hope it wasn't Dad," Lefty said.

"Two crews?" Sackerson was thinking it over.

"So, just how many of them are there?" Stu asked.

"There's no way to know that," Krys was guessing, "is there? These guys weren't supposed to be here either. Like you? *Not* 'historical' right?"

Sackerson nodded. He looked at her like he kept on doing, like she was the smartest person in the pickup. "Right."

Stu tried to scoff, but it stuck in his throat.

Chapter 32: Horse Thief Canyon Cabin

The radio had reported a good six inches of snow over the weekend, and Lark wondered how much thought Sackerson was putting into their travel plans. "Back roads," he had insisted, and it had taken them nearly two hours fighting drifts and slush and ice patches to get from Norman to the little Pump n' Go.

"Now we're fixing to really do some off-roading, eh Stu?"

"What do you call all this so far?" Lark asked. The four of them were grabbing up snacks. Lark had both pockets of the utility worker coat full of peanuts and jerky, and he fumbled a two liter of pop into the crook of his right arm.

"Paved," Stu said with a smile.

Krystal was carrying all the fresh produce she could. She looked utterly disgusted at the gas station pizza Sackerson was gorging on as they waited in line.

• • • •

"WHY COULDN'T WE GO into town?" Krystal asked as they got back in the pickup.

"Cameras," Sackerson said. "Didn't see any in there, did you?"

Lark thought about the big, curved mirrors that were in every corner of the convenience store, wondered if they had cameras behind them, but he said nothing. He eyed the storefront roofline and the gas pump area.

"Isn't that why you went outside?" Stu asked.

Sackerson had borrowed the key to the outside bathroom door. Lark thought nothing of it but now...

"Well, I am an electrical service technician," Sackerson smiled as he dropped it into gear. "See the jacket? The truck?" He chuckled. "I mighta done some creative work with their uplink while I was taking a whiz."

"What's an uplink?" Lark asked.

"All the franchise convenience stores uplink their financials, everything from the register, directly to their corporate office." Sackerson was rolling down a paved back road like he knew where he was going. "I don't want this rig, or us, in the record. So... no camera, no upload, no trace of four hungry travelers making a purchase outside of Perkins, Oklahoma, at roughly 11am."

Lark was really starting to admire Sackerson. He really did seem to be on their side, protecting them from all these Spooks, helping in the hunt for his father.

The road had some ruts for tracks. It was too far from anywhere to have seen a snowplow yet, Lark knew. The dash compass said they were headed due west. Some roadway signs announced they were nearing the Grider Farm Pumpkin Patch. He vaguely remembered a school trip, when he was in maybe fifth grade or so, and a visit to that pumpkin patch. He knew the Wiebe place wasn't far from there, for he could recall the bus had stopped at Stu's on the way back to town. It was a good memory. They had all jumped from hay bales and drank apple cider. Lark smiled. Stu's place was more a memory than the pumpkin patch itself.

"So, I haven't given you one turn on this whole trip, Sack. How do you know the way to the farm?"

"Dude," Sackerson said, "I know the way right to your *cabin*."

"Historical record, right?" Krystal said, doodling in the ice on her door glass.

"Actually, no," Sackerson said. "Oh, the farm's on the map, in the books, sure, but not the cabin."

"Soooo?" Stu pressed.

"I... I remember it, that's all."

"Here we go again," Stu groaned. "Listen, I know for a fact you've never been to Horse Thief."

"Facts, my boy, are a construct," Sackerson said.

"Dad says that," Lark said.

"I know," Sackerson smiled. "I suppose anybody in the sciences says that, though."

"You have *not* been to the cabin," Stu said again.

Sackerson wobbled his head, "Not lately, no."

"If you've been there, describe it," Stu challenged.

"I don't have to describe it," Sackerson countered.

"Ah, HA!" Stu almost capsized Lark's nachos. "You don't know squat."

Sackerson refused to be drawn in. He looked surprisingly sober as they rode along a few miles, past a cemetery road, past the pumpkin patch. Lark was getting uneasy with the silence. It felt like a quiet fight. Like a cold war.

That was pretty much his relationship with Stu too. Before the Guthrie Fall, Lark didn't really interact much with Stu Wiebe. He might have known him by name, maybe on some trivia list of big ranchers with big heads. If he was a football fan, he probably would have known Stu Wiebe as the big-time quarterback of Coyle High's little 8-man football team.

After the Guthrie Fall, however, it had been like this. Even though they sat side by side, there was nothing to talk about. The only thing they had in common was Krystal, and she was probably the number one reason Stu was such a jerk to him... if he had ever needed a reason.

Lark looked him over, out of the corner of his eye. He tried to remember that kid who'd had the class over to his farm. He could still make out a few freckles, that same smirk.

After a few miles, that smirk curled into a grin, and Stu looked past him to Krystal, then back to Sackerson. "You may not know the cabin, but Krys does, don't you?"

She rolled her eyes but did not reply. Lark figured there was a story there, but he wasn't about to pry into it.

Stu elbowed Lark. "Hell, Sackerson, I bet even Lefty here can describe the cabin better'n you, and he's only been there one time!"

Lark sighed. "Twice," he corrected.

"What?" Stu was taken aback. "I can only remember the school group, like from third grade."

"It was fifth grade," Lark corrected. "And... and one other time we came up on it by canoe."

"Ugh. River rats." Stu shook his head sternly. "You're a river rat?"

"I don't even—"

"Kinda people that sneak up on your property from the river. It happens a lot at our place. Way too much," Stu growled. "You did that, Lefty?"

"Just once," Lark admitted. "We were lost."

"Lost, huh?" Stu pressed back in the seat, dodging a downshift. "So. Tell us what you remember then... since Sackerson here's so full of it."

Sackerson pulled over suddenly. They weren't at any discernible crossroad, not even a farm or driveway. "Your turn, Stu."

"Doesn't even know the *way* from here, huh?" Stu was saying as he slid behind the wheel.

Sackerson was rounding the front of the truck, coming around to Krystal's door. Lark thought he saw something edgy in the way Sackerson was staring in the windshield.

Everyone shifted in the seat to allow for the rotation. As Sackerson slammed his door, he said, "We can't go up past your house. We have to take the long way. In from the west, riverside. Yes, I know the way," he said firmly, "but you'd be better at getting us there, I gotta admit."

• • • •

THOSE LAST FEW MILES to the cabin were a testament to Stu's driving ability and familiarity with the trail. It could have been a commercial for Ford trucks or for the Electric Cooperative. At times, Lark did not even see a trail, just snow, but Stu would plow ahead into it like the road was clear.

"I drive this all the time, guys. Shortcut to school when the river's dry."

Lark was certain they had run over a couple of saplings, maybe crawled over a downed tree or two, buried in a snowdrift. Krystal was clutching Lark's jacket with both hands. Neither of them had more than a lap belt to keep them from bounding to the ceiling.

They rounded a curve into an opening which looked onto a low place some thirty feet down, possibly 100 feet across. Now he knew what Stu was talking about. It was the riverbed. Before anyone could protest, Stu dropped the truck right down into it. Lark felt like they were on a Tilt-a-Whirl, for the pickup did two switchback turns, then lugged up the far bank.

"HA!" Stu said. "The ice really *is* solid enough. I told dad that a million times."

"You mean," Krystal asked, "you've never done that before?"

"Not exactly, not in the winter," Stu chuckled, obviously proud of himself. A tree clipped the side mirror off as he threaded the truck through a thicket. Then, the cabin came into view. "Here we are!"

It was as big as Lark's house, but it was finished out like a cabin with log siding and shake shingles. It had more of a peak to it, partially an A-frame structure. It looked just like he remembered it, with red curtains and an off-yellow porch railing. Snow trimmed it all out nicely. It looked like a cozy winter retreat.

Stu rammed through the snow recklessly, and they came to a sudden stop under a lean-to that sheltered the truck from view. That was smart, Lark thought, and said as much.

"Thanks, Lefty. I got a good idea now and then."

"Wait," Sackerson said, when Stu shut off the ignition.

Sackerson closed his eyes.

"What?" Stu popped his door handle.

"Wood furniture," Sackerson said, his eyes still closed. "Antler chandelier. Trophy heads on the walls and—"

Stu scoffed. "Like every cabin, ever."

"Red. Nice native rug, lots of red in it. Red curtains—"

"You can see the curtains from here!" Stu chuckled.

"Red leather on the furniture. Big American flag hanging from the peak in there... and a school letter jacket—"

"Over the mantle," Lark finished. "Like from the 1980s. Bluejackets."

Stu looked from Lark to Sack and back several times. "Huh!" he said at last and lumbered out of the truck.

Lark smiled. That was just as he had remembered it too.

Chapter 33: Fingerprinting

Context File

Fingerprints are formed in the womb. While twins may have matching DNA, their fingerprints will still be unique. The friction ridges of fingerprints contain pores attached to sweat glands under the skin. This sweat leaves behind a latent fingerprint.

In the late 1890s prints were matched, codified, and cataloged by various law enforcement agencies. By 1903, a standardized system was becoming recognized worldwide. These became digitally organized by the 1970s with the advent of the computer, and by the 1980s, more and more sophisticated, automated methods of print matching came online.

In 1997, at a NCAA D-1 football game, kits for the National Child ID Program were first distributed. That year, over a million of these kits were deployed. In just thirty years, over 70 million of the kits have been issued in the United States, most often marketed as a child safety initiative. To this day, some parents decline the offer to have the prints of their children on file. Typically, these are the same parents who guard their children from vaccinations.

Fingerprinting is one of the best techniques for identifying who was at the scene of a crime, but it is not without shortcomings. While registering fingerprints is common practice in government service and law enforcement, only one in six Americans are on file with the Integrated Automated Fingerprint Identification Systems (IAFIS).

Gloves and other appliances might mask a print, but more radical methods of ensuring anonymity also exist. A dedicated criminal can at least temporarily remove their fingerprints. This can be done by sanding, burning, and chemically altering the ridges, loops and whorls of their prints.

Interestingly enough, some people just *innocently* lose their fingerprints because of the abrasive environment of their occupation; for example, bricklayers wear off their prints. Even pianists and typists may lose their prints. Some people who work regularly with harsh chemicals like dry cleaning workers, hairstylists, and some, like farmers, lose the definition of their prints from a combination of hard work and harsh conditions.

Fingerprinting is just one method of biometric identification, which can include everything from blood typing to DNA, from retina and voice recognition to facial recognition. Many of these are in their infancy and cannot compare to the vast collection of easily identifiable fingerprints that have been collected for over fifty years.

Chapter 34: Gifted

K rystal was tired of it already. Stu was going on and on about the cabin, like he was some kind of realtor: "First part of it was built in the 1880s, you know, the *real* cowboy days, right after the land rush. The 1889 land rush, not the Cherokee." He was pointing out the walk-out basement that still featured sod walls. "That part survived a tornado, you know!"

No one seemed to know, so he continued, "When it was a fishing dive, back when the river was up, my grandpa used to spend a lot of time here. A lot. I think he built up most of this part of it." Stu was standing in what Krystal would call a Great Room, his arms wide, going in a circle. "I kinda think he lived down here, no better than he got along with Gran."

"Is that right?" Sackerson asked, taking it all in.

"He didn't do that fireplace, though. That was The Boys."

"Neighbors and friends, again?" Lark asked, though he was obviously not that into it.

"Yeah, them and my older brothers. Uncles, too. All native stone. Two stories high. I've seen a lot worse ones in the Better Homes magazines." He rattled on about how his mother had chosen "all the innards," herself, from the area rugs to the artwork. Then he was at the mantle, looking up at the letter jacket in the glass case. "That was dad's, you know," Stu said with reverence. "His team took state twice when he was on the team. Went to state all four years. Guy was a *beast* back then!"

Then he was off, with the two guys following after, continuing his tour. "Indoor plumbing before they even had it at the rez, I hear..." It didn't matter that the place had three bedrooms and a loft, two foldouts and a full kitchen. She could only think of the reputation the Wiebe cabin would never live down: it was the Shaggin' Shack. It didn't matter if they hadn't so much as kissed out there. If it were widely known that Krystal Price had visited, she would be ruined. Just the thought of it disgusted her. She avoided the Great Room and the not-so-great memories and took a stool in the kitchen, hoping to clear her head.

When they didn't return right away, Krystal set about cutting steak and vegetables for the kabobs Stu had promised. She snacked on a bell pepper.

She hadn't eaten anything of substance since Wednesday lunch, and though that was just over 24 hours ago, things had been so crazy, moving so fast, that it felt like a week. She knew her mom would be worried sick. Back when they swept her away for questioning after the Guthrie Fall, Krystal was only missing for two days, and her mom had practically called out the National Guard. She had actually contracted some private investigators, and they had just started looking for her when the feds had dropped her off at home.

All of that seemed so innocent now, just being at the wrong place at the wrong time, nearly getting killed in a meteor shower. It paled compared to being shot at and teleported by a time traveler! She shook her head and groaned. It all made her so tired that she trudged to a room where she could lie down.

She had chosen the loft, but Sackerson reclaimed it from her. He argued it would give him a better view if something should go wrong. She couldn't argue with that, so she took the bedroom with the single.

Krystal could hear them in the next room, but she couldn't make out all they were talking about. Stu still had on his showman voice, and Lark still sounded indifferent. She curled up on her bed with her carnival quilt and took a nap.

She could smell the steak grilling when she woke. Stu and Lark were outside, staying warm at the grill. Sackerson was tending to the fireplace. She shuffled through and plucked at some of the veggies they had not skewered.

"Oh, hi!" Sackerson said when he turned to see her there. "Good nap?"

"Guess I needed it," she said. "Do you ever sleep?"

"Live while I'm alive, sleep when I die," he smiled.

"Bon Jovi," Krystal chuckled.

"Really?" he asked. "How'd you know that?"

"My dad was in a cover band. Played lots of oldies."

They made small talk for a little while. She asked him about his taste in music, and he asked about hers. She got him talking about his love for milk for a while... and for fresh air. She worked the conversation around these 'safe' topics, always angling in to confirm her suspicions. When she got to his scalp tattoos, however, he drew it up cold. "Later," he said, "maybe after dinner. I'll tell you all a nice, long bedtime story."

"What do you want me to call you, anyway? Sackerson? Sack? Gary? *Something else, maybe?*"

"Names change to protect the innocent." Sackerson looked away, back to the fireplace. "Call me what you want," he said.

She got up from her stool and said, "Wait right here, Gary Sackerson. I have something for you."

Krystal came right back with something behind her back that she knew would surprise him. Before he could even venture a guess, she plunked it down on the table: the big silver gun that was dropped through the Hot Wire. "Bang Bang," she said.

She had not seen him so shocked, or so happy. "Now *this* is most definitely off-script," he said. He picked it up, incredulous, and asked, "Krystal, where did you find this?"

"It was in the backyard at Dr. Fortune's. I've been hiding it in that quilt all day."

"What?" He was, if possible, even more surprised. "In Norman?" He rubbed his jaw with his free hand, turned the gun every which way, and studied it. "That's not even possible, probably."

"*Probably not possible?*" she asked. "It is, or it isn't, right?"

"Hot Wire ports are—or I thought they were—single use. I only had just the one on the swing set... and you guys used it like *hours* after we ported out ol' *Bang Bang* from the barn."

The joy of giving was fading as he kept trying to figure it out. When the guys came in, tramping the snow off their shoes, carrying big platters of food, Sackerson hardly noticed. Throughout dinner (and a half gallon of whole milk), Sackerson was puzzling over it, sometimes aloud.

Neither Stu nor Lark really cared that the gun was back, or that she had found it in Norman. In the big picture of all they had been through, it didn't even make the list. The travels of the crow were more a curiosity. Stu asked why she didn't pull it on the utility guys, but she argued she could barely hold it up. Lark and Sack both queried as to exactly where she had found it. No matter how they asked it, the answer was the same: on the deck, in the glass, by the back door.

Sackerson seemed to forget about the promised long story, and she let it go for now. It was getting close to dark when Krystal asked Lark if he would go outside with her for more firewood.

"Got a bunch in the lean-to," Stu offered. "And there's plenty here for the night," he gestured toward the hearth. "You don't gotta go hunting for it."

"Yes," she said to him, firmly, "we do."

"Suit yourself," he said, and settled back with an old magazine.

She went to her room, bundled up, and met Lark on the deck. They warmed at the grill for a while in silence.

"Firewood?" he asked, finally.

"I've been wanting to talk with you," she said.

Lark raised his eyebrows but continued looking at the hot coals. He shook his head a little. "Where to start, right?"

"I know you have to be so worried about your dad..." she stopped, for she saw him swallow, blink rapidly. "I'm sure he's okay, Lark, and we are going to find him."

He scoffed. "What can we do? We're fugitives, ourselves." He tried to smile. "What could we do, anyway, against all these creeps?"

"We have Sackerson," she said, cautiously.

"And now we have a whole arsenal," he said, though it didn't sound encouraging. "Stu showed us the gun cabinets while you were asleep."

"See?" she encouraged him. "That's something, right?"

"Whatever." Lark said, warming his hand, "Besides, maybe dad doesn't want to be found. He got canned from the Installation. He quit taking calls. He even stopped answering the door when mom would bring him stuff."

"I know, I know, but maybe he was just... I dunno... busy?"

"It got to where she'd leave him a casserole in the fridge, and it'd still be there, days later when she brought him another."

"Maybe he was really onto something, Lark. Maybe Sackerson—"

"I like you, Krystal... a lot... but it really bugs me you take up for them."

"Take up for who?"

"Sackerson... and Dad." He shut the lid on the grill. They were left in the dark, with only the muted amber light from inside shining on them. "I mean, he ditched out. He went all eccentric on us. He just didn't remember anything. Didn't call mom to thank her. Didn't give me the time of day."

"He remembered you at Christmas," she smiled.

"No," Lark said, "he didn't."

"Yes," she said, "he did." At that, she took the box from the folds of her quilt. She had retrieved it when the boys went down to the hidden lab.

Lark looked at the gift for a long time. He read and re-read the tag. "Huh."

"Aren't you going to open it?"

"I haven't gotten anything from him for Christmas since the divorce," Lark said. "How old is this? Where did you find it?"

"It was in the study at your dad's," she said. "Now, open it!"

He clutched the gift in his right arm, and he tore the paper off like an eager child. It was a cigar box. He set it down on the grill's side table and opened it carefully, as if he expected it to explode with novelty snakes.

Instead, it was filled inside with little tubes. Each tube was full of the little white tablets like those Sackerson had used to make a Hot Wire.

"Wow," Lark marveled. "There's a lot of them here."

"Let's show Sackerson!" Krystal said.

"I dunno," Lark said, in a hushed tone. "Remember what he said about dad's journals falling into the wrong hands?"

"Yeah. So?"

"What if *his* hands are the wrong hands?" Lark asked. "I don't know that I trust him this much."

"Lark," Krystal put a hand on his shoulder and pulled him to face her fully. "Lark... do you trust your dad?"

"I guess so."

"Okay. Good. He gave you these. Remember that." She held his other shoulder now too. "Do you trust yourself?"

He was searching her eyes. She thought he was about to move in for a kiss. She did not know if she would mind. She jostled him by the shoulders.

Lark had turned his attention back to the box. He was gazing at it. She had only met Dr. Fortune once, but she imagined that this might have been what his obsession had looked like. Lark was so distracted that she thought he had missed her question, so she asked it again.

"Yes," he said, ultimately. "I trust myself."

"Good, then." She braved a quick peck on his lips, not knowing if she would have another opportunity. "It's good you trust yourself, Lark, because that's what you're doing when you trust Sackerson."

"Wha?"

She did not know if he was more dumbfounded by the kiss or the comment, so she persisted, "Sackerson is you."

Chapter 35: Conscience Corner

Stu looked up from his magazine a time or two. Nothing changed. Sackerson was at the kitchen island, pouring over Doc Fortune's lab books. Lefty sat staring at the fireplace, mesmerized. Krys had gone off to take a shower.

The October issue of Car & Driver had laid around the cabin for about four years. Stu knew every page, even the ads, but it gave him something to do. He growled at the feature of upcoming models, too damn many EV cars for his liking. He tried to think of something they could all do together, but it all seemed so dumb. Play a board game? Cards? Go out and have a snowball fight in the dark?

He was about to put in a movie, when Krys came padding out into the room, barefoot, her hair dripping. Stu put down the magazine. Sackerson looked up from his lab books. Only Lefty was ignoring the entire scene: a smoking hot babe wrapped in a bath sheet.

"What are we supposed to wear?" she asked.

"Well..." Stu had thoughts but caught his tongue. "Well, in the master bedroom dresser, there's some clothes we keep around. Help yourself."

"Thanks!" she said, but before she left, she looked at Lefty. He was still ignoring her.

"What's with him?" Stu asked.

"I don't know," she said, though Stu would have bet she was hiding something. She changed the subject, "Can we wash our stuff, maybe overnight?"

"Yeah," he said, picking up his magazine again. "Sure."

She shimmied up to him, and she leaned over a little too obviously. He was just admiring the view when she grabbed his magazine and flipped it over. "Upside down," she said, then sashayed down the hall.

Stu grumbled and buried his nose in it again.

Probably half an hour later, Krys was back. She even made flannel look good.

Sack and Lefty had not moved, but when she sat on the red loveseat, Sack perked up and came around the island. He flopped down in a leather mission-style chair and smiled at them, one by one.

"What?" Stu said, when Sack beamed at him.

"I'm just capturing this moment," he said casually. "Before it changes."

"Get anything out of Dad's notebooks?" Lefty asked, finally looking from the fire.

"Sackerson here promised me a story," Krys said. Her eyes reflected the fire and the pinpoint lights of the chandelier. Before Sackerson could respond, she interjected, "I can hardly wait!"

"A story?" Stu sighed, then stretched.

Lefty asked, "How about twenty questions, instead?"

"I don't know..." Sackerson said, "I think this story's—"

"We could play Truth or Dare," Stu grunted. He had some dares for Krys in mind. Nobody seemed to like his idea. He had eaten too much. He felt like going into hibernation. He reclined his chair further back and said, "Better get on with it then."

• • • •

"WE'RE WHAT... SEVEN years after the pandemic?" Sackerson began. "And how's the world turning?"

The three of them just looked at each other and shrugged.

"We came through, and the world's a better place, right? Lots more attention to health and hygiene. Am I right?"

Stu cleared his throat. "Dad calls it the biggest crock—"

"So, imagine if this trend were to continue. *More* attention to what's good for us." Sackerson stood and walked in front of the fireplace. "Wouldn't it be great? If people lived by their beliefs? Their convictions?"

"Where's this going?" Lefty asked. Stu wondered too.

"Okay. Okay. It's like this. About 2032—"

"Uuuuughhh," Stu groaned.

"It's a *story*, Stu, just give it a listen," Sackerson said. "Just a story."

"Whatever," he said and turned his attention to watching Krys.

"By 2032, just a couple years from now, you won't believe the changes. The EPA doesn't matter. Greenpeace doesn't matter. There's no need for people telling us how to live right. Know why?"

"A miracle?" Stu couldn't help himself. "Second coming?"

"Because people, by and large, *everyone*, even corporate big shots, just turned a corner and started living by principles."

"This is a fantasy," Lark said.

"I kinda like it," Krys said. "Keep going."

"The cool thing is, this started playing out at home too. More recycling. Eating better. More than that, eating *right*." Sackerson leaned against the mantle, taking in his audience. "They called it the Conscience Corner."

"Who called what the Conscience Corner?" Stu asked.

"Once people started turning the Corner, everything started to change. Consumer demand for processed food—gone. Support for corporations with a big ugly carbon footprint—gone. It's like, overnight, the economy was reeling from the Corner."

"You mean McDonald's went under?" Stu chided.

"All fast food was tanking," Sackerson said. "Tip of the iceberg."

"What could be worse?" Stu asked.

"People were taking ownership, not blaming big business, not relying on buying their way out of trouble."

"What do you mean?" Krys asked.

"That's a good thing, right?" Lefty asked.

"Fat people quit buying diet fads. Everyone started putting their money where their mouths were. Eating better. Living better. Drinking less. Sleeping more. Think of all the businesses affected by that!"

"What about gyms?" Stu asked.

"Belly up. Oh, I know, you'd think turning the Corner would send everybody to the gym, right? But no. You don't need a stair climber, just climb the stairs. You don't need a spin class. Just ride your bike."

"And bicycling trumps driving on two counts," Krys said. "Fitness and environment."

"I like it. Everybody's taking their body seriously," Stu said. He flexed his abs.

"You're not thinking it out," Lefty spoke up. "If people are conscientious, then they're putting down the remote."

"Yeah, so?"

"They're becoming more active," Lefty added.

"Great," Stu said.

"They started being *participants*, active in their own lives and accountable for their own circumstances, no longer victims, no longer *spectators*," Sackerson said it and waited.

"Okay..." Stu said, looking around the room. "Am I missing something?"

"*No longer spectators*, so no need for spectator sports," Krys jumped in.

"Oh, hold on. Hold on now," Stu said. As if the rest of this wasn't a little farfetched, this was just hog wash. "Like what?"

"Like everything. No more NFL, no more Olympics, no more high school sports," Sackerson said, softer and softer with each one. He came to sit in the chair right next to Stu and added, "No more NASCAR."

Stu got up and marched to the fridge. He grabbed a can of Coke and popped it open. It was a dumb story. *The world would never go that far.*

"So," Krys said then, "if everyone was living right, they must've gotten lots healthier, I'd bet."

"I know, right? You'd think so." Sackerson gave her that 'you're a genius' look again. "And I really think it was headed that way too."

"Except...?" Lefty pried. "What happened?"

"Records show that obesity was down. Heart attacks—for that matter all heart disease—was trending down. High blood pressure was no longer an epidemic." Sackerson stood again, for he couldn't help himself. "Guys, it was like people just realized we could *beat it all*... without so much health care and medicine and—"

"And now I see where this is going," Lefty interrupted. "Big Pharma."

"Yes!" Sackerson exclaimed, so loud it echoed in the A frame. "All this clean living, all this improved physical health, was also playing havoc with prescriptions, with drug dependency in mental health care too. The whole of the medical industry was taking it harder than food, entertainment, and transportation, combined."

It was quiet then as they thought about it. Stu could hear the fire crackle. Krys spoke up, asking, "All because of... the Corner?"

"The Conscience Corner," Sackerson nodded his head rapidly. "Right."

"Conscience Corner," Stu joked, "sounds like a time out."

"Exactly, Stu," Sackerson clapped his hands together. "A huge time out. It was like—the economy had been the biggest brat in the playpen, and suddenly it was put in its place."

"That couldn't have been good," Lefty said.

"Not at all," Sackerson said, solemnly. "Think about it, kids. What's that leave you?"

Chapter 36: Reflection

Lark was only half listening to the long yarn Sackerson was spinning. He was, instead, putting together everything he knew about the man, trying to match it to himself. Yes, they were not that dissimilar. He could imagine Sack might be his half-brother, for example, or from the same family tree somehow or another.

In their visit at the grill, Krystal had run through a dozen similarities she had discovered. Similar tastes in music, in food, in entertainment, from what she knew of the two of them. Sackerson always seemed to know where Lark was going with things, to the point he finished his sentences with uncanny accuracy and frequency. He knew things that Lark would have known and remembered, like the cabin itself. Then, there was the obvious "our father," slip up in Mack's that everyone had seemed to forget.

Lark argued that Sackerson was older, ten years at least. How could they be the same person, yet not the same age? Krystal chalked it up to time travel. Then Lark countered with the most glaring distinction between them, a point of order that he considered immutable: Sackerson had his right hand. Krystal did not have a ready answer for that. She had gone back inside in a huff.

Whenever he looked at Sackerson, it was not like looking in a mirror. It was not like looking at one of those portrait aging web apps. Lark was seeing a distinctly different man with whom he just seemed to share a lot in common.

This Conscience Corner story, however, seemed more plausible. Lark could sooner believe it all than believe that he was across the room from his future self, even when Sackerson would drop another depth charge.

"They were all fighting, terrible in-fighting. There were a few years of heartless winnowing away of competitors, and with that, consumer choices. Food corporations were making it harder and harder to eat right. You had to grow your own, practically, and in some climates and conditions, that was tough."

"So, people moved?" Krystal asked.

"I think they would have, eventually. I think folks would have left the crowded cities, and those that stayed behind would have made every inch into green space. I think more and more people would have moved into more garden-friendly climates too."

"You think so, but it didn't happen?"

"Fitness and Health made a big break from Pharmaceuticals, too, and that was their undoing. Pharma had lots more resources..."

Lark was drifting again. He was listening to the voice and the word choice and the delivery, and he could not deny that he probably would have sounded much the same. Even watching Sackerson, the animated scarecrow, was too familiar.

"So, they made up another pandemic," Stu interjected. "One that would bring everybody to their knees again and make them beg for drug treatment."

Lark snapped his jaw closed. He couldn't believe Stu had made such a big extrapolation, something so very horrible and plausible at the same time. Of course, he felt it to be tainted with right wing conspiracy, the old tin hat party, but... regardless... he wanted to hear Sackerson's take on *that*!

After Sackerson recovered a beat, he said, "Not right away, but... yes... and no... well, you're jumping the shark here.

"You're right, there needed to be something outside of the very personal sphere of the Conscience Corner, something threatening, like a virus, that people had no personal control over.

"The economy, in fact the *world* economy, needed an enemy no amount of positive thinking and clean living could tackle."

"Like what?" Krystal asked softly.

"There is an industry that is, ironically, bullet proof. One industry thrives on group think and propaganda, ignorance and avarice, more than any other. Ladies and gentlemen, I bring you... drum roll please... the military industrial complex."

"World War III," Lark said, flatly.

"That's right," Sackerson said, grimmer than Lark had ever seen him. "And in the same way World Wars are the product of fear, imagine what was waiting in the wings after that, after even a World War failed to crush Conscience."

"There's nothing worse, is there?" Krystal asked.

"There's a host of fears. Economic ruin. Borders falling. Plague. Pandemonium. Utter ending of one's way of life... but all that together isn't as scary as what's now beginning to rear up."

"Alien Invasion!" Stu shouted.

"Too far," Sackerson cackled. His 1000-watt smile was back. "Too far, my friend, but I like the way you think!"

Lark thought he had it. Something powerful that would bring down nations and economies and differences and consciences all at once. He drummed his fingers on the cigar box at his side, and he imagined the possibilities.

What if Transportation were instant, global, random, and free, like the Hot Wires? That would be so very disruptive, so very, very disruptive, it might even justify the resources of all the other corporations to be pooled together to engineer some way to go back in time and stop it.

Somebody needed to get the Genie back in the bottle and stop it up.

Lark looked at Sackerson and suddenly saw himself.

Chapter 37: Pillow Talk

Much later that night, Krystal was awakened by someone in her room. "What is it?" she said, like she might to an annoying brother. "Little late, isn't it?"

"Shhhhh," her intruder whispered, "outside."

Then, just like that, the shadow of a person moved through her opened door and was away.

About the last thing she wanted to do was get out of her warm bed, but she had heard urgency, even in the single word, "outside." So, she slipped into her shoes and pulled her carnival quilt again around herself, and she stepped quietly out into the hallway.

Her room was closest to the Great Room, so she did not have to creep past the others' open doorways. The shadow was already at the exterior door, and a blast of cold air told her he was already exiting.

She followed the familiar form, gently latching the door behind her when she moved out onto the porch. Nearby, she saw the dome light of the utility truck come on, then it was covered by someone's hand. She headed there, following him inside, settling in next to Lark. She pulled the door shut, and he removed his hand from the dome light.

He said softly, "I couldn't sleep."

"Why?" she whispered.

She could see their condensing breath. Lark was wearing oversized flannel pajamas and one of the utility service coats. They sat staring straight ahead for an eternity. The windows were already glazing over with steam.

Eventually, Lark held up his arm, and she snuggled right in next to him. It felt good. She did her best to arrange the quilt over both of them.

"Why are we here?" Krystal asked again.

"So much to think about," Lark said. She could feel him shaking his head. "All that about the future going wonky. It's just a lot."

That was true. She wondered what he was going through again. Now he was having to face the same impossibility she was: that time travel was real, that you could go back and even occupy the same space and time as your original self. It was the paradox she had fallen asleep thinking about, and it was again fresh on her mind.

"It's weird having him here, isn't it?" Krystal asked.

"It'd be weird if he was—I dunno—just some guy from the future, yeah. But to think that *he's me?* I just don't know..." he sighed a cloud of steam. "This is just bizarre."

"Have you told him you know... that he's you?"

"Doesn't he already know that I know?" Lark asked, "If he's future-me, then doesn't he know all of this already?"

"I don't think so." She said, "I think that when he says we're 'off-script' that then it's all unknown to him. I think he's as lost as we are."

Lark was quiet for a long time.

Krystal cuddled closer, hoping to share more body heat.

"Why is he here, Krystal?"

She had thought through this since they were in Norman. Now she had lots more to work with, and she had a sounding board. "What do *you* think? Why would *you* come back?" she asked, and in doing so, she realized she sounded a lot like her own mother—as if she were baiting a trap. That made her continue. "I think I'd come back if I had a personal reason. Not all this 'save the world stuff' he seems so hung up on."

"Like to save your dad?"

"Maybe. Yeah, I guess." She sat up and looked at Lark. "Is there anyone you miss, like presently?"

"Grandparents, sure—"

"Wouldn't it be something if you could go back a few years before they died and spend some more time together? Get in a good goodbye." Krystal was thinking about it, herself, and she had been since she'd first entertained time travel just the day before.

Lark was quiet. He had little to say about that, it seemed. She wondered about the reason for this visit tonight, but then, it was nice having this time, just the two of them, no matter what the reason.

"Maybe he's being nostalgic," she tossed out, finally.

"Oh, he's nostalgic about everything. Haven't you heard him? Reliving our glory days together. Drinking milk like it's some kind of fine wine. Going on and on about how pizza is his new guilty pleasure."

"True. But really—would *you* time travel to relive memories? I don't know if I would."

"I have to go back to what he said about something bad brewing," Lark turned the conversation. "I really do think he's buying his own story about saving the world."

"You'd save the world, wouldn't you, if you were him?"

"I'd save my dad."

"What if it's the same thing, somehow?"

· · · ·

THEY TALKED FOR WHAT seemed like timeless minutes that had to have been hours. She was sure they had dozed off together more than once. In all that time, they had settled on laying together on the bench seat, wrapped up like a burrito.

He had opened up about his thoughts on Sackerson's story of the future, and she shared his curiosity about exactly how all this with the Guthrie Fall and Lark's dad might fit in. They both realized that the Christmas gift, that box of Tic-Tacs, might be more important to some people even than finding Dr. Fortune himself.

"If this is the whole collection," Lark whispered in her ear now, they were so close, "if this box is all of them that are around, I mean—wow."

"And if you're right, if they somehow could tear up the future worse than a World War..."

"I'm glad I have them. Maybe I can, I don't know, use them for good." He shrugged. "I guess I'm glad you gave them to me, not Stu or Sack."

"Hey, he meant it for you," Krystal said. "That gift had your name on it. From your dad."

"Yeah," he said with a sigh. "It's the biggest, strangest thing he's ever given me, that's for sure."

It was quiet for a while again as they thought about it. Krystal's mind moved over a lot of things, but her thoughts often settled simply on how good it felt to be so warm and close.

"Lark," she said, surprising even herself with an epiphany.

"Yes?"

"It's about your dad's place."

He untangled himself enough to prop his head on his hand. "What about it?"

"Those feds—or whatever—called it a sloppy job. Remember that?"

"Something like that."

She continued, "Amateur."

"Right. So?"

"So, whoever did it, whoever ransacked the house, really wasn't very good at it, were they?"

"Why do you say that?" he said, and she could feel him fighting off a yawn.

"Because," she said, succumbing to a yawn now, herself, "they didn't leave with anything."

"Well, we don't know—"

"If they're a part of this whole thing with Sack, they really screwed up. They really are amateurs." She chuckled. "Not only did they miss the second basement, they didn't even think to open your gift."

"It's almost like—" Lark had some trouble finding the words, it seemed. "Like the whole thing was fake. Staged."

"Now that we're away from there, and the shock's worn off—"

"The way it was trashed seemed... too much," he added.

"Yeah, right?" Krystal could not have agreed more. "Like, why would they have smashed the TV? Tipped the refrigerator? I wonder if that blood stain was even real."

"I dunno," he said, nuzzling close to her again. His nose had gotten cold. "But I'd sure like to see what the cops have to say about it."

Chapter 38: Nothing on Earth

November 2029

Dr. Christopher Fortune chuckled to himself. How utterly ridiculous it would be to attempt writing his procedures up for a journal. He had thrown everything conventional and reasonable aside long ago and was left with the absurd. Chris just shook his head. Sometimes it took a little crazy to accomplish the impossible.

Yet that night, an almost invisible strand of fiber was glowing white before him. It was tacked to the open rafters of his hidden basement lab, and it dangled nearly to the floor, a yard-wide loop, a phosphorescent doorsill.

Chris had learned that if he crafted conditions just so, he could heat and spin a tic-tac into a thread not-unlike that of the fiber optics he had seen on television just weeks before. When he attempted to mount a paired tic-tac on that fiber, the result was a white-hot wire loop that performed like some kind of one-shot magic. It would vaporize anything within the loop the instant the filament was connected to both ends of the tic-tac.

He quickly learned that this worked with anything from wastebaskets and their contents to the bricks under his water heater. He made Hot Wire loops and threw handballs through them. He mounted one on a bed frame and learned he could pour a bucket of water through the loop into... into oblivion.

That was what had made him take pause, sometimes for days at a time, when he would come to question just what it was he could do now. His creation was unnatural, or perhaps supernatural. It made little sense, and it did not abide by any natural laws he could fathom.

In those ways, the Hot Wires would frighten him, and he would lock up his basement and stay upstairs for days, lost in thought.

However, his curiosity would not rest. Chris continued writing, doodling, ciphering, and talking to himself. He read voraciously online, brushing up on everything he had ever studied, stretching into fields far beyond his own.

Then he would return to the basement and try a little something new. He learned he could toss a 2x4 or a rake right through a loop, and that it would vanish as it cleared the loop's plane. He set up materials like this, from a stretch of rebar to curtain rod, on a cart, then he would pull the cart with the extended material right up to the loop. He would watch from the side, and use a pulley to pull the cart forward, while he observed. He found that if he retracted the length of material, no matter what it was, there was nothing coming back from the loop. The entrance side of the material would be unharmed, and it did not matter if he put a fluorescent bulb or a pool noodle through. There was never an explosive or adverse reaction. The loop would simply end whatever had gone through, leaving the rest a smooth cut.

When he did this with organics, however, he discovered the loop to not always be entirely benign. If he tossed a plant or an insect into the loop, it would disappear. If he retracted it partially through, only what had not entered would be left. Higher-level organisms would die if they did not go right on through a Hot Wire loop.

He came to believe that this was what had happened to Lark, that his hand had gotten tangled in a coil of wire and two tic-tacs—two matching tic-tacs—had ignited the Hot Wire as it was around his hand, in his pocket.

• • • •

ON CHRISTMAS EVE, 2029, Chris had his greatest breakthrough. On a whim, he spun out both of a matched pair into their filament form. He laid one out on the floor at the foot of the steps, and he eyed the harmless, nearly invisible loop for some time. He carefully arranged the other wire at the other end of the room, and when he joined the ends of the filament into a hoop, it happened!

Both Hot Wire hoops were aglow. They were sustained, bright blue ovals on his concrete basement floor.

Chris shrugged his shoulders, then dropped a pencil to the floor of the loop by the lab bench. As usual, it disappeared upon clearing the plane of the loop. He dropped a pop can in the same way.

And that was when he was surprised to hear the can hit the floor over by the stairway. He approached it carefully, studied it for a long while. In every way, it appeared to be the same can.

He did this again and again with the can, dropping it with some force through "loop A," as he called the stairway loop, and finding it would fly up out of "loop B" with the same force. When he just gently slid a paper into loop A, that paper would drift just above the plane of loop B until something jarred it, like another item he would pass through A.

The entire night he did test after test, learning eventually that even leaves, plants, insects and lab mice could pass through the two Hot Wire loops, unharmed. He wanted to jump into the glowing circle of a loop and experience coming out of the other, but he resisted the temptation.

Tests included those of range, and when his tests outgrew his basement, he would set a loop on the floor of his basement, another in his bathtub on the main floor. When experiments were proven to be successful at that distance, he arranged one on the second floor. Then on the back deck. Then in the tool shed.

In every instance, no matter what he dropped through A, it would pop right through at B. He was filled with wonderment. What distance might be the limitation? He thought and wrote about arranging a loop at the Installation, and he laughed at how surprised his former colleagues would be to someday find their facility filling up with rebar and handballs, cockroaches and kittens.

He referred to these loops or hoops or whatever as portals, and he wanted to suspend them like doorways, hoping to travel through from one to another. Of course, nothing could reliably hold the filament aloft, for if he tried to loop one over a nail, eventually the nail would vaporize. The same was true with any and every other material he tried. It was as if nothing on earth was impervious to the little glowing fiber.

Nothing on earth...

• • • •

"FORTUNE," HE ANNOUNCED, holding his photo ID before him, "Dr. Christopher Fortune. Colonel, USAF, retired."

"Oh, hey, Doc," the night watchman said through the little speaker at the gate. "Thought you'd been promoted or something."

"Or something, Paunch," he said, looking convincingly into the tiny camera lens. "Classified, you know."

"Oh, sure. Sure." The metallic 'clack' of the gate release sounded, and the arm raised up to let Chris drive right into the Installation by the main gate.

• • • •

IT WAS A CALCULATED risk. This was a low-level facility, it had been two years since the Guthrie Fall, and virtually nothing had come of it all. Most of the traffic now was routine. Most of the job, Chris knew, had become so routine that security would be lax.

He had hoped that the night shift was still shared by the two alternating guards he had befriended. This night, he was lucky it was the heavy, older Hispanic man who even referred to himself as 'Paunch de Leon.'

Chris had taken his time, like he had for every step of this, preparing. He found his old ID. He found his off-duty uniform and a lab coat. He cut his hair back substantially and shaved. He took the extra time to swing by the liquor store, and when he passed by the little kiosk where Paunch huddled over a space heater, Chris handed him a fifth of good whiskey.

The caper had been so anti-climactic that Chris Fortune actually did leave a Hot Wire circling inside a bathroom stall on the floor in the crack. Harmless, inert, likely undetectable, at least until its partner would light up and complete the circuit. It made him smile, though he did not know if he would ever actually follow through.

Instead, he turned his attention mostly to the materials he had come to retrieve from the Installation. In a matter of days after the Fall, contractors had carved out a large basement they went on to line with lead. They had built a clean room and a climate-controlled storage facility too. Chris' ID mag strip still opened them all, and he was able to load a cart with several lengths of metal, pipe, and wire that had been collected on site.

He had loaded it in his car and driven out the gate with little more than a hat tip to Paunch.

It did not matter to him that his every maneuver would be on record, every key card swipe, every compartment opened. It was all recorded and would be reviewed, he guessed, within a matter of days.

They would likely come by his place and put out a warrant for him when they failed to find him home.

They would not find him at home. They would not be able to keep up with him. He smiled broadly... provided everything was working as he knew it might.

A few days later, he had made what was his last recorded discovery. The foreign material did seem to be just right for holding his little fiber optic hoops in mid-air. He positioned his portals over several doorways in his house, on the back deck, and wherever it caught his fancy. All he needed was to station slivers of the alien metal elsewhere, so he sent it to several locations by several carriers, even the post office.

As he went about hanging portals on the outskirts of Norman and Guthrie, and burying and otherwise storing the strange metal nearby, he was euphoric. All the months and months of meticulous work were now to bear fruit. He would test his discovery on a broader and broader scale, seeing what limits it might have.

February 2030

That last night, he was aimlessly tossing pencils and pens through a series of portals that surrounded him in his basement lab. He speculated that, maybe, there was a way to generate power from Portals in series, but he had not put it all together yet. He had never written that down yet. He would never get that chance.

As always, he had closed off the lab carefully, and he had switched on all his home security measures. Until that night, nothing had sounded any alarm. Nothing had ever been on his monitors that was suspicious.

At the first alarm, Chris started dismantling his ports, carefully disconnecting each loop and even more carefully stashing them in little cellophane envelopes. They would appear to be nothing more than guitar strings or lengths of fishing line.

When he heard crashing upstairs, he looked around his lab for anything else that might give away his work. The notebooks were too bulky to deal with, and besides, they were impossible to decipher. Most of the devices in the room would make no sense to anyone.

Then he laid eyes on his cigar box and almost yelped out loud. He picked it up and scanned here and there. No corner of the room seemed to offer a good hiding spot. In a flash of insight, he found some old wrapping paper on the shelf with Christmas decorations, and he hastily wrapped it up as a gift. He held onto the box as he fretted over the intrusion.

It was shortsighted of him not to have a mobile phone here in the basement lab. It was, he had to admit, poor planning to not connect his alarms to local sentry services, not even that of his neighborhood. At the time, it had been an exercise in frugality and privacy, but now it seemed foolish.

Returning to his lab bench, he confirmed monitors were not that helpful. He would catch glimpses of the intruder from time to time, darting from room to room, flipping over furniture and rummaging through cabinets. He could not, however, get a good look at him in the grainy displays. It was terrifying and exhilarating at the same time.

He heard the heavy footsteps bounding downstairs, and it made his hair stand on end. The thief was just a sheetrock wall away from him now. Chris stepped carefully to the wall and put his hand on it, put his ear to it, listening.

The man on the other side continued to throw things around wildly. Chris was a little frightened by his violence... or was it panic? When the man returned to the main floor, Chris returned to watch him passing from monitor to monitor. He concluded this person was frantic, like a meth addict, but it did not seem like he was interested in the usual valuables. He passed up the wallet on the kitchen counter, even the jewelry box in the bedroom. Everything the man touched ended up across the room.

The only time he seemed to calm down was when he found the safe in the closet. After only a few tries, he actually figured out the combination. Chris could hear the audible beeps, even the man's voice when he exclaimed his success... but when its contents did not satisfy him, he returned to his crazed dance of destruction.

Chris waited him out, hoping against hope that the madman would not find and trip the latch to his hideaway.

He kept the last Hot Wire up and ready, just in case he needed it.

Chapter 39: Refreshing Mints

Context File
The Tic Tac breath mint has been a popular candy world-wide for over sixty years. The confectionery brand was launched under the name "Refreshing Mints" by an Italian candy company, Ferrero, in 1969. That parent company is also known for owning Nutella, a popular hazelnut and chocolate spread. Once rebranded as the Tic Tac, supposedly named after the sound of the candies bouncing around inside their container, the treat took off. Today, Ferrero generates over 400 million Tic Tacs annually. They claim that each person on earth consumes an average of 8 Tic Tacs a year. Over half of the Tic Tacs produced annually come from a plant in Ireland.

Traditional mint Tic Tacs are the most popular, but over the years the brand has expanded to include a range of flavors, including cinnamon, spearmint, peppermint, Powermint, sour apple, mandarin, tangerine, berry, fresh orange, strawberry, wintergreen, pink grapefruit, cherry, passionfruit, pomegranate, mango, lime, and popcorn. Additional flavors, including banana, Elaichi, and Mintensity have been popular in smaller markets.

Originally, the Tic Tac was marketed as a breath mint that was low calorie. Though largely sugar, the serving size is so very small (only 0.49g) that it does not register with the Food and Drug Administration. A Tic Tac is made of sugar, fructose, maltodextrin, peppermint essential oil, rice starch, gum arabic, and carnauba wax. They are gluten-free and contain no GMO ingredients.

Maltodextrins, contained in the Tic Tac® core, are medium-long chained carbohydrates. They are obtained from cereal starch (such as corn, wheat and rice) or from tubers (potatoes or tapioca) and have a moderate sweetening effect, a good solubility and a good degree of absorption of the essential oils. Maltodextrins are effective in the production of the pills, in particular because of their fluidity, compressibility and low hygroscopicity, i.e. the capacity to absorb water molecules. A tiny pill is generated at the heart of the product, which is coated with hundreds of layers of sugar, alternated with aromatic layers, forming the crunchy outer layer and transforming the pill into a comfit. In the same way that the oyster turns sand grains into a pearl, the particular Tic Tac® production process, which takes about 24 hours, transforms a simple pill into a unique and inimitable product.

A Tic Tac hosts 8 kJ, or 2 kcal, of energy.

The energy quotient of the alien Tic Tac has yet to be accurately quantified.

Chapter 40: Wires Crossed

February 2030

Shae hated mornings anyway, and this morning greeted her with a throbbing headache. She felt like garbage. She was comforted only by the aroma of the coffee that she guessed Rob must have gotten for her recently. He was nowhere to be found. "Probably out for a run," she grumbled. Morning people!

She was grateful she had taken extensive notes before she crashed for the night, for these captured lots of details that she now had trouble calling up. As she flipped through, she noticed tally marks she did not at first recognize. A receipt was tucked in at the end of her notes, as if she could get a reimbursement for a few rounds of drinks, out of county. Her eyes ached when she saw the total: over $250.

Counting the steak dinner, the nostalgia trip for lunch, the hotel room, and now the bar tab, this Valentine's was not only the most special but also the most expensive. Rob had put it all together for her, had even egged her on in her detective work. She could still see him looking over her notes, encouraging her to write things down, even asking questions himself. This was beyond him just being encouraging. He was really getting into it too.

She showered, got dressed, and downed her coffee as she watched the headlines scroll on the television. She was thumbing through messages on her phone when she saw that Burns had called several times. She shrugged and called him back.

"Shae," he said immediately. "Where are you?"

"I took a vacation day. Why?"

"Chief thinks you're nosing around," Burns said. "You aren't, are you?"

"Burnsey," Shae sighed, "me and Rob just tied one on last night at the Cherokee Strip. Celebrated Valentines, okay? Tell Chief Gibson that."

"Uh, you mean the Strip in *Perry*?" The accusation was dripping through the phone.

"Why've you been calling? What's up?"

"News," he said, then gave her a rundown. Trace from the farm was inconclusive. Ballistics, still not all in, but what they had back, didn't tell them anything new. Witnesses all had said the same thing.

"Nothing new there, Burns," Shae said, taking a swig of her coffee. It was still delicious, even if it was cooling. She looked around the room for a microwave.

"They never have caught up with Mr. Fortune, you know," he said. "The former Mrs. Fortune, though, said he'd been acting strange for a long time." He cleared his throat. "Too bad you're on vacation and all because I guess there was shots fired in Norman... you know, at his house."

She sat up.

"That *is* news... what'd Norman PD find?"

"Nothing official," he said. "Bottled up, again. They cain't say anything."

"What do you mean?"

"I mean, I know there was gunfire, and I know they found a Suburban wrecked in the backyard, but that's it. Even my brother-in-law isn't talking. He had a kid with him on a ride along and they got called over to the scene, but he won't tell me anything."

"Suburban?" Something jolted her. She flipped through her notes.

"Lissen. Chief put me on full time while Cole's on leave. I have to knock it out of the park, you know?" he said anxiously. "It's my chance to prove myself."

"The best police work is just nose-to-the-grindstone, Mike. You can prove yourself by taking your time, following your leads..."

"I know, I know," he said. "But you, *Detective*, being on vacation and all, maybe you can, you know, throw me a bone. Help a brother out."

He was annoying on his best days, but when he started talking like he was cool, it made her roll her eyes, and that made her head ache more.

"So, you called to get me to Norman?"

"I never said that," Burnsey backpedaled. "But if I did, accidentally, give you the address, you know, to your phone... maybe you'd get something crossed in your GPS or something, and—"

"I'll talk to Rob," Shae said. "We may be up for it."

"Okay then," he sighed. "Thanks... and Shae, I got more news. Remember those burned up wires Cole had when you talked with him?"

"Yes, why?"

"Feds didn't end up having the other one. Sheriff's office, Logan County's got the other one."

"Has the other what?" Shae was pacing now, trying to wake up, shake it off.

"The third Hot Wire," he said. "They found it strung up in the car wash out north."

"Out north, where?" she asked. "North of Guthrie?"

"Out on 77, between the mini-mall and the high school. I guess it was still smoldering when they got on the scene."

"How do they know it's not just some shorted-out wire in that shabby car wash?"

"I dunno but get this. My ex is dispatch for the Sheriff's office, you know, and she told me the strangest thing ever."

"Go on," she prodded.

"Truck tracks," Burns mumbled, but she could barely make it out. He had cupped the phone around his mouth. "Suburban, witnesses say. Tracks go right up to the wire, not past it."

She massaged her temples with her free hand. "Mike, what are you saying?"

"I dunno, Shae, but it's like that truck went barreling into the car wash, crossed that burned wire, never been seen again."

"That's just—"

"I know, right?" he chuckled then. "Just thought you ought to know."

• • • •

SHE FOUND ROB AT A five-dollar Blackjack table. He was surrounded by Dollarhide's carnival crew. He was smiling so big when she approached, she couldn't even question the frugality of his actions. She did not know such a small stakes table even existed anymore.

"We've been at it a couple hours now, right, Mabel?"

From the name tag on her vest, Shae figured out Mabel was the dealer. "Yeah, and you never stop talking," she growled in a smoker's voice. "No offense."

"Tip the lady, and let's go, Steamboat Robbie."

"What about waiting for the Suburban?" he asked.

"I have a feeling it's not happening," she said. Those around the table looked surprised.

• • • •

ON THE ROAD, ROB WAS recounting all the little tidbits he had picked up on. He was delivering them, she noticed, in ascending order. Each seemed more fantastical than the previous. Olga was telepathic... Oleander was over 100 years old... They were millionaires several times over.

Then he put his hand on her shoulder and squeezed a little to get her attention. She looked from the road to his crinkled smile. "What?" she asked.

"Here's the kicker. You know the oldest one, that one that's like Slavic or something? We were having breakfast together, and her great grandson was interpreting."

"Interpreting?"

"Yeah, she's probably the most talkative of the lot of them, but nobody ever listens because she doesn't speak any English. But Toby, he was having trouble keeping up once she opened up on me."

"And?"

"She told me the craziest thing."

"Go on," she said. She could tell by his delivery that this was big.

"Our guy, Sackerson. I guess she saw him spin a glow-in-the-dark lasso over his head and drop it down over himself—and get this—and disappear."

"What?" Shae chuckled.

"Yeah, I guess it was some kind of rope light or something. Toby couldn't get it right. Anyway, what do you make of that? Disappeared?"

Shae shook her head. "Not the strangest claim about him, but..."

Rob nodded his head. His brow was deeply furrowed.

"Where did she see all this, exactly?"

"Out at the train wreck, she said," Rob replied. "But people said they saw him all over, right? He never disappeared."

"Nah," she said, but she wasn't so sure. "No. Nobody just disappears."

Chapter 41: Snakes in the Woodpile

Lark was sure he heard something outside. He roused Krystal. He scrambled up to look out, but the windows were frosted over on the inside. He scratched at the ice, peered outside, caught his breath. "You're not going to believe this!"

It was Henny, peeking in the cabin windows.

Lark's pulse was pounding. Kenny Hinman, the guy that about got them killed by a train—back again!

"Let's get that bastard," he told Krystal.

She reached up and switched off the dome light, just as he was prying the door handle, slowly, quietly. The upholstery protested as they slipped across it. The snow was crunching way too loudly with each careful footstep.

Lark's eyes never left Henny's back. The guy was going from window to window, peering inside, his face lit by the glow of the fireplace. He looked to be consumed by his task. A lecherous peeping Tom. A betrayer, at it again.

It had taken an eternity to close the gap, but they were now just feet behind him. Henny was at what had to be a bedroom window. He cupped his eyes to the glass.

Lark was suddenly aware, when he was close enough to tap Henny on the shoulder, that he had no plan. No weapon. No idea what to do.

Krystal, however, swung a fireplace log, thick as a leg, and cracked Henny hard on the back of the head. He fell hard against the windowsill, then dropped to the ground, stunned.

"That's for ratting us out," she screamed.

He cried out, whirled around, and stumbling to get up, he fell in the snow. As he was scrambling to his feet, Henny was trying to wipe the blood from his forehead. Krystal gave it to him again, a full swing at his gut. He doubled over, cursing.

"That's for coming back for more!"

Lark stood stock-still. Wide-eyed.

"Krystal?" Henny gasped. He pulled a full breath and winced as he stood up. "Lefty?"

Lark still had no plan.

Krystal hefted the log menacingly.

"Guys, I came to tell you something." Blood was trickling from his nose. His eyes were pouring tears. "Don't trust him. Sackerson. Not one bit."

"Like you can talk!" Krystal growled.

"He's why I told the feds—"

Before he could finish the sentence, another person crashed between Lark and Krystal, throwing a full body block into linebacker Kenny Hinman, who was crushed into the log cabin wall. The man had unbelievable power. He just grabbed up Henny and hefted him overhead. Then, he summarily tossed him through the window and into the cabin.

"I was afraid of this," Sackerson said as he turned to face them. "Better pack up."

• • • •

STU HEARD A HORRIFIC crash down the hall. He heard voices. He hurried from his bed and down the hall to find Sackerson crouched over a body on the floor. The window was broken. Blood and glass were everywhere.

Sackerson rolled the body over and grabbed his victim by the neck. He pounded the downed man's head on the floor.

It was Henny!

"Hey!" Stu yelled. "Stop it!"

Sackerson sat back on Henny's chest and withdrew one of his guns. "Go pack," he said in a terrifying tone.

Stu was backing out the door just as Sackerson flipped the gun around to hold the barrel. He was pistol-whipping Henny then, and the sound and sight of it were too much. Stu kept backing away.

He backed into Krystal and Lark out in the hall.

"Gun," he warned. He cleared his throat and said, "Getting a gun!"

But no one moved. They all listened from the hall, petrified.

"Never did like you!" Sackerson said, then whacked Henny with the gun again. "I needed you, and you came through, alright." Another meaty smacking sound.

Stu was about to throw up. From the look on the other's faces, they were feeling about the same.

"Real snake in the woodpile, you are, Henny!" Sackerson was yelling in a high pitch, almost like he was crying it out. "Why? Why're you here? More importantly, how'd you get here? Car? Wire?" Horrible smacking sounds punctuated his monologue again and again. "Why didn't you just walk away?"

Stu couldn't stand it. He rushed down the hall and retrieved a shotgun.

Krys and Lefty had gone inside, so he did too. "Stop!" he shouted and pumped the gun.

"Oh, c'mon. That's not even loaded." Sackerson sighed, laying down his bloody pistol. He put his hands up.

"Well, leave him alone, anyway."

"Didn't you hear him? Did you? Hear what he just said, Stu?" Sackerson asked. "Guy's a double-crosser."

"Oh, is he?" Lefty asked. "*He's* a double-crosser?"

"You set him up." Krystal was shaking a log at him. A log?

"Ok, ok, yeah. I paid him off to tell the Spooks we were heading to the border—"

"Told you so," Henny burbled.

"—but just to misdirect. Buy us some time. Just so I could see who was onto us... not to get us all killed."

"Kilt?" Henny asked. He rolled his head away from Sackerson and toward them. "I never meant to get anybody—"

"So, you ARE a dirty double-crosser!" Stu pointed the shotgun then at Henny. "No... no... that makes you a triple-crosser. You sold us out for Sack, then told them where to whack us with the train!"

Henny was protesting, but Sackerson backhanded him.

"We don't have but minutes, guys. Minutes! No matter how he got here, they'll know it by now. Grab what you can. They're probably already at the farm."

Sackerson returned his attention to Henny. In his face. Threatening his life. Telling him about Hot Wire tortures and worse.

Lark and Krystal had disappeared down the hall.

Stu stood in his place, surveying the blood and violence in his family cabin. *At his farm.*

"You *will* help me find him. You'll tell me everything, be a big hero and not the pig you are right now... and if you don't..." Sackerson picked up the pistol and wiped it on Henny's letter jacket. "Next time it'll be worse."

Stu was reeling. *Already at the farm?*

He bolted from the room, shotgun in hand, and he burst out the back door. Barefoot in the snow, running with all his might.

"I'm with you, Stu," he heard Sackerson yell. "Right behind you."

Chapter 42: Hope

Krystal watched the two of them running off toward the farm. She closed the back door and turned, only to be confronted by Lark. "What was all that about?"

"Aren't you a little bit—"

"I mean, you, and Sackerson... and Henny?"

"Lark," she shook her head and dipped around him. "He had it coming."

"He's here to warn us," Lark said.

They rounded into the room where the beating had happened. It was breezy and cold, the floor bloodied and covered in shards of glass.

Henny, however, was gone.

"Great!" she said. If only she had her phone, she could have called the Wiebes, or Stu, and warned them. The rat was again on the loose.

"Gone?" Lark seemed so surprised. He picked his way to the window and looked out, as if expecting to see Henny there. "Where could he have gone? And how?"

"Maybe a better question is why? What's he running away from?"

"Oh, I don't know, another beating maybe?"

"We could have died! Henny gave them our location. He was working for them."

"He was doing what Sackerson told him to," Lark said. "That's the way Henny operates."

She knew he was right about that. Sackerson had admitted to as much.

"So that Sackerson could smoke them out?"

"That didn't work too well, did it?" Lark said. "In fact, *that's* what almost got us killed. If he hadn't told Henny to tell the Spooks where we were headed, and if we had not gone back for Henny—all Sackerson's fault by the way—we would be safe and sound somewhere right now, maybe in Kansas."

"Okay. How would *you* have handled it differently?" Krystal asked.

"Starting now, because that's all we can do, I say we bail," Lark said. She followed him as he continued on into the kitchen. "Let's take that truck, right outside, and go find a better place to set this out. Just the two of us."

"What about your dad?"

"We'll think of a better way of going about finding him on our own."

"What about Sackerson?"

"You mean, *future me*, right?" Lark stopped packing to look at her. "Easy. We go somewhere that I do *not* know, somewhere that you *do* know, but that you've never been in recorded history."

"You've been thinking this out," Krystal said. "Haven't you?"

"All night."

"So, maybe he couldn't find us," she had to agree. "What about Stu, though?"

"What about him? He's probably home by now. They'll probably run off Sackerson and Henny and whoever else comes around. The Wiebes aren't exactly weak, you know. And they have The Boys."

"What's gotten into you?" Krystal asked. "You just want to run and hide and leave everyone behind."

"Not everyone, Krystal."

"An hour ago, you seemed comfortable following Sack's lead."

"An hour ago, he wasn't beating a high school kid to death."

"You really serious about looking for your dad?"

"Of course. Why?"

"Sackerson's your only hope," Krystal said. "What else do you have?"

Just then, Lark's shoulders sagged. He had a radioactive smile on his face. "I have an idea," he said. Then he looked at her with certain confidence and said, "I know where he is!"

• • • •

SHE CLAIMED SHE DID not know how to drive a stick, and Lark was unable, because of his disability. That was her first winning argument. She continued to work on him as they walked toward the Wiebe farm. Even if Sackerson was off script, at least *he had read the script*, she argued. Stu was good to have around, for he knew about everyone in the region one way or another. Whoever was after them had a lot of influence. She reminded Lark of the arrival of the Spooks—that kind of influence that could derail trains—and they seemed relentless this time.

It was strangely quiet when they reached the farm. The house was lit up, warm and inviting, but they had expected a firefight, at the least some standoff between the Spooks and the Wiebes. Sackerson met them at the door and deflected them from the kitchen, where Stu was sitting. Stu did not even look up. He was looking at a paper on the table.

"It's bad," Sackerson said, when he had pulled them off toward Dale Wiebe's study.

"What do you mean?" Krystal asked. "Bad?"

Sackerson looked back toward the kitchen, then pulled them closer and said very low, "They got his family. Hostages."

"What? Running us down wasn't enough?" Lark asked. "Are they just pulling this crap with everybody now?"

"I feel so responsible..." she said, but looking back at Stu, she couldn't even finish her thought. She had never seen the spirit pulled out of him like this. Big tears were coursing down his face and onto the table.

"Note says they'll only trade for Doctor Fortune himself," Sackerson said. "Says they'll kill one Wiebe every day until we hand him over."

Stu was in the room now. "That gives us four days. They got Mom, Dad, Gramps, and my little sister, Annie."

"Stu, I'm so sorry—"

"Thing is," he cried openly, "*Henny* wrote this note. I know his handwriting." He held the crumpled page out to them. "What would make him...?"

Seeing him like this hurt her heart.

"The guy's way afield," Sackerson said. "He wasn't like this before...in my before."

"What do we do now?" Lark asked Sackerson.

"Start some coffee," Stu said, strangely inspired. He heard something outside that raised his spirits.

It sounded like a car horn playing Dixie.

They had trouble keeping up with Stu as he went through the house and out onto the porch. He wiped his eyes with his sleeve quickly as a dozen big pickups rolled into the yard. They spun around in a tight loop, revving their engines and billowing smoke.

The Boys had arrived.

Chapter 43: Unstuck

"What happened to you?" a large man with a bird's nest beard asked Lark. He pointed at Lark's missing hand.

He was large but also round. His nose was bulbous. His beer belly was substantial. Even his head was big and bald and round. They called him "Cue Ball," and Lark could see why.

"I... uh..." Lark was still not used to people being so blunt about his disability.

"Auger got me," a man on the other side of Cue Ball said. He held up a hook at the end of his arm. "But I like this now, anyway."

This created a conversation. They were wedged back in a corner of the kitchen, a place Lark could not escape. He was sitting on the countertop's corner, pressed in by Stu's family and friends. Those near him were comparing scars, missing fingers and teeth. The stories were gruesome but engaging.

Lark felt the stories were all aimed at him, since clearly, they all knew each other very well already. Each man would model his injury in a storm of one-up-man-ship and seek something then from Lark. He would nod or look aghast, and then the next man would go. Sometimes, by way of introduction, a man was pressed Lark's way with, "Shot to hell in Iraq, this guy. Meet my buddy, Dwight."

This bravado, this show of pain endured, was exactly what Lark expected of a band of brothers known as The Boys. They looked like a bunch of misfit boys too. They drove loud, audaciously modified pickups. They were all armed, even in the Wiebe house. They drained the coffeepot as if it were a keg of beer, over and over.

Otherwise, however, these men were nothing like he had thought. Two of them worked at the grocery in town. His old middle school shop teacher was in the mix. Krystal had said hello to two clergymen and a shoe store owner. When she and Lark compared notes, before they had all squeezed into the kitchen, they had both been surprised at the roster of The Boys.

Several were neighbors. Several more were Wiebe family from up and down the road.

A loud caw of the crow perched on his shoulder led to a moment of silence. Just as their questions were rearing up about the bird, someone waved his arms to get attention.

"Stewey's got something to say!" A teenager Lark knew as Schmitty stood up a little taller in the middle of the room. "Listen to him!"

Schmitty and a couple of others hefted Stu up on the kitchen table. He moved down the length of it to get out from under the lamp that hung in his way.

"We found this note," he began. Lark was surprised he sounded so small. Stu cleared his throat. People were getting quiet with expectation. "By the time we got down here from the cabin, this note was all that was left."

"That's when you called."

"That's right. When I read they got mom and Annie held hostage, that's when I called."

The room was abuzz. "Who got 'em?" A man leaned in and asked Lark.

"Well, let's go get 'em!" shouted someone else. There was a rumbling of agreement.

"They say they're going to kill a Wiebe a day," Sackerson goaded the crowd. "Are we going to take that?"

"Who are you?" Cue Ball asked. A murmur of questions circuited the room.

"Yeah, who the hell are you?"

"I've seen you," an older man said. "At Mack's." Lark recognized him now. He was the Hot Roast Beef man. He was there every Sunday at Mack's, before the church crowd.

"I've been protecting these kids for the past day or so," Sackerson said. Lark chuckled and shook his head. He did not know he had been so obvious about it, but a couple of the surrounding Boys nudged him to speak out. One tossed his head Sackerson's way, then squinted his eyes at Lark.

"What?" someone else asked him, softly. "Is he fulla shit?" The guy had terrible coffee breath. Lark looked him up and down and recognized then that it was Mike Burns, the cop. He was wearing coveralls and muck boots. He looked like any other farmer in the room.

Lark shook his head, no, despite himself.

"Point is," Stu said, "I need your help."

The room burst out in bold pledges of support, chest bumping and growling around.

Even Sack's crow was flapping its wings and making noise.

Lark shrank back on the counter a little farther, his back pressed against the upper cupboards. Krystal had found her way over and climbed up to sit by him.

Over the next few minutes, various men called out directives. Lark couldn't keep up with it all, but he had to admit, it sounded more organized than he would have expected.

The bidding for zones continued, accompanied by what Lark assumed might be radio channels or roadways. "Wescott. We'll be on 14... Caulder's Bridge to County... on 17."

"We'll take Riverbend," called out a man beside Krystal. His voice was the lowest that Lark had ever heard. He had to lean around Krystal just to get a good look at the man who owned that voice. He had bushy black hair, and an impressive full black beard. "On 19."

"That's Chief," Burns said, noting Lark's interest.

"Police Chief?"

"No. No. No. County Fire and EMS," Burns said. "He oughta be in charge, if you ask me."

"Of course," Cue Ball said, "We ain't asking you."

When the meeting disbanded, several men invited Lark and Krystal to ride with them. They hadn't talked it out. Lark did not know what to do.

"We're riding with Sackerson, I figure," Krystal fended them off, "and with Stu."

Once they jostled with the crowd out onto the porch, however, Lark could not pick Stu out of the crowd that was loading up and rolling out. Sackerson looked back and waved them on, but then even he was absorbed by the masses.

"Hey, Lark Fortune, right?"

Lark turned and finally saw a familiar face. "Tom!"

"You two, ride with me?"

Lark sighed with relief. "Krystal, this is Tom Chan. He's my PA, helped me out after..." he raised his wrist.

"Hi," she said, then was nearly bowled over by two men moving past her with what looked like a cannon. They chucked it in the back of a pickup, climbed in the back, and waved as they roared away.

"Hi," Tom said, and shook her hand. "It gets a little strange out here, I know, but they mean well."

· · · ·

LARK WAS MORE CONTENT than he had been in days. The three of them were riding in Tom's late model Toyota. It still had that new car smell. As they rolled down the highway, the sound of the tires competed with the Electronica pulsing in the cab. Like the other trucks, this one was lifted and lit.

"Nice truck," Krystal called out.

"Totaled," Tom said. "I rebuilt her myself."

As Tom rattled on about the ten-inch lift and oversized tires, the Cherrybomb exhaust, and bass speakers, Lark was continuously surprised. In the year they had worked together, none of this had ever come up. Tom had taught him everything from buttoning his shirt to shaking left-handed, but he had never mentioned he was a motorhead.

"They about wouldn't have me, you know," Tom told them.

Lark did not know.

"Foreign," Tom explained.

"What?" Krystal asked.

"Toyota," he grinned. "But I can go places none 'the rest of them can." A bit later, he asked, "Did you see the plate when you got in? The front license plate?"

They had not.

"Unstuck." Tom said. "That's what I called her. That's what she is. Never been stuck yet."

Tom turned down the volume some after he realized they had been yelling, and he continued filling them in. "The Boys" was not a car club. It was not even a club, or any proper organization, really. If you had a tricked-out truck, or if you were related, it was better for you. If you had gone brawling with some of the rougher ones or on a rescue with some others, you were pretty much in.

He went on to tell them about a couple of their exploits, but sobered eventually, and finally asked, "Who are the guys little Wiebe keeps calling Spooks, anyway?"

"We thought they were feds or cops," Krystal offered. "Now I don't think so, do you, Lark?"

"They could still be government," Tom interjected.

"All I know is they're after my dad," Lark said, "And obviously they're desperate."

• • • •

TOM WAS STILL AT A half tank when The Boys had a refueling stop. They were at the Stillwater interstate exit, at a place called the Smokey Pokey. It was a truck stop, but it featured good BBQ and an indoor pirate ship. Lark had met up with several of his friends there from time to time. It was something of a landmark.

It was Krystal's first visit. While The Boys were visiting, fueling, grabbing a bite to eat, Lark took her on a quick tour of the ship, then led her upstairs to a quiet part of the building that overlooked the Wall of Pickles, the pirate ship, and restaurant. He could easily see anyone coming from this vantage point.

"Krystal, I really do know where he is!"

"Who?"

A lot had happened since the cabin when he had first said it. Lark tried not to judge her confusion. *"Who do you think?!"* he wanted to say, but he continued: "Thanks to you, I know where Dad's going."

"Me? What did I...?"

"You said, 'Sackerson's our only hope,' remember?"

"Yeah, but—"

"So, it just clicked. You're a beautiful princess, like Leia, and—"

"Who?" she asked, blushing.

"Really?!" Lark took a step back. "You do know who I'm talking about, right? Princess Leia? Star Wars?"

"Sorta..." she said.

"You said 'only hope' just like she does. That made me think of the whole movie, the whole scene, you know, where she begs General Ben Kenobi on the hologram?"

"The Jedi guy, right?"

"Yes, yes, a Jedi, in hiding on Tatooine... but the point is, Dad's supervisor was his last hope, his only hope. He used to make a joke of it. *'Ben Canole, you're my only hope,'* he'd say. I remember him riffing on that from time to time before he started getting so—well, anyway, I think Dad's going back to talk to Ben at the Installation!"

"So..." she looked over the railing at some of The Boys. They were punching each other in the arm, hard, as they waited outside the men's room. "So do we tell them?"

"Listen, I know where he's *heading*, but I don't know that he's there. I don't know if it's a sure thing, like we can just announce it or anything." He sounded less sure of himself, and the more he talked, the less sure he was becoming. "Besides, I don't know that I could—I dunno—sell out my own dad!"

"I get it. I do... so what do we do now?"

"Now, we get Tom to make a little detour for us," he said.

When they returned to the parking lot, however, Tom was gone and the two of them were relegated to separate vehicles. Lark watched Krystal roll away in an old antique flatbed. He was left with a guy named Scooter, who was not the type to consider detours.

Chapter 44: Bedlam

February 2030

It had been an hour and a half, and Chris Fortune had not heard a sound. There was nothing on his monitors, just grainy-gray, empty, ransacked rooms. Though it disturbed him, even to look at the images of the ruination, he was relieved to have sat it out, to have evaded the robber.

He decided to spend another half hour studying the scene, listening for trouble. It was stark still and quiet, stunning compared to the recent wreckage. In his boredom, he resumed his hobby of tossing things through the portal. He was always amazed at how anything would simply disappear when passing through the glowing white loop.

This was Portal 22, and its partner was hanging discreetly in a park pavilion in Guthrie's Mineral Wells Municipal Park. Chris imagined a disgruntled park worker picking up all the debris: pencils, paper clips, paper planes. He quit tossing things abruptly and pulled down the filament from the ceiling. The loop returned to its inert state, looking like a handful of flimsy fishing line.

He absently stuffed the cigar box in his lab coat pocket and ascended the stairs quietly. He triggered the mechanism that released the hidden door and carefully opened it out onto the hallway. Chris wished now for some kind of portable monitor, so he could see each room again as he approached it. He was as stealthy as he could be, yet he crunched broken glass and debris underfoot despite his efforts.

As gently as he could, he snapped the secret door back in place and shuffled his foot to randomize the clean path the door had swept in the hallway trash.

The destruction was much more shocking when he was standing amid it. On the monitor it had been a distant set design, but as he made his way over broken chair legs and piles of books tossed on the floor, it was all too real. The faint light of the toppled fridge helped him navigate through puddles of condiments and broken casserole dishes.

In the hall, he dared flip on a light switch, only to learn two of the three ceiling fixtures were destroyed, the third dangling by a wire, casting light cockeyed down the hall. Even the ceiling fixtures had met the wrath of the intruder!

He crunched his way into the den and caught his breath. The destruction here had seemed most particularly malevolent. Even the spines of some books had been split and ripped in two. Carpet in the room's corner had been ripped back from the floor.

"What in the hell was he after?" Chris asked aloud.

"Answers," someone said, stepping from the shadows.

Chris fell backwards through the remains of the closet door and scrambled to his feet. He grabbed the first weapon he could find and swung it wild and wide at the intruder.

Comically, the bowling ball dropped out of the bag between the two of them.

The man smiled with his hands spread wide. "I mean you no harm," he said in a calming—simultaneously terrifying—tone.

"No harm?" Chris said, looking all around them. "Look what you've done here!"

Chris wasted no time. His military training came back to him like a jolt of adrenaline, and he waylaid the lanky robber. Surprisingly, the downed man sprang immediately to his feet and bounced like a cage fighter.

"Good one," he said, then he dove at Chris.

In a space with more room, he might have dodged the move, but in the confines of the closet threshold, he had nowhere to go. The man clasped his arms around Chris' arms and chest and lifted him off the floor. He pressed him against the back wall of the closet. "I'm not here to hurt you. I'm here to help."

Pinned to the wall, his head and neck crimped awkwardly by the closet wall, Chris had few options. All he had were his legs, so he kicked hard at the tall man's shins. Then he regained his footing and planted a crushing knee strike into his opponent's groin.

The man doubled over but grasped Chris by the lab coat and again pulled him into another, less reserved bear hug. This time Chris kept a hand free, and with it, slammed his attacker's head against the door frame. Stunned, he partially released Chris, clutching still at the coat. Chris spun out of it and ran for the hall.

"That hurt, old man!" the robber shouted after him. Chris heard him close on his heels. He slid into the kitchen, quickly flowed into a defensive stance, and chambered a kick.

The assailant rounded into the kitchen, stopped abruptly, and put up his hands. Blood was coursing down the side of his head, yet he continued to smile.

"Forgot all about the karate," he said with a gasp. He stepped into the kitchen, rounding past a broken chair.

"Close enough, you!" Chris said.

"Where were you hiding?" the man asked, astonished. "And where's all—"

"Just leave," Chris said, "or I'll... I'll..."

The other man just smiled and shrugged. It was true. Chris had little to threaten with.

He noticed the portal fiber was still clutched in his hand and lowered his threatening fists. "You leave," he said, "or I will."

"Oh no," the skeletal face got serious. "Not after what I've gone through to find you."

He dove at Chris, but again it was not a violent gesture, obviously one uninformed by any hand-to-hand training. Chris sidestepped the opening arms, then grabbed the man's bald head again, and, using his own momentum against him, slammed his skull on the countertop.

The man groaned and rolled on the floor, bleeding even more profusely. When he saw Chris shake loose a filament loop, plug it together in an arc of glowing white, he scrambled away and cried out, "Please don't!"

Chris whirled it overhead and let it drop around him.

Instantly, he caught his breath in the cold night air. He was standing in the gazebo in the Guthrie Park that celebrated "Bedlam," the Sooners vs. Aggies football tradition since 1904.

He picked up the Port 22 wire and snapped it apart. He tossed pieces of it with the random office debris.

"Go team," he said, patting the monument as he walked by it and out into the moonlight.

He had never felt so free.

Chapter 44: God's Country

Stu had been on these before. Most recently, they had tracked down Lydell Scruggs, a guy who had opened fire in the Guthrie Wal-Mart, killing two and maiming several others. His shooting spree had ended at the Wal-Mart property line though, and once they found him, huddled in a dugout along the river, he came along peacefully.

Stu had felt pretty good that day, joining the posse to catch a killer. They had roared along full-bore in their trucks once the location was over the radios. They had taken position on the creek bank, hidden in duck blinds and lying prone for the best shot. Even Stu had Scruggs sighted in. He figured he could have pulled the trigger without remorse.

The Sheriff had been along on that one, however, and he talked Scruggs into coming along without further incident.

This was different though. Stu was sharing this with Sack in the back seat of a crew cab. These strangers in town were stranger than strange. They kept showing up: at Mack's, near Perry, on the Kansas border, even in Norman... in utility trucks and hospital helicopters and out sabotaging trains... and most recently... right in his own home. Four of them were dead, but it seemed like they just kept coming.

"The audacity!" Sack said, pulling it to a fine point.

"Right!" Stu said. "I mean, who the hell do they think they are?"

"They came to the wrong place to pick a fight," the driver said. He was a Catholic priest they all called "Father."

The passenger sang a lyric from an old country song: "*Devil went down to Georgia, but he didn't stick around.*"

They all joined in chorus, "*This is God's country!*"

"Well, I doubt there's thirty of 'em, anyway, like us," Father said. "And I know they're not prepared for the likes of us."

"Sheriff's actually letting Burnsey's ex run dispatch for us on this one," the passenger said. "I hear he's out and about, has been since you called it in."

"Gotta love Timberton. Best Sheriff we ever put in office."

As the sun had come up, Stu finally felt they could really surveil the countryside. In the dark, it had all been adrenaline and KC lights, but now, if there was a trace of those Spooks, Stu was sure they'd be on it in no time.

The way The Boys liked to run things was tight but unusual. Since they all knew the region well, and they all knew every diner, truck stop, and home kitchen supporting their cause, The Boys would assemble in little clutches every two hours. They called it "Fess Up and Fuel Up." The veterans among them just called it FUFU. When the time was announced on the radios, everyone rolled to the nearest coffee spigot. That way, they could compare notes and swap stories and do their business, then be back out on the road, all while maintaining some sense of order. Sure, sometimes there would be eight trucks at a stop, then only two at another, but the point of regrouping regionally had proven crucial to their previous searches.

There was always a good deal discussed over coffee that they wanted to keep off the airwaves too, and these meetings allowed for that. Sometimes they swapped passengers around to stay awake and keep fresh. He had heard that in times of actual confrontation, these meetings were great for equipping one another with ample ammo and intel too.

They had just come off of their second FUFU, at Lake Langston, exchanging one of Stu's aunts for Father. Stu knew the truck belonged to the passenger, that no matter how much swapping around happened, that man and this pickup would be together. Everyone knew the rig, and that old Cole Grant, a body shop owner, had fabbed it himself. It was a six-wheel drive Chevrolet 3500. On another occasion, he would have told Sackerson all about it, for it was truly a one-of-a-kind truck.

At the moment, however, he was keeping a sharp eye on every side road, scanning for fresh tire tracks.

"Don't the State Troopers have a chopper?" Grant asked. "Why don't they get it out and about?"

"There are four people being held hostage," Father said. He looked over his shoulder at Sackerson, adding, "And... Sheriff Timberton's looking for you and the kids too, you know."

Sackerson held up his hands, palms facing Father. "Not guilty, I'm telling you. We're on the run from the very same people who took the Wiebes."

"I heard that," Grant said, "but I don't get it."

Some radio chatter interrupted them for a moment. Father whipped the truck around and followed a new directive, soon turning south for Meridian.

"Sack here has got us out of some tight spots, it's true," Stu said, slapping Sackerson on the back. "Saved my life."

Almost killed my friend, Henny, he did not say. That was still haunting him.

"What's your story?" Grant asked, turning around more fully to study Sackerson.

"Doc Fortune—you know him, right? Air Force guy? He is on the run with something these creeps want," Stu interjected. "They want it bad, so bad they have been hunting us for two days now."

"Why's that?" Father asked.

"That kid with the red hair, that's Doc Fortune's kid," Stu said, "so they figure his kid might know where Doc's hiding—"

"So, they're doing all they can to nab him," Sackerson said, rounding out the idea. "I'm here to protect him. All of them."

"Because?" Father asked, looking at Sackerson in his rearview.

"Lark Fortune's my... cousin," Sackerson said. Then he continued, surer of himself, "And of course, so's Doctor Fortune."

"So, you're in from out of town to help out family?" Grant asked.

Father held up a hand to silence everyone, then he turned the radio up louder: "Possible sighting, currently in pursuit, north of Bear Creek."

"Roger that," someone said.

"Picked 'em up by Cooper Cemetery," the voice said, strained. "Moving fast now."

It seemed the cue they'd all been waiting for.

Father downshifted.

Grant and Stu fastened their seatbelts.

Sackerson, Stu noted, seemed oblivious as to their current condition.

They were one of the closest vehicles to the sighting.

Chapter 46: The Law

Context File

Guthrie's Police Department (GPD) was right sized in 2022, then doubled with the next president's agenda and administration. There were 40 on staff, 22 of which were actual officers of one sort or another who saw action. These men and women served within the city limits of Guthrie.

On special request, GPD provided assistance for the Logan County Sheriff's Department. The Sheriff's office and staff were tiny, merely six employees, radically understaffed considering 750 square miles it covered and the 11 various towns it encompassed.

Oklahoma State Troopers had a broader jurisdiction yet. Charged with patrolling Oklahoma's 111,994 miles of city, county, and state-maintained roads and highways, the 800 Highway Patrol troopers kept busy. In addition, they were called upon for trivial parade routes and keeping the highways free from obstructions. They were also tasked with being first responders, whenever possible. All this, while struggling to keep good relationships with local authorities.

These three law enforcement organizations collaborated within a hierarchy; the Highway Patrol was the governing body, though all participants operated autonomously. The Highway Patrol did the bidding of the governor of Oklahoma.

When the governor hunted in the fall of the year, he always leased a cabin at Horse Thief Canyon from Darryl Wiebe.

When the FBI would come poking around intent on taking over from the locals, a strong governor like Jeremy Black never let that happen.

When Black learned vigilantes had been loosed on Logan County to find those who kidnapped four members of the Wiebe family—one of them being Darryl himself—he issued two missives. One, for the media and the feds, praised the combined efforts of regional law enforcement. The other was issued via a select social media channel, encouraging the locals to redouble efforts before there was an intervention from Washington and an influx of out-of-towners.

The Boys took heart from their strong governor's support. At the next FUFU, they toasted him. Then, en masse, the dozen pickups gave chase to a black SUV with Texas plates. Unlike their brethren who had city, county, and state boundaries to attend to, The Boys were in this for the duration, like a pack of hounds giving chase.

Chapter 47: Processing

Her squad car was her second home. When she was nestled in that cockpit, surrounded by instrumentation—radios, mapping, a laptop with a windshield heads up display—she felt omniscient and omnipotent. She nicknamed that car "Omni."

The minivan, however, made her feel like a soccer mom. It was an old model that Rob had talked her into, and he had been right. Despite its age, he had run a CARFAX and studied it through Consumer Reports, and sure enough, it was a bona fide gem. Thirty-two miles per gallon, always reliable, all the comforts, but being over 20 years old, it was missing what she needed most in the moment: onboard GPS.

Shallowbrook was one of those HOA neighborhoods that lived by the code. Identical houses on nondescript, winding roads with pastoral names she could not keep straight (Stoney Creek, Mossford, Dalton's Bridge). Distinguishing characteristics were covered in snow.

So, she was getting directions from Rob over her earbuds. "No, no, no," he said, "you should have turned *right* back there. You're on Riverview Court, you want Circle, hun."

It would have been easier had he not needed to go home to tend to the kids. Twenty miles into their big adventure, "following a hot lead" as Rob had said, his mother called about Hester and Opal being sick.

She could have tried following the map from her phone, but she took digital distractions seriously, having been on too many accident scenes. Besides, she had to admit, having him in her ears was almost like having him by her side.

"There is no Circle," Shae said again.

Rob was fussing with one of the girls.

Shae just had to make it on her own a bit and not feel guilty about her baby girl crying in the background. She navigated out of a cul-de-sac and back onto a thoroughfare she had been up and down repeatedly.

"Ah," he said after a bit. "You're back on Glenn Aire. That's good." The live time tracking from her work laptop was spot on.

"Now what?"

"Now in about two... three little side streets, you'll see—yes honey, that little dot's your mommy—you'll see Dundiddy, and then it's just a few houses—"

"Rob. Rob. I see it. Thanks."

She saw vehicles, such a splash of color in an otherwise slushy, beige neighborhood. They were backed up to the thoroughfare on both sides of the street.

It was Processing. The usual suspects. Some unmarked police cars, a Sheriff's SUV, and two crime scene vans. There were too many others though. This was not released to the public yet, but she guessed there had to have been four or five more vehicles on the scene. One was a bright orange car from the power company. Another was with a towing service. Three, however, seemed like they did not belong: black full-sized cars with dark windows. She could only guess that these might be Federal. As she drove past, the plates confirmed it: government issue.

Shae parked a few houses down, not wanting to be associated with the minivan. She pulled on her GPD service coat and hoped she could just flash her badge at the door and go in, jurisdiction be damned.

The officer at the door, however, was not having it.

"Fine. Let me talk to the Officer in Charge," Shae said.

"OIC's at lunch. You can wait in your... van." He was a judgmental little man, and she wanted to elbow past him and get on with it. "Move along," he said, sounding to her like he would be more suited to be a crossing guard.

"Who's here?" a voice inside asked. The door swung open wider, and Shae relaxed and smiled.

"Shaelyn Lawton!" proclaimed a jaunty detective. "As I live and breathe!"

"Dalton!" she beamed and pushed past the officer at the door. "Is this your scene?"

"I'm assigned, yeah, but I'm under the Trooper on this one." He touched her elbow and led her toward a knot of men. "Captain Banks? Meet Shae Lawton, Guthrie PD."

"Guthrie?" he said, turning his attention to her. He was a very tall man, carved of granite. "What brings you here, officer Lawton?"

"It's Ward now," she said apologetically to him, then glancing at Dalton. "And I'm on a related case."

"Another one, huh," he grunted. "There's people here from the base, from that Installation out your way, city, county, even Oklahoma Electric," he wagged his head and turned back to the table. "File your log entry and have at it."

"It's a shit show," Dalton said, hovering over her at the logbook. "But it's great to be working with you again."

"Same," she said, "It's been a while."

"Twelve years, outside the Academy," he said.

"So," she said, stepping around evidence markers and extension cords. "What's the story?"

He shook his head, put his hands on his hips. "Wish I knew. This is an odd one."

"How so?" Shae was taking in details. Obviously, the place had been broken into and tossed.

"Just a lot going on. A lot that doesn't lock in."

"This looks a little strange, if you ask me," she said in the trashed family room. "A little... *much*, maybe?"

218 MARK LANDON JARVIS

"I know, right? But it just keeps getting more bizarro," Dalton said. "Come look out back."

She was not encountering any of the resistance Burns had cited. Two minutes in, and she was getting the whole tour.

In the yard, it appeared someone had driven an ice cream truck through the back fence and crashed into the deck. "Dollarhide's suburban," she said aloud.

"What?" Dalton exclaimed. He glanced at his watch. "Not even five minutes and you've got something?" He chuckled. "Yes, the vehicle's registered to Dollarhide's Amusements, a carnival outfit out of Texas. How'd you know that?"

In the yard, two uniformed officers were folding up a white tarp. Two men in suits were peering inside the vehicle. Another officer was visiting with a military officer and the man from the towing service. All of them were mincing around, as if attempting not to corrupt the scene worse.

"I met the owner," Shae said. "And the people I'm interested in were seen in that vehicle."

"You're kidding me. When? Where?"

"Last night in Perry."

"We got this pegged to last night, maybe yesterday. Depends on the timeline."

"Everybody's here," Shae said. "Why?"

Dalton said softly, wheeling her back inside, "The homeowner seems to be everyone's person of interest."

He led her down a hallway to an office. Like the rest of the home, it was in ruin. "Found blood here too," he pointed to the frame around the walk-in closet door. "Shop thinks it's the same as in the kitchen."

Then, in low tones, he continued, pulling her close. "Ever seen so much attention, Shae? I mean, there's guys here above Captain Banks, I mean, DC Feds."

She loved how he spoke, like a teenager, even to this day. Dalton had been a godsend in school, and she was happy to be with him again.

"I saw the cars," Shae said, "but it's just a robbery, and I'm working on a possible kidnapping, a double homicide, and—"

"Homeowner was some kind of a big deal, they say, out at Tinker."

"Yes, Dr. Christopher Fortune."

"That's right..." Dalton said.

"He was married to a nurse in Guthrie. I think he lived there until recently."

"That's what we've learned too."

"And the kidnapping I'm on? One of the kids was theirs, Larkin Fortune."

"But still," he whispered, "Feds?"

"I'm guessing it's got something to do with his research."

Dalton's eyes got big, and he hunkered in closer. "Research?"

"Really, it's just work on that meteor shower. He was part of the research unit out west of Guthrie."

"People are getting killed over that?"

"I think it's all related to my alleged kidnapper."

They both looked around the room, as if it might tell them something. Finally, Dalton said, "Double homicide, you say? We had two on the floor. C'mon." He led the way to the front room. "Two guys from the power company... well, the OEC guy says they're not company men. Coroner's got them now."

"I can save you some time, if it's anything like my scene."

More loudly, he said, "Oh yeah, bloodstains, there and there. Blood in the kitchen. More back here. Right this way."

Back in the study, he looked intently at her.

"You won't find anything on them. No ID. No records," she said, "and if they're anything like we have in the fridge, they won't have prints or any distinguishing characteristics."

"What?" Dalton smirked. "Nothing?"

"Nothing much. Common blood type. Average height and build. No scars, no broken limbs, no tattoos. Not even any food in their stomachs. Nothing."

"This is your local M.E., right? You don't have much back from state, right?"

"Laugh if you want to, Briggs, but I think you'll find I'm right about them."

A couple of techs came back in the study to take pictures. Dalton resumed in his official tone, "Yes, yes. Hella domestic disturbance, but nobody reported anything before the gunfire."

"So, the carnival truck slams in the yard," Shae said, as they traipsed down the hall, "then what?"

"I don't know. Maybe the passengers tore the place up? Roughed up the homeowner? Somewhere in there—and it is no end of irritating that not one neighbor admits to seeing anything. At *some time*, this OEC truck pulls up, probably the guys we found in the front room. But then the truck leaves in a hurry, circles back, leaves again. At least that's what we had in the snow before everybody got here, and it warmed up. It's going to be impossible to tell much outside, come tomorrow."

"Nothing else? Just speculation?"

"It's like we have trace on the homeowner everywhere, of course, but there was a lot going on, a bunch of others in here too."

"A *bunch* of others?"

"Counting Fortune, we have footprints from six, maybe seven individuals."

"So, if one's Doc Fortune, and two sets are the gunshot victims... maybe four others? Maybe *my* four?"

"Do you have anything on them?"

"We have blood and hair for the kids, shoe sizes too. The other guy, we have nothing at all."

"Want pictures?"

"What are you talking about?"

"We're going to walk back through, and I want you to look at all the tiny cameras, Shae. Whoever finds the footage wins the day."

"What?"

"Banks wants that footage so bad; he's giving first view to whomever finds it. Even over the Feds. Hell, the tow truck guy could get first dibs."

"Strange," she said, "how you city boys roll."

Dalton Briggs scoffed. "Didn't you work out of New York?"

"L.A.," she said, as she began looking for cameras.

"Same thing," he said.

Chapter 48: Boys into Men

Krystal Price knew why they called themselves The Boys. From the first "woot, woot," to this latest cross country drag race, they all lived up to their name. They were acting like children.

Somehow, between the first and fourth rest stops, she had been separated from Lark and had met a new combination of The Boys every two hours. She had most recently been riding in a teetering pickup that required a retracting ladder to get into. The driver liked talking about "G forces," and kept cranking the wheel this way and that to cause the truck to lean. When she was able to get out at the next stop, what they called a Foo Foo, Krystal learned she had been riding in a truck fondly known as *Lurch*.

She made a mental note of that, to never ride in *Lurch* again.

Krystal was determined to find Stu or Lark or even Sackerson, but it took her until the fourth stop to spot one of them.

At last, she and Lark were reunited in one of the three Federal Express van conversions. On the outside, this one looked like any of the defunct delivery vans she had seen around, though this one sat much higher off the ground. Their seats had what the driver called "5 point safety harnesses," which were impossible for Lark to fasten without help. Krystal had to admit, of the vehicles she had been in, this one felt a little safer. It even had a metal cage inside, a roll cage, in case the van ever flipped.

The Boys in the front were very engaged with some of their friends on the radio. The passenger seat was overflowing with Officer Burns, and this, too, gave her a little comfort. She had gotten the impression that this impromptu group was at least unofficially sanctioned by the law, and that made her relax some.

The van was careening around, vaulting into the air, bouncing off the snowbanks it would hit. It seemed to have an unnerving ability to crash land on a single front tire, then find its balance and drop back to all fours, blasting onward. Once, when it came back down, it nearly tipped side-for-side, but the driver, a woman Krystal almost recognized, was skilled, if not also unhinged.

Lark was extra pale. He looked like a kid riding out a horrible carnival ride. He was clutching his harness and kept his feet planted against the back of the seat in front of him. Krystal thought he looked like he might throw up.

Out the windows, she saw they were flanked and following several other 4x4s. All were bouncing and bolting after another vehicle. Their prey was hard to see from the clouds of snow it was kicking up. That vehicle, according to the radio reports and the front seat commentary, was the prize. Inside, everyone knew, were Wiebe family members and their captors.

• • • •

"IN CASE WE DON'T MAKE it," Lark said through gritted teeth, "I want you to know I'm sorry I got—" the van slammed hard into a snowbank, then plowed through—"I got you mixed up in all this."

Krystal stared straight ahead, not sure what to say to that.

"Things could get messy up here, kids," Officer Burns said over his shoulder. "When we stop, you just stay buckled in, okay?"

Someone was yelling something unintelligible through the radio.

"I'm the one who wanted to help," she said, turning to Lark. She put a hand on his shoulder, then clutched his shoulder as the van pulled radically left. "I think I got *you* into this."

"It's all about my dad, though, so—"

"So maybe *he* got us all into this," Krystal said. "Doesn't really matter, now, does it?"

Lark closed his eyes again and kept them squeezed shut.

The van was bounding down a long slope. Even those up front were commenting on the steep incline and the long drop.

"If we aren't going to make it—just playing to your theme here—I'd want you to know something too."

"What's that?" he asked.

"I'd want you to know that I think trying to save your dad is kind of, I dunno, heroic."

Lark peeked at her out of one eye. "How so?"

"That's them! That's them!" the driver shrieked. She was racing neck and neck with their quarry, a black SUV. After the last six hours riding with The Boys, it was no surprise to Krystal that the driver was angling the FedEx van closer and closer, as if to side swipe that SUV.

"Think about it," Krystal said more loudly, competing with the straining sounds of the van's drivetrain. "If Sack's right and those Spooks are, like, from the future, and if they're trying to kill your dad, then they probably don't care about us or the Wiebes either."

Lark's eyes got wider and wider as he watched out the windshield.

"So, what I am saying is, it's crazy brave to do this, to get in the way of these guys."

"Crazy, anyway," Lark said, and braced for impact.

"Twelve clicks. North, northwest of town. Yeah, near Crescent," the officer was screaming into the radio. "Pinned."

The van slammed sideways into the big black SUV they'd been chasing. The SUV's driver glanced at their van, then dropped back, as if he had slammed on his brakes.

Krystal heard a horrible crashing sound behind them. Their van did a tight twist back, and she could see what had happened. In trying to evade the van, the SUV had stopped suddenly, and two others rear-ended them. The Boys' trucks circled around the SUV in a lethal knot. Guns of all types were bristling out of pickup windows.

Officer Burns opened his door and used it as a shield. "Exit the ve—"

A blast from the SUV shattered his window, and Burns retreated to the inside, slamming his door and ducking down.

A second blast resounded like thunder.

"Move!" Several men were shouting and cursing over the rumbling pickups.

"Back!" one shouted. "Get back."

The circle grew broader as they backed up their rigs. One truck that had rear-ended the SUV did not budge. The driver and passengers ran back to the safety of other vehicles.

Smoke was rolling out of the SUV, not only from under the hood, but now also from the windows. Once windows—Krystal noted—now they were just gaping holes and shattered glass. Many of the vehicles around the circle, like their own, seemed to have lost windows from the explosions.

That man they called the Chief was the first to approach the shelled-out SUV. He high stepped through the snow, slowly, gun drawn. Krystal looked away. She did not want to see any more violence.

"Careful... careful..." the officer in their van was whispering.

She could not help but watch. Chief had reached a window, peered inside, then lowered his weapon and his shoulders. Without even turning back to The Boys, he shouted the all clear.

• • • •

"DALE AND HIS DADDY, Darryl," their driver huffed, returning with a report, "and two of them."

"Dead?" Lark asked the obvious.

She nodded, and in that curt nod, Krystal suddenly recognized her. It was the woman who taught her mixed martial arts at the rec center.

"How?" Krystal managed to ask. "What happened?"

"Chief says some kind of incendiary—a bomb." She shook her head, then looked long at the man in the passenger seat. "Wouldn't you say, Burnsey?"

"I... uh... yeah, probably so from the concussive effect of..." he seemed less sure of himself. Krystal was not surprised. When their window blew out, his scream was louder than hers.

"They killed themselves?" Lark questioned. He was seeking Krystal's attention, then mouthed to her, "Again?"

"Looks like it, but I don't get it. I'm EMS, you know. Seen a lot of wrecks. This thing burned out but never caught fire. Just a big flare and it was out." She was processing aloud. "Hot flash, too, like phosphorus."

A knot of men was tight around the cab of the Coyote Wagon that Krystal had been in previously. They were crowding in, arms over each other's shoulders, murmuring in deep, dark tones.

Krystal heard an angry wail surge up from there.

A harsh sobbing followed that made tears run from her eyes. Lark, too, was fighting it back unsuccessfully.

• • • •

KRYSTAL AND LARK HELD each other close as they stood shivering in the knee-deep snow. The Boys shuffled around, but they had not yet refocused. Many of them were openly weeping. Others were working it out for themselves alone. One man sat in his truck pounding his steering wheel. Another just walked off into the snow, his head hanging low. Sackerson sat on the tailgate of a pickup with Chief, having an angry, animated conversation.

After a good long while, one of the clergymen stood up on the back of the Coyote Wagon. "Men!" he said, "Men, would you join me in a moment of pra—"

Every radio in every truck squawked and screeched. Every mobile device rang and squealed at once. The sound echoed wild and wide. Loud static drew down to a whine, and then a voice rattled the speakers:

"We want Christopher Fortune." The voice was cold and mechanical. "We want the kid and the Bear, too, and if we don't have them by dawn, more will die. More and more will die until we get what we want." The radio snapped and popped, then the voice concluded with a cruel, "Thank you," an obvious afterthought.

Sackerson's crow, circling overhead, shrieked a warning caw.

Chapter 49: Twins

Context File

It has always been rumored that twins have a special bond of ESP, when in fact, it is simply an advanced, intimate communication. This actually begins for them in the womb, according to a study by the University of Padova, which found twins reaching for one another and then touching each other a few weeks later. The twins gestured and communicated.

More studies have been conducted on twins than any other humans, and even so, their heightened sense of communication remains baffling. What is known? Twins separated at birth do not have the communication skill, though they may have other disturbing similarities, mannerisms, and so on. Thus, scientists have a good hunch that twin communication, that is, cryptophasia, is more a product of them forming their own society than it is something genetically in common.

Cryptophasia is a phenomenon of a language developed by twins (identical or fraternal) that only the two children can understand. The word has its roots from the Greek *crypto*, meaning secret, and *phasia*, meaning speech. This is not a rare phenomenon, showing up in about 40% of all twins, but often disappearing in early childhood.

It is very rare for twins to preserve their secret speech into adulthood.

Chapter 50: Cavalry

S ackerson had barged into every grouping of The Boys, even visited with the loners. Lark was watching him. Even someone as odd as Sackerson should have known better than to intrude at a time like that. Lark was baffled. Even *he* knew better, so why didn't his future self? A couple of men just pushed Sackerson away, and a couple more turned a cold shoulder to him. Undaunted, Sackerson moved on, pushed his way in, making attempts to talk.

The last thing Lark wanted to do was mill around talking to people. He wanted to be alone with his thoughts. He needed to sort things out. Lark wished he could teleport somewhere far from all this. The smoke smelled horribly, reminding him constantly of the terrible deaths Stu's father and grandfather had endured.

Krystal, Henny, Stu and his family—none of them had anything to do with this. The running had been terrible but tolerable. If only he had run—alone—no one else would have been harmed.

Now, however, people were dying. *"...more and more will die..."*

It made him so angry. His fist was clenched, and for a moment, his phantom fist was too. It did not happen so often now, a year later, but sometimes it felt like the hand was still there. Lark was so mad at the Spooks, particularly the radio voice. He thought he could do some serious damage even with that phantom fist, alone.

Earlier, he and Krystal had almost joked about whose fault it was. Now, Lark had no doubt. It was his own fault. They were after his dad... and him... and a bear?

"...the kid..." Lark had been called out by the radio Spook. He was the one they wanted in trade for Mrs. Wiebe and her daughter. It was becoming clear to him as he watched The Boys. More and more of them had put together that *he was that kid*.

He was certain, too, that he knew where his father was, and chances were, The Boys had figured as much, just as the Spooks had. Grab the kid, get the dad. Lark looked over at Krystal, leaning against the van, wearing someone's down coat and wrapped in her carnival blanket. Had he told her? He couldn't remember in all the jumble of these hours and days on the run.

Would she tell if she was privy to the location?

"...*We want the kid and the bear, too...*" the radio Spook had said. Nothing was making any sense. What bear could they want, and what did it have to do with Lark and his dad?

He so wanted to give himself up, to give his father up for that matter, but the bear?

· · · ·

SACKERSON HAD MADE his way to them, finally, and he tried to pull Krystal and Lark into a hug or a huddle. "Ah, come in for it," he coaxed, but Lark was not having it. He needed to be alone, not cuddling with his would-be girlfriend and his would-be self. He shook his head at the very thought of it.

Sackerson pulled them up close to the van. He looked over his shoulder at The Boys here and there, then said, "It strains credulity," he said with a strained smile, "just how off the map we are right now."

"What are you talking about?" Lark snapped. He couldn't help it.

"He means this is not going well, not going like it ought to," Krystal said. She had been silent up to now. Lark wondered if he had snapped at her too.

"Not at all well. People are dead," Sackerson said. "Nobody's supposed to get hurt. I'm here to help—"

"Nobody hurt?" Lark interjected, "*You've* shot at least four Spooks!"

"Correction," Sackerson said. "*I have shot no one.* I have, however, been beaten and shot, multiple times."

"Let's not make it one more then," someone said, behind him. When Sackerson turned, Lark could see that The Boys had migrated to their van. A man who looked a lot like Stu pointed a rifle at Sackerson.

"Now fellas," Sackerson began, but several rifles were cocked then, and he held up his hands. They stepped closer, gesturing menacingly with their rifles. Lark and Krystal were herded closer to Sackerson. They pressed their backs to the van. Sackerson stood in front of them.

"Where's your dad, kid?" Cue Ball asked, from off to the side. He had not drawn a weapon. "That's all they want."

"It's true, Larkin," a man beside Cue Ball said in a cultivated calm. "We don't want anyone else getting hurt."

"Oh, I want some people getting hurt," the woman who had been driving their van spoke up. "I want some justice."

"That's my dad in there," someone else said.

"My uncle."

"My grandpappy!"

Lark felt the mob turning. It was one thing to be in the gang, even with the gang, when they were doling out their justice. It had been exhilarating chasing down the Spooks. Now, however, being the *object* of their justice was the new last place Lark ever wanted to be.

"Look. I know everyone's hurting," Sackerson said, "I know—"

"Shut up, you!" someone shouted.

Various other shouts followed.

"Boys," one of the clergymen said, coming to stand in the gap between Sackerson and the guns. "You haven't even asked for their cooperation, now have you?"

Lark cleared his throat and took a step forward.

Sackerson pressed him back. "Cooperation? Whatever could that mean? We give ourselves up, and Doctor Fortune, too?"

"Exactly that!" someone called back.

"We don't even know where Fortune is," Sackerson said.

"I do," Lark said, elbowing Sackerson aside. "I know where he is, and I'll help you get back Mrs. Wiebe too. You can turn us all in together at dawn."

"That's not going to happen," Stu's voice cut through the crowd. They stepped aside to let him through. Bearing down on Lark, he stopped short and stood with the clergyman. "Not like that."

"Stu, I'm so sorry..." Lark's voice trailed off.

Krystal was all over Stu immediately, hugging him, kissing his cheek, rambling.

Stu stood stiffly, staring at Lark.

She got the message and retreated to Sackerson's side. He threw an arm around her, and she sobbed into his chest.

Lark turned his full attention back to Stu.

The cocky jock was gone, replaced by a stiff, vengeful man. "We're not turning anyone in."

"But Stu!" some urged.

"Eye for an eye," another yelled.

"We gotta get 'em for this, for your dad!"

At that, Stu turned to whomever had spoken and glared at him.

Lark felt like the crowd was getting more and more agitated. He felt closed in. As he looked around, he noted a small clutch of people that looked as worried as he felt—the clergy and Mike Burns, Tom Chan and a couple of others he recognized—shrinking together as others pressed forward.

Lark realized The Boys had moved in from behind them as well. They were surrounded.

Stu took a deep breath and then shouted out to them, looking out at them as he turned full circle. "Listen. Thank you for all the help. You're family, and family helps family. Now, these guys are too. I signed on to help him find his dad because I didn't trust this one." He looked at Sackerson, then continued, "Thing is, they both saved my life, just this last day or so. They're alright, and we are not going to sell them out." His voice cracked as he gestured to the charred SUV, "Not for them, and not for Mom and Annie, neither."

"Sorry to disagree with you, cousin, but we *are* trading them out," said the man who looked so much like Stu. "For justice."

"Justice," most of The Boys shouted out.

"Try it," Stu said, drawing a large knife.

Lark did not see quite what happened next, but The Boys seemed to dive into one big fight.

He was nearly tackled, and he fought back as best he could, but the large man who had a hold of him was relentless. Lark was slammed against the far side of the van, smashed next to Krystal and the clergymen. It was Cue Ball. He pinned Lark by the shoulders and looked him in the eyes. "Bad to worse," he said. "You'd best get the hell outta here." He handed Lark a set of keys. "It's my Bronco. Now go."

Then Cue Ball was gone, around the van, and back into the fight. Lark had to hazard a glimpse, peeking around the corner in disbelief.

Three or four men, Cue Ball, the Chief, the hook-handed man, and some others, had sided with Stu and Sackerson. Members of that small group were struggling to ward off their attackers. Some were swinging improvised weapons, a tire chain, a shovel, but Stu waved his big knife defensively, slashing at those who would attack him.

Sackerson's crow was diving and whirling, a blur of black feathers. It was lashing about with its beak and talons, cawing a wild scream Lark had never heard come from a bird.

But it was Sackerson that held Lark's attention.

Sackerson was throwing men about, roaring at the top of his lungs. He raked his nails across men's faces and necks. He twisted limbs and growled in glee.

It was clear to Lark just then who the bear was.

It was Gary Sackerson.

They were simply outnumbered, however, and about the time Sackerson pulled his big pistols, other shots rang out, and it had a sobering effect. The Boys would not shoot their own.

It was all the distraction that was needed. Stu and his defenders were overwhelmed, and even Sackerson was brought to the ground.

Lark and Krystal were pushed around to join the others. After some kicking and cursing, Stu and Sack stood with them. They were back-to-back, facing The Boys. Stu's other defenders had accepted defeat and melted back into the mob.

Their ankles and wrists were being zip tied. Lark smiled at the woman attempting to tie him. "One of the few advantages," he smirked, referring to his wrist.

"Really?" Krystal said. "Cracking jokes now?"

"It's all I got," he replied.

"Last laugh," Stu growled. He resisted the people pushing him. They were being loaded into one of the FedEx vans.

Sackerson was not an easy fit in the doorway. Someone was pushing down on his head. Someone else kicked him in the back of the legs. He fell to his knees but turned for one last look outside. Past Lark.

"Now that's more like it," Sackerson beamed.

Lark turned to see what Sackerson was marveling over.

In the sky were three approaching helicopters. On the ground, snowmobiles and snowcats were rolling in from all directions. Every vehicle was shiny and black, government issue.

"Cavalry's here, kids. We're back on script."

Chapter 51: Sesquizygous Conductor

January 2030

Chris Fortune sat in the white wicker rocker watching the sunbeams glide across the floor, as if they were moving in a time-lapsed film. Once in a while, his brother Tristam would stir, roll over, then settle back down.

Otherwise, Chris was absorbing the peace of the sanatorium. He would breathe it in—the unnaturally clean, oxygen-enriched air—and let it pass from him quietly. In his days spent here with his brother, Chris had found his center of gravity. Here, time was a thought, a breath was a millennium, a day was the blink of an eye.

When evening came, he would unspool his thoughts into the room. In the dark, he and Tristam would have long conversations in their twin talk. No other being on earth would know what they spoke of. It was more intimate than sharing a womb, more expansive than dreams they shared.

Here with Tristam, he could blow out the most hyperbolic fantasies about space and time. He could tread on the edges of the universe and leave only his one set of footprints, carrying his invalid brother while his brother carried his burdens of heart and mind.

Even had they used English, Chris knew no one would follow them in their recursive treadmills of forethought and hindsight. They had modulated their conversation, even the tone of it, to a common whisper. No one could even discern two voices. They were one.

In this communion, Chris and Tristam strengthened one another. Chris's mind had expanded. His thinking was exponentially more vast than it would have been had they not maintained this ritual. Tristam, assumed to be catatonic, had learned to walk, talk, and lay aside his somnolent self for the length of these visits.

• • • •

CHRIS PUT THE LAST extraterrestrial pin in the fourth corner of the portal fiber he had hidden in the curtains. He briefly linked the loop and Tic Tac he had in his possession and was pleased to find it a perfect match of glowing blue. Satisfied, he stashed his end of the portal in his pockets and resumed his post at Tristam's bedside.

The conversation had been taxing on the two of them. Chris knew it was time to go when his brother curled up in a fetal ball and said no more. He pulled the blankets up around Tristam, assembled another Hot Wire, and examined it before dropping it over himself.

Over time, he had learned of three potential portal configurations. He named them after types of twins. The strongest bond was between two Tic Tacs that snapped magnetically, end to end. These were the ones Chris was using for *intentional* transportation. They were the Monozygotic, from one cell. He did not know if that was true, but these two acted as one most reliably.

The Dizygotic would share a lazier bond that was hard to see, yet no less potent. These were the unpredictable pairs he used in rigging Hot Wires. He had no idea which Hot Wire return field would be the destination. If they were up and connected, they were all fair game.

The last pairing configuration he had discovered he dubbed as Sesquizygous, "semi-identical," which had no bearing on their origin or composition, simply on the fact they were the rarest of twins, and so far, the rarest of Tic Tac pairs. These would snap together magnetically, sure, but then, like jumping beans, they would re-polarize and flip end for end. He kept them separated, for they had created quite a stir on his lab bench. He had only found a single pair of these, and he trembled at the thought of using them.

Now one of the Sesquizygous Tic Tacs was spun out and suspended in the curtains. He would keep the other with him, always, so that he might return to see his brother again no matter what might befall either of them... or so he hoped.

Chris let the white light lasso fall around him, and with it, his sense of foreboding fell away as well.

Chapter 52: Starkweather

February 2030

Stu knew The Boys would reject the idea that they were beat. Sizing up the vastly superior forces and firepower of the United States Government Special Forces, to a man, The Boys quickly loaded up and tore out, shouting "Next Time," and shaking their collective fists. The trucks roared away, grumbling all the while. Some exchanges of fire were traded between the government force and the locals, but it was just the occasional warning shot popping off.

This left Stu, Sack, Krys, and Lark standing by the wreckage.

The black vehicles glided quietly in to surround them tightly. "Electric," Stu scoffed.

"This does not look good," Krystal whimpered.

"Let me handle this," Sackerson said. He began bunny hopping toward the nearest snowmobile.

Stu did not like the look of it. Many guns were trained on them, from individuals with pistols to an overpowered gun he spotted in an SUV with a pop-up turret. "At the best, this is no better... wasting time. At worst, we're all gonna die."

"Don't be silly." Sackerson turned and said, "These are the better guys."

"Better guys?" Lark asked.

"Yeah. Now, *those* guys," he tossed his head toward the burned-out vehicle, "Those radio guys—" he hopped a couple of hops, "they're the bad guys." He hopped again. "These are the better guys." He turned to face Stu fully in his next hop, saying, "Us? We're the good guys."

At that, he tripped and flopped down on his back, but sprang back up to continue hopping, though simply hopping in place now, for the uniformed men had come to him.

"You're the one they call The Bear," a man surmised. He had not removed his snow goggles, so Stu could not tell much about him.

"Might be," Sack said, still hopping. "And you are?"

"Pendleton."

"Well, Mr. Pimpleton—"

"Pendleton," he corrected.

"Could you kindly release us?" Sack asked, turning his back to Pendleton and raising his wrists.

No one paid him any attention.

"Trucks are clear," one of the other men reported. "Four dead, and this one." He stood aside, and two more men dropped Mike Burns to the snow in front of Pendleton.

Burns struggled to his feet. Snow was caked on his belly. He half-saluted Pendleton, "Hello... officer... I'm Sergeant Mike Burns, Guthrie PD."

"What are you doing here?" asked another man, this one wearing reflective sunglasses and a pompom snowcap. "How's the police mixed up in this?"

"Obviously some local yokel, Forrester. He's probably one of the vigilantes," Pendleton said. "Isn't that about it?"

"He's family," Stu butted in.

Burns looked over at him and smiled meekly.

Pendleton sized up Stu, then looked at a bracer on his arm for reference. It had a little monitor like a cell phone screen. "You're the Wiebe kid. Stewart Wiebe."

"Yessir," Stu said.

"What did they want with you?" asked a square-jawed man. He wore a black cable-knit sweater, no parka, no snow cap, no eyewear. "Why are you out here?"

"Why were all 'you out here?" another man asked.

Pendleton looked at the rest of them. "Krystal Price," he read from his bracer and looked at her again. "And you're the one they were talking about on the radio, aren't you? Larkin Fortune."

Lefty nodded but kept his head down.

"And I'm Gary Sackerson," he said, bouncing back into view. "I've been protecting them."

"I see..." Forrester sneered. "Good job."

The last of the helicopters had landed, and more men were approaching. Stu shook his head at the show of force. What had kept them so long?

"We were in pursuit. Hostage situation," Burns offered. "Unsubs were holding two of the Wiebe family when their vehicle... exploded."

Everyone looked over at the vehicle for a moment, except Stu. He was watching the men closest to him. Even the ones with ski masks on were looking a little anxious, maybe trying too hard to look official as the helicopter teams approached.

"You and your 'boys' didn't do this?" Pendleton asked.

"No," Stu said.

"No sir," Burns said. "I think—"

"It just blew up, then?" square jaw asked. "Just like that?"

"*Detail*!" Forrester said, standing at attention. "Cameras down."

The men gathered there switched off various cameras on their helmets, body armor, and rifle sites. Pendleton receded into the group, and an older man approached. Stu recognized the suit from the Installation, Starkweather or something. The man removed an earpiece on a spiral cord and smiled at them grimly.

"You have my dad?" Lark asked before the man could begin.

The man took a breath, let it steam out of his nose. "Not at the moment, no," he said.

"Then where is he?" Lark sounded surprised.

Sackerson stopped hopping.

Pendleton made the slightest face that might suggest that was an inappropriate question to be asking.

Stu persisted, "Do you have Henny?"

"Kenneth Hinman," one of the flanking men offered.

"Yes, I know, thank you." The man cleared his throat. "Mr. Hinman fell in with the wrong crowd, it would seem."

"What's that supposed to mean?" Stu growled. "He's not with you?"

"Hardly," the square-jawed man said. "Dumb bastard—"

Starkweather made the slightest gesture, and two men broke off toward the man with the square jaw. He holstered his weapon and stood rigidly at attention.

"Do you recognize me, Mr. Wiebe?" asked the special agent in charge. "Starkweather."

"Sure." Stu shrugged. "I guess."

"You know I'm with the Installation, correct?"

"Yes."

"You know why I am here with these men, then?"

Stu glanced quickly at his companions. They had taken sudden interest in Sackerson's crow, circling overhead.

"You're a little late," Stu growled, and took the opportunity to dive forward to headbutt Starkweather.

The old man sidestepped, and another agent stepped in to clock Stu in the jaw on his way down. He fell face-first in the snow. He rolled over as someone kicked him in the ribs.

"Enough of that," Starkweather said crisply. Then, "Pendleton!"

"We're taking you back to the Installation," Pendleton announced, "where you will be fed, bunked, and sequestered safely."

Stu was brought to his feet, his knee bindings cut free, but they kept his hands tied behind his back. Lark and Krys were freed entirely. They were escorted to separate vehicles.

"Aww, c'mon!" Sackerson complained, for his bonds were not cut. Two men pushed him along and into yet another vehicle.

Starkweather was already returning to a helicopter, and two more men were guiding Stu to the same one, it seemed.

It was going to be an unpleasant flight.

Chapter 53: Through the Looking Glass

S hae was grateful when the technicians drew Dalton away. They were working on a hunch that, since the cameras were wireless, maybe they could get some reverse signal or something. She did not know or care. She was more of a hands-on empiricist. In her experience, hard work beat gadgetry every time. After walking off the entire house herself, she backtracked. The focus was room by room.

No one seemed to attend to the hallways, so she did.

The long hall she had been down again and again with Dalton yielded nothing. From boot print abrasions at head height, it was probable that the perp had done parkour jumps from wall to wall to swat out the lights. It seemed strangely playful too. He had been enjoying this far too much. Cameras were at each end of that hall, just little black buttons in the crown molding, and Shae smiled at one, thinking how odd that light smacking might look on film.

The other hall—the one that led from entry to back door, opened to the pantry and the upstairs—was virtually ignored. It had received the least damage from the break-in, and no one was examining it. This hall was paneled with thick walnut. It reminded her of a high-end attorney's office. The entire hall, floor to ceiling, was covered in random cabinet doors mounted edge-to-edge for that raised panel look.

"Anyone looked at comparables in the neighborhood yet?" she asked in the family room, where most of the activity remained.

A couple of people shrugged, but no one responded.

So, she did it herself. Even though she was out of her jurisdiction, even though it was a lame idea, Shae went door-to-door on a fact-finding mission. The neighbors who were at home grumbled when she flashed her badge but then obliged her request. A couple even offered her refreshments and small talk, mostly questions, about the situation.

She had six home tours, while ten other homes were not occupied. She confirmed what she suspected: identical layouts, identical builder's grade trim, identical fixtures, doors, everything.

It wasn't conclusive, but it was the lead she needed. Returning to Fortune's house, she walked it off again. Five of the six houses she had visited had full basements, while this one only had a shelter/mechanical room. None of them had elaborately trimmed hallways like the one Shae returned to explore. She ran her hands down the raised lips of the irregular panels, and she made a discovery.

She snapped off a little gasp when she learned one panel was hinged. Behind it was simply an empty storage cabinet. Nonetheless, it was something new, and she hoped to find the recording instrumentation, perhaps, behind door number two. Another cabinet door, one at floor level that extended up 3 feet, opened to a storage area under the stairs. It was full of empty moving boxes, broken down and folded up, nothing behind them. She closed this door quietly and looked up and down the hall discreetly. Whatever she was doing was likely being recorded, she knew, even now, so she did not want there to be anything fishy about her demeanor.

The other side of the hall hosted additional hidden doors and cabinets, all empty. She returned to the stairway side to discover a double-wide and doubly long door, fashioned from four cabinet faces. This clicked open when she pressed on the frame, and she stepped in immediately and shut the door behind her. Discretion be damned.

Detective Shae Ward had discovered a second basement!

• • • •

MOST OF THE ROOM WAS lined with shelves, and most of them were packed with random household stuff one might expect in any home. A portion of the shelving served as pantry overflow, it seemed, packed with bachelor foods like canned meats and freeze-dried pasta. A case of MREs was on the floor. None of that seemed odd. She had seen many Oklahoma basement shelters ready to ride out tornado season.

Shae noticed nothing had been damaged here. It had not suffered the senseless ransacking of the rest of the house. She wondered what all the devices were on the countertops. Some looked like toaster ovens and others like sonogram machines. Something looked like an old school Geiger counter. None of it was disturbed, but she got the impression things had been removed. Two bookends on the counter were left empty and apart. A drawer gaped open and empty.

So, maybe someone had been here, but had it been the destructive people or someone else?

Then she settled into the prize find: the monitors. They were on blue screens, and it took her longer than she wanted, but she soon had the knack of the system and was reviewing recorded footage.

Shae worked as quickly as she could, anticipating that people would soon miss her and become more diligent in seeking her out. They would find this space, and they would not honor the "first dibs" policy Briggs had bought into. State would not share.

She was impressed with how thoroughly Dr. Fortune had arranged his cameras and files. The default display was a collage of all eight camera views that ranged from the porches to cover every room in the house. She could click on any view for a zoom in.

She could scroll back along a timeline to revisit the scene before the damage. She learned to get more granular with the timeline and pull into focus the sequence of events she was after. Though she could not enhance the video quality, it was still informative.

In the video, the patio sliding door exploded, and the perp entered the kitchen. He immediately started tossing the place with no regard. He seemed intently searching for something, but he sought it out in the strangest of ways. He threw open the dishwasher, for example. "Who hides things in the dishwasher?" she said aloud. The man then wrenched on the washer, as if trying to pry it from under the counter. Giving up, he went on to rummage through the refrigerator, taking time to eat something that looked like a carrot. He pulled the fridge out of its alcove and then forcibly tossed it over and open. He examined the wall behind it.

Her neck tingled. The intruder was not looking for money or valuables. He was looking for an access point. He was looking for the very space she was in!

When he was in the pantry, tipping over shelves and kicking the mop boards, Shae was able to get a good look at him. The room was small, so the camera was close. He was a white male, easily 6'2", and lean. His face was lean, clean shaven, even his eyebrows were shaved. Though he kept smiling and perhaps talking to himself, he did not otherwise look to be without his wits. He looked nothing like a typical drug addict. He had on a Buffalo plaid Elmer Fudd hat, a black duster, and big boots.

His seemingly maniacal trashing of the house was to cover his tracks. She was becoming sure of it as she watched him work from room to room. He would thump at walls, rip up carpet, move large objects and explore behind them—all in addition to destroying everything in sight. He went about it like some frantic dance, and she was certain he was enjoying himself. His mouth was moving, but Shae knew there was no audio. He seemed to move in time to his mouth, and she was now convinced that he was, of all things, *singing* as he kicked doors, stripped beds, and did parkour in that other hallway.

When he cracked the safe, Shae replayed it several times. She wished so much that she could zoom in or pan around. She wanted a better look at his face. She wanted to see what combinations he was trying. That he tripped the safe in short order told her what she had suspected: the guy knew Dr. Fortune, knew enough about him that he had attempted obvious passwords, birthdays perhaps, or names.

He resumed his swath of destruction until he was visibly tiring, and that's when he did the strangest thing yet. Any robber would have left, lugging away whatever treasures he had come for. This guy, however, righted an office chair and sat down. He took off his hat, rubbed his scalp, and then crossed his arms and did not move afterwards. Who had that level of confidence and that lack of fear? It was as if he were waiting to be caught.

Tall, bald, tattooed. This was her perp. He *had* been here.

She kept the view of him on the big screen but fast-forwarded until something changed. Something caught his attention in the hall. He stood, this time being stealthy, and backed into a closet in the office.

A second man entered the office, and they fought. She stopped the film, opened up all the screens, and watched as the man came first into the paneled hall from the secret door, then made his way through the house. He was shorter than the intruder, but he was better built. He wore a cardigan sweater and slacks. He could have been anyone. Shae bet he was Dr. Fortune himself, for this man knew the house, and he was obviously shocked at the condition of it.

She resumed the video of the fight scene and noticed the ways each man moved. The tall bald one, the intruder, did not intend harm. Dr. Fortune, however, surprised her with moves she had learned at the Academy. The fight migrated to the kitchen.

"I'm not proud of this part," a voice said behind her. Shae turned slowly, catching the moment when Fortune had dropped the intruder, hard and fast. In the corner of her eye, she thought the screen blipped white, but it had simply reverted to the collage view.

• • • •

POLICE WORK IS MUNDANE. The Guthrie Police Department worked a homicide every other year. They averaged a robbery case every month or so. The crime index for her town was in the bottom 25th percentile for cities of the same size. In her entire career, Shae had never discharged her weapon.

She had spent endless hours in court, even more filing paperwork. She had commendations for what she considered trivialities like consecutive days on the job and years of service.

Still, Shae Ward had stayed sharp. She was the top scorer on their aptitude testing and term evaluations, always. She had the best stats and tightest patterns at the gun range. She could drop anyone on the force, she was certain. She had not let herself go, even after having two babies.

In the seconds she spent turning to face the man, she calculated. Her service revolver was on her hip, below counter height, and she would have to stand to draw it. Her backup was on her ankle, and that would be even slower to pull. Various things on the counter could serve as weapons, but they were at very close range, and even the time it might take to swing an instrument at the man would be far too long if he were inclined to shoot her.

She bit her lips together and fought back tears. She thought of Rob and the girls and of all the things she had yet to do with them. She thought of Dalton and all the others upstairs, too, and shuddered at what was about to happen.

Then, she inhaled, and did what she considered the smartest thing: she raised her hands and turned to face him full-on.

"Doctor Fortune!" she said, recognizing him.

"Let's keep it down," he shushed her, like a librarian.

He had on a heavy winter coat. His shoes and the cuffs of his slacks were wet with slush. He had no weapons she could see.

"Agents from every branch of law enforcement are right upstairs, sir," Shae began. "They want to visit with you, to clear this up and get on the trail of—"

"I don't need to visit with any of them," he said, "but I do need an accomplice."

"A what?"

Fortune smiled a faint half-smile, "And a confidante."

"What are you—Me? Why me?"

"I need you to reformat that hard drive," he said, glancing at the surveillance equipment. "And I need you to come with me."

"That's... that's out of the question. You need to come with me. Upstairs. We need to sort all this out."

Fortune shook his head. "Do it. Delete it."

She was running through options in her head. Destroying evidence was not an option. Information on that machine was vital to the case, as was his testimony.

"Can I... can we... take it with us?" she stammered. Apparently, he had some other entrance to this secret basement that had allowed him to come down unnoticed. The thought of taking his statement out in the van was appealing to her. She would have the case open and shut before all the other badges even knew what had happened. It made her smile just a little.

"Yes, sure. Just pull it and let's go."

Shae dutifully extracted the data port with some coaching. She was just wondering why he had not done it himself, being more familiar with his own machinery. When she turned back to ask him as much, she noticed a faint glow behind him, as if he were being backlit by a fluorescent light.

He stood aside, and she noted a thin strand of light, like the LED lights her girls had up in their room. This strand formed a rectangle the size and shape of a doorway.

"After you," he said.

Shae looked at him, picked up the hard drive, and did as he asked. She walked through the light like Alice through the looking glass.

Chapter 54: Men!

Krystal decided the only difference between the military thugs and The Boys might be the uniforms. Those in her Hummer were joking and bragging, like they'd bagged a deer. At least they had stowed her behind the back seat and not strapped her across the hood.

She was considering a private school, maybe a convent, where she could be done with men, once and for all. If she had learned anything in the last few days, it was that men were nothing but adrenaline junkies who just never listened.

Then, a guy in front of her reached back and handed her a Gatorade. "On the house, Miss Price."

"Thanks," she said.

"Sorry Cap stuck you back there. You comfortable enough?"

"Sure, fine," Krystal said. It was not altogether true. She twisted the lid off and took a sip. She expected to be repulsed by the stuff. *Salt water for jocks.* However, it was kind of refreshing. She took another drink. Then another.

"Good thing we stopped those boys, huh?" the guy said. "Looks like they were about to turn—"

Some commotion in front took his attention away. There was a round of laughter. Someone repeated a punchline. Then he turned back to her again. "Were they? About to turn you in?"

"I dunno," Krystal said.

"We'll make sure nobody gets to you, not the hillbillies or the others."

"The others... just who are they?" Krystal asked. "They're not with you, or the Installation, or the police."

"Oh," another man turned to say, "that would be classified."

"Classified!" the kind one laughed. "That would suggest we have our shit together!"

A couple more men laughed at that too.

"Don't you, though?" Krystal asked. She squirmed to her knees and held on to the back of their bench seat.

"Miss, we never laid eyes on them."

"We were just on orders to find you guys."

"And the kidnapper," the Gatorade guy added.

"He's not a kidnapper," Krystal corrected. "He's our friend. He's saved our lives from those other guys, like at least twice now."

Another one said, "Heard your friend called those other guys the Spooks."

"Are they spooky?" a third man smirked, from the middle row.

"Spooks—like spies," Krystal said. "They're always sneaking around."

A couple of them shrugged, as if there were always people sneaking around. The other guy in the back seat took interest. "What do you mean?"

"I mean, ever since the Guthrie Fall, there've been Spooks on us. It feels like they're constantly on us."

"On you and your friends?" he asked.

"Yeah."

Conversation went on and she explained the whole Guthrie Fall, what it was like to be there, how she had come into custody and later routinely returned to the Installation.

She learned her current escort was not some black ops unit, like Stu had said. They were National Guard. They told her how they had been brought in from all over the US overnight for this assignment. They were not much older than she was, Krystal was discovering. One guy was just married. Another had been at a nightclub when he was called up for action. Two of them were stationed somewhere (classified—*ha ha ha*) in Oklahoma. One man came in from so far away that he had not slept in two days. He was, much to her consternation, the driver.

• • • •

IT HAD BEEN SIX MONTHS since her last visit to the Installation. Krystal had tired of the routine and had finally come to just tell them whatever they already knew. In short, she was frank and honest. In the last two visits, they had only detained her for thirty minutes.

The questions always began the same way, with one of them asking her name, date of birth, all the vitals. Then the other would ask a series of questions that always ended with, "Is that right, Miss Price?" They were stupid questions:

"No one suspicious has approached you about the night of the Guthrie Fall, is that right, Miss Price?"

"You have not returned to the site of the Guthrie Fall, is that right, Miss Price?"

"There has been no contact between you and Mr. Fortune, right Miss Price?" With this, she could not contain herself and asked, "Which Mr. Fortune?" But generally, she was agreeable and efficient in her answers.

Her last visit had more of a sense of urgency to it than others. The interrogators were not working from computers or a list, and the questions were anything but routine.

"Has anyone threatened you lately, Miss Price?"

"Have you been feeling problems in your equilibrium?"

"Depth perception?"

"Smelled bleach?"

"Experiencing chronic fatigue?"

• • • •

THIS TIME WAS DIFFERENT even yet. Before, she was never left alone. Even when she needed to use the restroom, a female would accompany her. This time, she was never frisked or asked to change clothes. She was not kept waiting for hours on end.

She was not even in a familiar part of the Installation. There were no detention cells nor interrogation rooms in this area, but they did walk by many offices and labs. She was not volleyed between good cop and bad cop.

Instead, she was escorted to a conference room and instructed to sit at the end of the table. She was given another drink, even offered a snack. In only a couple of minutes, a man in a pressed white shirt and tie entered the room, showed his name badge to Krystal's guard detail, then dismissed them.

He did not sit at the far end of the conference table, as she expected; instead, he came right to her and offered his hand. "You must be Krystalline Price?"

"Krystal," she replied. Not even her mother called her Krystalline.

"I'm Dr. Benjamin Canole."

Ah, she thought, *their only hope.* She was skeptical.

She braced for the efficient question-and-answer mode that had earned her quick release before.

"I have a daughter your age," he said. "She's into tennis. Are you in any sports?"

"Golf," she said. She had played golf at first to humor her mother, but she lettered in it. They would know that, so why not tell them what they wanted?

"Now there's a game!" he said.

Krystal sat patiently. Most likely her mother was on site somewhere by now, or a car and attorney would be waiting soon. She was wondering what she would do next, whether she would help Stu find his mother or Lark find his father. Maybe she would jump through another teleportation hoop with Sackerson.

"...so that's why I'm so interested in what you may know."

"Pardon me?"

"I hear you've been in his house recently, so I am hoping you might tell me more."

"More about what again?"

"The way Chris is doing it," Dr. Canole was smiling broadly now. "What in the dickens did he figure out?"

"I... I don't quite understand," she said, flushed.

"He was just here a few hours ago. He just—appeared, you know—then had a coffee with me and asked me a few things. Starkweather came in like a wet hen, then POOF, Chris was gone!"

Krystal wondered how it was going to go with Stu and Lark. She worried Sackerson could not keep his mouth shut, that he would go on some big rant about the future.

"I'm sorry. I don't know what you're talking about."

"Candy?" he asked and fished a little box of Tic Tacs from his shirt pocket. He winked at her, glanced around the room, and said very quietly, without moving his lips, "from Chris."

He pressed the box of them into her palm.

Chapter 55: Reunion

L ark laid the ground rules. "We only say what we know they know, what we are okay that they hear, because..." he pointed around the room, "they're monitoring everything."

Krystal and Stu nodded.

The three of them were sitting in a research library at a round Formica table with chrome tubing for legs. Their chairs were boxy old utilitarian chairs, very retro. The floor was shiny green linoleum tile, and the rest of the furniture looked as if it were retrieved by a set designer for a 1960s office movie. It had to be the middle of the night, but no one was sleepy. Lark wondered if they pumped oxygen into the rooms.

Krystal was sipping on a pop.

Stu was dabbing at a wound on his cheekbone.

"Let's start with you," Lark said. "Looks like you have a story to tell."

"I fell getting out of the chopper," he said. "That's the official story, so that's what happened."

Krystal was clearly incensed by this, but she said nothing.

"I've been with Sackerson until they brought me in here," Lark shared.

"Don't they usually split us up?" Stu asked. "Why they letting us be together now?"

Lark and Krystal shrugged.

"When can we go?" he said, louder.

"I don't know Stu."

"And what the hell are they doing about finding my mom?" Stu said, a little louder yet, looking directly at the 'hidden' cameras.

"I wish I knew," Lark said.

Then it was quiet.

Stu was moving his tongue along inside his mouth, like he was feeling for missing teeth.

Krystal waited a bit for him, then asked, "So how did it go with Sackerson?"

"He was a little strange," Lark began, struggling for the right words. "I mean, he just came off this crazy fight, and I still don't know what happened on the way over here with him, but when we were in an interview room together, he was all smiles."

"He's a lot strange," Stu said.

"Was it his fake smile or a real smile?" Krystal asked.

Lark and Stu looked at each other, then at her. "He has more than one kind of smile?" Lark asked. He flashed on the full-toothed Cheshire cat smile that Sackerson was always making.

Krystal laughed a little. Even given the circumstances, it made his tummy do cartwheels.

"What did he say?" she asked. "When they questioned him?"

"You know how he always goes the long way around things? He kept doing that. It was really annoying the Installation guy."

"Did he share any... news?"

"Nope. Never explained a thing. Every question was answered with a question... or a joke," Lark shrugged.

"And you?" Krystal asked.

"Just the facts. Could have read them their own incident reports. We left before the gunfight at Mack's. We left the Wiebe place and visited Perry. We went to Norman, yes, then circled back around to the Wiebes, about when the demands were coming in. We rode with The Boys up until they decided to turn us in for that creepy radio message. Now we have about two hours until dawn left, and they're not doing anything."

"That was my story too," Krystal said.

"Same." Stu mumbled, "Pretty much."

"Meaning?" Lark asked, with growing concern.

"I told 'em about Henny, and I told them about how those guys in Norman threatened us."

"They also asked me..." Lark intimated, "about a train wreck in Perry."

"Huh," said Krystal.

"That is news to me," Stu said, as if he were reading a cue card.

They sat calmly, not speaking aloud, but their expressions were impossible to repress. Stu was angry. Lark knew he looked worried. And Krystal seemed eager to speak, but she was having trouble getting her thoughts together.

"So... they're really just keeping us here now for our own good?" Krystal asked, eventually. "Protecting us from... from whomever?"

"That's what they say," Lark said.

"Keeping me here is *protecting* whomever," Stu growled. "And it doesn't matter how long they keep me here. We will find those guys and they'll pay!"

Both of them placed a hand on his shoulder when he broke down in tears. Krystal was still eager to speak, but neither of them wanted to disturb Stu's sorrow.

When he lifted his head again, he looked possessed. "I need OUT of here!" Stu stood so suddenly his chair fell over. "What the hell TIME is it?"

Lark had noticed there were no windows, no clocks. The room seemed timelessly locked in the 1960s.

Stu pounded on the door then. "Let me OUT. We gotta find my mom, NOW!"

The pounding was quickly addressed by a group of soldiers who escorted Stu away. Lark heard him yelling all the way down the hall and out of sight.

Escorts were waiting in the hall for Lark and Krystal. As they were being led in opposite directions, Lark heard a commotion. He turned around and saw that Krystal had pulled away from her escort and was returning to him.

"I just wanted to tell you," she said, her eyes twinkling, "I met a Jedi!"

At that, they pried her away, leaving Lark both amused and confused.

Chapter 56: Confidante

When Shae was young, she used to love taking a bath, particularly the way the water flowed over her when she would submerge and emerge slowly. It was a very similar sensation walking through the light door, an almost-liquid-like curtain. Once on the other side, she stopped and gawked.

Dr. Fortune was right behind her. "Always important to move through," he coached. "Homegrown versions of these will slice you in two."

Slice you in two? That was not comforting. It might have been good to know before she had taken that first step.

She was taking in her surroundings, trying to place the location. She recognized it, but in the snow, and in the aftershock of teleporting, she was dumbfounded.

"Guthrie," Dr. Fortune clarified. "Mineral Wells Park."

She turned to look him in the eye. Nothing there but sincerity.

In an instant, she had moved from his basement in Norman to a park she knew! In a single step, she had traversed 60 miles. She gasped at the cold, outside air.

The lighted door frame was fading behind him.

"I... how?" She crouched and ran her hand over the snow at her feet. The chill of it heightened her awareness. The high cloud cover moving above and behind Dr. Fortune was convincing.

This had happened.

"I worked for months to recreate this very thing, and the first times I experienced it, even though I knew it was coming, I felt the same as you do now. It cannot be true, *but it is.* We have moved through space instantly. Miraculously."

A smile pulled at the corners of her mouth. She shook her head slowly, in awe at the magic of it.

"And in this little demonstration, Ms. Ward, you now have all the evidence you need, do you not, to be my ally? My confidante?"

She stood and turned another circle. Elements of the park were registering more and more. It was all "rezzing up," like one of Rob's video games. The gateway entrance. The gazebo. The Bedlam monument. The lake.

"This explains a lot," she smiled at him.

"Doesn't it?"

"More than you know," she said to herself.

"What's that?"

"The wires at the cafe and the car wash—they're doorways like this, right?"

"I call them portals, but yes. They are teleportation gateways. In one, out another."

"And that is how you have remained at large?"

"Yes," he said. "And it is, unfortunately, how others are moving about, I understand. Openly and without discretion."

"Like the man who broke into your house?"

He looked at her out of the corner of his eye. "Yes, I believe so."

Shae thought of the many reports she had taken in from witnesses, from the kitchen staff, even Davis Cole's unpublished alley report. She had written them all off as unstable, but now she knew otherwise.

She had seen it on video when the robber flashed into the kitchen. She sensed it to be true when Dr. Fortune had gotten the drop on her in his lab.

Now she had experienced it too.

"And this is what the Installation is all about then?" she asked.

"Let's walk," he said, and he took her arm in his, guiding her onto the lake trail.

• • • •

AN HOUR LATER, SHE was still finding it all hard to believe. Dr. Fortune had engineered a way to make random teleportation into practical transportation, for he had mastered a pairing arrangement with special materials. He had "spun out" (as he called the process) hair-like filaments from little white rocks (Tic Tacs, he called them) found at the Guthrie Fall.

They were not taken seriously by anyone else at the Installation, and when he was fired, he just took as many as he could get away with. He had spent the last year tinkering with them, and now he had a sophisticated network of these portals spread around. In just one day, he had used two tanks of fuel going farther and farther afield, hanging portals and testing them out.

"The miles don't matter. Travel is instantaneous. It defies all the laws of physics and reason itself, but teleportation is fast, free, and thanks to my research with pairing, one can *intentionally* move from point A to point B."

"So... they're connected, point A and B?"

"The portals at either destination are related to each other. If I keep a map of them, which I have been doing, then I know which connects to the next. If I set up point C near either A or B, then have D be another 100 miles away, then I can move fluidly from A through B, then C to D—all as simply as walking through doorways."

He explained the other ones again. He called them Hot Wires and said that they were *not* paired up specifically. Enter a Hot Wire and you might exit at any other Hot Wire portal rigged up anywhere. These were plentiful but impractical.

"Imagine that you enter a Hot Wire portal, dressed as you are now, thinking you might end up, say, in a nearby neighborhood or even a neighboring state." He shuddered. "You're dressed for it, but due to the randomness of the Hot Wire, you could end up in the tropics. And worse, you might have a terrible time getting home."

"Not only that," she said, "you might materialize somewhere you're not wanted, or somewhere you're not supposed to be."

"You might be perceived as a terrorist or a thief," Dr. Fortune added to her growing list. "Or..." he held up a finger, "in all innocence, you might accidentally spread disease. Say you're eating a mango in South America and absent-mindedly carry it with you when you pass into Canada."

Shae stopped walking and Dr. Fortune did too. "The other guy's using those, the Hot Wires."

"Yes, I have heard," he smiled sheepishly. "I can come and go and overhear quite a bit... plus I visited a good friend today and heard much, much more."

"So, have you heard your son might also be associated with the man who wrecked your house?"

"Yes," Dr. Fortune said, "and I hear they are both in custody."

"Your friend's well-informed," Shae said.

"He works in high places."

"You know that you're a suspect, too, particularly in the shootings in your own home. That same man who trashed your house, the one you fought with, might be the same one using Hot Wires and shooting people."

"He most assuredly is," Dr. Fortune said. He resumed walking, and Shae fell in step with him again.

"Doesn't that *bother you* that your son is with him?" she asked.

"You would have to know my son," he smiled. He cocked his head, "But something tells me he could not be in better company."

"Dr. Fortune, again, why me?" Shae asked. She felt inadequate at absorbing all this. "Why not take it all back to the Installation and give them this same demo we just had?"

"Why you? For one thing, you have a very analytical mind. I've been watching you. You really stand out."

"Thanks," she said, unsure of when or how he might have picked up on that.

"You have been on this since the beginning, and you would have pieced this together, even without our little talk."

"I would not have. This is—"

"Science fiction?"

"Yes, and... if I hadn't just now done it, I wouldn't believe it."

"You are empirical in your detective work, and you work outside of bounds. I know, for instance, you are the only law enforcement officer to have spent any real time with the Dollarhides. And you discovered my little lab. No one else has proven themselves so worthy, Detective Ward."

"Well... I... I'm methodical. That's how cases get solved." Shae felt herself blushing.

"Methodical," he chuckled. "You are also known to 'jump the shark' as they used to say, again and again. That's not methodical. That's intuitive."

"I might jump to conclusions now and then."

"And yet, you don't go blathering it all over, causing false alarm and widespread panic. "

"Well, in this instance," she said, "I'm still trying to figure it all out."

"And I will help you. I can get you to key players in strategic places... the keys to the kingdom. But I need you as my confidante," Dr. Fortune smiled. "Are you up for it?"

"A confidante, as in somebody you tell things to? Isn't that what you're doing?"

"This is just what we can *prove*, what we can lay our hands on," he said, gesturing at a park bench that had been cleared of snow. "I would like to tell you more. I need to tell someone more."

"Why not your friend at the Installation?"

"He's too involved. Try as he might, he's a scientist working on a government contract, and he can't quite be trusted with all this. He can't be expected to embrace all this."

"Why not just talk it all into your cell phone recorder?"

"You're more credible than a recording. You're a decorated officer of the law," he said. "And you're local, trusted, and dedicated."

"Okay, okay," she sat down beside him. "What else could you possibly tell me to top all this?"

"I can get you access to my son and the others, including your suspect."

"You can?" Shae squinted. "But... they're at the Installation."

"And in exchange, I need you to be my vault. I need to tell you my worst suspicions and greatest expectations for these." He held out a little container of Tic Tacs. "For the future."

Shae shrugged. It seemed like an opportunity she could not let pass. Then again, something seemed familiar about it all that she could not quite put a finger on.

"Okay," she said at last. "I'm in, under one condition."

"What is that?" he asked, his interest piqued.

"We have to get my van back here in time for dinner," she said.

Chapter 57: Secure

Context File
   What the locals called the Installation was actually the Guthrie Fall Asset (GFA), under the jurisdiction of the 137th Special Operations Wing of the Will Rogers Air National Guard of Oklahoma City. Since its establishment, October 11, 2027, guardsmen had been stationed on site. However, as of February 15, 2030, that provision was superseded by a platoon of federalized Special Operations Wing commandos. This released the lax guardsmen of duty.

In transferring responsibilities, new protocols for egress and access were instated, much to the dissatisfaction of the civilians and science officers who had been on the site for some time.

The GFA was a 70,000 square foot rectangular brick of a building that was erected in less than a month. Formed of reinforced precast modular concrete units, with the rest of it poured by a massive 3-D printer, the facility was rated to withstand 200 mph tornados, although that had not yet been tested. The twenty doors were the weakest aspects of the building from both storm safety and overall security.

Prior to the February 15 transfer of power, only the main entrances were secured, and that was by key card and closed-circuit camera. The main gate was more a formality than anything, but the kiosk was always manned. Now every major entrance also had an armed guard, and the main gate was now fortified with attenuation barriers, extra fencing, and armed guards.

For a research site, even a top-secret facility as the GFA was purported to be, the new security measures seemed like overkill to those who worked there, even to those who were stationed there to guard the place. Even tighter security, however, would have had little effect on those who infiltrated the GFA.

Chapter 58: Space Candy

Stu was not good company. He was not a cooperative captive. He did not feel the Installation was doing him any favors, "protecting him." He wanted out. He wanted to find his mom and sis and just go back home. He wanted to talk revenge with The Boys too.

Instead, he had been stonewalled.

No matter how much he hollered or fought, no matter who he talked to, no one would listen. "We're doing all we can," they would say, or "We have this under control."

Meanwhile, some assholes were holding his family hostage.

Killing his family.

He had been going through this cycle since they brought him in, a painful cycle of anger, then sorrow, and then amplified anger because of his sorrow.

Since he had been a problem, they had taken everything from him and made him wear an orange jumpsuit. Even this was made of paper, and he knew all the reasons from lectures received during his previous stay. No belts, laces, metals. Anything he would be given, from clothing to a sheet, would be lightweight fiber designed to tear under load... as in hanging oneself or using the cloth to strangle someone.

Stu's frustration was coming to a peak. He had grown up farming, and he intuitively knew when the sun was coming up.

Dawn.

They were going to kill his mom or his sister any time now.

The door to his cell clicked open, and several armed men entered. Starkweather was front and center.

"You again!" Stu grumbled.

"Good morning, sunshine," Starkweather sneered.

"Piss off."

"Is that any way to treat an old friend?"

Stu felt his muscles straining. He was trying to contain himself. He knew that anything else would be painful.

"Men!" Starkweather said over his shoulder.

The door opened again, and a cart was rolled in. It looked like a room service cart, covered with a white cloth, arranged plates with bounties of food. A big silver plate, covered with an inverted chrome bowl, was in the middle of the arrangement.

They parked it between Stu and Starkweather.

"Go ahead, look under the cloche," Starkweather said. "Check out the main course."

Stu looked at him, then at the cart, puzzled.

Finally, the soldier snapped the chrome bowl away, revealing a tablet device on the plate. "Voila!"

Stu stepped closer and saw live footage of his mom and sister hugging each other. Mom was crying, but she looked relieved. Sissy was clinging to her, bawling into her jacket.

"Pan out," Starkweather said into his sleeve mic.

The image grew broader, pulled away from his family to encompass a surrounding group of soldiers dressed like those in his room. In the foreground, on the ground, were two other men in a pool of blood.

"You got 'em!" Stu exclaimed. "You saved them!"

"All in a day's work, Wiebe." He slapped Stu on the shoulder. With a very uncharacteristic smile, Starkweather joked, "Now eat up so you and me can go another round."

"Thanks..." Stu said, handing the tablet back reluctantly.

As everyone filed out of the room, one lingering soldier paused and set a blue racquetball on the corner of the food cart. "It helps," he said, and followed the others out the door.

• • • •

STU ATE ALL THE FOOD on the cart, even the garnish slice of orange. He was so relieved he found he could breathe freely again. He wanted to talk to Krys and Lefty, even to Sackerson, and tell them all the good news.

After the food was gone and someone had rolled out the cart, Stu laid on his cot and his thoughts returned to the remains of his dad and granddad. There would be hell to pay, he would see to that. Whomever was behind all this was going to regret it.

He was squeezing the racquetball so hard it should have popped. "Who does this?" he asked himself. Before they'd kidnapped his family, Stu might have thought it was the government. They might have been spurred to take their usual harassment to a new level.

Not likely, though, for even they weren't dumb enough to shoot up a restaurant. All the creeps out here at the Installation were soldiers, and they lived by a code. It wouldn't have been them.

Someone new was doing all this. Someone desperate.

Stu began tossing the ball up and catching it. The repetition of it helped him think. Everything had gone nuts about the time Sackerson showed up, so something about him had brought these guys around. From the moment he'd been in town, Sack had been fighting Spooks. He'd called all the shots that sent him and Krys and Lefty on one wild ride.

He sat up and started throwing the ball at the wall and catching the rebound. Sackerson's teleporting ended up being the real deal. He had transported them *and a Suburban* with one of those stupid wires. Even though they wanted to get to Doc Fortune, it seemed the Spooks had left him alone before Sack came along with his teleportation tricks.

Whomever it was wanted it all, that was obvious. They wanted Fortune, Sackerson, and the kid... all to themselves.

They said on the radio that they wanted Lefty too? Why him? They'd said nothing about Stu or Krys—just Lefty. Sack acted like he needed Lefty too, but why?

Everything that held them together as a group had started that night the hippie kid lost his hand. Sackerson had said something about how Hot Wires and Tic Tacs had taken Lefty's hand into some unknown place or dimension or something.

The racquetball was zinging hard into the wall with loud popping sounds now, then ricocheting back fast. "Tic Tacs!" he scoffed. "Space candy."

Chapter 59: Ally

February 2030

Chris Fortune had tired of driving. The tedium of traffic and stops at intersections—it was all becoming an inconvenience. Worse than anything was the *time* that conventional travel cost. It was 45 minutes from Guthrie to Norman, straight down the Interstate with no stops, but it was less than a heartbeat to port there. He was getting spoiled, and he had only been porting for a few days.

He told Shae as much, but she had good counter arguments. "I'm old school, Doc. I still think the journey's as important as the destination," she said. "And besides, it feels like I've spent a lifetime behind the wheel of my squad car. It's as comfortable as an old pair of shoes. I think people are going to need cars for a long time."

"Think of the carbon footprint cars make," he said. "Even electric cars are costly to the environment. Manufacturing a car is costly to the environment. And that's to say nothing of roadways and all that goes with them."

"What are you saying, that we'd not have cars, period?"

"Exactly."

"We're a car culture. My brothers run a custom body shop out in California, and they can't keep up with the demand." Shae said, "I can't see a time when we'd choose Hot Wires over hot rods."

"Ports could make travel possible for everyone. Even the most impoverished person could someday be freed from the shackles of their environment."

"'Freed from the shackles...' You've cooked all this up in the last couple of days?"

"I've had a year to think about it." Chris smiled. "It's all I can think about."

She was thinking about it. He could see the wheels turning. They had talked the whole drive, and it was a conversation he wished was not ending soon, but then, it was not. Not if she remained his confidante.

"So... what if this takes off? What if, say, my husband and I wanted to eat out? We could teleport to—

"Theoretically, anywhere on earth!"

"Paris or something like that?"

"For dinner, and be back to tuck in the kids."

She smiled at that.

"Date night doesn't have to begin and end at dinner, either. You could watch the sunset on the Pacific, enjoy the cityscape from the Empire State Building, and swim in the gulf with dolphins... and still be back in time for that bedtime story!"

"That sounds like an itinerary Rob would dream up."

They had cleared Oklahoma City. They were over halfway to his house. Chris had something else he wanted to share.

"I know I can trust you, Shae," he began. "With my life."

"What? Really? We hardly—"

"Some people, I believe, are natively good. It's your nature, and you don't stray from it. Ellen, that's my ex, she's like that too."

"I've been a cop too long to buy that, Doc. I've seen lots of good people do really bad things."

"But there's so many others who are good. Always."

"Maybe," she said, "but I'm not even sure that's me."

"I am." He took a deep breath and extracted a cellophane envelope from his pocket and handed it to her. "Know what this is?"

"One of those Hot Wire things?"

"It's one of those you can pair and count on." He took another envelope from the breast pocket of his coat. "This is the partner port."

"Okay..."

"I want you to set up that port somewhere for me. Do not tell me where."

"Set up... I don't even know how to set it up... and why wouldn't I tell you about it?"

"See those little black pins in that envelope? Those are, well, they're special pins that you just tack up, then hang the filament on them."

"And that sets up a teleportation machine? That easy?"

"It's that easy."

"What if my cat or something jumps through it?" she half smiled.

"Somewhere safe, remember? Private. And please, don't pin it on a wall. That makes for an abrupt entry."

They both got a chuckle out of that.

"And the reason I don't want to know the location is... well... if ever I use this port, it means I'm in trouble. Someone on the other end might be trying to forcibly extract information from me. It might threaten your safety. Are you willing to do this for me, Shae?"

"Forcibly extract information—you mean—*torture* you?" she asked. "Over this?"

"I have a feeling that whoever is chasing me doesn't share my morals, if you know what I mean."

She was biting her lip. She looked the envelope over closely as she was processing. Chris knew she would not take this responsibility lightly. He was glad about that. He was relieved at her answer. "Yes, I will. I'll hang it and forget it and protect us both that way."

• • • •

THEY WERE PARKED BEHIND her vehicle, which was around the corner from his place. The sun was low in the sky, smothered by gray clouds. Chris shut off the engine and enjoyed the silence between them. Finally, he spoke, hoping to lift the burdens of their heavy conversation. "Sporty van."

"Yeah," she said. "I'm sure they've run the plates, even sitting back here. I'm sure they are being very thorough."

She was all business... not gaining altitude. He tried again. "Want to race back to Guthrie? Your van versus my rental?"

Shae turned to him and shook her head no. "You're not going back to Guthrie. You're going to lie low here, aren't you?"

Chris smiled. She was that savvy.

He reached into his coat to extract a thick envelope and handed it to her. "This is what I promised. Keys to the kingdom."

"What?" She unfolded the metal hasp and peered inside.

"There's a blank proxy card, see? And a guest ID, only not like the ones they used to give at the gate. Ben says this is like an all-day pass. You're already signed in."

"Signed in, where...?" Shae began. "Oh! At the Installation. This gets me inside?"

"Better yet, you have an appointment. It's all set up."

"What do you mean?"

"You're now Lark's attorney. Court appointed, of course."

"Attorney?"

"You want to see him, right? You have questions? My end of the bargain."

"Yeah, but won't they be looking into my records? Won't they figure out I'm not—"

"Records are fixed. Ben took care of that. The fact is, a couple of research nerds can do amazing things on a computer, things no soldier's going to think twice about."

"Dalton said they had Troopers and Feds and Special Ops all on this—"

"They do, but this is a little thing. They won't suspect this. Besides, you'll be in and out before they even smell your perfume."

"I don't wear perfume," she said, defensively.

"You do now," Chris said. "It's all in your profile." He tapped the envelope. "You might want to stop in OKC and get some professional clothes."

"I have the clothes..." she said absently, reading over her profile.

"You're good. You guys planned all this out before you even spoke with me? Before you even knew I'd sign on with you?"

"Like I said. It was a safe bet. You're one of the good guys." Chris smiled, and she smiled back, looking up from the paperwork.

"Astonishing, really. Height, weight, eye color... you have all this right. How'd you do that?"

"Records," he said. "Science."

"Okay, Doc," she said, collecting her things and opening the door. "I guess the rest is up to me. Good thing I took that acting class back in school!"

• • • •

AFTER SHE GOT OUT AND safely on the road, Chris took the car for a few laps around his neighborhood, constantly looking out for anyone suspicious. There was one squad car parked out in front of his house, but that appeared to be it. Chris doubted that to be true.

After all the turnout earlier, he suspected there might be a man or two inside, maybe even someone patrolling the neighborhood, just as he was now. They probably had the entire area rigged with surveillance devices.

He sighed and made another pass.

Somehow, he had to get to his Tic Tac horde in the basement wall, and his precious gift box of paired ones... unless they had already discovered it all, which he doubted very much. If he could take all those and then go somewhere, they'd never find him... just the thought of it made him grin openly.

Chapter 60: The Mission

T he spy had been told that the GFA security system was almost entirely meat-based. The facility did not have motion sensors, infrared detection, or night vision cameras... not even the slightest external surveillance cameras. Instead, there were soldiers, actually National Guardsmen, and as the spy had learned, they were only Air Force pussies, even at that.

They were armed though, and they could surely pose a problem should the spy slip up in the least. He was very aware of that. It had kept him hunkered down in the snowbank behind the cement barrier for far too long. His clothes were soaked, and he was freezing, but he had a mission to complete.

The spy was not only let down by the lax security gadgetry; he was also unhappy with his choice of apparel. He was wearing black, from his sneakers to his snowcap, so that he could blend into the night. The coveralls he wore were too tight in the shoulders—too tight all over—and he worried it might restrict his movement, should he need to break out and tackle anyone headlong.

He was even more unhappy with the all black ensemble now, for it was daylight, and he was afraid he was too obvious in the snow. He wished now that he had worn layers, not only because it was cold, but because any good spy would have been prepared and simply stripped out of the black layer only to have on a stark white, or snow camouflage, outfit underneath.

The spy cursed himself again for not calculating how very far the GFA was from where he parked. It took him forever, due to the snow, to cover that distance in stealth.

So, there he was, studying Door 8 with a toy periscope from behind the cement embankment. This short wall surrounded the building ten yards out. They said it was to stop terrorists from crashing into the Installation. The wall was an obstacle, but the spy had prepared for this. He had packed the periscope, some dental mirrors, binoculars, a flashlight... even some energy bars.

He had thrown in nun chucks and brass knuckles for good measure.

He was pouring sweat, despite the cold. Traversing all that snow had been exhausting. He took a gulp of Gatorade and resumed his observations. Door 8 had had no action of any kind in the last 90 minutes. Snow outside drifted up against the building and door. The spy was undaunted. Oklahoma snow could drift right back in place. Door 8 might have been accessed just before he arrived on the scene.

In his recollection, this door was one which the men often used for smoke breaks and, conversely, to get some fresh air. It opened onto a hallway that adjoined the room where his target would be staying. He was sure of it.

His mission was simple. Infiltrate the Installation, locate the Asset, deliver the package, then get out. He was certain he could do all that as sneaky as a ninja.

The spy double-checked his watch. It was a dial watch that had special features ranging from a camera to a code breaker to being waterproof to 200 meters. It was a gift from his direct report. He pulled off his ski mask and made a quick video: "Captains Log, 9:43 a.m. I've been in position now for over two hours. No activity at Door 8. I'm gonna make my move at 10 hundred hours. Stay tuned. Out."

He huffed and scrambled to his knees now to look directly over the barrier at Door 8. He had a pry bar in his duffle, and he fished it out, hefted it to appraise the weight of it. Best $30 he ever spent at Harbor Freight.

The spy zipped up his coveralls and pulled his ski mask back on, taking care to align his eyes with the holes. He zipped his duffle.

Then, as if he were doing drills, he rolled over the concrete attenuation barrier and army crawled the distance to Door 8. His watch read 9:59. The spy got to his knees and wedged the tip of the pry bar into the door frame and put his weight behind it. The door gave way with remarkable ease. The doorknob assembly seemed to be an everyday household model.

He whipped the pry bar up and spun inside. His memory had failed him. Door 8 opened into a mechanical room. A very large air handling system was humming in one corner. A complicated water manifold was on the opposite wall. The room was cluttered with boxes and discarded office furniture.

The spy opened the exterior door and looked at it again. Then he pulled back his glove and examined the number he had written on his palm with a sharpie. This was Door 8 alright. His palm, however, read a blurry 13.

He let out a big sigh and relaxed. Easy mistake, he said to himself. Stenciled numbers. The spy was happy that this door had not opened onto a busy corridor, for then he might have had to muscle through the soldiers on guard. He imagined a violent fight scene with himself, center stage, fending off soldiers with his nunchucks, or swinging his pry bar madly, all with incredible speed and absolute silence.

Someone was opening the interior door. The spy dashed behind the air handler, squeezing in between it and the wall as best he could. Now his black clothes were spot-on, for he could blend into the shadows. A worrisome idea jolted him, however. *What if his socks were white?*

One soldier traipsed into the room, and he was carrying a rifle.

The soldier crossed the room to examine the door ajar. He went outside for a better look around. The spy was counting on the drifting snow to have covered his tracks. He bolted for the interior door and darted down the hall in search of his target. His sneakers were anything but sneaky, for they were squeaking on the glossy floor. Behind him, he was leaving wet footprints.

Fortunately for him, the target was behind the third window he peeked into. He tried the knob, surprised to find it unlocked. He threw himself inside and shut the door behind himself, careful to stand out of sight should anyone else look in the door glass.

Krystal turned from whatever she was doing. She was about to scream when the spy pulled off his ski mask and begged her in a raspy whisper, "No, no! It's just me!"

"Kenny?" She was clearly surprised and relieved to see him. Though he could not risk taking her away to safety, he was here as her hero, anyway.

"Yeah, it's me," he said with a smile. "I ain't got much time, neither."

"I thought you were—beat up or something. Where have you—"

"I got this for you," he said, wrenching a phone from an inside pocket. "It's a beater."

"Burner?"

"What?" he said. "Anyway, you keep this hidden, but keep it with you all the time, okay?"

"Why?" she asked, screwing up her face.

"I'm a double agent, okay?"

"A double..."

"Yeah, and if there's trouble, you'll be notified."

"What kind of trouble, Kenny?" She just wasn't getting it.

"Any kind of trouble."

"Does Sackerson know you're here?"

"Sack's in on it," the spy said, narrowing his eyes. "He's had me working both sides of the aisle, all along."

"Both sides of the..." she tipped her head. "Kenny, what's this all about?"

He chuckled. *Spies don't give away all their secrets.* He had to give her something though, so he said, "He paid me to nark you out in Perry. He paid me to fake you out at the cabin. I ride with the Spooks, but just to scope them out. I'm there if ever Sack needs my advice."

"Has he needed your advice?" she asked, puzzled.

"No, not yet." The spy was reserved. He crossed his arms over his big chest. "But if he ever does, I'm his man."

"And this phone?"

"That's all my idea. So was breaking in to see you. All my own purgatory, see?" He pulled back on his ski mask. Then in a whisper he added, "No one knows I was here," he waved his hand between them as if he were blanking out her memory. "You *never* saw me."

Krystal nodded, looked first at the phone, then back at him.

"Okay?" The spy stood there a little while, thinking maybe he would get a kiss.

"Ooooohkay," she said eventually. "So, I guess you should be going now?"

"Yeah. I suppose so." The spy shuffled his feet, looking at his watch. It was now 10:05.

• • • •

BY 11:00, HE WAS BACK in his mom's Civic, eating an energy bar. Mission accomplished.

Chapter 61: Twenty Questions

S hae hated impractical shoes, but she had to look the part. They filled with snow, and she almost broke off a heel just crossing the lot. She was wearing her Valentine's dress and over it, a long black wool double-breasted trench coat that she was surprised she had not donated to the thrift store years ago.

The guardsmen at the front doors each took a door and together swung them wide for her. No ID check, no passes or permits. So far, so good. She approached a reception table, careful not to let her heels slip too much on the wet floor.

The clerk was in fatigues, but she was all business. She looked up from her computer station and raised her eyebrows. No "Hi, how are you?" or "State your business." When Shae simply looked back at her, waiting, the clerk nudged a clipboard that was on the counter between them.

"Sign in," she said, then returned to her monitor.

Shae shrugged and signed in, using the pseudonym assigned to her. Attorneys had already come and gone for Stuart Wiebe. Another had signed in and out for Krystal Price. Shaelyn North fit right into this parade.

On any other day, she and the clerk would have been sisters in arms. Shae knew the sexism this woman had to endure daily, and she knew the disdain that clerk, that *soldier* who had earned her stripes, was harboring for the fancy-dressed girly-girl in front of her. In her younger years, Shae had felt similarly about such women, primped and primed to look like models they could never really be.

Shae stood to her full height and cleared her throat.

"Enter the time," the clerk said, then sighed with exasperation when Shae looked for a clock. "It's 11:30 a.m."

Shae dutifully marked the time, then extended the clipboard. The clerk glanced up at her, then immediately back to her computer screen. "Take a seat," she said.

Shae walked slowly around the foyer. The tile floor was high gloss, pristine condition...slick. Though the entire facility was not even two years old, and in her reckoning new, it was outfitted with military surplus furnishings, right down to bulletin boards and (empty) trophy cases.

Before she could figure out how to sit in that dress gracefully, another woman approached. This guardsman was probably thirty, easy-going even in the way she moved. "Morning!" she said, extending a hand. "Welcome to Guthrie Falls." She even knew the locals' joke, that this place was a town in and of itself, named after the meteor shower.

"Good morning," Shae said, shaking hands.

"You're here to see the Fortune boy?"

"I am," Shae said. "I am his attorney."

"Sure. Sure. This way," the guardsman gestured, and Shae fell in beside her as they strode down the hall. "I'm Staff Sergeant Washington, by the way."

"Shae... Shaelyn North," Shae said. "Are you career?"

"Oh no. Lord no." She smiled, "I'm with a PR firm in OKC. Got called up for this when it first started, before the building was up."

"A lot's changed," Shae said. She had toured the site when they were first fencing it off. She had stood watch at that fence before the military even got involved.

"Everything's changing. Just this week we cinched up. Nerd wing is *not* happy."

"Nerd wing?"

"Ah, we just call them that to mess with them. 'You here to see Doc Fortune's kid, right? I really like ol' Doctor Fortune." Washington glided them down two halls and stopped at a door that looked like all the other doors in sight. "This is you then. Think you can find your way back?"

"I do, thank you," Shae said. She waited for Staff Sergeant Washington to unlock the door, but the guardsman just turned and walked away, humming.

The door was unlocked, and Shae let herself in. "Larkin Fortune? I'm your attorney." She smiled and held out her hand.

Then she withdrew it quickly.

"I didn't order an attorney," he quipped. He was tall, almost a head taller than Shae, and he had a full head of unruly red hair. She could see his father in him, the set of his nose and eyes. "You must be court-appointed?"

"Court... no, no." She stepped in close. "Your *family* asked me here."

"My family, eh?" He was suspicious. "My mom couldn't afford you, and my dad doesn't even know I'm here... so... try again."

The room reminded her of a dorm room in college. They stood in the middle, having something of a face off. Shae knew it would be out of character, but she stepped in Lark's personal bubble. "Your father *does* know you're here."

He stepped back then and scanned the room, causing her to do the same. He caught her attention and nodded toward a small black plastic bubble. Shae nodded, approached the bubble and looked it over. Then she fished her car keys from her coat pocket and pried the bubble from the wall. She addressed it directly then, saying, "This is still America, assholes. Attorney-client privilege." Then she pulled the bubble until the attached cables snapped free of it.

"Humph!" the teenager said, then slumped back on the bed.

Shae stood, waiting for someone from the Installation to take her away, someone on the other side of the camera, but no one came. Finally, she asked, "Is that the only one?"

He pointed to an open drawer, and the contents made her smile. Five or six other bugs and cameras had likewise been found out and dismantled. She tossed hers in with the rest. "I'll take that as a yes?"

"Yeah, but at least you had an excuse. Legal precedent and all that. I'm just sick of being watched all the time." He smiled for the first time, and now she could clearly see the resemblance to his father.

"Just in case," she said, "can I sit by you? Can we talk in muffled whispers?"

"You mean, spy talk?" he chuckled, patting the bed beside him. "Sure."

She gave up on gracefulness and just flopped down beside him. Everything orthodox was out the window as soon as she had pulled the camera anyway. Doc Fortune had coached her on this, that the boy was a bit of a rebel, so play to it.

"So, what're you in for, kid?" she asked, having a little fun with him. "Crimes against the state?"

"Originally, I was on a date," he began, but when this piqued her interest a little too much, his ears turned red, and he switched gears. "I'm here for my own protection, they say."

"The ol' lock up the victim instead of the assailant routine," she laughed. "Yeah, I know that one."

It was quiet for a beat.

"You're a cop," he said then, and Shae felt a little flushed. Even more quietly he said, "I waited on you, at Mack's. You had a little Christmas party in the back room with the rest of the police department."

Shae sat up then, not knowing quite where to take things. She had forgotten about that party. This kid was good.

"Still," she said finally, "your dad *did* send me."

"Why?" Lark asked.

"I wanted to ask you some questions."

"You and everybody else!" he crossed his arms. "And here I thought you were different."

"I can be different," she said. "I'll ask you only yes/no questions. How's that?"

The smile returned, this time with caution. "We can play twenty questions."

She thought a bit, looking at the ceiling for inspiration. "Do you know why they want you?"

"The Spooks?" he asked for clarification.

It made her smile then. "Yes, *the Spooks*. Do you know why they're after you and your dad?"

"That's two questions," he said. "But, for the record, yes and no."

"You know why they're after you, then?"

"Yes."

"Does the other guy know why they're after you?"

"You're not very good at this. Who's the other guy?"

She thought through her notepad. "Sackerson, the Bear."

"Yes."

"I think they are after you to get to your dad, but you don't yet know why. Is that about right?"

"Qualified yes," he smirked. "I don't really know why. No. All I know is what Sack says, and when you meet him, you'll know why I don't know anything, really."

"Does this Sackerson say your father's in danger?"

"Yes."

"Did he tell you that your father had made a big breakthrough?"

"Yes."

"We think that's it. We think they're trying to get their hands on his breakthrough."

"That's not a question, but yes."

"Do you know what that breakthrough is?"

"Yes."

It was so challenging, playing his way, but she was determined to win him over and to learn more. Shae licked her lips and asked, softly, "Is it related to... travel?"

He nodded his head.

"Unconventional travel?"

He nodded again.

"I've recently traveled with your father, myself," she offered. "Have you?"

"No," he said.

"With Sackerson?"

Lark thought for a moment. "No... not actually."

"Been to Norman lately?" she asked with care.

"Yeah," he said coyly. "Traveled in a Suburban."

They shared a secret smile.

"You know any good cryptographers? Because if you did, you could just read all about this for yourself, you know."

"Oh?" she said.

"Tell him all his journals are out at Stu's."

"Really?"

"Yeah, in a couple of suitcases in Stu's cabin. In those roll-on type suitcases you take on a plane."

"Have you told anyone else about this?"

"No."

"Why me?"

"That's not a yes/no question," he said impishly.

"Do you trust me?"

"Yes." He said it as if that surprised even him.

She pulled in close enough to whisper in his ear. "He's working on getting you and your friends out. Said you're just sitting ducks here. He told me to tell you to do whatever Ben says. Okay?"

"Yes. Okay." The boy's eyes were wide now. "When?"

"He didn't say," Shae said. "Soon."

They looked at each other for a while. It was like telepathy, yet no ideas were exchanged. Just feelings. Sympathy. Trust.

Finally, she regrouped. She wasn't just here as Fortune's ambassador. She wanted some answers.

"This Sackerson, is he safe enough?"

"Yes," he said at first, "and no."

"No?"

"Nope." Lark Fortune bounded up off the bed, beaming. "That was your twenty questions. Thank you. I'll be here all week."

"Lark. I *really* want to know everything about this Gary Sackerson. Where's he from? Why's he here? I think you're the guy to ask, Lark. I think you're in the know more than—"

"You wouldn't believe me if I told ya," he said.

"Try me," Shae replied.

Chapter 62: Good Show

Lark let out a huge sigh and put his back to the door when the cop left. He hadn't realized he was holding his breath, like a middle-aged guy, sucking in his gut. He relaxed his shoulders and let his head loll around on his neck a bit.

He had never entertained a career in law enforcement, but then, he'd never entertained a career in anything. Statistics were solid on the fact that most people change careers a dozen times, and people in his age group seldom held a job over 10 months. When the school hosted career days or aptitude tests, Lark always hacked them, having his fun when the test would tell him he should be a ballerina or work the bomb squad.

Had he met Shae North—or whatever her name might be—before, police work might have made it to his maybe list. All the other lawmen he had encountered had been self-righteous and far too by-the-book. Then again, he had to admit, all the other lawmen had been men.

He wondered what she might *really* be like. There were layers here. She was posing as an attorney, and if she was worth her salt, she had been posing some for him, too. What did they call that in psych class, modeling or something?

Lark didn't really care at the moment. He had had a close encounter with the first cop he could really respect, and it didn't hurt that she was beautiful, too.

He replayed their encounter in his head. She'd played his games. She'd risked being tossed out on her can when she jerked the camera from the wall. He smiled, remembering that. Even if it was all for show, it had been a good show.

He thought about her questions. Some, like those about the situation that had led him here, were predictable. Others, the discreet ones about porting, were well-crafted and let the both of them learn a lot between the lines. Most, however, were related to Sackerson. This made sense, for a Guthrie cop would be addressing first of all a Guthrie crime, like whatever had happened at Mack's.

Then his thoughts went to her reactions to all he shared, the whole info dump he poured out, about Sackerson. Lark really did believe she had 'traveled' via Hot Wire, for otherwise, his story would have registered as a tall tale. He knew from her reactions, however, that she was the real deal. She had teleported, and she believed his every word... even the stuff about time travel... even the potential that he and Sack were *related*.

"Related," she had repeated. Repetition must have been her best technique for drawing out people, for she used it all the time. "Well, that doesn't work for me. You're an only child, and even if you weren't, your folks aren't old enough to be his parents. He's also too old to be your son, even if I did buy into this time travel thing."

"What if I told you he was me? Aged to perfection."

Lark was proud of that quip. He was thrilled with her laughter. From their whole hour together, he would file that laugh and the way she wiped tears from the corners of her eyes. He thought even then that she must have been overdue for a good laugh.

"I haven't met the guy, but if he's your idea of perfection... well... I think I like current-day you better."

"Future-me has both hands though," he had said. *He is whole.*

"Ah, but what is the sound of one hand clapping?" She smiled at him, continuing her Zen master/Yoda shtick, "I think I'd be content as you are, young padawan."

He asked her a question then, that had been burning a hole in his head since Mack's. "So what if he is me, you know, down the road... is that inevitably me? Do you think people can change?"

"And more," she added, "can a time traveler change history?"

It was that kind of talk that had elevated their conversation far beyond anything Krystal Price could think about. Shae North was sharing ideas with him that he hadn't even entertained. His own mom wouldn't have had that level of mindful dialogue with him. It made Lark wish he had had an older sister. It made him eager to visit with her again.

Lark forcibly turned his thoughts to the things he had learned from their visit. His father was not just wandering about with his head in his books. He was aware of Lark's situation, and he was doing something about it. His father's obsession had paid off, it seemed, though the payoff had mixed results.

More and more of the things Sackerson had said seemed validated now, for it was a matter of fact that teleportation worked. It was obvious that it was being explored by his father. And it was, without a doubt, the reason the Spooks were suddenly coming out of the woodwork.

Lark had also learned that his hunch about Ben Canole was accurate: an inside man. Not only that, but Lark had learned through casual exchanges with his guards and inquisitors that Canole was the top civilian here.

He realized then that his father's strategy was very carefully arranged and balanced. He was in hiding, yet he had powerful players helping him. People had to believe in Dr. Canole. They had to believe Shae North was an attorney. They had to have confidence in the military guard. It was important that nothing wonky upset the balance of it all.

He studied the drawerful of cameras and mics and was struck by something else. What had changed here? Why didn't they keep him in the detention room, like before? Why didn't they go off when he and Shae had deloused the place? "Destruction of government property," and all that? Even his door was not secured, not by lock or guard.

He thought maybe they had bigger fish to fry. Then he pondered that very saying: *When you're frying fish, do you ignore the small fish and focus on the big one? What was a bigger fish than the catch of the day, the fugitives from justice?*

Lark had heard the argument that they were being held at the Installation for their own good. The Special Ops guys weren't saying much, only that they were "detaining them at the most immediately accessible government stronghold." He looked around his room, and he thought about the rest of the place. It did not seem like a fortress to him, even though he had heard the whole thing about it being a tornado and bomb shelter.

Besides, if the Spooks could port in and out of places, how could foot-thick reinforced walls possibly protect anyone?

Chapter 63: Crazy Eights

Krystal sat the phone on the table in her room. She was sure it would only be a matter of minutes before some overzealous soldier would dart in and take it away. After all, they had probably apprehended Kenny just moments after he had left her room.

Time passed. A lot of time passed. She was getting hungry for dinner and checked the phone's display. 15:45. She sighed with exasperation. Why was it set to military time? She did the math, figured out it was 3:45, and sat then at the desk, holding the phone idly.

Kenny had covered the camera lenses with nail polish, it seemed, and that was alright with her. She had become just suspicious enough to think of the phone as yet another surveillance device. How could she disable the mic?

She took the case off the phone. It was a good quality case, and removing it was no simple task. As she worked at it, she decided the case was likely worth more than the phone. At least, that was her conclusion from the limited apps she had seen on it. She found a little wire and microchip stuck inside the case. The way things were going, nothing much surprised her anymore. She was sure it was another tracking device, so she promptly flushed it down the toilet and resumed her work.

The phone was actually the very latest model, refabbed to look like a junker. Had she the time and interest, she could have unlocked and loaded a nearly infinite number of apps. Outside the case, it felt sleek and new in her hands, and she was growing to like it.

16:00 and still no one had taken away the phone.

She shrugged her shoulders and risked a phone call to her mother. No one answered, of course. This was an unknown phone.

293

Her mother was a busy woman. Krystal cleared her throat as her mother's voicemail message droned on.

"Mom. Thanks for Earl. He was out this afternoon, and we filled out paperwork. I'm okay. Things have been crazy, but I am okay. Please don't get too upset. They're treating me well here. Even brought me a TV, and now this phone. Call if you want to talk. Love you."

She clicked off and again sat the phone on the table, now sure some sophisticated system had noticed the outgoing signal. Surely now many soldiers would kick open her door and take that phone away.

By 17:00, she was bored. Nothing on the television was relieving her boredom either. She decided to make something happen. Anything.

Out in the hall of doors, she began knocking on each one in passing. In her wake, doors would open behind her intermittently. People would stick out their heads, spot her and frown, then return to their quarters. These people, every last one of them, looked like some kind of science geek. Goofy glasses, frumpy hair and clothes... most of them in their 30s, she guessed.

One door, however, opened to reveal Lark Fortune.

"Krystal!" he said from down the hall behind her. She turned, and they smiled at each other. "What are you doing?"

He caught up with her, and they made small talk as they walked the rest of the corridor. Looking behind her, she guessed it to be about half the length of a football field, maybe more.

They found the library again, and a friendly guardsman there agreed to go get Stu Wiebe for them.

"It's like the Twilight Zone," Lark said, when they were alone inside. "Does this seem anything like before?"

"No," Krystal said, glad to hear someone else putting her thoughts into words. "Not at all."

"I mean, there's more soldiers, but—"

"But less security."

Lark smiled. "They don't even care that I tore out their cameras."

"You what?"

"Took out all the bugs and cameras and everything—and they don't even seem to notice. I took a stroll, maybe an hour or so ago, and no one even cared. It's like we've always been here or something."

Krystal shook her head. She wanted to tell him about her visitor and the phone, but she was sworn to secrecy. Instead, she said, "They brought me a television."

"A television!" Lark was obviously jealous. "Did they bring you a masseuse and some of those guys that fan you and feed you grapes, too?"

"Attendants," she fancied the word. Some day she hoped to have attendants.

"Whatever," he said. A moment later he asked, "So... are we all over the news?"

"Not a word, not even on the local channels. Even the train wreck has fallen out of vogue, and that was what—yesterday?"

Lark shook his head. "Twilight Zone, just like I said. One minute we're fugitives and outlaws. Next minute, we don't even make the news at all. They didn't even talk about the Wiebes?"

"Not a word. I finally just flipped to the shopping channel."

It was quiet between them for a longer stretch. Lark perked up and shared, "I met my attorney."

"Mine came out today too. Injunctions to sign. Statements to take. The usual."

Lark seemed especially amused.

"What is it?"

"Aww, nothing," he said. "We didn't do any of that. She's just building a case."

"It's a little early for that, isn't it?"

Just then Stu came in. He was smiling brightly and looked genuinely happy to see them.

"Hey guys!" He patted Lark on the back and gave Krystal a quick hug. "Guess you heard?"

Krystal shook her head.

"Mom and Annie—they found them and they're alright!"

Krystal and Lark both celebrated with him as he recounted the story of his big breakfast and surprise. About the time that was all played out, there was a rap on the door. Several people brought in plated dinners for them, complete with table service, napkins—even a candle.

Stu dug right in.

Krystal, likewise, could not resist. The meal was a scrumptious salmon on cedar plank. She tasted a delicious soy mustard glaze. It was served with rice pilaf and a side of steamed mixed vegetables. She sampled it all, then noticed Lark had not touched his food.

"I'm telling you," he said, shaking his head, "Twilight Zone."

· · · ·

WHEN THE FOOD HAD BEEN polished off and conversation tapered off, Krystal suggested they play a card game. She had found a deck of cards on the library shelf. Stu was characteristically competitive, even at Crazy Eights. What Krystal paid more attention to, however, was how very capable Lark was at playing with only one hand. She had never thought of it before. She had never really thought of any of the things he must have had to do with just one hand. She tried not to stare.

After two rounds, Lark motioned them to come in close. He was still suspicious of someone listening in. That much was clear when he leaned in, his eyes darting from face to face, and he whispered: "We're going to get out."

"Released?" Stu said, a little too loud for Lark's preference.

"Of course, we are, probably tomorrow. The law is swift to—"

"Another way," Lark confided.

"What are you talking about?" Stu asked, shuffling the cards.

"There's an inside man," Lark said, "working with my dad."

Stu scoffed.

Krystal did not. Despite her big talk, she knew it could be days before her mom could leverage anything, especially out here, where even the feds were involved.

"When?" she asked.

"Dunno. I haven't even seen the guy yet. You have though."

"What guy?" Stu asked.

"The Jedi?" Krystal asked, keen to be on the inside scoop again.

Lark nodded.

"Aw, for crying out loud," Stu said. "Who?"

Chapter 64: Homecoming

C hris felt he could not wait any longer. He needed to get into his basement lab, but he did not have the paired portal. It was back in Guthrie. From his room at the OKC Super 8, he lassoed up a random Hot Wire and took his chances. Random porting, do your worst!

He was suddenly in a pitch-black room. It felt bigger than his basement, and it sounded big, too, by the way voices echoed off in the distance. He stood stark still, in case he might stumble on something and give away his position. Eventually, his eyes adjusted, and he found himself in a warehouse. High ceilings, large pallet decks all around the walls, cement floors. He was curious just why Sackerson would have placed a portal here. He felt around for the wires, dangling, but they were nowhere to be found.

Chris shrugged and slowly, cautiously, made his way to a wall at the end of the large rectangular space. An odd idea came to him that this could be the lower level of the Installation, and that made him want to explore even more.

The wall had a very large garage door, but next to that, a standard industrial door that he gently tried. It opened onto a much smaller space that was lit at the far end. He caught motion and voices there, so he took cover behind the crates and machinery in between.

This room smelled like solvent and oil. It was some kind of machinist's shop. In the low light, he came to recognize lathes, grinders, welders. He crept closer to the lighted zone, and as he drew nearer, he heard more and more of the conversation.

"...at this too damn long already."

"Nothing. That's what we've accomplished..."

"Gentlemen, the enemy of victory is mediocrity," the voice of a leader said over the others. "Mediocrity and impatience."

"And we cannot afford either," another voice stated flatly.

Chris strained to hear more. Someone was continuously concerned with being found out. Another voice was repeatedly negating what others said. He could hear that just in the man's tone of voice.

"Hey, I do not care," someone said. Chris could see he was getting up from a seat at the table. "I came here to do a job. A real important one."

"It just sucks!" a booming voice said. "Bad enough we gotta hide out all the time, but we're missing what made the 20s great!"

"Beer."

"A good porterhouse steak!"

Chris was watching the men at the table as they came into view as he rounded machine after machine. They looked very much alike. There were seven of them, and they all had short cropped black hair. They all wore identical clothing: grey suits, white shirts, black ties. They shared features variously, like blood-related family at a dinner, not identical, but obviously from a very strong gene pool. He was coming to think of them as cousins.

Then he tripped over a misplaced tool. The tool, a large wrench, spun just enough to clank against the leg of a nearby lathe. He froze.

"Driving! I'm having a..." the man was hushed by his colleagues. They all were standing now. Chris was crouched low, taking cover behind some crates, holding his breath.

Chris was frantically trying to assemble another Hot Wire. He had to get out of there, and fast.

The men were fanning out, pulling weapons. One called out, "Benson? That you?"

He received no answer.

Chris had one end of the wire affixed to the Tic Tac, but his hands were so sweaty he was continuously dropping it. He knew he was making too much noise in his struggle, but he was desperate.

"Whoever you are, you're outnumbered. Give it up and show yourself."

Finally, he had it. The Hot Wire was warming up fast when he heard something behind him. A man kicked out at him.

"Found him," shouted the man behind Chris.

On impulse, Chris whipped the Hot Wire into a big loop and swung it at the kicking man. It instantly cut through his leg, severed his torso from his pelvis to his shoulders. That part of him disappeared in the Hot Wire's flash. The rest tumbled down all around Chris, causing him to cry out.

The Hot Wire was still aglow, however, and much as he dreaded doing so, he stood up and spun the lasso overhead. Shots were being fired, loud and fierce.

Then it was silent. His eyes adjusted to the blinding snow. He was in a white field. Trees lined the perimeter. He was standing in a big splash of blood. Body chunks, still dressed in the cheap gray suit, were piled at his feet. He retched but immediately broke out into a run.

PT had always been easy for Chris Fortune. He was a natural athlete. Even into his 40s, he was active, playing Ultimate Frisbee and cycling long distances. He ran full tilt, not really sure what he was running away from, other than the remains of who he assumed to be Benson.

Then his mobile chirped.

He did not even slow down to extract it from his pocket.

Shots were being fired again. He saw bright flashes of white, washed out some from the snow, but they were teleportation flashes, he knew. Flashes were now happening in front of him as well as behind him. Bullets whistled past him.

The incessant phone was chirping again.

He tapped his earpiece. "Might as well stop running, Dr. Fortune."

A cloud of snow puffed up right in front of him, a stray bullet.

"What?" he huffed as he ran. "What do you want?"

One man flashed in front of him, and Chris just bowled him over and kept running, full force. As he ran, he was again struggling to get a wire and Tic Tac together, fearful that it might dice him up if he did it incorrectly.

"We can trace you. Stop trying to escape," the phone voice said.

He ran as best he could, holding his arms out in front of him, opening the Hot Wire portal as wide as he could manage. Another shot zinged past his ear. He dived headlong into the portal.

. . . .

CHRIS FORTUNE FOUND himself in a spot that he had prearranged. It was just outside Ellen's apartment, in the parking garage. Though it burned his hand, he grabbed the filament and jerked it down, wadded it up and ran. Maybe they would not trace this one, he hoped. If they did, at least it was unusable now.

Bright flashes like lightning scorched his vision. He ran on blindly, crashing into the stairwell and feeling for the handrail to scale the stairs.

"We could split up. Some of us go fetch your ex-wife too," the headset threatened.

Chris had his sight back, and he knew where he was going now. He had also learned a thing or two about porting. Hot Wire ports were indiscriminate, porting him from any Hot Wire to any port, be it paired portals or not. They were device-agnostic. He had set this port. Someone else had rigged the Hot Wire in the field.

A bullet cracked into the cement of the stairwell and peppered him in the face. It stung like buckshot.

At the top of the stairs, one man had just flashed into being, and Chris shouldered him over the top of the retaining wall. He did not stop to listen as the body hit the parking lot three floors below.

He ran hard for the other stairwell and elevator alcove. It was only two hundred feet but could have been miles. His right lens on his glasses was cracked from the stairwell shrapnel, and he was feeling increasingly disoriented... but he had to make that elevator. He had mounted a port there.

Chris was nearly there when his feet were knocked from under him. He fell headlong onto the pavement, scraping his palms and cheek. His glasses now were lost to him, but he did not care. He scrambled up, learning he could not put weight on his left foot. A glance at it told him he had been grazed by a bullet.

"You are outnumbered, Dr. Fortune. Stop running."

He did not. He vaulted into the elevator shelter and ported to his backyard shed. Chris threw up again. He did not know if it was the pain in his foot or the over exertion. He didn't have time to think about it. He kicked the door to the shed open and ran out through the Suburban-sized hole in his fence.

It seemed to take more and more time for them to catch up to his location, particularly when he ported from one Hot Wire to another. He had a theory to test, if only he could keep ahead of them.

"We don't want to kill you. We simply want your invention." The static on his headset congealed to say. "We want your schematics."

"I don't have anything," he yelled, his voice raspy.

"We know differently."

He wanted to tear the earpiece away and never hear the voice again, but it was valuable to know when they had ported into his latest location. He theorized that there would be no signal if they were not nearby. His cell phone was lost in one of many pockets he did not have time to explore, and he bet they were dialing him in via Bluetooth—or something like it—directly.

Once in a while, he would turn to glimpse his pursuers. They did not seem phased by the running. It was always as if they were gaining on him, almost to nab him, when he would throw another Hot Wire lasso and port out of reach.

He appeared in the Installation and immediately regretted it. He did not wait for them to pursue him in here but dove right back into the port he had just entered from.

"Mistake!" he grunted aloud as he doubled over in a powerful abdominal cramp. He felt stuck in between ports for an instant. His head was swimming.

He hoped it might confuse their tracking, maybe not even register the Installation port. He tumbled in a slushy alleyway on the outskirts of Guthrie. His heart was beating hard. He was panting. His throat burned and his foot was a bloody, throbbing mess—but he was close to his goal. *At least they're far from Lark*, he thought, *and from Ellen. And the Installation, I hope.*

He ran a good half mile before he heard the voice again. "How do you hope to evade us? We're better equipped than you. We know this system. You're a Neanderthal, Fortune. You don't even know what you're doing."

He cursed.

He sobbed.

He kept running, even when he could see the flashes of them porting in nearby. He kept to the alleys of the old residential neighborhood, hoping to draw less attention, to keep others safe from the constant gunfire.

Finally, just ahead, he saw the park. He had come up via the least direct route to Mineral Park, hoping if not to throw them off, then at least to make it less obvious. If they were tracking his ports, they knew the one in the gazebo. He intentionally avoided going anywhere near it.

Instead, he ran flat out toward the playground.

A man in a gray suit flashed in between him and the equipment. He was raising his gun toward Chris.

With a guttural curse, Chris dove the distance between them and drove the man hard into the ground. Then he was up again, closing the gap to the giant caterpillar equipment. Made from a series of old tractor tires, half buried, it was a great crawl-through for kids, and it had been for decades. The tires were spaced a yard apart, painted varied hues of green as they had been replaced at different intervals through the years.

With all his might, Chris tried to pick up a last burst of speed.

A bullet pierced the tire he was nearing, but he did not care.

He dove headlong into the caterpillar, into a series of Hot Wires he had strung inside of each tire. If he had not pushed himself hard enough, had he not dove far enough, any one of the Hot Wires could have sliced him in two as he fell to the ground.

Chris winced and squeezed his eyes and entire body, bracing for the final pain. Instead, he met a sudden and unforgiving impact with the ground. It was now warm. He was on carpet. He was whole. But he was sick. Very sick. He vomited again and wished for a moment that he had died.

He rolled over on his back and laid there, taking in his surroundings. Everything was lavender—from the ceiling, which featured hand painted clouds—to the curtains. The room was lit by small lamps, one stationed at each bedside. Posters of astronauts and animated cats covered the walls.

The door to the bedroom burst open and framed the person entering in bright hallway light. "What the hell!" she shouted, flipping the light switch.

Chris Fortune shielded his eyes from the light but sat up and made himself known with a wave.

"Doc Fortune?" Shae exclaimed.

"This! This is your idea of hiding the port?" he panted, then flopped flat on his back and groaned. He could only hope those six successive ports had toasted their tracking entirely.

"I was in a hurry," she said, apologetically. "I-I had to fetch groceries."

"Honey, who's your new friend?" a man asked casually from behind her. He was bouncing a little girl on each hip.

"Rob, meet Dr. Chris Fortune," Shae said. "Doc Fortune, this is my husband, Rob."

"Pleasure," Chris managed, still trying to control his savaged breathing.

"He smells bad," one of the girls said.

"He's leaking on our floor," said the other.

"So..." Rob asked, "staying for dinner?"

Chapter 65: The Siege

Another blast shook the walls of the Installation. Stu knew the weapon well. It was the cannon The Boys had been lugging around with them for years. The civilian in charge of the Installation had received a phone call an hour ago that shot everyone into high gear. It was a threat to the facility, and they took those very seriously. That man had also rounded up the kids and Sackerson and taken them all downstairs to shelter. Starkweather had retrieved Stu from the basement, and now Stu knew why.

They stood with a contingent of soldiers on the flat roof of the facility, taking it all in. Trudging through snowdrifts, they moved close to the western edge. The walls extended a yard above the roof, providing something of a parapet. Special Operations guardsmen were stationed all around this roofline, aiming at the instigators below.

American flags were hoisted from most of the vehicles. The Boys had parked at every odd angle behind the cement barrier surrounding the building. Some trucks, like the one sporting the cannon, were backed up to the wall.

Two large dozers were approaching from the north, slowly rumbling across the field toward the Installation.

Stu followed Starkweather on around to the east wall. Below, a man stood in a pickup bed with a megaphone on his hip. Stu knew him by his hat. It was his cousin, Keith Wiebe.

A mic click chimed loudly from an enormous bank of loudspeakers mounted on poles at each corner of the roof. They reminded Stu of the speakers on the football field. Starkweather spoke into a handset, and after a brief delay, it was broadcast loudly for all: "This is an Air Force research installation under the jurisdiction of the United States Government. Cease and desist immediately."

Below, several of The Boys shouted back slurs and blew raspberries.

"They're not going to listen to that," Stu advised.

"No?" Starkweather squinted at him. "Got a better idea?"

An empty beer bottle cleared the wall and tinkled across the roof before settling in a snowbank.

Keith Wiebe offered the official response from The Boys through his megaphone: "We don't recognize your authority. Vacate or die."

"Commander," someone said, marching up double time. Stu recognized him as Pendleton from just the day before. "Craft are hot, sir."

"Put them up, Pendleton. Keep them out of range. They're worth more than this whole pissant complex."

"Yessir," he said and ran away, shouting commands to others.

Stu walked over to the north wall. The heavy equipment was not far out now. He dreaded thinking about what they were going to try with it. Starkweather joined him there. "Really. Do you have any ideas, kid?"

"You could let me talk to them, maybe." Stu shrugged.

"Protocol," Starkweather protested. Then on his mic he said: "You will be rounded up and summarily charged for committing an act of aggression on the United States. Return to your homes and we will not pursue."

Stu thought the offer was poorly timed with the launching of the three intimidating helicopters that roared up over the roofline. The wind generated by them alone was blowing off seed caps and cowboy hats below. The choppers hovered overhead, then rose much higher and circled, kicking on dazzling searchlights.

It was sundown, and the lights of the Installation were blinking on too. Altogether, it cast The Boys in an eerie blue white that washed them out some. It reminded Stu of scenes from C.O.P.S. when crackheads would be chased down by similar lights.

• • • •

MANY MORE ANNOUNCEMENTS were made about protocol and many responses returned from below, but nothing changed. When the dozers arrived, however, Stu pleaded with Starkweather. "C'mon. I have a bad feeling about this...sir. Let me give it a try."

Starkweather looked down at the dozers. They were Caterpillar JD-40s, and he looked to know their power.

"Go for it," he said, "but just know I can cut you off at any instant, if I feel I must. This all has to go down... correctly."

Stu cleared his throat and clicked the mic off and on twice. "Guys!" he said. His voice echoed over the fields. "Guys, it's me, Stu."

A squawk from the megaphone was followed by, "We gotta take your friends, Stewie. Uncle Darryl says so!"

Stu took a few stumbling steps back from the wall. *His dad?*

Starkweather shook his head. "Bullshit."

Someone humping a lot of electronic gear was approaching. He was wearing a big headset and a specialized helmet.

"They're misinformed, sir." The man turned quickly to Stu to explain further, "I'm in Comm. This is all over the news, all over the web." He held out a tablet that displayed a newscast with his father talking. The captioning displayed over the news ticker was ranting about the rights of the American people. Stu felt tears welling in his eyes. He fought them back. A lump was aching in his throat.

"It's an old school deep fake, but it's been tricked out. Our boys haven't seen anything this good."

"Who's doing it?" Starkweather asked, "Who the hell's behind this?"

"We don't know, sir," the Comms officer said meekly.

"Tell them it's fake," Starkweather told Stu. "Tell them—right now—it's all bullshit."

Stu stood up and wiped at his eyes with his knuckles. He looked out over the wall at his cousin, up and down the way at the others. He pocketed the handheld then and hefted himself up to a sitting position on the wall, his boots hanging over the edge.

"Keith, that's not dad. That's some tech fake out."

The boys were shaking fists and calling out. Several revved their trucks and launched clouds of diesel smoke. Rolling coal.

Blasting over the loudspeakers, the voice of the Comms officer stated, "What you have seen on social media and television today has been a very professional rendition of a deep fake. Video and audio are altered and synched to—"

The cannon blasted the east wall again. Surely, if successfully aimed at the doors, it had blown them wide open. Stu worried about those guarding the doors below. The reverberation had nearly knocked him off his perch.

"Guys..." Stu started. "Boys... Dad's dead. You saw him for yourself. Everybody in that 'burban. Remember?" There was grumbling and discussion barely audible above the rumble of diesels and helicopters. "That's some real assholes, anyone that would make that fake of Dad. It's... it's a sacrilege."

"Those guys who took your mom and sis demand we give up your friends, Stu. We got no choice." It was the deep, powerful voice of the fire chief. He needed no megaphone. "Family first."

Stu shifted, so he could directly address the Chief. "They're safe. Air Force saved them this morning."

This caused a lot of commotion below. "Lies," was what Stu heard most of all. "You're a stooge, Stewie!"

"Boys," he said, now almost yelling into the handheld. "Boys! This can't end well. Look up there. Fighter choppers." He was down from his perch now, marching along the inside of the wall, gesturing wildly to them below. "Stand down. What could you possibly hope to do here? Die martyrs?"

Now the curses and barbs were more profane and volatile. More beer bottles were being tossed up on the roof. One bounced off the helmet of a soldier near Stu. A few of the Boys popped off guns, up in the air, three pops, the final warning. Stu had trained with them. Three pops was the last chance.

The other rumbles were drowned out now by the two dozers. Stu admired the sound of the turbos. They sounded like jets on the runway. He looked at Starkweather wearily.

Then Keith Wiebe said it for the rest of the Boys. "Dig 'em out, Boys, dead or alive!" He did the family 'whoot whoot' then added, "For Aunt Grace and Annie!"

The dozers rolled up big clouds of black smoke and charged into the building, alternating in 1-2 punches. Men on the roof were struggling to keep their feet.

Starkweather wasn't worried. He was angry. He swiped the handheld from Stu and switched channels. "Shut 'em down," he commanded. "Every one of them."

• • • •

A PAIR OF SOLDIERS hoisted enormous weapons over each of the four walls. Stu was yelling for them to stop, but he could barely hear himself over all the roaring engines and gunfire from below and the helicopters descending from above.

As if they had it synched up somehow, all four wall cannons and all three of the chopper-mounted cannons fired at the same time. It made the choppers rock back and forth from the blast. The walls and floor of the Installation trembled.

"Percussion cannons," Starkweather explained. "Sonic warfare." The gunfire and bravado, even the dozers, were all silenced now.

"And EMPs. Laser point accuracy. We can kill their power, down to wrist watches and cell phones, and never miss a beat in our ranks."

Stu looked below. The Boys were collapsed on the ground, curled up like babies, hands on their ears. "Effective and non-lethal," said another man nearby.

"What about pacemakers?" Stu said with a start. "I know for a fact there's three ol' boys down there with pacemakers."

"See for yourself," Pendleton said. Soldiers were darting around below, man to man, checking them, reviving them.

"Strap 'em up," Starkweather said over the loudspeaker. "Then haul off the trash."

"Strap them up?" Stu repeated. "Haul off the trash?"

Starkweather strolled away.

Pendleton explained, "In this case, he just wants them off our land. We're obligated to restrain them and tow their vehicles off site. In this case, they'll probably hog tie a few, for good measure."

The helicopters passed over one more time, then settled back on the helipads. Stu followed the last of the guardsmen inside.

That, he thought to himself, had been close.

Chapter 66: Televangelists

Context File
Trial runs were so terribly unpredictable that test subjects were most often drawn from death row inmate volunteers. In the United States, ten percent of prisoners on death row typically volunteer for execution. Initially, twice that number volunteered for port tests. Most of them were never seen or heard from again. The few who returned suffered horrible symptoms. Common side effects of large-scale, highly repetitive porting were: nausea, vomiting, nasal congestion, mouth dryness, acute sensitivity to sound and light, weakness, exhaustion, organ failure, psychosis, amnesia, insomnia, extreme sexual appetite, or lack of sexual desire, and anal leakage. Some who ported too much—a measurement that was never clearly established—experienced paralysis, brain damage, irreversible coma, suicidal feelings, extreme paranoia, rapid aging, intracranial hemorrhage, mania, or seizure disorders.

A very few who seemed resistant to the torments of porting were relegated to every kind of testing and questioning. Those who told researchers what they wanted to hear—wild stories of how fantastic porting had been—found their sentences revoked and they walked free. One in a thousand became seasoned celebrity porters. These men and women could port with impunity, seemingly unaffected by the harsh conditions they were subjected to. These people were referred to in a few publications as "Televangelists," as in teleporting champions (evangelists), and the term stuck.

The Televangelists title was not far off the mark. They were all flamboyant, outspoken advocates of porting, *and their voices carried.* Funding was increased for porting. Public interest continued to soar.

When a Televangelist ported into town, large crowds gathered with questions. They had been places and seen things that no one could imagine. They were excellent storytellers, and when they were not, as they were after all death row criminals, they were managed by firms with excellent promotional engines.

Most Televangelists traveled in tight-knit groups. They were often packaged on tours together, and even though they were violent inmates, they tended to get along famously. Literally famously. Many of their relationships grew beyond platonic. Some married and quit "the life." Others found the thrill (and profit) too hard to walk away from.

Televangelists often had a spokesperson from their ranks or hired someone to do their press releases. These people would also call crowds to attention, prompt audiences to file to the mic with their questions, facilitate panel presentations, and pass the collection hat. In the tradition of carnivals and sideshows of old, these spokespeople were known as "Barkers."

Once in a while, a Televangelist and Barker would fall in love and marry. The most famous of these were renamed after a pair of gangsters of 100 years ago: Bonnie and Clyde. (Though their real names are lost to history, they were rumored to be Mary Beth Scranton and Lloyd Smith, both previously and separately sentenced for crimes against the state.) In their professional lives as Televangelists, Bonnie and Clyde were experimental thieves, porting from place to place, stealing large quantities of cash with great fanfare. It was later revealed they would simply port to predetermined spots, be loaded by stagehands with bags of cash, then port back to tell their latest story.

The stories, like the Televangelists' entire careers, were hype cycle thrills that continued to draw more and more people to the excitement of porting. The side effects were muted and eventually forgotten by everyone, except those who could afford lavish porting itineraries and the Televangelists. The former would tut-tut away their illnesses in regal denial. The latter, however, would be whisked away at the first sign of major illness. Other, more memorable and vainglorious Televangelists would be plugged into place, and the show would go on.

Porting was becoming the sole form of transportation for the elite. They would arrange ports to move through their own mansions. Ports came to replace elevators, golf carts, even wheelchairs. The illnesses suffered were on the rise, but the uber-rich continued to wave away medical advice.

Those who opposed excesses of porting often disappeared when they became too outspoken. Though they raised important questions, their message was not en vogue. It was not good business to ask, for instance, what would the consequences be if death row inmates were being ported freely and widely all over the globe? What of those actually were surviving the traverses of time travel porting? What would the world be like if even the boundaries and borders of nations and time were no longer respected, and a mighty, well-informed criminal element surfaced, say, in the past?

What if half of the glowing stories Televangelists told were lies? What if it were all a big lie?

• • • •

WHEN A CERTAIN STRAIN of teleportation materials was discovered, testing of it became nightmarish. Eventually, not a single test subject came back.

Televangelists came to refuse it. Common inmates balked at it. Public interest was souring.

Only one body of people (so they had been determined by the courts, not public opinion) was left.

It was time to send in the clones.

Chapter 67: Up in Smoke

Doc Fortune hobbled through the house. "I'm sorry, no, there's no time for that." He was roving, looking for an exit. His depth perception seemed off, but Shae could attribute that to missing his glasses. "Detective Ward, we gotta go. You all must leave."

Rob stammered about spaghetti.

The girls groaned.

"Shae," Fortune said more emphatically. "They're following me. Here."

The tumblers fell in place in her mind, and suddenly it all registered for her. *Forcibly extract information. Imminent danger*, and she did not need to know the details. *Her family was in danger.*

"Take the girls to Mom's," she said and rushed to grab her coat and keys. "We have to split up. I'm going to get him as far away from you as I can."

"But..." Rob read her well, and he nodded when she shoved her backup into her boot. They exchanged a quick look that said it all: *be careful... I love you... see you soon.*

Then he bundled up some things for the girls, swept up the van keys, and led the way. "Let's all go to Gramma's," he strained to sing. "C'mon girls."

Shae helped Fortune into the squad car, then coming back around, intercepted the van as Rob was backing out. She leaned in his window, and they shared a passionate kiss. "I'll be fine," she said.

He nodded, and they rolled away.

Shae would like to have changed into her uniform, but her coat and lanyard would have to do in a pinch. She was wearing a sweatshirt and leggings, her police-issue boots, and a snowcap she had found on the counter by the back door.

"Where's Stu's cabin?" Fortune asked when she got in.

"It's the Wiebe cabin, hunter's retreat, out at their farm," she said. As the car warmed, she called it up on the Onboard. "About half an hour."

"Just go," he said. "I do not want them getting my books."

What about your kid? Shae thought. Lark was bright, funny, edgy like his old man. She didn't want anything happening to him, either. She'd told them around the dinner table about meeting Lark. She had shared that the kids had secured Doc Fortune's journals, that they were hiding them at the cabin...but he didn't care about them? Her old Mother Hen instincts were surging.

As they rolled through town, she called into dispatch, "Code 3. Notify County. On route to Coyle, then going rural."

"Do you need assistance?"

"Under control," Shae replied, "but they could clear Highway 33."

She kicked up the overheads, splashing the fast-food restaurants they shot by with red and blue.

Doc Fortune was staring out the window, his breathing still irregular. She let him rest a while.

Once they cleared Interstate 35, she switched on the sirens, and she sped up considerably. It was dark now, and road conditions were questionable. Local 33 was clean, but she watched for patches of black ice. She was mentally listing all the chases and emergency runs that had been botched by bad roads when Fortune twisted in his seat.

"How much longer?" he asked.

She glanced at the Onboard and shrugged. "Ten miles to Coyle, then it gets a little slower. Probably twenty minutes tops."

"I wonder if they're tracking us? If they'll get ahead of us?"

"How would they?" Shae thought about it, then looked at her radio and considered her call-in. Anyone on a scanner could know they were headed to Coyle. "How about an alternate route, a little more off-the-radar?"

Fortune nodded, then closed his eyes again.

She had only been out that way a few times, but she had a great mind for roads and topography. In two miles, she had reconfigured in her head and was rocketing straight east on county 105. It was a lesser road, but it had been bladed, and it had no traffic at all. She punched in every random destination within ten miles of the Wiebe place on the Onboard. Red Herrings, if anyone was monitoring.

• • • •

FINALLY, SHE JUST *had* to know. The girls weren't around. No recording devices. Just the two of them. She had just turned north onto a country road that had not been bladed, but it had melted off fairly well. "Doc, what happened?"

He looked at her, measuring her up again. She was familiar with the locals doing this before trusting in their 'lady cop,' but she did not expect it from Fortune.

"You've been exposed to some strange things. I don't know if you're ready for more."

"I can handle it," she said, fighting the wheel a little.

He was studying her, and she was evaluating him. He looked pasty and pale in the dashboard lights. His face was pockmarked with punctures and road rash on the left side. Without his glasses, he looked ten years older.

"Well?" she asked.

"I'm sure now that someone has taken this teleportation technology far beyond what I have."

"I thought you... invented it?"

"Someone's beat me to it. Somehow. I don't even think they need wires or ports or anything. They just pop up in a flash."

Shae frowned at this. "I thought that was the whole thing, point A to point B with the matching Tic Tacs or whatever?"

"So did I," he said, shaking his head. "And these guys can *trace* porting. They were chasing me."

"You're sure?"

"Positive," he said. "I was back and forth from Guthrie, to OKC, to my place. I went through ports that weren't even mine, even some Hot Wires I thought were single use. Every time, they caught up."

"Good thing you got us out of the house when you did," she said.

He nodded. "They'll catch up."

"Just who are 'they,' anyway, Doc?" she said after mulling it over a bit.

"I do not know, but I have a theory. A crazy theory."

The radio sputtered, then, "Ward, what's your 20?"

Shae raised an eyebrow. That was not GPD dispatch, and it did not sound like the Sheriff's department dispatch, Mike's ex, either. No call numbers.

Fortune had recognized her concern. He shook his head when she picked up the mic.

"Haven't seen anything of you on 33," the radio voice said.

She shut off the radio entirely.

"Throw your phone too."

"I can't do that," she protested. "Rob. The girls."

She did shut off the siren, then the flashing lights too. They had not seen another car in miles. *No reason to make it too easy for them*, she thought. The road was getting gradually worse, but she did not slow down. Fortune's sense of urgency was contagious.

"Your theory?" she asked. "And don't spare me anything. I'm a big girl."

"You will not believe me, but here goes. I think the guys after me are... expendable. They just dart right into harm's way, and there's no fear. They are reckless and not terribly smart... and... they all look almost alike... I'm sure they're related."

"Like brothers?" Shae asked. "You have a pack of brothers after you? How many did you say?"

He seemed increasingly agitated. Putting him behind the partition, back in the cage, crossed her mind. "Seven... maybe eight."

"Eight brothers are after you," she repeated it back. Not *necessarily* crazy. "Describe them."

He did, and Shae could not help but do a double take. He was describing the men at Mack's, exactly. His description matched the photos Dalton showed her on his phone of the guys in Norman too. She told him about this, and they both were dumbfounded.

"Twelve brothers. Twelve identical twins. That's not likely."

"I think they're more than that. I think they're clones."

Shae scoffed. "Right."

"Run the DNA, you'll see..." He waved his arms. "There's another one in Guthrie, Sunset Apartments. He fell off the parking garage... and another, for that matter, at least most of him, in a field west of town."

Shae's eyes were getting wider and wider. It crossed her mind again that Dr. Fortune might not be the best companion riding up front.

"*And*," he went on, his tone drawing up for the kicker, "I think they were sent here from the future."

She smiled broadly. "Your kid already broke it to me. He thinks his future self is coming back in time. He thinks Sackerson is a version of him."

Doc Fortune nodded, "I think so too."

• • • •

SHE WAS SLIDING THROUGH the last curves less than a quarter mile from the Wiebe farm when she lost control of the car. Here the road had dwindled to mud, and it had recently been heavily traveled and thus was rutted. It had not frozen back over for the night, though temperatures were dropping. Fighting with all her wherewithal, she managed to get the squad out of the ditch, but then it bolted over the road and into the ditch on the other side. It took out a few yards of fence and became high-centered on the hump of the fence line.

"Now what!" Shae said aloud, but Fortune was already forcing his door open.

"Now we walk," he said, pulling Rob's coat up around his neck. Shae watched him move out in front of the car, listing from side to side in the bright headlights. Fortune was still hurting, still avoiding his left foot, but otherwise he moved well through the snow and mud. He seemed to have renewed energy or had at least willed himself for this final trek to the farm and cabin.

She quickly caught up and directed him into the Wiebe driveway.

"Car was probably a beacon anyway," Fortune huffed as he moved ahead. "They're no doubt tracking it."

That made sense to her. She stopped in her tracks and powered down her body cam, radio, and cell phone. By the time she caught up to him again, he was wandering around the farmyard. "Which way to that cabin?" he asked.

"This way," she said and took the lead.

Once they had arrived, she pulled her pistol from her boot. The back door was wide open. A room had been broken into, and there was evidence of a struggle. Glass. Blood... coagulated.

"Here!" he called out.

Shae rushed in to find Doc Fortune slumping at a counter dividing the kitchen from the great room. He was swiping at notebooks, opening some, sliding others around.

"Stoke up the fire," he said, short of breath.

"Are you alright?" she asked. "Are you sure about this?"

"Please, Shae."

She did as he asked, worried more now about his well-being than possible intruders. Whatever had happened here earlier seemed to have passed. Whatever was going on with Fortune was not going away. When the fire was restored, she approached him at the counter. He raised his head, looked beyond her to the fireplace, and smiled. They each carried a bundle of notebooks to the fire.

"Feed them in, one by one. Make sure they burn. All of them."

Shae was curious why this was so important to him, but she did not ask. She fanned one open and tore it along the spine, then tossed it in. She watched the pages curl and catch fire. The flames grew in heat and intensity.

"I think it's too much porting," he explained after the third book was burning well. "I might have overdone it back there... but I just wanted to get away from them, maybe confuse them some. Instead, I led them right to your house."

"That was my fault," she said, shredding another notebook.

Fortune tried pulling one apart, but he was too weak. He grumbled but began tearing out individual pages and wadding them up. He would stop to look at some of them first. "All that work," he said, "but it's all in here anyway." He tapped his temple.

He looked at her and shook his head. "If they get here, I'm no good to you. Put a bullet in me first."

"I will not do that, Doctor Fortune," Shae said firmly.

They worked in silence, save the roaring fireplace, for quite a while. Doc Fortune continued to fade. Finally, he was just sitting there, his back against the fireplace stone.

"Why don't you get some air," she suggested. "I've got this."

He looked at her for a bit, as if he were seeing her for the first time. "Yeah," he said. "I'll do that."

She had to help him up, even had to help him walk across the room and outside. They shuffled in the snow on the large cedar deck.

"Right here," he said and found a place to lean against the railing. "I'm fine right here. Finish the job."

Shae looked back at him again and again on her way back inside. His condition was not unlike others she had seen at roadside emergencies. The shock was wearing off, exhaustion setting in.

Now that she was alone, she flipped through the books as she burned them. She was surprised that she had not noticed the strange characters and numbers before. It was just as Lark had told her—encrypted. It was fascinating. She lingered on illustrations she could not hope to understand. Mathematical equations stretched on for pages. Some entire notebooks were nothing but 1s and 0s.

Dutifully, she continued to burn it. Page by page, book by book, even though it grieved her to do so, thinking of how much time and effort Doc Fortune had obviously invested in it all. She felt what he must be feeling, that it was all for naught. He had invented something someone else had also invented. It was something so amazing and powerful, yet a dozen men had been sent to take it away. Lives were threatened and had been taken, all in this struggle to control... what? Teleportation?

A rapid honking of a vehicle horn stirred her to her feet. She tossed a whole handful of the journals in the fire, then rushed out on the deck to see if Doc Fortune had heard it too.

"Over here," she heard him call. She stepped out of the light of the windows and could clearly see Fortune standing beside an orange utility truck.

"Yes?" she said.

"We might still have a chance at getting out of this alive," he said, his spirit somewhat renewed. "Know how to bypass the ignition?"

She looked back at the cabin door, wide open, and the fireplace inside, the flame smoldering as it tried to catch up to the big load she had dumped on it. She looked back at Doc Fortune and shrugged.

"Don't they teach the police that?" he cocked his head.

"No..." Shae replied. "But I've seen it done enough. I think I could probably—"

"Great," he said, struggling into the truck and sliding over to the passenger side. "This won't even be on their radar. It's from the electric company."

"I see that," she said as she fished around for tools. She found an oversized screwdriver and hammer in the first compartment she checked, and in a matter of minutes, she had pounded and pried the ignition out of the steering column. A few minutes later, she had it running.

He huddled over the heater, and she returned to the cabin to burn more journals. In a few minutes, he was honking again, and she just tossed the rest at the fire and left to join him.

Get out of this alive, she replayed in her head. She had not realized that was ever an issue until he had said it. Somewhere in her swollen head, she had thought she could handle anything this case tossed at her... but seven or eight clones from the future? How had Fortune bested all of them?

Chapter 68: Tied with a Bow

Lark, Stu, and Krystal stayed behind after the all-clear. The basement was vast and empty and gave them room to both walk and talk together privately. They were making laps as Stu shared first.

Lark listened to Stu's recounting of The Boys and their siege on the Installation with rapt attention. It turned out that all the soldiers and protocol had paid off. They really were holding him there for his own protection.

Air Force 1, Boys 0.

"What about the Spooks, though?" Lark asked.

"I still don't feel that safe," Krystal said.

"Yeah, they're not letting up, even using a fake of Dad to stir up The Boys."

"They're not letting up at all. It's like they're coming unraveled," Lark said. "They're coming at us from every angle."

"I was just thinking the same thing," Stu added. "It's like all this is all about you, somehow."

"Just because I'm his son," Lark said quickly. "I think they want me for more leverage on him."

"Okay, then what about Sack? Why him? The Spooks want all three of you." Stu went on, "And Sack won't make a move without you."

"I think they want Sackerson because he knows a thing or two about teleporting," Krystal offered.

Lark nodded. "I think he knows something about the Spooks too. And if he's really from the future, he's a threat to them, right? Since he knows how this all ends up, he could probably rat out the Spooks right now."

"Tell them the reason they're really after you, Larkin Fortune," Sackerson said from behind. They all whirled on him. He was beaming ear to ear.

"And what reason is that?" Stu asked. He squinted at Lark.

"Where have you been, Sackerson?" Lark asked, redirecting. "No one's seen you since lunch yesterday."

"I don't like lead room basements, even if they are shelters," he said, looking all about. "I wouldn't have done well down here with 40 guardsmen. We would've all gone a little stir crazy."

"Like the two at dad's house, the way you 'have that effect' on people?"

"Yep, stark ravin' mad. Somehow, I get under people's skin! Crazy!"

"I think we're already there," Krystal smiled.

Stu stopped their walk. "So, Lefty, what *is* the reason they're after you?" He held his arms wide, as if to prevent anyone from walking on.

Lark was looking at Krystal, then at Sackerson. The former was shaking her head no. Sack was nodding his head, saying, "Tell him."

"They're after me... I think, anyway... because now they know Sackerson's their very real problem."

"And?" Sackerson prodded more.

"And they think the best way to stop him is to... to stop me."

Stu shook his head, as if to clear it.

"Stopping you," he pointed to Lark. "Somehow stopping you stops you, Sackerson?"

"Let the kid talk," Sack said, bowing.

"If they capture my father," Lark said, "they can get a monopoly on this Tic Tac teleporting. They can get the inventor, his notes, and his materials, and turn the future whatever way they want to."

"They know Sackerson's here, from the future, too," Krystal said, "and he's got a different agenda, right, Sack?"

Sackerson nodded his head.

"But YOU," Stu asked again. "Why you?"

"If they can stop me, now, in 2030, they'll never have an older me in, say, 2050."

"Wait." Stu's arms fell to his sides in resignation. "What?"

"I am Lark Fortune," Sackerson said, finally. "I'm him, all grown up."

"That's another thing," Stu interrupted. "Ever since Mack's, I've been thinking about you being a grown-up version of... of Lefty." He darted over and held up Lark's right arm. "What'dya *grow it back*?"

Lark pushed Stu away and asked, "More than any other reason, *that's* why I doubt you're me."

Sackerson looked past them, around the room, then said conspiratorially, "Yeah, guys, that's exactly what I did. I grew it back."

"You're kidding," Krystal asked, stepping closer to look it over.

Sackerson held up his right hand and wiggled the fingers, turned it over, flexed the joints. "Really? This is why you've doubted me?"

The three of them nodded.

"It's just grafting. Easy as gettin' stitches where I'm from." Sack shrugged. "Sometime I'll tell you the whole story on that."

"I can hardly wait," Stu said sarcastically.

Lark could hardly wait, himself. It posed a promise he would look forward to, having both his hands back. It seemed too good to be true.

• • • •

"SO, THEY CAN GET THE formula, the inventor, and leverage on the inventor by taking his son, Lark," Krystal tried to sum up, obviously trying to get them all back on track, "who *just happens* to grow up to be the man who stirs up the whole thing?"

"Exactly. There will never be a complication if they deal with Lark. That ends this timeline for the man I become," Sackerson said, "which would be a pity, don't you think?"

Stu shook his head and walked away, whispering through it all. He looped back around to them. "So, they want you, because you become him?"

Everyone was nodding.

"And they want him because he is back here messing everything up for them?"

More nods.

"So, they don't really want me and Krys at all, other than to get to you..." he pointed to Lark. "And getting you..." he pointed to Lark again, "gets you too?" He pointed now at Sackerson.

"That's my thinking," Sack said. "And his, for that matter."

Lark nodded.

"So, what's to lose?" Stu said. "What's to stop me from turning you in right now?"

"Well, now... I'd have to stop you, Stu, and I was just starting to really like you again," Sackerson said. "Besides, that's not how it all plays out historically."

Stu humored him, "Oh, really? Just yesterday you were all sideways because you said things were... offbeat or whatever. How do you know how it's supposed to play out?"

"And why are you so sure you can change anything?" Krystal asked Sackerson.

"Guys, I am not sure of anything," Sackerson said. "I am sure there are goons out there who will stop at nothing—like we've seen over and over—to get what they want. Right now, what they want is us."

"Sooooo?" Krystal said.

"So, we make a rendezvous spot," Sackerson continued, "somewhere that gives us advantage and gets them exactly what they want, all tied up with a bow."

"What?" Stu and Lark exclaimed at the same time.

"The journals are at the cabin," Krystal reminded them. "We could go to the cabin and invite your dad, somehow, Lark. Maybe we could get the Boys to stake out the place, sneak up behind the kidnappers, and be done with it."

"Except we are still wanted by the authorities," Stu reminded them, "and The Boys are hellbent on turning us over to the Spooks, and, oh, yeah, we're being detained in a government outpost."

"Pragmatic! That's what I've always liked about you, Wiebe." Sackerson clapped. "Limited only by, oh, everything!"

"What's that supposed to mean?"

"I mean, it's your best and worst trait," Sackerson said. "You could MacGyver anything the rest of us could dream up, but you can't do the dreaming yourself."

"MacGyver?" Krystal asked.

"Never mind. Point is, Stu, you need to live a little in the gray, buddy. It's good in the gray, right Lark?"

Lark had actually said that very thing before, talking to his father. He nodded slowly, mystified.

"Right," Stu said. "The gray."

"We could brainstorm—"

"Ugh, I feel like I'm in school!" Stu said. "Brainstorming!"

"Play along," Sack said. "You toss out a negative pragmatical thing, and the three of us will give you workarounds. Then we can trade around, let you get a feel—"

"Whatever. Whatever gets us the hell out of here and back to normal life," Stu said.

"Good start. Let's take that." Sackerson was pacing now, hands behind his back, like a university lecturer. "Stuart, I would postulate that you would be bored out of your mind if things went back to normal."

"That's just bull—"

"Aside from your patriarchy, rest their souls, I would offer that this is your best life."

Lark nodded. "It's not boring."

"We are getting to know each other better," Krystal added.

"I'm seeing sides of each of you I never saw when I was here before." Sack said, smiling.

"Whatever," Stu said. "Okay, take the fact we're locked up. How does the brain trust plan to get us out of this one?"

"Attorneys," Krystal said immediately, then regrouped and threw out, "or... or magic."

Stu just laughed. "Magic. What's next, a dragon?"

"Well," Lark smiled, "that new series of helicopters outside *are* named after dragons. Dad used to talk about it." He looked from face to face. "You know, Mal, Falcor, Shindig, Drogon, Smaug..."

Stu and Krystal shrugged at the same time.

"The point is, yeah, you could call it magic. What if we jack a helicopter and tear out for the cabin?"

"What if pigs fly?" Stu scoffed. "Who here knows how to fly a helicopter?"

Sackerson raised his hand meekly.

"The point is, guys, now you're cooking with gas." Sackerson smiled. "What else?"

"We could... dig our way out," Krystal said.

"We could dress like guardsmen and walk right out," Lark said.

"We could help with the cleanup and sneak away," Stu said, surprising even himself.

"Yeah, yeah!" Sackerson applauded. "Good stuff."

"Okay, so we get out. There's still The Boys."

"*Your* Boys," Lark said. "What would it take to change your mind if you were out there?"

"Nothing would change my mind," Stu reflected. "That's just it, isn't it?"

"You said they came at us because of a video, right?" Krystal asked.

"Yeah, so... what, are we going to make one of those fake face things?"

"Show them the other video you told us about," Lark said, "with your mom and sister and all—"

"Maybe they're here somewhere, you know, protected like we are," Krystal said.

"Didn't see them during the lockdown, did you?" Stu replied. "I don't know where they're at."

"So... *would* they believe the video?" Sackerson asked, prompting him. "They believed the other one of your dad."

Stu shook his head. "They're too committed now. And besides. They say that one of Dad was all over the news and everything."

"Let's say we did, somehow, get them on our team," Sackerson said. "Now we're free. They're with us, and we all go to the cabin. We bait the trap with me, mini-me, and the notebooks. How's that grab you?"

"It's back to magic," Stu said. "You're really jumping to conclusions, jumping right over the Boys."

Lark scoffed. "Hell with The Boys then. We get the law involved."

Everyone looked at him funny.

"What?" he said, defensively.

"That's just... not something you'd normally go to," Krystal said.

"I'm maturing," Lark said. "And I know somebody."

"So do I, I guess." Stu nodded. "Burns."

"Burns, the part-time guy?"

"Yeah, and he's also with The Boys..." Stu was thinking aloud, "and he's also pretty easy to, you know, convince."

"Okay, okay," Sackerson smiled, "look what we're doing here, Stu, we're knocking down barriers left and right. Doesn't matter if we dig out or walk out, doesn't matter if it's your Boys or the cops..."

"We still don't have the missing piece, the one person they seem to want most of all," Krystal said. "Dr. Fortune."

"What can we do about that, kids?" Sackerson asked.

"I think," Krystal said, not too sure of herself, "I think I know somebody."

"The Jedi," Lark smiled.

Stu groaned.

"The what?" Even Sackerson was aghast. "The who?"

"The man upstairs," Krystal added. Lark enjoyed this moment with her, playing them along.

"Jesus! Starkweather?" Stu asked.

"Either could help," Sackerson cackled. "Jesus or Starksy."

"No, not him," Krystal said, "the civilian leader. The brains of the outfit. You know, Dr. Canole."

Sackerson looked legitimately surprised.

"She had a talk with him," Lark said. "Like, first thing when we got here."

"And he's got access to Dad?" Sackerson asked, still slack jawed. He shook away the shock and said, "So Dad's working with Canole, and has been all along?"

"I dunno, but I think he can get a hold of him."

"Well, well, well..." Sackerson resumed his professorial pacing, now rubbing his hands together. "So, we get out, we get help, and we get all our bait together. We're all set."

"What about the Spooks?" Stu questioned.

"How do we reach them?" Krystal seconded.

"I have a feeling they'll be all over this," Sackerson said. "I think they're monitoring everything." He looked at Krystal pointedly and said again, "Every. Thing."

Lark was puzzled by that.

Krystal shrugged and said, "Whatever."

"It's all just talk," Stu said gruffly. "We're never going to get out of here, not in a million years. Not even with magic. We're just locked here, just sitting—"

"Maybe not with magic," Sackerson interrupted. "But maybe..." he pulled something from his pockets, "with *science*!"

"Is that what I think it is?" Lark said, looking at the little coil of wire Sackerson extended in one hand and the Tic Tac he had in the other.

"My last one," Sack said.

"Where would it take us?" Krystal asked.

"If it even works," Stu said.

"It could take us somewhere we don't want to go," Krystal argued. "Like, I don't know, pop us right in the middle of the Spooks, right?"

"I really don't know, but wherever it goes, it's out of here, right?" Sackerson said. "And now we have a plan!"

"I say we go for it," Lark said.

Just then, metal doors, like roll-top desks, rolled down over every exit to the basement and snapped loudly into place. They heard a dull hum, like that of fluorescent lights, then over that, an intercom click. "Know what a Faraday cage is? You're standing in a very large Faraday cage, designed to limit electromagnetic fields."

The voice was familiar, Lark thought. He had heard that accent before, the way the words were clipped a little too precisely. He just could not place it.

"Who are you?" Krystal shouted, "What do you want?

"You are being detained for your own protection. By your own confession, you have been plotting crimes against the government, including escape and sedition... use of illegal and unregistered materials..."

The list was going on and on. Sackerson was looking at the ceiling, nodding in agreement at each accusation.

Tears were streaming down Krystal's face.

"Welcome back to the black and white," Stu said, kicking the wall.

Chapter 69: Kiss Your Babies

Chris Fortune had once suffered a terrible case of COVID-19, one which even led to his hospitalization. The worst of it had been a raging fever that would spike, then leave him in chills and sweats, then return with a vengeance. He felt he was experiencing this again, and he had been getting worse since crash landing at the Wards' home.

Even worse, he was hallucinating. When he had settled into the passenger's side of the cab, he was sure he had seen his cigar box, the one from the basement lab in Norman. When they drew closer to the Wiebe farm, Chris was sure he saw someone on the side of the road, though Shae did not. Passing through the Wiebe farmyard, he saw a flash of light through a crack in the barn door. Shae had not seen this, either.

"That was port flashing," Chris said.

"What? I didn't hear you," Shae said with a look of concern.

"That flash in the barn back there..." Chris found it difficult to speak up over the rumble of the truck. "I think they're already closing in, porting in to hunt me down."

"I think you're being a little paranoid," Shae said.

They passed the patrol car, and she did not give it a second glance. It was clear to him that something else was foremost in her mind. He could tell she was in a hurry. She had navigated to a different route, and she was forcing the OEC truck through snow drifts and mud holes with no reserve. "Glad it's four-wheel drive," she said, downshifting. "Good ground clearance, too."

"And dual rear tires. Probably can't get stuck in this."

"Jury's out, Doc. There's a lot of weight back there, though, so we ought to be good." She looked him over and changed the subject. "I'm worried about you. Feeling sick?"

"Better. Lots better now," he said. "I think I just need some rest."

"You do that. We'll be back in Guthrie just as soon as I can get there."

• • • •

HE WOKE TO A STEAMY, warm cab and country music blaring on the radio. Shae was shaking him. "Phone," she said. "Your phone's going off."

Chris rummaged around in his pockets, then remembered his comm implant. He tapped his temple and leaned up to turn down the radio. It seemed the whole vehicle folded in on itself. Then again, it was normal. He was woozy. "Fortune," he answered.

"Christopher! It's Ben. I'm so glad I reached you."

"Keep it short," Shae whispered in his face. He wondered how she could be that close and still be driving. Then he realized she was not driving. They were stopped in the parking lot of a Gas n' Go. "Like a minute, tops."

"I gave the girl the Tic Tacs, like you wanted."

"Good," he said. "So, they're out?"

"They're missing."

"Good... that means they're out, right?"

"Maybe, but she left the Tic Tacs in her room."

"All of them?"

"Who's to say?" Ben sighed. "We lost track of them this afternoon. We ran into some trouble."

"Trouble?" Chris was flexing his jaw, trying to get a better sound from his earpiece. "What trouble?"

"We were raided by those rednecks, you know, The Boys."

"Raided?"

"Bulldozers and bullhorns, mostly, some shots fired, but the ANGs shut them down fast. We hid the kids in the Lead Room."

Chris' head was swimming. *The Boys, that vigilante group, had shot up the Installation?* He thought he had not heard right. He wanted to know more, but Shae was tapping the clock on the dash.

"Listen. Media was here for The Boys' raid, but now they've been run off by somebody on the perimeter. Looks like the FBI or something. ANGs scrambled. They're not telling me anything official, but a couple of officers gave me the 'kiss your babies and say your prayers' routine."

"What?" Chris did not want to cut this short. Not now, but it had been over a minute. He knew a telephone trace could already be underway. That had to be Shae's concern too.

"Sounds crazy, I know, but I think there's something big going down. I'm not sticking around to find your kid, Chris. I'm heading home to Jill. All of us are leaving."

Chris shook his head. "Is it that bad?"

"I've been around bases my entire career, and I've never seen anything like it. This is not a drill." Ben Canole took on an even more serious note, suggesting, "Maybe you ought to go see Ellen. Just saying."

"End it," Shae commanded, and he did. He powered down his communications implant, then switched his attention to the radio in the OEC truck. None of it was making any sense. News was blaring about security threats and bomb shelters. He tried to dismiss it as talk radio fare.

"Who was that? The GFA captain?"

"No. Ben Canole, Science Officer at the Installation," Chris said. "Said there was some kind of emergency, 'something big.'"

"How big?"

"A national emergency," he said. "The whole air force is mobilizing."

"Oh my god," she said. She wasted no more time. She ground the truck into gear and took off, throwing Chris back in his seat.

"Heading out there?" he asked. "To the Installation?"

"Hell no," she said. "I'm going to my mom's. I have a really bad feeling about this."

"Me too," he said.

• • • •

NORMALLY, RADIO STATIONS would pitch rivalries, do everything but slander competing stations. They would stick to their formats and trash talk the others.

However, during emergency weather situations, all the channels of a conglomerate would simulcast. Tonight was such a situation, but it was not the weather. It was nothing he could understand. Chris was punching the buttons up and down the radio dial and found them all to be telling the same stories.

Complications at the highest levels were leaked. All military personnel had been called in, even reservists, to active duty. People were urged to stay in their homes, but that, of course, had caused mass hysteria. Stores were reportedly ransacked, and shelves were bare. Traffic snarls around OKC had ground to a stop.

All this had seemed to happen in the hour they had been going out and back to the cabin. Chris still thought he was hearing it all wrong. Nothing moved so rapidly. It had to be a hoax, a la War of the Worlds.

"Except it's on every station," Shae shook her head. "Every station! Listen to the OEC band. I bet it's on there too."

She was roaring over intersections and passing on the wrong side of the road, breaking all manner of law she normally would uphold. She had turned on the utility truck's flashing yellow light bars, and she laid on the horn when people would not get out of her way.

Chris struggled to keep upright, but he tuned the high band radio to various channels, listening intently. Without all the hype of commercial radio, the message was still one of anxiety and immediacy: "Grid might fail south. Nothing we can do if it comes to that... Where's the main station for... If that gets hit, we'll go black all over the Midwest..." He did not understand much of it, but what he could put together was grim.

"Think we're actually under attack?" he asked Shae.

She shook her head. She was biting her lips.

She looked at him. "Fish my phone out of my jacket, will ya?" The truck went through another daring twist and turn as she cut an intersection short, ramping up into a car dealership on a corner lot, cutting across and down the intersecting street, barely slowing down. "Maybe they're not onto my line yet, and maybe with whatever the hell this is, they'll be too busy to run a trace."

He got the phone out, and as she coached him, he punched in her code, then her mom's speed dial digits. He had to hold it to her head, for she required both hands to manage the truck.

"Mom," she said, sounding nothing like Detective Shae Ward, but everything like a concerned mother. "Wake up Rob and the kids. Get to our house, to the basement."

Chris almost dropped the phone when the light of streetlamps and store fronts illuminated the floorboards. The cigar box from his house was broken open, spilling straws of paired Tic Tacs all over the floor. He tried to reach for it as he kept the phone at her ear but failed. He wanted to touch it, for he was sure it was another hallucination.

"Not a tornado. We're not sure what it is, but I want you safe. I'm still ten minutes out."

Holding the phone felt oddly intimate, Chris thought. He could feel her hair on his knuckles, the warmth of her face on his hand, even her breath, the brush of her lips.

"Where's Dad?" she asked, already shaking her head. "What? Since when?"

Chris thought her driving reflected her rising ire. She was losing it.

"I. Don't. Know." Shae honked furiously at someone in front of them.

The voice on the other end sounded hysterical. He could hear it over the radio and the truck noises. A tinny, emphatic tone, though he could not make out the words.

"No, don't bother. No. Rob's stocked it up." Shae tried to look over at him, rolling her eyes for him to see, but she snapped back to attention when running through a red light.

"Please, Mom. Don't start... I'll see you in a few... and Mom. MOM! Tell them I love 'em, okay?"

He felt her tears on his hand when she nudged the phone away. "Mothers, am I right?" she said, sniffing, trying to laugh it off.

70 Michael Faraday's Cage

C ontext File
    Benjamin Franklin, a polymath by any measure, is renowned for bringing forward the printing press, the public library, and any number of inventions (including the bifocal lens). He was a statesman, a politician, a wordsmith, and yes, an inventor—but more importantly a scientist, dabbling in everything from armchair meteorology to electricity. The words used to this day—battery, charge, plus, minus, and conductor—were first used by him in the context of electricity.

Thoughts of Franklin and electricity seldom venture beyond the famous kite and lightning experiment—one he may not even have conducted, merely conjectured. He did, however, place lightning rods on his roof, and he did many experiments with electrical current that are underappreciated.

In 1755, Franklin observed the effect by lowering an uncharged cork ball suspended on a silk thread through an opening in an electrically charged metal can. That the cork was not drawn to the inside of the can was a phenomenon he found intriguing.

Franklin may have first attended to the phenomena, but Michael Faraday duplicated the cork and can experiment, furthering the discovery and popularizing it so that now it is named after him, not Franklin (who had, after all, the Franklin stove and over twenty counties and thirty cities are named after him)

Michael Faraday's "cage" was much like the charged bucket. Items within the charged cage were inert and not susceptible to the exterior charge. Radio waves and other electromagnetic radiation are also blocked by the cage, which can be a solid metal surface (like the walls of an elevator or a tin hat) or a metal grid (like the rebar in a building that causes trouble with communication signals). Some buildings—prisons and private facilities—are built as a Faraday cage because they have reasons to block both incoming and outgoing signals.

Other structures, like the Guthrie Falls Installation, were retrofitted with Faraday cages. The thinking was that sensitive equipment and warehoused materials there would be protected from an EMP or other disturbance. The underground bunkers of the Installation were rumored to also be fitted with Lead Rooms, impenetrable by any signal, even the Earth's magnetic field.

Chapter 71: Dumb Luck

"We're done for," Krystal cried. Trapped without a prayer. Whether it was Spooks or the military, they weren't going anywhere.

"Ah, Krys! Now these Air Force buffoons are really limited in their thinking," Sackerson said, unaffected by their circumstances. "You're right, though, Stu. They are all black and white. Thing is, we're *technicolor*, baby!"

"What do you mean?" Krys asked, but Sackerson was lost to some mad dance in which he was jumping high and slapping at the ceiling.

"What *does* he mean?" Stu asked.

"I think he's in denial," Lark said.

The three of them watched Sackerson roam the room. He had resorted to running a finger along a wall. He licked his finger, as if tasting it, then continued to trace the perimeter. The ceiling was high, a raw unfinished cement ceiling with exposed beams. Some beams were steel girders. Others were wood. He was jumping in a bizarre dance, touching the beams as he again rounded the room.

In reality, she realized he was rigging up their port.

He was being flamboyant in his discretion.

No one else in the world would have taken him seriously. At no other time in her life might Krystal have taken him seriously, but she fell in with his merry dance, urging the other two along.

"No way," Stu said.

"I...I don't dance," Lark said.

She joined Sackerson in his singing, picking out keywords. They were having a private conversation in the guise of a babbling nonsense song.

Hey nonny, nonny, nonny
A penny for your money, money
Thinking thoughts for ticking tocks
Ricki Ticky Toc Tacks
Baby's got back...

It was so liberating to be so goofy and free when trapped in the most dire of circumstances they had ever known. She laughed with Sack while the other two just stood there.

"Stop that," the intercom voice broadcast. "Your behavior is unbecoming—"

Stab a needle in my eye
Needle and thread, and a bottle of rum
It's portabella time
It's margarita time

She got right in their faces. "*It's time we go, fellas!*"

She hooked her arms in theirs and dragged them along. They shuffled and half-ran, but they lacked the grace and mirth that she and Sack were displaying.

The intercom's voice continued to berate them.

She laughed, giddy and free.

Sackerson was facing them, doing a little jig backwards and singing some unintelligible language. As they drew near, he stopped and, like the finest ringmaster in all the world, he waved his arms to showcase an otherwise imperceptible port wire and glow.

With a twinkle in his eye, he sang more beautifully than ever:

Hope to see you soon, buffoons,
On the other side of somewhere.
Up the ante, down the dregs,
Around the corner from anywhere.

• • • •

IN A FLASH, THEY WERE back where they had started, it seemed. From basement to barn, Stu's barn, bumping into each other from the momentum of the dance that had brought them here through Sackerson's portal. Krystal knew it by the smell, and the chill, and she was happier to be here than at that Installation, any day, but then—-

"Where's Sack?" she asked, her smile fading fast.

The barn was dark, save the light coming from the familiar cracks, light streaks from the farmyard lights, and that of some passing vehicle strobing by.

Stu threw open the door and looked after the vehicle. "Dually, not one of ours."

Lark was still taking in his surroundings. "Sack?" he called out.

Krystal joined in. She even heard Stu out in the yard, calling for Sackerson. She was shocked he had not teleported with them. "Where is he?"

"No surprise," Stu said, snapping the barn lights on. "He never comes right with us."

"Maybe he's trapped somehow," Lark ventured.

"You mean the cage thing? The Installation?" Krystal asked. "It didn't stop us."

They prowled around for him in the barn, then the house. The lights were still on, but it was strangely empty now. Half empty cups and bottles were strewn where The Boys had left them. Stu picked up a couple of revolvers and a box of ammunition. He led the way back outside.

"Does it ever surprise you guys?" Stu asked, turning to them. "We were just talking about this great scheme, and now Sackerson zaps us here—I mean right here! Doesn't that even seem a little strange to you?"

"It's all strange," Krystal said, "but I'm starting to like it."

"Speaking of strange," he said, "what was with you back there? You went a little loopy on us!"

"I dunno..." Krystal admitted. "I really don't know." It made her laugh. "I guess I was just feeling it. I was happy because he had a secret plan to get us out, and it was... fun flying in the face of authority or whatever!"

"Whatever," Stu said. "It's just getting way outside my comfort zone."

"Let's check out the cabin," Lark said. "Somebody's been up there."

"How can you tell?" Krystal asked.

"Stands to reason," Lark said. "That truck just came from up there,"

Stu said he did smell the cabin's fireplace. "No car, no phone, nobody around... I guess it's worth a try," Stu said.

"Or," Krystal offered, "we could just stay in the house... maybe wait for—"

"For what?" Stu spat. "My folks to come home?"

He stomped off in the snow.

Krystal understood. His father and grandfather were dead. His mother and sister were... where? Detained back at the Installation, maybe? She wondered if he might have some hope they were at the cabin, but she said nothing.

• • • •

STU HAD BEEN RIGHT. Someone had just been at the cabin. He was doing a room-by-room search.

Lark was fiercely angry, and Krystal couldn't tell why. "What's wrong with you, Lark?"

He glared at her, then waved his hand at the fireplace. "Can't you see?"

The fireplace was smoldering. She realized it had been overloaded with—the journals!

"Oh, my god!" she rushed over, poking at them with the fireplace tools. "Who would do this!?"

"The truck that went by? Our OEC truck's gone. That had to be it...." Lark said. "And with it, my present."

"Your present... you mean that box of—that's right! We were talking about them when Henny showed up. Are you sure that's where you left them?"

He gave her a sour look.

"Well," she offered, optimistically, "I bet the power company found their truck and took it back."

"At this hour?" Stu said, rejoining them. "Can't get OEC on a call on a perfect summer's day, let alone the middle of the night."

"Well, what do you think?" Krystal asked.

"I think Henny took it," Stu said through gritted teeth. "Guns are missing. Journals are burned. Truck's gone... how else do you explain it?"

"What is it with you? Why's it always Henny all the sudden, when you guys—"

"Shut it!" Lark rasped, pointing to the loft. "Someone's up there."

Stu drew his gun and led the way upstairs, cat quiet. Lark followed next and Krystal brought up the rear, looking over her shoulder. It was suddenly worse that someone might be there than when the place seemed empty. She worried someone was going to come up behind her.

The stairs seemed infinitely long. Every time one of them creaked, she was worried they'd be found out. It was a three-run staircase, winding up to the loft. Stu was out of sight at the last turn. "Whaaaa?" she heard him gasp.

"No way," Lark said, as he rounded up the last flight.

Krystal skipped a step to round the corner and see what the two boys had been so surprised at.

Sackerson was standing there, hands on hips, beaming like usual. "Slight detour," he said, "but now the gang's all here!"

The boys were peppering him with questions. Why hadn't he gone with them? What was his detour? Why here, in the loft? That wasn't really his last Hot Wire, was it?

Krystal, however, made some excuse about needing to go to the bathroom, and she returned to the fireplace. As she forked through the remaining journals stacked on the logs, she found some were still intact. The fire had not yet caught on them. She used some oversized tongs to pull some of the least-burnt journals off to the side. In doing so, she gave the fire its air, and it gradually came back to life.

Krystal got black all over her hands as she flipped through to confirm her thoughts. Many pages were just fine, just burnt around the edges. All was not lost.

The three were now laughing upstairs. They seemed preoccupied. She grabbed up several journals—one or two still smoldering and warm—and spread them on the counter. Looking back to make sure they were still busy upstairs, she then extracted Henny's phone and snapped pictures of as many pages as she had time for.

If this stuff was so valuable, why hadn't they done that in the first place? She thought it only prudent now, especially since someone was trying to get rid of them.

"...bet those guys were surprised by that!" Stu said, coming down the stairs.

"I think they didn't know I had it in me," Sack was laughing. "I didn't know I had it in me." He turned to Lark and asked, "Would you have thought so?"

Lark was still not over the cigar box. It was obvious to Krystal, for he disregarded them and walked straight to the fire. "What are you doing?"

"Look," Krystal stashed her phone, then held up a well-preserved page of a journal. "They didn't get them all!"

"Oh!" Sack said, more surprised than pleased. "We still got 'em?"

"Some," she said. "Maybe most of them?"

"That's good, right?" Stu asked.

"Yeah, it's... it's great... it's just not historical."

"What do you mean?" Lark asked. "How do you even keep it straight anymore? Doesn't it make you dizzy?"

"I mean, there were no pages of the journals preserved before. In my day, we just worked off rumors and tests. Lots and lots of tests." He shrugged and assumed his happy-go-lucky demeanor. "This is much better!"

They stood around the kitchen island admiring Krystal's handiwork.

"How'd you do it, Sack? How'd you get us right back here, all according to plan? We even have the journals now," Lark asked, at last.

"Dumb luck," Sackerson said.

"We haven't had the best luck lately," Stu offered. "I think you had this planned."

"*I do protest*," Sackerson said, with mock injury. "I might have known, say, that there was a Hot Wire up there. I knew there was one in the barn too. I might have been pretty sure they were the last ones... but a plan? Hardly."

"You knew they'd work in that basement trap, the Faraday Cage," Lark said. "How'd you know that?"

"Guys, remember, I'm on your side. I'm here with a wealth of experience and charm." He smiled reassuringly. "Sure, I knew a

Faraday wouldn't even matter to porting. I'm light years—well, a good hundred years, anyway—ahead of your Air Force buddies."

"Whatever," Lark said. "So, what's next in your plan?"

"In *your* plan," Sackerson corrected, "we'd need Dad here, and we'd need to alert the Spooks or wait for them otherwise, and we'd need the posse bringing up the rear."

Krystal wondered how to get Dr. Fortune to the cabin. He really was the missing ingredient. She didn't have a number to reach Dr. Canole. Maybe if she did, he could get Lark's dad to come out...

"It's a trap, right?" Stu said. "They don't need to know exactly what cards we're holding. We just need to make it attractive enough that they'll come after us. We don't need Doc Fortune. We still have you guys as bait, and we can lie about the rest."

"How?" Lark asked. "How are we going to let them know we're here?"

"They traced us, right Sack?" Stu asked.

"They will, if they haven't already."

"So that's taken care of," Stu said. "I could call in a favor with Burns, if only we had a phone."

"If only we did!" Sackerson said, looking at Krystal.

She felt her face flush. They were all looking at her now. It was too much pressure.

"Okay! Okay!" She pulled the phone from her pocket and sat it on the counter. "But I don't have his number."

Just then, the telephone rang. She was sure it had been on silent. It continued to ring and vibrate, not to be ignored.

Chapter 72: Duck and Cover

Rob Ward was a smart coupon shopper, but even so, he had amassed ten bottles of shampoo, gallons of cooking oil, and enough toothbrushes for a lifetime. They had finished a room in the basement for his overload, and during every tornado drill and warning, they were at least sure they'd have enough to get by. There had been freakish shortages in the five years they had been married, and every time Rob's coupon overages had seemed prescient and wise, always expecting a run on bleach, masks, and toilet paper. The last had been an unfounded report that spices would be in short supply, and Rob did not even flinch. He had two shelves dedicated to quart containers of every major spice in their cabinet.

"Canned meats," Grandma Willow observed. "You're low on SPAM and deviled ham and tuna too. Canned meats are protein, you know."

Shae was trying to ignore her mother. She had spoken with Cole and dispatch, learning little. She dialed up Dalton Briggs, and for the last five minutes, one or the other of them had been interrupted non-stop. Shae had to struggle with her daughters, Briggs with his detail, on location at the Installation. Ultimately, she went upstairs, claiming she was going to fill the sinks and tubs with water, just in case. It had pacified her mother and given her a break.

She had better phone reception too, full bars, from the second floor. She was pacing the hall when she spotted her father in their bedroom. He was rummaging through a cedar chest.

"Dad? Did Mom send you up for more blankets?"

"Hmm. Something like that." He looked like a rookie thief, or like Opal with her hand in the cookie jar. "She sent me up for keepsakes." He cocked his head toward the window, adding, "You know, just in case."

Why didn't people keep their treasures in the basement in tornado alley? Shae had always wondered about that. Instead, at times like these, people rushed around the house grabbing up whatever struck them as priceless at the moment. He did not show or share them with her, but she recognized what he was holding, the belt and pistols he hid under the bed and Shae's first rattle and blanket.

It was an odd combination.

Shae's phone vibrated just then, so she stepped away to take Dalton's latest call. He went for a drive, he said, telling his men he needed to take in the perimeter again.

"Dalton, I have kids in jeopardy out there. I can't just abandon—"

"Your kids?" he asked.

"Well, no, but they're integral to—"

"Shae, if they're not yours, they're not worth it."

"Just fill me in," she pleaded. "What the hell's going on?"

"Stay by this number," he said and clicked off.

By the time the tub was full, the phone rang. She did not recognize the number, but she picked up.

"I'm calling from a phone I had to lift." Dalton spoke quickly, "All I know is, we're evacuating everyone east of Coyle, through Perkins and on northeast."

"Isn't that the sheriff's job?"

"This is big, a cooperative effort."

"Like Fortune's house," she said. "Coincidence?"

"Why are you on this one, Ward? Go duck and cover."

"I can't just leave this to someone else. Besides, it sounds like everyone's a hot mess right now, got their hands full. Look, I'm just trying to help some kids, just three troubled teens out of a whole county."

"Your three that were also in Norman?"

"Maybe... yes. And they're at ground zero, or will be soon, according to our informant at the Installation."

"Informant? Who?"

"Doesn't matter right now, does it?"

"Ground zero? Like the Wiebe spread?"

"Yes, Wiebe's—how'd you know that?" He had certainly picked up on the local scene quickly.

Shae's father cursed from the hallway.

She opened the bathroom door immediately and gestured him in. The room was all his, if he needed.

"I gotta step out, Shae-baby," he whispered, avoiding the phone. He put a hand to her cheek and told her he loved her.

She held the phone loosely in her hand and watched him bound down the stairs. "Love you too," she murmured. The surprises kept stacking up. *Where was he stepping out to at a time like this?*

"...like I said, it's a collaboration," Dalton was saying when she put the phone again to her ear. "Look, I don't know what else I can tell you, Shae."

"Tell me what you *think*, Dalton. I've never even trained for evacuation. What do you think's going on?"

"I think anytime now they'll call it an anhydrous leak or maybe some freak virus in the wind. It'll be all over the news." He cleared his throat. "But I think it's worse. The way everyone is overreacting, I think it's something to do with the Installation. You're going to think I'm nuts, but I wonder if we're in for another air raid."

The locals had colloquially called the Guthrie Fall an *Air Raid*.

She would run that one by the astrophysicist in her basement, the first chance she had.

"Your last one took out several square miles."

"I know," she said. "What are the chances there'd be another like that, so close to the last one—in the same *county* as the last one?"

"All I have to go on is panic, Shae, and from what I'm seeing, from the highest offices right down to my detail—this one could be county wide. Could be even bigger."

• • • •

DOC FORTUNE WAS NOT much good to her. He was going on and on about craters two miles across in Argentina, about statistical improbabilities and how if another Fall like the one they'd had were to hit this close again, then it had to be intentional in design. It would not be random.

This, as he was arranging the shelves like a stock boy, checking expiration dates, and cooing at the girls.

"Doesn't matter," she arrived at this herself, without even a quick consult with Rob. "It doesn't matter. The point is, your Dr. Canole says they're heading for Horse Thief Canyon, and my informant says that's right into harm's way."

"Your informant must be well-informed. I've never been able to predict a meteor fall with that kind of accuracy. To even know the when and where? I seldom even get the state correct. I'll admit, I've been out of pocket for a few months now, but we..."

Shae wasn't listening anymore. She was hugging her girls, her mother, and working her way to Rob.

"What do you think you're going to do, Shaelyn?"

"I'm going to get those kids and get back here, fast."

"I'm going with you," her mother said.

"No, you're not." Shae had never been so firm with her mother before. It did not sit well. Willow turned sharply and went back upstairs.

"Shae? Really?" Rob had her by the shoulders, looking her in the eyes like he always did at times like this. "Don't want to pass on this one?"

"Listen, it took me half an hour last time, but I can spin hard, take 33, and be there in half that. I can beat whatever's coming."

"Then *I'm* going with you," Doc Fortune ducked in, as if cutting in on a dance. "Lark is my son."

"No," Rob said, turning on Fortune. Rob was a very large man in a small basement. Dr. Fortune was half his size, and in his current condition, could have been bowled over with a glare.

"Honey," Shae said calmly, "he's just worried."

"Well," Rob deflated some, smiling down at Shae, but continued. "Well... he got to go last time." Then to Doc Fortune he said, "And she's my wife."

"Stay here, Chris," Shae said. "Get feeling better."

"I'll be fine," Fortune said softly. "It's the kids I'm worried about."

"You and Mom can listen to the scanner. If there's something to worry about, you'll be among the first to know."

"Right," he said, with resignation.

She gave him a hug, whispering, "And watch my mom and the kids for me."

Fortune nodded and shrank away.

Shae and Rob were gearing up for the trip just as fast as they could. Willow stopped them at the door. "Fine. I talked to your dad. Just go for it but come back with some canned meats."

"Got it, Mom," Shae said.

Her mom grabbed her elbow and forced something into her palm. It was a strange weapon she hadn't seen since she'd snooped in the cedar chest years and years ago. "Just in case," Willow said coldly, "take my plasma pistol."

"Yeah. Okay," Shae nodded, and then she and Rob climbed into the minivan.

He noticed it immediately and snatched it off her lap. "This is cute," he said, pointing it at the road ahead. "Pew-pew," he added. "Pew!"

"It's not a toy, boy toy. Now, buckle up."

Chapter 73: Technology

Nothing but surprises, Stu thought. It was getting to be too much!

They all looked at the phone, then at each other. It continued ringing. Finally, Krys took the call on speaker.

"Krystal, it's me. You gotta beam out of there or whatever."

"Hinman?" Stu moved toward the phone to crush it.

Sackerson raised his hands, coaxing everyone to calm down.

"Stu? Oh man, am I glad to hear you!" Henny said, "You guys gotta leave your place, and now."

"Wha?" Stu couldn't believe what he was hearing.

"Why's that?" Lefty asked. He looked especially confused.

"They know you're there, that's why. They followed you, somehow, when you teleported."

"Why should we trust you, Henny?" Lark asked.

"They know your dad was there too, Lefty. I heard them talking about it." Hinman huffed into the mouthpiece. "It's going to be bad. That's all I really know. They're going to do something really, really bad."

"Kenny, what are you talking about? What are they—"

"Listen, Krys, I gotta go. Tell Sack I'm still on the job."

The phone went dead.

"You guys don't think he's legit, do ya?" Stu asked. "What if he's still double-crossing us?"

"He's the real deal," Sackerson said, "and this is really big."

"What do you mean?" Krystal asked. "Really big?"

"If my spy called this number, and he just did—putting his life in peril again for you three—then yes. It's big."

"Like?" Krys asked.

"Like a host of assassins might come to snuff us out before sunrise," Sackerson said.

"What can we do?" Krys asked. "Where can we go? Even the OEC truck's gone."

"And I really am fresh out of Hot Wires."

Krys felt her pockets, then made a terrible face. "I left mine at the Installation."

"Your what?" Lark asked.

"Canole gave me a whole bunch of the magic Tic Tacs," she groaned. "But I left them when they rushed us to the bomb shelter."

"So, now what?" Lark asked.

"So, things are moving faster, but still our way, right?" Stu said. "Trap's springing. We need to call for mop up."

"You want this?" Krystal slid the phone toward him on the counter.

"Someday I want to know how you came by this," Stu said. He snapped up the phone and called Burns.

· · · ·

WHILE THE REST OF THEM stood around feeling sorry for themselves, Stu moved. He was back from the farmyard in just a short while and called them all out of the cabin.

They came out to see him standing in the moonlight on the open blue snow, surrounded by horses. "Leave that damn phone inside, and let's ride," he said. "They can track teleporting and all your fancy technology, but they're not going to track us on these. We'll be back in Guthrie before they've even figured out we're gone... and by then, they'll be surrounded."

Sackerson approached a horse. It was clear he had handled them before. He was stroking one's neck. He looked at Stu like he was made of gold. "Now you're thinking outside the lines, Stu. This is genius."

• • • •

IT TOOK TOO LONG TO get everyone into their saddles and on the trail, but after some coaching, they were riding as hard as Stu thought he could keep them on their horses. He took them across the Cimarron and almost directly west, over two of the Niles' pastures and another creek.

In a different situation, it would have been beautiful. Even though the snow made the roads a slushy mess, out on the prairie and in thickets of trees, the snow was a beautiful, radiant blue. Pristine. He liked words like that, when they fit just right. The snow was new and clean and white and... pristine.

Tonight, however, it didn't matter. He was pressing them on, pulling them through tough spots. Lefty threatened to walk more than once. Krys was swatted in the face by a tree branch somewhere along the way, and she was difficult after that.

Sackerson rode at ease in his saddle. His gelding was the most spirited of the lot, but Sack kept him reined in nicely. Stu rode alongside him when he could and asked again and again just what big trouble they should be expecting.

"I missed this," Sackerson said, changing the subject. "Riding. I haven't been on a horse in... a long time."

Stu wondered where this was going. He noticed that damn crow was back on Sack's shoulder. He was going to ask how, but Sackerson continued.

"I know you grew up with them, but have you ever thought about it? Now dogs, you know, we bred the wolf out of them and made them docile. Horses, however, we never really tamed. Did we?"

"These are broke," Stu said. "What do you mean?"

"I mean, we have this symbiotic relationship with horses. What other animal do we ride like this? They're big animals too. A thousand pounds or more, right?"

"Yeah, at least—"

The crow cawed frantically and took flight. It spooked them all, and the horses bolted and bucked. Stu reined his horse and kicked to pull her up to Krys's horse, so he could reach down and grab the bridle. Sackerson had done the same with Lark's horse.

The horses were blasting great geysers of steam and whinnying. Stu talked them down as best he could. He was not having much luck.

"Earthquake?" Stu asked. "Think that's what spooked them?"

"Worse," Sackerson said, pointing to the sky.

Chapter 74: Collateral Damage

D r. Chris Fortune heard the long wind up of tornado sirens from several directions, just out of sync. They came into their disturbing, harmonious wail and held the tone.

"Well," Shae's mother said, "I guess this is it, eh?"

"I don't know that—"

"*Warning. This is a warning from the Emergency Broadcast System and Wireless Emergency Alerts,*" Chris was hearing it ambiently throughout the house, over the basement television, but also through his earpiece in a disorienting simulcast. "*There is an imminent threat to life and property. Take shelter immediately. Move to an interior room...*"

Chris clambered to his feet, his military conditioning snapping him into action. In a calm but firm tone, he approached Shae's mother, asking, "Willow? It's Willow, isn't it?"

She nodded, holding her granddaughters close.

"I'm going to need you to—"

"*Stay away from windows, doors, and walls that face the building's exterior...*" the announcement droned on. He struggled to think over the noise of it all. "*Go to a sheltered area, such as a basement or the lowest level in the building. If there is no basement, go to the center of an interior room...*"

"Willow, we're going to be fine. Just fine, understand?"

Her face was pale and void of expression. "I've been through worse," she nodded again.

"*...away from corners, windows, doors and outside walls. Put as many walls as possible between you and the outside. Get under a sturdy table and use your arms to protect your head and neck...*"

And kiss your ass goodbye, Chris thought.

He conducted them into a tight corner of the basement, then took the stairs two at a time to the main floor, grabbing up couch cushions and a quilt, then returning to tuck the three of them in. They were sitting on 100-pound sacks of beans and rice, surrounded now with cushions.

The broadcasts and sirens had ended, and it was deathly quiet. In his experience, this was when one listened for the tornado. He expected to feel the telltale changes in air pressure in his ears, and for them to pop.

"What about you?" she asked.

Chris tucked a wind-up flashlight/radio in the quilt with them. "I'll be right out here," he said. "Going to watch it on the news."

"Drag that TV in here!" she said, and he did it without protest. "Now get in here." She spread her arms wide, opening up the quilt and cushions for him.

Again, he obeyed, wedging in between the two little girls. The sirens and announcement cycled again. When it was quiet, he could hear the girls sobbing and their grandmother trying to console them. It smelled of patchouli and Kool-Aid.

The television screen went from the EBS screen to a live broadcast. A haggard newsman was in the foreground. His mouth was moving, but there was initially no sound.

"...all we know." The newsman glanced at his crew, not the camera, then said, "I understand we had some sound problems there." He slicked back his hair and began again, talking into the camera, "A major break in the story. This is no tornado. We have confirmation from the National Weather Service. Instead, we—" he looked away again, then up and to his left. "Get this? You getting this?"

He stepped offscreen, and the cameraman attempted to focus on the night sky. The aperture struggled with the lights of the parking lot where the news crew had set up but eventually adapted to the black. "Did you see that?"

Chris saw it. A streak of light sliced the sky.

The camera man struggled to keep it in focus.

"Meteor?" the newsman asked. "Can we get confirmation on this, guys?"

Chris knew it was no meteor. It was a missile.

• • • •

WHEN THE EMERGENCY Broadcast again took over the television, it did not take over Fortune's earpiece. Instead, he heard static so loud he was struggling to free himself up to shut it off, but then it stabilized and a cold, familiar voice, the same voice as the one haunting him when he had tried to evade them, came in loud and clear.

"Dr. Fortune, you have left us no choice. It is imperative that we neutralize the problem once and for all."

He stammered, sat up between the little girls, saying, "Wait. Wait. What are you talking about?"

"We have targeted you and the infiltrator Sackerson to be at these coordinates: 97410928740615-1213690123-18236402134. We will eradicate the problem, including you, your accomplices, your resources, and notes."

"I thought you meant us no harm," Chris said. "*What have you done?*"

"We have verbal confirmation that all three of you have ported to the determined coordinates. It is a rural location affording allowable collateral damage. We have photographic images of your documents from that same location. In a matter of minutes, everything will be incinerated."

"Please," Chris begged, "I'll come in peacefully. I'll bring everything. Please, just let—"

"Resources have been deployed. We are notifying you as a courtesy, out of respect for your outstanding achievements in teleportation. Make right with your maker, Dr. Fortune. And thank you."

The television again featured live footage. The newsman was in the foreground, speculating as to the streak in the sky.

In the next instant, a massive explosion glowed on the horizon behind him, then the broadcast went blank, and the television screen turned blue and silent.

"We should put in a movie," one of the little girls said. "This one's over."

"Now your eyes are leaking," her sister said as she wiped at his face.

He held them both up close and whispered over and over, "It's okay. It's okay. It's okay."

Chapter 75: Heroes

Shae was driving their van flat out. Though she knew the way, Rob had taken the role of navigator, if nothing else than to provide moral support. He was not scolding her about burning up the engine. She grazed a mailbox that took off the passenger mirror, and still—he did not criticize.

He did, however, hold a little tighter to the armrests.

Highway 33 was a four-lane, divided highway, and Shae abandoned it after ten miles. She cut to paved roads, and then gravel, and now muddy, rutted, red dirt roads. It seemed their progress was throttled down to nothing.

She reminded herself this was not the OEC rig, not even her patrol car, and that she was subjecting the family van to rigors that even the off roaders would respect.

Rob did his best to keep it light, to play along. "Whoo-hoo! Caught some air on that one," he said, as they bound over another hill. "Tighter, tighter, tighter," he coached when Shae drifted the van around a slippery curve.

"That was the old Prospect Church," she narrated as she drove. In the dark it was difficult to tell, but she had assisted County at that location once when they found a body. They sped past it, and Shae forced a little more from the van as it pushed up a hill.

"Oh, no!" Rob said, preoccupied with something behind them. "We have traffic!" In her rear-view mirror Shae saw several vehicles closing fast. She edged the van over as far as she could, creeping to a stop as the tires fought the rocky edge.

Shae gritted her teeth. If these were the Spooks, she wanted to crank the wheel of the van sharply and bring them to a stop, blocking the road.

She waited, her arm muscles knotting.

She revved the engine.

Then, squinting, she could see lots of lights on the approaching vehicles. She rolled down her window to look behind, and they were nearly on top of her then. Pickups, four-wheel-drive vans and trucks, all festooned with light bars and spotlights. Half a dozen of them roared past them on her side. Two others fought through terrain on the passenger side. They honked and hooted as they passed.

She knew them. It was The Boys.

Her eyes adjusted as the taillights rocked and rocketed out of sight. She shook her head as she pulled back onto the roadway now carved with fresh ruts.

"I'm so glad you're not one of those bozos," Shae said, risking a quick pat of Rob's shoulder.

"What are they doing out here?" he asked.

"They probably think they're saving the day," she said, bringing the van up to speed again as best she could.

"I thought *we* were saving the day," Rob looked a little put out. "Aren't *we* saving those kids? Who do they think they are?"

Shae saw a glimmer that made her brake. These roads were haunted by deer—often their eyes reflected headlight beams. Then again it could be one of The Boys or maybe someone on foot. Maybe the flash of a phone. It could have been nothing more than interior lights playing tricks on the windshield. She couldn't tell how far ahead it had been, but surely, they had passed it. She shrugged it off and continued, a little more attentively.

"Heroes," she said. "They think they're heroes."

He flipped down Shae's visor and tapped a picture of their girls. "You know, so long as *they* think we're heroes—"

A fire burst flared around the visor. A blast wave blew out their left side windows. They were tossed off into the ditch. Airborne. Weightless. Glass fragments floated in every direction.

Rob whooped like a rodeo clown.

Cabin lights on? Some other light?

Her eyes were tricking her. Was it the end? The light at the end of—

The seatbelt cracked at her collar.

Rob smiling. Her daughters playing.

Mom, teaching her to shoot. *Concentrate.*

Dad. Awash in blue-white light. Concern etched his features.

Blood and bleach.

The steering wheel punched her hard in the face.

Air bags—she knew—were deploying.

And that was the last thing she knew.

Chapter 76: Silence

Lark heard Stu's constant narration up ahead. He wondered if he were sometimes just talking to himself, but at other times, Sackerson seemed to take an interest, and they would ride side by side.

"This sandbar's the three-mile mark," Stu said, pointing off toward the river. "I used to camp there sometimes."

Lark adjusted in his saddle. Three miles. It had been a hard ride, constantly jostling and swaying. He wondered if his horse was running or stomping and tripping along.

"We're on the Niles place, still. You guys know the Niles family? Their great grandpa was a doctor. I think there's a dentist in Guthrie named Niles, even today. Probably related. Anyway, he traded doctoring for deeds, see. That's how they—"

The trees and trail, Krystal Price and her horse, and all ahead of Lark flashed blank. A tremendous explosion sounded behind him.

Lark was airborne, then pounded into the ground. He couldn't catch his breath. Trees were bent nearly flat. All the horses were knocked off their feet.

Stu started to say something, but Lark was too deafened from the blast to make it out.

Then a second blast rolled over the horizon, leaving everything in silence and cinders.

Chapter 77: Low Impact

Context File

On February 17, 2030, at 22:22 a LGM-30G Minuteman-III U.S. land-based intercontinental ballistic missile (ICBM), was launched as a routine test from Vandenberg Air Force Base, northwest of Lompoc, California. This missile was commandeered by unknown forces or malfunction which redirected the guidance system toward an assumed target of Tinker AFB in Oklahoma. Equipped with W62 Mk-12 thermonuclear warheads, having a yield of 170 kilotons, this missile missed its mark by over seventy miles, detonating in a rural area of northeast Logan County, Oklahoma.

The immediate blast radius and subsequent fallout required that the town of Perkins, Oklahoma, be cordoned off. All traffic, including air traffic, was rerouted to further isolate the effects of fallout. It is estimated that only 20-30 fatalities occurred in the incident, with an additional 70 suffering injuries from the limited blast radius of only 3.88 miles. Low winds from the southwest reduced fallout in populated areas to the northwest, including Stillwater, Oklahoma, which resumed normal operation within twenty-four hours.

Political fallout was dampened by the release of a cover story that a toxic gas leaked from experimentally deep petroleum drilling near Logan and Payne counties. It is expected the region will be restored within fifty years. Meanwhile, reparations have been made to area farmers and ranchers.

Chapter 78: Coyle

Stu Wiebe found himself looking up at a view he had never hoped to see: the ceiling of the Bluejacket's gymnasium. In all his years of wrestling, he had never spent any amount of time on his back. At the moment, he could not command himself to move, however, so he closed his eyes to the bright lights again and waited for the count.

"Stu," someone said, and he felt it had not been the first time he had heard the voice. Someone shook him. He raised his hand to brush theirs away, but it fell to his side.

"Stu, it's me, child. Wake up, son." It was his mother's voice, but when he tried to open his eyes now, the lights above were so terribly bright he could not make out her features. She was backlit by heaven. *He was in heaven with his mom.*

"Mom?" he said.

"Yes, right here. I'm right here." He knew her voice. He smiled. He was right. It was her. "You're singed, boy, your whole left side. Just be still."

"Annie?" Stu slurred. "Where's Annie?"

"Your sister's just fine," the Chief said off to his left.

"Chief?" Stu struggled now to sit up, feeling gauze on his cheek and tape on his arm, feeling an IV tangling with his cot.

"That's right, Stu," Chief rumbled. "It's me. Can you open your eyes? We need to check your pupils."

A nurse in a surgical mask was on his right, the Chief on his left. Stu tried again to sit up.

"You just calm down now, Wiebe," another familiar voice said, but Stu did not get the chance to see who it was.

The scene became clearer to him when they were done with his pressure cuff and the stethoscope. They *were* in the Coyle High School gym, alright, along with 20 or 30 other cots. The room was buzzing with activity.

Most of those attending to patients were in military scrubs, but he saw some familiar faces working among the cots too. He recognized more people who were on the cots, his neighbor to the south, the new guy with the Sweet T ranch. His cousin, Keith, and several others of The Boys. Off by himself, Lark Fortune sat on a cot, his head palmed in his hand.

Stu turned his attention back to his mother. She was sitting calmly at his side, smiling at him. "I'm so sorry, Mom," Stu said, and felt himself turning to tears. He could not stop.

"Stuart," she said, "it's not your fault. There's nothing you could have done."

"We did try, ma'am," said someone from a nearby cot. "We was just too late for poor Dale."

The Boys were grunting to sit up all around them, expressing their condolences and expressing deep apologies.

Stu watched his mom stand and rise to her full 5'3" as she surveyed the room. "Gentlemen," she said firmly. "Thank you, one and all. I'm so grateful to you all. We all know Dale and his daddy are in a better place. And... to have my Annie and my Stewie back... that's a blessing."

Manly rumblings echoed throughout the gym.

"Now, the fact they killed and wounded dozens of my neighbors and many of your friends too," she said, more emboldened, "and that they poisoned our family's land for the rest of our lives, *burned* our land, and *killed* all our livestock... that's the work of Satan himself!"

Louder voices rallied around her.

Stu noticed the people in scrubs were having a hard time keeping The Boys down. Some of the men, even those heavily bandaged, were coming to their feet. Others were shaking their fists and grumbling curses.

The exits filled with men in uniform, but Stu could not make them out. They did not look like the guardsmen from the

Installation, but he could not be sure. They were armed, however, and very serious-looking.

He saw his mother looking at them, too, from door to door. "You lost people, too, didn't you?" she addressed them. "From the radiation and the rescue effort."

There were nods from a few of them.

Others acknowledged her by holding her eye contact.

One man, not much older than Stu, himself, was crinkling his mouth and chin, obviously trying to fight back tears.

"I don't know who these people think they are, what kind of cowardly scum of the earth they are, dropping bombs on us instead of fighting us face to face," she snarled bitterly. Tears were creeping from the corners of her eyes too. "I do not know who they are, but they should know that we *will* find them out, and we will make it right!"

Through the cheering and commotion that followed, Stu noticed that Lark had been joined by Sackerson, and that they were slinking out a side door. They were not his problem anymore.

It was family first.

• • • •

AS HE TALKED TO THOSE around him, Stu gradually pieced it together. A nuclear missile had misfired and destroyed his place. Guardsmen swore it was aimed at OKC, but it seemed too likely that it had been fired by the Spooks. This was the very bad thing Henny had caught wind of. He was sure of it now.

He had seen Lark and Sack, but as it wore into evening, he had yet to see Krystal. When he asked about her, no one seemed to know anything. He strained to recall the bomb, just the night before, but it felt like a forever-ago memory. He could see them on horseback. He could see Krys on a horse, even, but he could not put the details in place.

On the order of his doctor and his mother, Stu had slept off and on through the day and evening. He was more curious and concerned than he was sleepy now, so he carried his IV drip with him and worked the room. Most people just wanted to hug him or give him their condolences. Most everyone had their share of losses to talk about too.

He came to learn more about the incident, though it was like it was someone else's story. The blast blew fallout to the north and east, so Coyle and Stillwater were spared. The route he had been riding, west along the river, had been safe. They were well outside the 'blast radius,' but shockwaves had knocked out windows clear to town.

No one had been to the site of the Wiebe farm, but the Guard had flown drones crisscrossing the area and found nothing. Whomever had attacked them had done a very thorough job, leaving behind scorched earth and flattened trees and smoldering corpses of horses and cattle for a three-mile stretch.

Guardsmen, along with civil defense workers, had poured in as close as the perimeter allowed, running sweeps and finding survivors. Those who were far from the initial blast and not irradiated or suffering burns were here in the gym. More serious cases were at an emergency hospital set up in Langston, just a few miles away. Stu worried Krys might be there... or worse.

Outside the gym, in the ball diamond and the parking lot, a village had sprung up. Stu learned that The Boys, even weakened in strength and numbers, had rejected FEMA units for the displaced, favoring instead RVs trucked in by area dealerships. On his second day, he was able to join his family in an RV, and he got his first solid sleep.

He had not seen Sackerson, nor Fortune, nor Krys.

He began to wonder if he ever would again.

Chapter 79: Pure Imagination

Krystal Price had a private room in a hospital that was managed by very quiet people. No one would tell her anything, not even—literally—the time of day. They called her Jane, even when she protested and offered them her real name. They brought her excellent food, even though she told them repeatedly that she had no appetite.

The only relief came when an attractive man in a nice suit came to visit. He was obviously *not* a doctor, and he made no effort to hide the bulge of the service revolver slung under his arm. He came into the room and waited out all of her attending staff, then settled on a stool at her bedside.

"We already had the room swept for bugs," he said by way of introduction, "so you and I can speak freely, Ms. Price."

"Who are you?" She sat up a little in bed. "Are you with the FBI?"

"No," he chuckled, "I'm Dalton Briggs, OKC PD. I'm here on something of a personal matter."

Krystal nodded.

"I'm worried about a friend of mine, a detective from here in Guthrie. Shaelyn Lawton Ward. You know her?"

"I don't think so, no... unless she's that one from the city. She was my DARE officer a few years ago."

"Real cute? Tall..." he smiled wistfully. "Tough-gal-type, maybe?"

"Yeah, that's her." Krystal liked his description. It was spot on. The DARE officer had looked like she could have beaten down anyone on the force... but she was pretty too. "But I haven't seen her in years."

Dalton looked down then and swung his feet back and forth under his stool. "We lost track of her out where we found you... well, a few miles south, anyway. I was just hoping you might tell me anything you might know about her whereabouts."

"No, I'm sure sorry... maybe you can tell me more about mine?"

"Sure," he smiled again. "You had a severe concussion. Still have a good lump on the head, I see."

Krystal felt her forehead again. The swelling had gone down considerably, but it was very tender. She didn't know she had been concussed. She was puzzled, trying to remember.

"When our team found you, you were on horseback," he laughed openly. "I guess they had a time of getting you down."

"Horseback?" she was recalling now. Riding from the cabin, trying to escape whatever Kenny Hinman had warned about. "*Where* did they find me?"

"Funny thing," he said. "You were at Langston University, on the quad."

"Langston? That's a long ways from—"

"From the blast site... I know, right? You must have been riding all night. Had some problems with hypothermia too. You didn't know your own name." He shook his head, continuing, "Eventually we found the brand on your horse and the tooling on your saddle placed you at the Wiebe ranch, a Dale Wiebe's place east of Horse Creek Canyon."

"Stu Wiebe," she mused. "What happened to him?"

"He and your friends were found in Coyle, but since you had some head trauma, we've kept you here. We've talked to all three of them already." Briggs leaned in. "We know about the Tic Tacs *and* the journals. We have uploads of the pictures you took at the ranch. We have just about everything now, Ms. Price, just about ready for a perfect erasure, but we're looking for Shae—and more importantly—Dr. Fortune."

He stood and stroked her hair back from her head wound, still smiling at her, but it was a smile void of humor, at least anything humorous she readily understood. "I've been waiting here in this shithole state, in this backward, backwater time for *fifteen years*, you squatty little pip." His fingers closed on her scalp, and his thumb pressed her head wound. "My patience is gone," he gritted his teeth and pressed harder, "you understand me? Gone!"

She tried wrenching away. She growled and shrieked. The pain was causing her vision to flare and fade to black. It felt as if his thumb was about to stab through her skull. "I. Can't. Help. You." She was pushing him away with both hands and a knee.

"Where. Is. Fortune?" he growled.

"Wouldn't you like to know?" Sackerson said from behind and then beat Briggs to a pulp with a bedpan.

She changed out of her hospital gown in the adjoining bathroom, feeling the pain of every bruise and abrasion. Her head was throbbing, particularly after the Spook's little gesture. She had a quick and quiet cry. She just didn't know who she could trust.

Sack and Lark had trussed up Briggs, mopped up his blood with bed sheets, and stuffed him in a closet.

"I thought you were out of Hot Wires," she said.

"We visited Dr. Canole at the Installation. He gave us your Tic Tacs," Lark held them out to her.

"How'd you know—when did you put a Hot Wire in here?"

"The morning you arrived," Sackerson said. "I was your primary physician." He put on a facemask for effect and wiggled his bald eyebrows.

"But how..."

"We can worry about all that later," Sackerson said. "Let's go see Dad."

She stood waiting for a port to open up.

"No, no, no," Sackerson said. "They're still hot for us. Tracking teleportation. We're going in old school this time."

• • • •

"TO THE RESIDENCE OF Detective Ward, please," Sack said to Lark in a flourish. As the three of them tried to fit on Lark's moped, he added, "Stat!"

It was a harrowing, cold, and horribly uncomfortable ride into town from Mercy medical. Krystal was sure the suspension was going to collapse under their weight when the moped dipped through potholes on old 12th. It moved slowly uphill; she thought she could have walked alongside. Engine straining, Lark rode on, Krystal sandwiched between him and the giant Sackerson bringing up the rear.

At a stop sign, seemingly out of nowhere, the crow, Aha, joined them and took position on Sackerson's shoulder. He spread his wings when Krystal looked up at him and turned his head to give her the eye. "Whaaa?" he cawed. If he had eyebrows, she was sure he was cocking one, as if to challenge her. "Whaaa?"

They arrived at a split-level house on a hillside. Krystal had never been in the neighborhood, but she liked the way the homes opened back with big decks looking over the woods. This house seemed abandoned, but when they forced themselves in, they finally found an older woman and two children at the lower level. The woman led them to the basement, and there they found Dr. Christopher Fortune curled up on a stockpile of beans, babbling incoherently.

"He's been like this since the bomb," the old lady said. "Feels it's all his fault, as best as I can get out of him."

"Dad," Lark said, bending down to him. "It's me."

Dr. Fortune just stared off into space, mumbling.

"Daddy-o," Sackerson sang, "it's me!"

Dr. Fortune continued to move his mouth randomly.

"We're okay," Krystal said, crouching down too. She put a hand on his shoulder and jostled him. "We all got away."

Fortune stopped muttering and looked at her.

"My Shae didn't get away," the old woman said sharply, "now did she?"

Fortune resumed his crazy talk, now with greater intensity. He wasn't saying anything at all that Krystal could understand.

It sounded like a foreign language.

. . . .

"WELL NOW, THIS IS VERY disappointing!" Sackerson said, pacing the basement. He was so tall that he bumped his head on the joists above, yet he did not seem to notice. His bird was on his shoulder, ducking even when he did not.

"Dad. Dad. Dad. I had a speech prepared for you on this." Sack cleared his throat. He seemed to not care that Dr. Fortune was curled up in a fetal position, drooling. He ignored everyone else in the room, even as he shared his secrets. "Dad, listen. I don't want you going down in history as civilization's greatest tyrant, or even as the man who invented the *tool of tyranny* that porting becomes," Sack said. "I want it to stop, now. I'm here because I love you, and I love America, and I can't let it crumble and fall into the wrong hands. Our nation was just on the mend after the Corp Wars, and then the Port Authority rose up, and it was all built on your tech!"

He looked at Dr. Fortune then, then at Lark, and then Krystal.

"And that's about the size of it, kids. I came back to save the world."

"By getting rid of porting?" Krystal asked. She was sidestepping toward the old lady and the little girls. The crow was watching her closely.

"Exactly," Sack said with a bob of his head.

"Just like the Spooks... or are you *with* the Spooks?" she asked.

Lark looked at her wildly. "Are you kidding?"

"I do not agree with their methodology," Sackerson said. "But I guess, in the end, we were after the same result, eh?"

Lark then looked at Sackerson, "What?! Are *you* kidding?"

"Think about it, Lark. Thanks to their ham-fisted efforts, there's no trace of *anything* left. Not even us. We're lost to history, and with us, so's the last trace of this whole nightmare."

"I'm not buying it," Krystal said. "Why would you have fought with them this whole time if you're on the same side?"

"We're *not at all* on the same side, sweet'ums. We do have the same endgame, it's true... but really... clearly, I work with laser-like precision, while they swing in *a nuclear bomb*! I mean, c'mon!"

"The problem is," Krystal argued, her back to the stairs, "we are *not* yet lost to history. We're all alive and well. At least for the moment. Now that you have everyone here, including Dr. Fortune, you really can snuff this out and us with it."

Sackerson jerked up in astonishment. Aha cried out in surprise and fluttered off his shoulder. Sackerson had hit his head hard on the joists, interrupting what was sure to be another bit of empty praise for how astute she was.

Krystal wasn't going to listen. She was going to run. She was going to drag the grandmother and the girls and run for her life.

Lark was standing between her and Sackerson, like a referee at a boxing match, trying to decide whose glove to raise in victory.

"I have a present for the giant," one of the girls said. "It's from the sick man." She pulled away from her grandmother and handed a tattered Christmas gift up to Sack. Krystal recognized it immediately—it was Lark's cigar box of Tic Tacs.

When Sackerson opened it, his face went through several expressions, as if he were an actor in front of a mirror, trying them on. Curiosity. Surprise. Suspicion. Happiness. Ecstasy.

Lark was stuck on surprise.

"Ohhhh pumpkin, this makes this giant very, very happy!" Sack said, crouching down to smile at her. "Thank you so much."

He stood again, struggling to take his eyes off the box. "You know what this is, Lark?"

"More Tic Tacs," he said. "So?"

"Let me show ya," Sackerson said, fingering through them delicately. He sang softly as he picked out a Tic Tac that looked to Krystal just like all the rest.

Come with me
And you'll be
In a world of pure imagination...

...you know the song, Lark. If I know it, you know it!"

Lark was not singing, but he was clearly fascinated with Sackerson now, watching him take that Tic Tac and some pins from his jacket and form a portal. It snapped to a white glow, not just the wire, but the skim surface of the entire portal.

"C'mon, Lark. Let's leave these women to their knitting."

Lark looked at Krystal and shrugged. "It would have never worked out between us anyway," he said and followed Sackerson through.

"Men!" Krystal stomped her foot.

"You'd best go after him," the old woman said. "I'm calling the Villas to fetch this one."

Chapter 80: I am the Outcome

Sackerson had Briggs' service revolver out, waving it all around in the poorly lit room. Lark recognized them to be in the secret basement lab in Norman.

"Now, how'd we end up here?" Lark asked. "You said you'd never been here. Right?"

"That's just the start of it," Sackerson said. He chucked the gun on the island bench, then sat down and began unlacing his boots. "With these, little Lark—the last remaining teleportation Tic Tacs known to man—we can go anywhere there's a port, maybe even anywhere there's ever been a port."

"Why here?" Lark asked. He was looking around the room for anything they had missed before.

"Oh, this place was just a lucky break. Dad must have rigged it up." Sackerson shed his jacket then and was taking down his pants. "I just wanted some privacy."

The port had faded to a dim neutral gray, but it flared again as Krystal stepped in to join them. Sackerson's crow was on her forearm.

"Aha!" the bird declared.

"What's going on here?" she asked, taking in Sackerson in his boxers, socks, and t-shirt.

"Ugh. You are persistent, aren't you?" Sackerson said, straining the usual merry tone. "And you brought *him* too?"

Sackerson shook his head, stepped behind a bench, and continued to strip.

She looked at Lark, and he shrugged. "I... I have no idea."

The bench was concealing his privates, but Lark found it no less disturbing that his future self was standing over there naked.

Sackerson turned his attention back to them once he tossed his socks on the table. He looked down at the cigar box nestled in with his clothes. "Theory is, Dad found some premium Tic Tacs... a finite resource. Interstellar stuff, you know, that he collected because he had... drumroll please... *foresight*. That's just been a theory, until right now, of course, for these were not part of the historical record."

"And you're going to keep it that way, right?" Krystal asked.

Lark looked at her, puzzled. She seemed miffed for some reason.

"Yeah." Sackerson was scrubbing himself with what looked like a bar of soap.

He couldn't stand it any longer. "Sack, what are you doing?"

"Pumice," he explained, and nothing more. It seemed so bizarre, possibly the most bizarre thing he had done in the days they'd shared, though that would be a difficult contest.

"By getting rid of us?" Krystal asked. She had edged to the table and then slipped the revolver from it. Sackerson had not noticed.

Aha did, however, and jumped to Sackerson's shoulder. "Ack!" he warned.

"No need now," he said, then looked at her. "Records are expunged, and I'm going to dial back and really clean house, now that I have these babies."

"What's that supposed to mean?" Lark asked.

"Dad also figured out some way to match these in processing so that you could know *where* you're porting... and they are two-way tablets, not burn outs. It's the game changer, right? With this design, porting can be revolutionized."

"It's also bad, though, right?" Lark asked. "Because whoever owns the port circuit owns the world!"

Sackerson was scrubbing at a foot. Aha was awkwardly perched, splaying his wings to keep balance. His sharp talons were not digging into Sack's bare shoulder, at least not enough to get a reaction from him.

He continued talking. "In all good conscience, I can't let there be a transportation monopoly. You're right about that."

"Yeah, but *in the right hands,* we could manage transportation and make it a real utopia!" Lark smiled. "We can make it Dad's legacy!"

"That's right, mini-me. And *these*," he held up his hands, which were reddened from scrubbing, "are the right hands... give or take."

Lark felt a flutter in his stomach. He did not even know how to put it into words, but something did not feel right. Krystal gave him a look, and he couldn't process that either.

Sackerson continued, "Here's the rub. Dear old Dad wrote the formula in some wackadoodle code. If I'm going to run this show right, I gotta risk another detour."

"You mean..." Lark felt it coming to the surface now. "You meant to say that *'we'* would take a detour..."

"Nope. You're not coming." Sackerson picked the crow from his shoulder and set him on a countertop. "And you're not either."

"I'm not—what about the 'world of pure imagination' you just promised." Lark balled his fist. "What about us building Dad's legacy?"

"Another time," Sack said absently. He was picking through the Tic Tacs again, seeing something in their similarities. "Ah! Here we go."

Lark pressed. "What do you mean? I thought we were in this together."

"You," Sackerson said, pointing at him, "are irrelevant. Like a Cotyledon." When both Krystal and Lark looked puzzled, he added with exasperation, "*You never get my metaphors.* Cotyledon... first leaves on a seedling? You might have pushed through, got us where we are today, but *I am the outcome.* The real deal. The fact is, now, all of this is irrelevant." He waved around the room. "There's no reason for any well-meaning, time-traveling clones to shut it down.

No reason for *me* to shut it down. Why? Because I'm going to be in charge, and I'm going to do it right!"

"Sackerson, I don't know what you're talking about," Lark felt the frustration roiling inside him.

"Oh God, Lark! Want me to lay it out for you?" Krystal asked. "He's ditching us! He's going to pre-empt us. Isn't that about right?"

"Babe, if only... I just never realized how sharp you are!"

"Ditching us?" Lark said.

"Yeah, I am going where it's not safe for you to go." He lit up the port, this one glowing aquamarine. "Hardly anyone has ever survived these portals. It plays hell with your immune system. Leaves most people, if they survive, covered in second-degree burns."

"Where are you going to?"

"More accurately, I'm going *when* and where it's not safe to go. In Televangelism, we call these bad boys 'Hot Spots,' but I'm trusting in the Tic Tac."

Sackerson absently rubbed his palm over his head, and Lark looked at the tattoos again, illuminated in the blue of the Hot Spot. He realized the illustrations featured one thing more than any squiggle or number: Tic Tacs. Stu might have been right all along. Maybe Sackerson was in a Tic Tac cult.

"He's going back in time, even farther, now that he's got the box," Krystal said.

Sackerson nodded.

Everyone dived for the box at the same time. Sack snatched it up and edged toward the glowing portal. "Next time I see you two, I'll be old enough to be your grandpappy!"

"What? Where are you going?" Lark asked. He shook his head, trying to ask again more clearly, "*When*?"

"I'm going back to 1975," he said. "Going to check in on a couple of twins. Learn me some code. Chum around with Christopher Robin and his half-wit brother."

He jumped naked through the port, and it went black in a pop.

"Aww!" the bird shrieked, finding himself ditched by his master.

Lark growled and upended the table, tossing all of Sackerson's junk on the floor. He whirled on Krystal and said, "That guy, for the record, is NOT me."

"I never said—"

"He's a liar and a… a *megalomaniac*!" Lark threw over another bench, swung a stool into the wall. "He left us, Krystal! That crazy, goofy, freaky—he just up and left us!"

Aha flapped around the lab, cawing in agitation.

Lark kicked the wall. His foot went right through it, and thousands of Tic Tacs poured out.

They looked at each other and smiled.

Chapter 81: Awakening

Context File

Guthrie's Villas of Benedictine Pointe served previously as Logan County Hospital from 1925 until the new county hospital came along in the 1970s. For twenty years, the building was idle, attracting vandals and falling into disrepair until it was turned into luxury apartments in 2020. During the grand reopening, one resident's arrangements were made covering rent and care in perpetuity by a generous grant from an anonymous donor.

In that way, Tristam Shandy Fortune came to be known by others in the Villas as the vegetable in residence. Visited regularly by his twin brother, the two of them would sit in silence for hours, then babble in a foreign tongue until late at night.

One February morning in 2030, Tristam rose from his bed and enjoyed a long, languid stretch. He felt his toes tingle on the cold wood floor. He breathed in the frabjous day, then sang out clearly, "Coming, dear brother!"

He stepped into the curtains at his bedside and disappeared in a white-hot flash. He was never seen or heard from again.

Chapter 82: Late to the Party

They were all seated around a coffee table at Buzz and Willow Lawton's. Lark was happy to share a love seat with Krystal. Stu and Henny were on opposite ends of a long couch. Had Sackerson not gone, his gigantic personality might just fit in the space between them. It was ample room for the Lawtons, but Buzz was not around, and she was a dynamo who could not settle down. Willow insisted on feeding them, and she was constantly moving back and forth from the living room to the kitchen. She was probably in her sixties, but she moved more fluidly, and she acted more like a soldier than anyone had at the Installation.

She was sharp, but Lark doubted even *she* could see what he found to be so painfully obvious. They sat in the same room, eight knees against the same coffee table, but they were not together.

The old gang was reunited, but Lark thought they were different people than they had been just days ago. They were done with the mystery of Sackerson and his hijinks. They were still hiding from Spooks and creepers—maybe for the rest of their lives—even though no one had seen or heard from any of them in days.

No one seemed interested in the four of them anymore. Local law enforcement and civil defense worked out east of town, as they had previously on the west with the original Guthrie Fall. News vans, food trucks, rubber-necking onlookers—all eyes had been diverted to the new crisis. They were all too preoccupied to care about four teenagers.

Even parents behaved as if the kids were off-limits.

Grandma Willow, however, seemed to follow a different directive.

She had invited them over to mine them for their answers. She served them Kool-Aid, finger foods, and questions. She wanted to know more about the tall bald man. How was it possible that Dr. Fortune had disappeared? Why had Dr. Fortune been so sick?

They were doing a competent job of tag-teaming on her questions, improvising with colorful flourishes even Sackerson would have admired. No matter how many ways she inquired, the incident made little sense. Willow was insatiably curious and surprised by it all. The others around the table, however, were less surprised. Once in a while, Lark would catch someone's eye. Even Grandma Willow did not seem to be saying what she was speaking aloud. It was as if the subtext of their conversation was a complicated game, but he did not know the rules.

The back storm door clapped closed, hard.

Everyone stood. Action poses.

Stu had his hand on a pistol in his belt.

Willow peeked into the kitchen, and her shoulders relaxed. "Where have you been?"

Buzz Lawton hugged her tightly. He smiled over her shoulder at the gang.

"Out," he offered, as he looked her in the eyes again. "I told you I had to go out."

"*That was days ago*!" Willow said through gritted teeth. "And what are you tracking into my house?"

Lark smiled and waved. He knew Buzz from Mack's. The guy was a regular. Always talking, always smiling. Tonight, he was his usual animated self, shaking hands with everyone, teasing his granddaughters. Willow was alternatively scolding him for tracking in red mud and then doting and fawning all over him.

Buzz was also avoiding his wife's curiosity (and ferocity). That was clear. When she asked him into the kitchen for some help, he invited the girls along too. When she confronted him again about his whereabouts, he switched it up, asking the gang how they were doing. Buzz Lawton seemed interested in talking about anything other than the last few days.

Willow went downstairs to fetch something, and Buzz turned on him. "Your dad's long gone, Lark, but I guarantee ya, he's gone to a better place."

"Yeah, right." It was the same sentiment people always shared... but it sounded different when Buzz said it.

Lark felt the others were watching him. They expected him to say more. *What could he say?* His dad was gone. Sackerson, the man who called himself Lark's "chronologically-askew doppelganger," was gone. Shae Ward, whose family home he was sitting in... gone. He didn't know if he believed in a better place, but Buzz Lawton made it sound so real.

It was quiet for a beat.

Krystal put a hand on his knee and squeezed. "No one's really lost to us, you know. We always have their memories."

"That's a truth," Henny said, glancing sidelong at Stu, then bowing his head.

"Yeah, you're right," Stu said. "I know you're right... but I'm still finding those guys behind the bombing... and I *will* get even."

Willow was back in the room. She handed a journal to Lark. "This won't explain anything, but... it was his. It must've slipped out of his pocket when we were in the bunker."

Lark held it tightly. These were his father's last words. He wanted to wait as long as he could to open it. Maybe he could hold out for years.

Buzz gave him a meaningful nod, then slipped away again into his grandfatherly bliss. Willow continued with questions. She asked more about Stu's situation. She felt for him and offered her condolences on the loss of his father and grandfather. If their ranch was no longer an option, what would he do next? She wanted to hear more about the land out east, about the memorial Burns had been talking about when he had been by earlier.

"It'll be out on the median on 33. They're going to make a turnabout there, since it's a dead-end road now." Stu darkened at the thought. "It'll list everybody, missing and... dead."

"Shaelyn and Robert should be on that plaque too," she said sternly.

"Yes, ma'am," Stu said, swallowing hard. *His father and maybe his uncle, too.*

Though she had put them to bed twice, the girls were out and snacking again on the finger food. They delighted in their grandfather's return. Opal had the cutest red Kool-Aid mustache. Lark smiled at her, and her smile back made him feel a bit better.

Aha threw a fit on the porch.

"He's back!" The other girl, Hester, shouted, then ran to the door and looked out.

Her sister joined her, and they jumped up and down with glee. "Mommy's home! Mommy's home!"

Lark and Willow were there immediately, looking out at the street. She turned on the porch light, and he saw it clearly for himself. The family van was wobbling and squeaking up the driveway. The paint was scorched, and several windows were missing. It was pretty mashed up, as if it might have been rolled. Red Oklahoma mud was still caked on it.

Rob and Shae Ward smiled and waved as the van hobbled to a stop.

Everyone poured out on the porch and down the stairs.

"Sorry we're late to the party," Rob said. "We got caught in a nuclear war."

• • • •

MAYBE IT WAS JUST GETTING late, or maybe things were as lopsided as Lark felt the world to be. The Wards had no explanation for where they'd been the last couple of days, and nobody seemed to care. Whenever a question about it came up, Willow would just sweep it away with a quick, "Now, now, let's be glad everyone's safe."

It gnawed at Lark.

Rob was off putting the girls to bed. Shae was playing cards with Henny, Stu, and Krys. The Lawtons, he guessed, had gone off to bed themselves. Everything was assuming the shape of just another night.

He should have been relieved they were back and that everyone was together. Alive and safe. He should have felt safe in the home of a police officer. Lark knew all that, but anxiety was coursing through him. He frittered and stewed until he came up with a course of action.

He'd go home and patch things up with his mom. He hadn't been home since the day of the restaurant shootout. He thought he'd hit the bathroom one more time before he left. He closed the door and looked in the bathroom mirror. *He was not himself.* That's what came to mind as he stared at his reflection. He tried a smile, but it looked fake. He ran his fingers through his ratty red hair. On a whim, he palmed his hairline and questioned how much he might resemble Sackerson.

Then he heard them in the next room. Buzz and Willow.

"Listen. I love you a thousand times over. Thanks for bringing them back."

"Couldn't live without my Shae."

Lark pressed his ear to the wall. He'd missed something. Willow was speaking again, "...but this is nothing. It's all moot."

"Again, with the *language*," Buzz chided, "Moot?"

Debatable, uncertain, not a clear and final decision, Lark said to himself. Also colloquially... irrelevant.

"Sackerson," she said, as if that were any kind of explanation. Then again, Lark thought, being around Sackerson seemed to explain a lot of things. "Nothing's as it seems, and now *everything is nothing at all*."

"You spent too much time at camp in the 90s, Sugar Lump."

"I mean it. If Sackerson's back, who knows what's different."

"Nothing. *It's always never the same*," Buzz said, "and no matter what he tried, it obviously didn't matter. The Guthrie Fall fell, babe, and the Tic Tacs are out. That's on me."

Again, she argued, but it was something Lark couldn't discern, even more muffled, as if she were crying into a pillow, or maybe, he thought, Buzz's shoulder. He adjusted his ear placement, leaning over into the shower stall. The tile was cool on his flushed cheek.

"Hey, hey," he was consoling. "At least the Spooks are spooked and the whole thing's covered up for a while. Maybe they'll buy it."

Lark's pulse was pounding. Buzz's voice was loud and clear here, as if Buzz were talking directly at the wall between them.

Something about Buzz seemed so disjointed. He didn't talk like an old guy, some antique Einstein like he always did in Mack's. Then again, they'd only talked about food and school in the diner. He'd not been talking to his wife in private either.

Lark stepped back and took in his surroundings, trying to get grounded. An everyday bathroom in anyone's home. Shampoo on the shower shelf. Toothbrushes in a cup on the sink. Old magazines on the lid of the toilet tank. He rolled his eyes at himself in the mirror. Who knows what he was really hearing through the wall.

He heard Buzz's voice again. It was more strident. Lark pressed his ear on the wall again and caught, "See for yourself."

Willow's response was to burst from the room and down the hall. Buzz was following.

Lark shut off the bathroom light and opened the door just a crack.

They were standing in the threshold to the living room. Beyond them was a tableau of a pseudo family night, the five of them huddled over a game of cards. Rob was dealing. Shae was studying her hand, the tip of her tongue poking between her lips. Krystal was holding her cards to her chest, wary of Stu, who was craning his neck to get a peek at Henny's.

Lark felt a pang of separation from them all, but he pushed it back and crept down the hall after them. Something unresolved between the Lawton's stirred his curiosity. They looked on at the gamers for a long while.

"You're right," Willow said to Buzz, taking his hand and leaning into him. "The future is in good hands."

"And ultimately, it's all up to you again," Buzz said over his shoulder with a wink.

Please visit marklandonjarvis.com for all the details of the Endless Tempest series. Readers can learn so much of the lore and backstory there, as well as hoover up behind-the-scenes making-of, dreaming about, and hoping-for's. The website also hosts character sketches, short stories, and acknowledgements of all the many people who have been instrumental in putting this book—and all the others—into play.

I am eager to hear from readers, always. Follow the contact information at the site, get on my newsletter list, and let's swap some mail. I am available for book clubs and readings, and I answer every email.

Thanks for reading,
Mark Landon Jarvis

Don't miss out!

Visit the website below and you can sign up to receive emails whenever Mark Landon Jarvis publishes a new book. There's no charge and no obligation.

https://books2read.com/r/B-A-QYDU-JCNAD

BOOKS 2 READ

Connecting independent readers to independent writers.

Also by Mark Landon Jarvis

Endless Tempest
Future Fugitives
Lightning's Hand
Bewildered
Lost and Found

About the Author

Born when the world was black and white, when a phone was simply something one talked on, Mark Landon Jarvis appreciates modern technology and yet abhors its abuses. Most of his speculative work is from this vantage point of concerned enthusiasm.

Jarvis is from the rural Midwest. He lives on a hobby farm with his wife and four teens, along with seven goats, five dogs, four pigs, and a flock of chickens. He is a college professor and Spam connoisseur.